# DOCKSIDE AT WILLOW LAKE

# DOCKSIDE AT WILLOW LAKE

Susan Wiggs

CHIVERS

British Library Cataloguing in Publication Data available

This Large Print edition published by AudioGO Ltd, Bath, 2012.
Published by arrangement with Harlequin Enterprises II B.V./S à r.l.

U.K. Hardcover     ISBN   978 1 4458 3024 7
U.K. Softcover     ISBN   978 1 4458 3025 4

Printed and bound in Great Britain by
MPG Books Group Limited

For boat commutes to our writers' group in the summer, for treacherous drives through frozen winter nights, for sticking together through spring floods and autumn rains, for my fellow writer and friend for all seasons—For Sheila! For Joy!

# ACKNOWLEDGMENTS

Many thanks to the *real* innkeeper, Wendy Higgins of The Ocean Lodge in Cannon Beach, Oregon. Deepest appreciation to fellow writers Elsa Watson, Suzanne Selfors, Sheila Rabe and Anjali Banerjee; also to Kysteen Seelen, Susan Plunkett, Rose Marie Harris, Lois Faye Dyer and Kate Breslin for their humor, wisdom and patience in reading early drafts.

Special thanks to Meg Ruley and Annelise Robey of the Jane Rotrosen Agency, and to my terrific editor, Margaret O'Neill Marbury.

'A lake is the landscape's most beautiful and expressive feature. It is earth's eye; looking into which the beholder measures the depth of his own nature.'

—Henry David Thoreau
*Walden,* 'The Ponds'

## Part One

### Now

'You are part travel guide, social director, advertising and marketing specialist, housekeeper, chef, accountant, public relations specialist, buildings and groundskeeper, and local historian all rolled into one. If . . . you are willing to work hard, are dedicated to creating comfortable accommodations for visitors, have a love of your area and a desire to share that passion with others, then you may want to consider owning and operating a bed and breakfast inn.'
*—The Bed and Breakfast Association of Alaska*

# ONE

After Shane Gilmore kissed her, Nina Romano kept her eyes shut. All right, she thought, so he wasn't the world's best kisser. Not every man was born a great kisser. Some had to be trained. Surely, Shane Gilmore was trainable.

She opened her eyes and smiled up at him. He certainly looked like a good kisser, with nicely sculpted lips and a strong jaw, broad shoulders and thick black hair. Maybe he was just having an off day.

'I've been waiting a long time to do that,' he said. 'Your term in office couldn't end soon enough for me.'

He didn't mean it as a dig. Did he? The fact that her term as mayor of Avalon, New York, had concluded in scandal still stung; maybe she was just being paranoid. She decided to laugh it off. 'All right, now you sound like one of my political enemies.'

'My reasons are romantic,' he insisted. 'I was waiting for the right time. It wouldn't have looked right for us to be together when you were mayor, not with me being president of the only bank in town.'

You look like such a hunk, she thought. Don't act like a dork. And yes, she *was* being paranoid about the scandal, which was odd,

3

because given her background, Nina was no stranger to scandal. As a young single mother, she'd held her head up and gone to work for the town of Avalon, eventually serving as deputy mayor. The salary was almost nonexistent, and hadn't improved much when Mayor McKittrick fell ill and she became the de facto mayor, the youngest and lowest-paid in the state, as far as she knew. She'd inherited a city-finance nightmare. The town was on the verge of bankruptcy. She'd cut spending, which included her own salary, to the bone and eventually found the source of the leak—a corrupt city administrator.

Enough, she thought. This was a new chapter of her life in so many ways. She'd just returned from three weeks away. She and Shane were on their first date, and quibbling with a first date was a no-no. And aside from that kiss—awkward and way too . . . slobbery—things were going all right. They had shared a Sunday afternoon picnic at Blanchard Park, on the shores of Willow Lake, the town's best asset. Afterward they had taken a leisurely stroll along the lakeshore, and that was where Shane made his move. He'd stopped right in the middle of the path, cast a furtive glance left and right and then pressed his mouth in full lockdown mode upon hers.

Ew.

Snap out of it, Nina scolded herself. This was supposed to be a new beginning for her.

4

While she was raising her daughter, she'd never had the time or energy to date. Now that she was making her belated entry into the world of dating, she really shouldn't ruin it by being hypercritical. She had ruined more first dates by being hypercritical than . . . come to think of it, she'd ruined all of them. First dates were the only kind Nina Romano ever had, because there was never a second. Except that one, years ago. The one that had resulted in her getting pregnant at the age of fifteen. After that, she'd concluded that second dates were bad luck.

Everything was different now. It was time—past time—to see if a date could actually turn into something besides a disaster. Nina's daughter, Sonnet, was grown; she had finished high school early, at sixteen, and had been accepted at American University, neatly avoiding every youthful mistake Nina had made.

Don't, she thought, feeling herself starting to drown in thoughts of Sonnet. In a moment of insane self-deception, Nina had convinced herself that it would be easy to let go of her daughter. To let go of the child who had been Nina's whole world until high school graduation a few weeks ago.

Trying to pull herself back into the moment with Shane, she quickened her pace and felt a fiery sting along the length of her leg. Too late, she saw that she had strayed too close to a clump of thigh-high nettles.

Even when she gave a soft hiss of pain, he didn't seem to notice as he strode along beside her, filling her in on his latest round of golf.

Golf, thought Nina, gritting her teeth against the stinging sensation. Now, there was something she'd always wanted to try. There were so many things she'd put off learning and doing. Now that Sonnet was gone, it was Nina's turn to take her shot.

The thought put a spring in her step despite the nettles. It was a gorgeous Saturday afternoon and people were out in droves, like creatures awakened from hibernation. She loved the sight of couples strolling along the lakeshore, families picnicking in the park, catboats and canoes plying the clear blue waters of the lake. Nina loved everything about her hometown. It was the perfect place to launch the next phase of her life.

Though not financially rewarding, serving as mayor had brought her friends and allies who far outnumbered her enemies, even after the finance scandal. These connections, and Shane's bank, were the key to her new endeavor. Now that Sonnet was gone, Nina was about to resurrect a long-buried dream.

'So you've been waiting for me to free myself of the mayor's office,' she remarked to Shane. 'That's good to know. How are things at the bank?'

'Actually, there've been a few changes,'

he said. 'I was going to talk to you about that later.'

She frowned at the way his gaze shifted as he spoke. 'What sort of changes?'

'We've got some new personnel who came on board while you were away. And can we not talk about business?' He touched her arm, sent her a meaningful look. 'On the path back there—' he gestured '—it felt like we really clicked. I missed you. Three weeks is a long time.'

'Uh-huh.' She reminded herself to be fair, to give this date a chance. 'Three weeks isn't that long, not to me. I've waited for years to get going. This is it. My new life. I'm finally starting a future I've dreamed about ever since I was a little girl.'

'Um, yeah. That's great.' He seemed uneasy, and she remembered that he didn't want to talk about work, so she dropped the subject.

'I'm glad I got to make the trip with Sonnet,' she told him. 'I can't remember the last time we had an actual vacation.'

'I thought maybe you'd be seduced by big-city life and never come back,' he said.

He didn't know her at all, then. 'My heart is here, Shane,' she said. 'It always has been. Here in this town where I grew up, where my family is. I'd never leave Avalon.'

'So you got homesick on your trip?'

'No, because I knew I'd be coming back.' The day after graduation, Nina and Sonnet had taken the train to Washington, and they'd spent three glorious weeks together, seeing the nation's capital and the colonial monuments of Virginia. Though Nina wouldn't admit it, she was also reassuring herself about Sonnet's father, Laurence Jeffries, and his family. Sonnet would be spending the summer with him. Laurence was a high-ranking army officer, a military attaché. He'd invited Sonnet to travel with him, his wife and two daughters to Casteau, Belgium, where Laurence was assigned to the Supreme Headquarters Allied Powers Europe.

Having a father who worked at SHAPE was a wonderful opportunity for Sonnet, who would be serving at NATO as an intern. It was a chance for her to get to know Laurence better, too. Laurence and his trophy family. He was a shining star, an African-American graduate of West Point. His wife was the granddaughter of a famous civil rights leader, and his daughters were honor students at Sidwell Friends School. Yet they genuinely wanted to make Sonnet feel welcome, or so it seemed to Nina. At summer's end, Sonnet would matriculate at American University. Simple, thought Nina. All kids left home, right?

The fact that Sonnet would be living with her father, stepmother and stepsisters was simple, too. Blended families were the norm in this day and age.

8

So why was it, every time she imagined Sonnet in that so-perfect Georgetown brick house or the quaint Belgian town filled with SHAPE and NATO personnel, that Nina panicked? She felt her daughter becoming a stranger, more distant with each passing day. Stop it, she admonished herself again.

Letting her go was a good decision. It was what Sonnet wanted. It was what Nina wanted, something she'd been waiting for—freedom, independence. Still, saying goodbye had been a leap of faith. Thank goodness, Nina thought, she had something to come back to besides an empty house. She had a new life, a new future planned, a new adventure. Nothing could take the place of her daughter, but Nina was determined to move forward. There were things she'd given up, things she'd missed by becoming a mother at such a young age. No, she reminded herself. Not given up. Postponed.

Shane was talking again, and Nina realized she hadn't heard a word he'd said. 'I'm sorry. What were you saying?'

'I was telling you, I'm pumped about going kayaking. I've never been.'

Pumped? Had he really said pumped? 'The lake's a good place to start. The water's pretty tame.'

'Even if it's not,' he said, 'I'm prepared. I bought some gear, just for today.'

They arrived at the town dock and

9

boathouse, busy with people out enjoying the best weather of the year so far. She saw couples and families strolling or splashing in the shallows. Her gaze lingered on a couple sitting on a bench at the water's edge. They were facing each other, holding hands, leaning forward in earnest conversation. They were ordinary people—he had thinning hair, she had a thickening waistline—yet Nina could sense their intimacy, even from a distance. There was a certain posture people took on when they loved and trusted each other. The sight of them made her feel wistful; she was no expert on romantic love, having never experienced it firsthand before. One day, though, she might unveil that mystery for herself.

Glancing over at Shane, she thought, probably not today.

He mistook her glance. 'So after we go kayaking,' he said, 'I thought we'd go to my place. I'll fix you dinner.'

Please, she thought. Please stop trying so hard. She smiled up at him. 'Thanks, Shane.' Once again, she reminded herself to loosen up. In a way, dating was like being an explorer, setting off into unknown territory.

'Nina,' someone called. 'Nina Romano!'

There, in the picnic area near the boat shed, was Bo Crutcher, the star pitcher of the Avalon Hornets, a Can-Am Baseball League team. As usual, the long, tall Texan

10

was drinking beer and hanging out with his buddies.

'Hey, darlin',' he drawled. His accent flowed like sun-warmed honey.

'I'm not your darling, Bo,' she said. 'And isn't there a rule about drinking before a game?'

'Why, darlin', I reckon there is. How'd you get so smart?'

'I was born that way,' she said.

'Seems like you know everyone in town,' Shane remarked.

'That was my favorite part of being mayor— meeting so many people.'

Shane looked back over his shoulder at Bo. 'I don't know why he hasn't been fired from the team.'

'Because he's good.' Nina knew Bo Crutcher had been cut from other teams thanks to his party-animal ways. The Can-Am League was pretty much his last chance. 'When you're good at something, people tend to overlook a lot of other flaws. For a while, anyway. Eventually, though, they catch up with you.'

The sound of boyish laughter carried across the water, catching Nina's attention. She immediately recognized Greg Bellamy and his son, Max, launching a canoe.

Every unattached woman in town recognized Greg Bellamy, the ultimate in recently divorced guys. He was ridiculously handsome in a white-teeth, sparkling-eyes, broad-shouldered, six-feet-something way. For a long time, Nina had had a secret crush on him. He wasn't for her, though. He came with too much baggage in the form of two kids. Nina knew and liked Max and Daisy, but she kept her distance. She had finally reached a place in her life where she could just be by herself. Taking on another woman's children was not in her plans.

Besides, Greg wasn't interested. When he first moved to town last winter, she'd invited him to coffee but he turned her down. Nina reminded herself of this when someone else joined Greg and Max—a woman in breezy white capri pants and a lime-green sweater. She appeared to be about eight feet tall and very blond. Although she wasn't close enough to see, Nina knew she was attractive. That was the only type Greg Bellamy seemed to favor. Italian-American women under five foot two, known for their fiery tempers, cropped hair and lack of fashion sense, didn't appear to interest him.

Resolutely pulling her attention from Greg Bellamy, Nina led the way to the boat shed where she kept her kayak. She'd had the kayak for years because she loved being on the water. Willow Lake—the Jewel of Avalon, as it was known in chamber of commerce brochures—was ten miles long, fed by the Schuyler River and bordered by the wooded rise of the Catskills. One end of the lake faced the town of Avalon and was fringed by the popular city park, which Nina had been instrumental in funding when she was in office. Farther along the lakeshore were summer homes and the occasional bed-and-breakfast hideaway. Privately owned property on the lakeshore was exceedingly rare, since the land was now part of the Catskills Forest Preserve. The few places that had been built before the preserve stood like storybook settings from another time. In the shape of a long, curved finger, crooked as though beckoning, the lake stretched deep into a pristine wilderness. At its northernmost reaches nestled a place called Camp Kioga. The property had been in the Bellamy family for generations. Of course it had. Sometimes, it seemed to Nina, the Bellamys owned half the county. The camp had recently reopened as a family resort. At summer's end, it would be the setting for a much-anticipated wedding.

As she and Shane brought the kayak from its berth in the boat shed, she felt a surge of nostalgia. She had bought the two-man kayak years ago at the annual Rotary auction. It was perfect for her and Sonnet. Remembering those rare summer days when she stole time from work to go paddling on the lake with her daughter created a pang of longing so unexpected that Nina caught her breath.

'Something the matter?' Shane asked.

'I'm fine,' she said. 'Just excited about getting out on the water again.'

He went to his car to get his gear. While Nina launched the kayak at the dock, she tracked the progress of Greg Bellamy's canoe. He and his boy, Max, paddled in tandem while the blonde sat like a Nordic princess in the middle. Wasn't she bored? What fun was it to just sit there, keeping every hair in place, white pants unwrinkled?

Nina wondered who the woman was. Thanks to the upcoming Bellamy family wedding, there had been lots of visitors to town and to Camp Kioga—event planners, florists, caterers, decorators. The bride-to-be was Greg's niece, Olivia. Perhaps the Nordic princess was going to be his wedding date.

Since she came from a huge family, Nina was no stranger to weddings. But of course, she'd never been a bride. Maybe now that she was truly on her own, she would get married. Turning away from the scene on the lake, she glanced at Shane Gilmore, returning from the parking lot. Then again, she thought, maybe not.

He had geared up for kayaking in a crash helmet and float coat, a protective spray skirt that circled his waist like a floppy tutu, a VHF radio and amphibious shoes.

'Well, look at you,' she said. Fortunately, serving as mayor had taught her to be diplomatic.

14

'Thanks,' he said, preening in his gear. 'I got everything at the preseason sale at the Sport Haus.'

'Lucky you,' murmured Nina. 'You probably won't need the helmet and skirt today. Those are usually only needed for extreme whitewater kayaking.'

He disregarded her advice and eased into his seat while she held the boat steady. 'Ready?' he said, banging the fiberglass hull against the dock as he settled in.

'Not quite,' she said, and picked up the paddles. 'We don't want to be without these.'

'Dang,' he said, 'I feel like this is going to tip over any second.'

'It won't,' she said. 'I had Sonnet in this when she was five years old. In good weather, there's no safer way to be on the water.'

He clutched at the side of the dock as Nina got in. She told herself not to be so critical of this guy. He was the bank president. He was educated and good-looking. He said things like, 'Do you know how long I've waited to ask you out?'

She showed him how the rudder worked and demonstrated a simple paddling technique. So what if he was a dork? So what if he was wearing a crash helmet and spray skirt? There was something to be said for exercising caution.

Besides, she could tell he was enjoying their outing. Once they paddled away from shore and glided across the smooth surface of Willow Lake, he relaxed visibly. This was the magic and beauty of being on the water, Nina reflected. This was why the lakes of upstate New York were so legendary, having been sought after by harried city dwellers ever since there was a city. The water was dotted with catboats with sails like angels' wings, other kayaks, canoes and rowboats of all sorts. The weeping hills, veiled by springs and waterfalls, were reflected in the glassy surface of the lake. Paddling across the sun-dappled lake was like being in an Impressionist painting, part of a peaceful and colorful tableau.

'Let's go over here,' she suggested, indicating with her paddle. 'I want to take a look at the Inn at Willow Lake—my new project.'

A beat of hesitation pulsed between them. 'It's kind of far,' he said. 'Clear across the lake.'

'We can be there in just a few minutes.' She tried not to feel annoyed by his hesitation. The Inn at Willow Lake was going to be her life. As bank president, Shane was one of the few people who was privy to that dream. The inn had gone into foreclosure and the bank now held the title. Thanks to Mr. Bailey, the asset manager, Nina had been given the management contract for the place. She would oversee its reopening and operation. If she did a good job, if things went as planned, she'd qualify for a small business loan and buy the place for herself. That was what she wanted. It was something she dreamed of doing all her life.

Without meaning to, she went faster, her rhythm out of sync with Shane's so that their paddles clashed. 'Sorry,' she said. But she wasn't really. She was in a hurry.

As she paddled toward the historic property with its long dock projecting out into the lake, her heart lifted. This was the only hotel on the lake, thanks to deed restrictions that had been enacted after it was built. The property consisted of a collection of vintage residences around a magnificent main building, which lay upon the emerald slope like another place in time. The Stick and Italianate architecture was a superb example of the irrational exuberance of the Gilded Age. There was a wraparound veranda and gables along the upper story. There was an incredible belvedere rising like a wedding cake, its turret crowned by an ornate dome. The mullioned windows offered a matchless view of Willow Lake. From her perspective on the water, Nina could imagine the place in the old resort days, when the grounds were dotted by guests sunning themselves or playing croquet, and lovers walked hand-in-hand along the shady paths. There was a part of Nina that was a shameless romantic, and the inn fed that fantasy; it always had. Her favorite building was the

17

boathouse, built in the classic style of the lakes of upstate New York with covered boat slips at water level, and living quarters above. It was made of the same whimsy and luxury as the main building of the inn.

In accordance with her agreement with the bank, the upper level of the boathouse was to be her private residence, and she had plans to move within the week. The boathouse had originally served as a lavish playroom for the children of the original owner, with quarters for the nanny. Lately, however, it had been used for storage.

Ever since she was a little girl, she'd pictured herself here, warmly welcoming guests from the world over as they gathered for lemonade and croquet on the lawn in the summer or for hot chocolate and cozy reading by the library fireplace in winter. She had always known exactly how each room would look, what low-key music would be playing in the dining room, what the baking muffins would smell like in the morning.

Her plans had been derailed by a teenage pregnancy and the responsibility of raising a child alone. No, she thought. Not derailed. Delayed. Now an opportunity had opened up and Nina was determined to seize it. She was ready for something new in her life. With Sonnet gone, she needed it.

To some people, being an innkeeper might not have sounded like much. To Nina, it was

18

the start of a long-held dream. As they glided close to the dock, she felt a warm thrill of excitement, not unlike the sort of thrill she was supposed to feel for her date.

'So there it is,' she said. 'I can't wait to get started.'

He was quiet. She wondered if he was checking her out and twisted around in her seat. 'Shane?'

'Yeah, about that,' he said, jerking his helmeted head in the direction of the inn. 'There've been some interesting developments at the bank.'

Nina frowned. ' "Interesting" sounds a bit ominous.'

'While you were away, Bailey retired and moved to Florida.'

She relaxed. 'I know. I sent him a card.'

'And we brought in a new asset manager from the main branch, a woman named Brooke Harlow. She made some changes in her department. She had orders from the home office to improve her bottom line.'

Nina's heart faltered. 'She's still going to honor my contract, right?'

'Rest assured, that contract is considered a valuable part of the package. You have a fantastic reputation. No question you're the best general manager for the job.'

'Why doesn't this sound so good to me, Shane?' she asked.

'Well, actually, it could be very good. The

Inn at Willow Lake has been sold, and your contract with it.'

She turned again and scowled at him. 'Not funny.'

'I'm not telling you to be funny. It's just something that happened.'

'It can't happen.' Yet the churning of her stomach told her that indeed, it could. 'I expected the bank to give me the option to buy the place as soon as I'm able to qualify for a loan.'

'I'm sure you knew it was a possibility that the bank would divest itself of the property if a buyer came along.'

'But Mr. Bailey said—'

'I'm sorry, Nina. That's what happened.'

She'd been aware of the risk. She'd known it when she signed her contract, but Mr. Bailey had told her the possibility was highly unlikely. As soon as Nina qualified for a small-business loan, she would be in a position to buy the place.

The Inn at Willow Lake. Sold.

For a few moments, she couldn't get her mind around the reality. It just seemed like such a foreign concept. Of course the inn would be sold one day—to her. That had always been the plan.

'Anyway,' Shane went on, ignoring the fact that every word that came out of his mouth was another hammer blow, 'it belongs to someone else now. You won't believe who the buyer is.'

Nina Romano felt something snap inside her. This clueless man, this spray-skirt-wearing lousy kisser, was sitting there informing her that her entire future, the one thing she had counted on to fill her life now that Sonnet was gone, had been taken away. It was too much.

'Hey, are you all right?' he asked.

Not the smartest question to ask an Italian-American woman with steam coming out of her ears.

Nina's body was not her own. As though possessed by demons, she reared up in the kayak and went for his throat.


## TWO

'Isn't it a bit early in the season for swimming?' Brooke Harlow asked Greg Bellamy.

Curious, Greg turned to see what she was pointing at—a couple with a kayak in the distance. A dark-haired woman and a guy in a crash helmet appeared to be locked together in the kayak in a passionate embrace, churning up water all around them as the craft bobbed and rolled. Stillwater kayaking was supposed to be a relaxing sport, Greg thought. But it was none of his business. Whatever floats your boat. Ha-ha.

He tried to shake off his sour mood. It

was a blue-sky, summer's-coming day and he damn well better enjoy it. He was spending the afternoon with a woman who looked like a lingerie model. His twelve-year-old son was actually behaving like a human being for once. It didn't take long for Greg to figure out why. Max was . . . Damn, he was checking out Brooke Harlow. The kid was only twelve. That was way too young to be interested in women. Wasn't it just yesterday that Max was playing with Tonka trucks, making motor sounds with his mouth?

Brooke shook the water from her hand. 'Brr. I think I'll wait until later in the season to try swimming. How about you, Max?'

'I don't mind cold water,' he said.

Greg suspected Max would be agreeable to walking across hot coals if Brooke suggested it. He tried to send his son a telepathic message—you're too young to be thinking what you're thinking. But Max was oblivious to everything except Brooke.

Greg told himself not to worry about the situation. But of course, these days, he worried about everything, including the fact that later in the summer, Max would be going overseas to visit his mother. Which was more depressing for the kid: having his parents together, but miserable, or having them an ocean apart? Also depressing—the fact that Greg was thinking about these things when he was supposed to be on a date.

22

This wasn't a date, not technically. That wouldn't happen until Greg took her to dinner tonight. She was the new asset manager of the bank, and she'd recently overseen a major transaction for him. For better or worse, Greg now owned the Inn at Willow Lake. He had paid cash for the place and Brooke had expedited the transaction so it took place in a matter of days. His ex, Sophie, would probably be the first to tell him he was crazy, which was why he hadn't told her yet. The place had been vacated and was now closed for renovations. He'd dived in headfirst, hiring a contractor and spending his own days—and nights—hard at work on the place. The idea was to reopen as quickly as possible. Greg and his kids, Max and Daisy, had already moved to the premises and now lived in the owner's residence at the edge of the property. The boxy Victorian house was a far cry from their first home, a luxury high-rise in Manhattan, but the three of them were adjusting well enough, all things considered.

He dug in his paddle and, at the front of the boat, Max did the same. Working as a team, they paddled in tandem and soon had the canoe gliding through the clear water. For a few blessed seconds, Greg felt connected to his son, the two of them engaged in a rare moment of cooperation. They used to live their lives according to the same rhythm, but since the divorce, they'd been out of sync.

'Holy crap, Dad,' said Max, pointing at

23

the people in the kayak. 'I think that guy's in trouble. We should go check it out.'

'No, they're just horsing around,' Greg said. Seconds later, the woman went overboard. A fount of water exploded around the kayak. The woman in the water was trying to hold the kayak upright while the guy flailed and shouted.

The kayak bobbed, then toppled sideways in a roll. The guy in the helmet yelled a word Greg liked to pretend Max didn't know, then crashed into the water.

'Oh, my lord,' Brooke said, 'I think that's Shane Gilmore.'

The bank president. And, as Greg and Max paddled closer, he realized that the woman in the water was Nina Romano. Damn. What were the chances?

The dude in the crash helmet seemed to be shoving at Nina with a paddle. Maybe he knew something Greg didn't about her.

'You guys need some help?' Greg shouted, bringing the canoe alongside the kayak. Stupid question. He extended his oar toward Nina.

She ignored it and said, 'Help me hold this upright. He's panicking.'

Great, thought Greg, his skin shrinking as he thought about the water temperature. 'Hang on,' he said, then sucked in a big breath of air and dove into the lake. He emerged a few feet from the rolling kayak.

'The kayak's taking on water,' Nina shouted.

24

'He's stuck and he won't stay still.'

'Get him the hell out, then,' Greg said, going numb from the shock of the cold water.

'His spray skirt is caught on something,' she yelled.

The guy was flailing and coughing. 'Can't . . . swim.' His face was white, his lips a chilly blue. The crash helmet was knocked askew. His hands were locked like vise grips in the cross straps of the kayak.

'You don't need to swim,' Greg said. 'We're going to get you to that dock over there, okay? But you have to sit still.' In his mind, he added, you pussy. A grown man who couldn't swim, even with a flotation vest. What was up with that?

They made it to the dock quickly because it was so damn cold that Greg kicked at high speed. The dock, projecting from the grounds of the Inn at Willow Lake, had definitely seen better days. Some of the planks were warped and the nails rusted, and a fine film of algae covered the piers. A rickety ladder was attached to the side.

Shane clung to it, shivering, while Nina hoisted herself out of the water and bent over the hull of the kayak. 'Hold still,' she said. 'Let me figure out what you're caught on. I think this cord—'

'Screw the cord.' With safety assured, anger took over. Shane clawed a pocket knife from his pants.

'Hey, don't—'

Ignoring her, he sawed through the carrying cord of Nina's kayak and clambered out onto the dock. 'Thanks, Nina,' he said. 'It's been . . . real.'

'I'm sorry,' she said faintly. 'I had no idea you didn't know how to swim. You should have said something before we launched.'

'Nobody can swim hanging upside down underwater.'

'I know. I said I was sorry . . .' Nina gazed up at Greg, her eyes watering and her chin trembling. Poor thing, Greg thought. He was confused by a sudden urge to pull her into a soothing hug. He wanted to tell her the guy was being a jerk, not worth crying over. Then, seeing a tremor in her throat, he realized she wasn't fighting tears, but holding in laughter. In the spray skirt and crash helmet, Gilmore looked like a grotesque, angry ballerina.

Don't make eye contact, Greg cautioned himself. Too late. He and Nina looked straight at each other and immediately lost it. Between guffaws, Greg saw the bank president's color turn a furious red.

'Happy you're so amused,' Shane said.

Greg struggled for control. 'Hey, it's just relief, buddy,' he said. 'We're glad you're okay.'

Nina giggled helplessly while still shivering with cold.

'Yeah, I can see that,' Gilmore muttered.

Brooke and Max arrived in the canoe. She clambered out and ran to Shane, clucking over him like a mother hen.

'You're freezing,' she said.

'So am I,' said Greg, but she almost stepped on him as she rushed toward Shane.

Greg eyed Nina, who was hugging herself, teeth chattering. She was a small, intense-looking woman. He found her oddly attractive—oddly, because he wasn't usually drawn to her type. Yet there was something about Nina. He'd always been intrigued by her. And now he had big news to share with her. He'd pictured a different sort of meeting about the inn, though.

'Is he the first to wear a crash helmet on a date with you or have there been others?' Greg asked.

'Very funny. And clearly, it doesn't help.'

'Listen, I'm parked at the inn,' Brooke said to Shane. 'If you want, I can give you a lift to your car.'

Shane's lips had turned from blue to indigo. 'That'd be good.'

Brooke said her goodbyes to Greg and Max. Then she turned to Nina, offering the dazzling smile that had inspired Greg to ask her out in the first place. 'I'm Brooke Harlow.'

'The bank's new asset manager,' Nina said, her eyes narrowing. 'And you've parked your car at the inn.'

'Sure. I drove myself over.'

'Shane was just telling me about you.' Somehow, despite being soaked to the skin, Nina managed to summon a kind of icy dignity. 'Nina Romano.'

'Oh, you're Nina! I've heard so much about you. We'll have to catch up, but I should give poor Shane a lift before he freezes.'

'You do that,' Nina said.

Brooke offered Nina an uncertain smile. 'Nice to meet you. I'm sure we'll meet again.'

'Count on it.' Nina thrust up her chin as though trying to make herself taller.

'I'll call you,' Brooke said to Greg.

No, you won't, he thought. He could see it in her eyes, because he'd seen it before. His life was way too complicated to appeal to a woman like Brooke Harlow, a fresh transplant from the city, looking for a simpler way of life. He was divorced, had custody of two kids and was about to launch a new business, all of which meant he didn't have unlimited time to give to a relationship. Okay, he had maybe five minutes a day to give to a relationship.

Still, he watched Brooke leave with a twinge of regret. She had runway-model legs, long blond hair, a great smile and . . . He tried to figure out if he liked her personality. Did she have one? With those looks, did she need one?

Max tied the canoe to a cleat. 'I'm going to go fishing, okay, Dad?' he asked.

'Okay, but stay on the dock,' Greg said, glad that the kid wanted to do something more wholesome than checking out Brooke Harlow.

Greg turned to Nina. She was facing the inn, her dark eyes diamond-bright with . . . He couldn't read her expression, but he could tell she wasn't happy. Dripping wet, she looked even smaller than she usually did, her jet-black hair hanging limp and her spandex shorts and T-shirt clinging. He could tell at a glance that under the shirt, she was wearing one of those heavy-duty athletic bra things. Whoever invented that garment lacked imagination.

'Well,' Nina said as she bent down and started bailing water from the kayak. 'Well, doesn't this just make my day?'

Greg wondered why—besides being soaked to the skin—she was acting so hostile. This was not a good sign, since they would soon be working together. One thing he had never figured out was how to penetrate a woman's anger. He hadn't been able to do so back when he was married, and he wasn't able to do it now. He'd known Nina off and on over the years—mostly off. He remembered her as a lively kid some years his junior, a local girl he saw when he came to spend his summers at Camp Kioga. He recalled more about her than she could possibly know, but it was probably not a good idea to bring that up, especially with her in this mood. When he'd first moved back to town last winter, she'd made what he thought might be an overture, but he'd been reeling from the divorce and hadn't taken her up on it. Now, looking at her, he called himself a fool. There was more fire and appeal in a wet, angry Nina than in a hundred blond Brookes.

The old planks of the dock creaked as Nina bent to hoist the kayak out of the water.

'I'll give you a hand,' said Greg. He felt mildly annoyed that she hadn't asked for help. The kayak was heavy, and as they upended it a slew of water soaked their feet all over again. They set it up on the dock to drain some more. Greg watched Brooke and Shane cross the broad lawn. For their first—and apparently final—date, Brooke had brought her own car to the inn. Although he hadn't been divorced for long, Greg had learned the separate cars ploy right away. When arranging a rendezvous—date, hookup, whatever—it was safer to arrive and depart separately. This evening, Greg had planned to leave Max with his older sister, Daisy, and take Brooke to dinner, after which—please God, it had been so damned long—he would get laid.

But no. Clearly, that was off the table. Now he was wet and cold and stuck with an equally wet, cold and ticked-off Nina Romano.

The last time he'd seen her was at high school commencement a few weeks before. He and Nina each had a graduating senior. Sonnet Romano and Daisy were friends, but the future lying before each girl couldn't be more different. Sonnet was headed for travel and adventure and college, as he recalled, while Daisy was—

'I'd better be going,' Nina said, interrupting his thoughts. 'My car's clear across the lake at the municipal boat shed.' She bent to relaunch her kayak.

'Forget that,' Greg heard himself say. 'Let's go inside and dry off.'

He gestured toward the inn. The main building was a house of wonders, having been built in the 1890s as a vast family summer compound by a railroad baron with more money than common sense. Over the generations, the place had undergone a number of transformations, ultimately becoming the sort of cozy lakeside resort people thought of when they needed to escape somewhere.

'What do you mean, let's go inside?' Nina asked. 'The place is closed.'

'True.' He dug in his pocket. 'Luckily, I have a key.'

She gaped at him. Her face paled and her voice was a rasp of disbelief as she said, 'I don't understand. What are you doing with the key?'

Oh, boy. This wasn't the way he'd planned to tell her. He'd envisioned a business meeting, both of them in dry street clothes. What the hell? he thought. 'The Inn at Willow Lake belongs to me now.'

Not only did Nina Romano have a Sophia

31

Loren face, with those large, gorgeous eyes and full lips; she had an expressiveness about her that showed every emotion. She wasn't reserved and cool like the girls Greg had grown up with—bloodless, sleek-haired schoolgirls or the queen of all suppressed emotion, his ex-wife, Sophie. Nina instantly expressed everything she felt. Maybe that was why Greg found her a little scary. Unlike the Brooke Harlows of the world, he sensed Nina could be a real threat, because she might actually make him feel something besides plain lust.

At the moment, she had an entire succession of emotions on display—shock, denial, hurt, anger . . . but no acceptance.

'So you're the one who bought this place while I was away,' she said, anger shaping every word.

'Gilmore didn't tell you?'

She glared at him. 'I didn't actually give him a chance.'

Greg didn't know why she was so pissed off, or why he felt defensive. 'It's probably serendipitous that we both ended up here. I know you hold the general management contract. We'll need to renegotiate that.'

Still radiating fury, she said, 'Renegotiate.'

'You made the agreement with the bank. The contract was sold with all the other assets, but we'll have to change some things.'

'No shit,' she said, and marched toward the

inn.

*      *      *

The moment she stepped from the wraparound porch into the sunroom of the inn, Nina was transported. Even though the place had seen better days, an air of faded gentility and elegance lingered in the arched doorways and carved wooden mouldings and railings, the tall ceilings and carpenter-Gothic window casements. She had spent a lot of time here, both in person and in her dreams. The smell of fresh plaster and paint indicated that renovations were already underway.

When she was a little girl, she and her best friend, Jenny, used to watch the Rainbow Girls in their white dresses and gloves going there for their monthly meeting. The Rainbow Girls were a group of privileged young ladies who gathered to work on charitable pursuits, and they'd always seemed like a breed apart to Nina, like fairies who lived on a special diet of meringues and cream. She never actually wanted to be one of them—they seemed a bit boring to her—but she wanted to be their hostess. When she and Jenny would ride their bikes past the inn, she'd say, 'I'm going to own that place one day.'

The owners, Mr. and Mrs. Weller, lived on the premises and ran the place as a quiet retreat for tourists and people from the city. Nina had worked there each summer, beginning when she was thirteen. The work was not glamorous, but she'd been fascinated by the operation of the hotel, the array of guests from all over. Later, as a young mother, she'd moved up from housekeeper to desk clerk, bookkeeper and assistant manager, learning every aspect of the business. Even dealing with plumbing woes and cranky guests hadn't discouraged her. After Mr. Weller died, Mrs. Weller carried on, but never with the same spirit she had when he was alive. When she passed away, she left the place—along with its mortgage—to her only living relative, a nephew in Atlantic City. He entrusted its management to a contract firm that let everyone go and sent in their own staff. Nina went to work as the mayor's assistant while she finished her education. The experience had led to her being appointed to office when the mayor had been incapacitated by illness. Her friends and family thought her head would be turned by city politics, but she always came back to the idea of the Inn at Willow Lake.

Due to neglect and mismanagement, the inn went into foreclosure. It seemed a perfect opportunity for her, a time to take a risk, to start something new.

Her first step had been to approach Mr. Bailey, the bank's asset manager, and propose to him that she reopen the inn, managing it on behalf of the bank while she applied for a small-business loan. It seemed like the perfect arrangement.

Now she stood dripping on the faded cabbage-rose carpet in the salon and stared at Greg Bellamy, the new owner of the inn.

Funny, he didn't look like the kind of guy who stomped people's dreams into the ground. He looked—God—like Mr. Nice Guy. Like Mr. Nice Guy with an incredible body and killer smile and hair that was great even when it was wet.

Still, she had no trouble hating him as he hurried to a supply closet and grabbed some towels and a spa robe and slippers. 'You can dry off and put these on while I throw our stuff in the dryer,' he said.

The man was clueless, she thought, grabbing the bundle and heading into the closest guest room. The Laurel Room, it used to be called. Oh, she remembered this place, with its beautiful woodwork and lofty ceilings, the white porcelain sink set into an antique washstand. Apparently, Greg had wasted no time fixing the place up. The walls bore a fresh coat of sky-blue paint and a new light fixture hung from the ceiling. From the window, she could see Max out on the dock, casting with a fishing rod.

She tried to numb herself to all feeling as she peeled off her cold, clammy things and put on the robe. The thick terry cloth fabric felt wonderful against her chilled skin, but she was in no mood to feel wonderful. Bitterness and resentment filled her up like poison, and it was hard not to feel utterly persecuted by fate. It seemed that every time her turn came up, something happened to snatch it away.

All her life, she had made every choice for practical reasons, governed by what was best for Sonnet. Finally she had reached a point where she could take a risk. If not the inn, then something else. It was true that because of area covenants, there could never be another inn on the lake, but there were other options. She could become a painter, a bookseller, she could train for a triathlon, open a dog-grooming parlor, drive a bus . . . a thousand possibilities lay before her.

The trouble was, she wanted this. The Inn at Willow Lake. Nothing else would do. Only she wanted it on her terms, not Greg Bellamy's.

Snap out of it, she scolded herself, cinching the robe's belt snugly around her waist. She had a great kid, a loving family, the chance to serve as mayor. She ought to be counting her blessings, not tallying up her losses.

Yet when she marched back to the lobby with her clothes in a squishy bundle, she was far from calm. She was still a seething ball of fury.

Greg had managed to scrounge up a pair of painter's pants and had paired them with a slightly-too-tight T-shirt. His hair was attractively mussed. The fact that he looked

36

completely hot only made her madder. The friendly, warm gas fire he'd ignited in the salon's fireplace made her madder still.

'I'm glad I ran in to you,' he said. 'I'd heard you were back from your trip. Is Sonnet okay?'

'She's fine.' All right, so he was being nice, asking about her daughter. Of course, he could afford to be. He already had what he wanted.

'I wanted to set up a meeting this week. We have a lot to talk about.'

Hugging the oversize robe around her, she went to the settee in front of the annoyingly cheerful fire. 'I don't think there's anything to say.'

He smiled. *Smiled.* 'This is an opportunity for both of us. I'm going to need a general manager, and the bank already had a deal with you. Now, about your contract—'

'The contract.' She rubbed her temples, feeling the beginnings of a headache. 'It was supposed to be so simple. How did this happen?'

'It *is* simple. Bailey retired from the bank and Brooke took over the asset management. She sold me the inn.'

Nina glared at him. 'What did you do, sleep with her to get a good deal on the place?'

He glared back. 'That's none of your business.'

All right, Nina thought, that was probably a low blow, but she didn't care. 'I don't get it. What on earth do you want with this place?'

'It's exactly what I've been hoping to find. A business that keeps me close to home for my kids, something I like doing. And I know you're the ideal manager. You've got a history with the place, experience running it. You're perfect.'

This was so classic. The Bellamys were a favored family. It seemed to Nina that every last one of them had been born with a silver spoon in their mouth. It seemed that fortune denied them nothing. While ordinary people like the Romanos struggled for everything they had, the Bellamys swept in and helped themselves.

For Nina, even traveling was bad luck. 'The deal's off,' she said tightly.

'Are you always this angry, or is this something special, just for me?'

'I had plans,' she snapped. 'I know that doesn't matter to you, but—'

'Come on, Nina. At least hear me out.'

'Why should I?'

He didn't react to her challenging tone. Instead, he said simply, 'No reason. We barely know each other. For what it's worth, I had plans, too.'

*Plans.* 'You probably want to turn this place into some kind of overpriced corporate retreat,' she said. 'And wouldn't that be just charming.'

'Whatever gave you that idea?'

'I've seen the numbers. It's the best way to

38

turn a profit.'

'And that's what I'm all about. Turning a profit.'

To be honest, she didn't know what he was about. She didn't know much about him at all. That hadn't stopped her from jumping to conclusions about him. She took her fury down a notch.

'So tell me. I really want to know.'

He studied her, and there was something in his gaze, some level of trust and confidence. 'All my life, I've done what I thought I was supposed to do. Ten years ago, I started my own firm in Manhattan because it seemed like the responsible thing to do. What I ended up with was a job I didn't like and one that made me ignore my family.'

All right. So he wasn't a complete selfish bastard. But why on earth did *his* act of redemption have to step on *her* toes? 'There are lots of ways to do that,' she told him. 'You don't need this place.' *I* do, she thought. I always have. When she was fifteen years old, the roadmap of her life had unfolded, and she'd always known her final destination was here.

'You don't know what I need. Maybe this will give you an idea.' He went to the front desk, already furnished with computer and phone. She heard the breathy whisper of a printer, and then he brought her a copy of the contract. She'd been so excited the day she'd signed it. Now she felt sick to her stomach.

'The modifications are in bold,' he said.

'You think you can come in here with your money, buy this place and me along with it, a single woman with limited options,' she said. 'Well, think again. You can't—'

'When you buy a business, you buy all its assets and liabilities. This contract with you is one of its assets.'

She grabbed the document from him and studied his suggested changes. She blinked to make sure her eyes weren't playing tricks. He had increased the salary and added a profit-sharing option and pension.

Just for a moment, she wavered. This was real money. For once in her life, she would be financially secure. She could help out Sonnet, because even with the scholarships she'd won and her father's contributions, it didn't mean her education would be without cost.

No, Nina thought. No. She recoiled from the contract as though it had turned into a snake. For all the incentives he'd added, he'd still taken away the one thing worth having— the possibility of owning the place one day.

She got up and went to the window, knowing she probably looked completely undignified in a robe three sizes too big, but she didn't care. She studied the view outside—a broad, sloping lawn dotted with Adirondack chairs, the belvedere, carriage house and caretaker's quarters, the boathouse, dock and the lake in

40

the distance. Max had apparently grown bored with fishing. A pole lay abandoned on the dock. 'I'm not signing that,' she said over her shoulder. 'Find someone else.'

'I suppose I could opt for a commercial management company from out of town, but I'm hoping to avoid that. I want you,' he said simply.

She swung around to face him. 'You can't have me.'

His expression indicated that this was not something he often heard from a woman. Well, of course not. He was a Bellamy. He looked like the American Dream come to life. He was not the kind of guy a woman refused. 'You were perfectly happy to make a deal with the bank,' he pointed out.

'That was different. I—' She stopped herself. She wasn't going to tell him her hopes, the future she'd imagined for herself. It was none of his business, and she already looked pathetic enough, standing here in her borrowed robe. 'I have to go,' she said, heading down the hall to the laundry.

'Your clothes aren't dry yet.'

'I'll live.' She'd survived worse.

He intercepted her in the hall. For a second, his nearness shocked her and she didn't know why. Her skin flushed and her heart sped up, and all he was doing was standing there. He smelled of the freshness of the lake, and unlike some guys, he looked even better up close.

41

Kissing Shane Gilmore hadn't affected her like this, and Greg wasn't even touching her.

She glared at him. 'You're in my way.'

'I'm just not getting the rage, Nina. What is up with you?'

'You don't get me, that's what. This was supposed to be my time to shine. My whole life has been reacting to a change of plans. I never dreamed I'd be realigning my thinking about this and now here I am . . . I don't walk away from a challenge.'

'Then why would you do that now?'

'There's nothing here for me, nothing but a job, working for you. I don't need this. I don't need you. I have options.'

'I want you to stay,' he said, still close enough that she could feel the warmth of his breath. 'Let's talk about this.'

She suspected he started a lot of sentences with 'I want.' She kept her gaze steady as she said, 'There's really nothing to talk about. I suggest you get busy trying to find someone to sign your contract.' With that, she pushed past him with as much dignity as she could muster, and ducked into the laundry. She slammed the door and opened the industrial-size dryer. Sure enough, her clothes were at that lukewarm, half-dry stage that made them clammy and supremely uncomfortable. She didn't care. She had to get the hell out of here.

She could feel the fury and resentment pouring off her as she returned to the salon

42

with the damp clothes stretched over her, probably in the most unflattering fashion. Greg either didn't notice or didn't care about her appearance or her state of mind as he followed her outside, across the lawn and down the dock.

'Let's put the kayak on my truck and I'll give you a lift back to your place.'

'No, thanks,' she said, pulling on her vest. Such a gentleman, ripping her future to shreds while offering her a lift to nowhere. In one angry movement, she launched the kayak, got in the rear seat and pushed off.

'Nina,' he called.

Forget it, she thought. He can beg all he wants. In so many ways, he was still that too-handsome, too-lucky guy she remembered from the past. She wondered what he remembered about her. Sure, it was a long time ago, but still . . . Clearly the meetings had meant more to Nina than to Greg, which only fueled her anger at him.

'Nina.' His voice was a bit more urgent. 'I don't care how pissed off you are,' he said. 'You won't get far without this.'

She glanced back in time to see him standing on the dock, holding out a double-ended paddle.

So much for her exit. Leaning forward, she reached for the paddle. She couldn't quite touch it, so he leaned a little farther over the water until she was able to grasp the blade.

At the same time she gave it a slight tug—an accident, of course. For a split second, they engaged in a tug-of-war, angry gazes locked, the paddle between them. Seized by a childish impulse, she gave one final tug on the oar. He wobbled for a moment, then pitched forward into the water, making a splash that didn't quite drown his curse.

'Nice, Greg,' she murmured, then dipped in her oar and glided away.

## THREE

After dinner that evening, Greg sat with his daughter, Daisy, going over the hundreds of photos she'd taken for the inn's new brochures, ads and website. He studied her as she concentrated on the images. Current mood, he assessed, was cooperative. With her face bathed in the pale glow from the computer screen, Daisy was fully absorbed by the task. She was so beautiful, his daughter, and at eighteen, so heartbreakingly young.

He wished he could talk to someone about what it was like, picking his way through the minefield that was his relationship with his troubled daughter. Since the divorce, he and Daisy had grown close, although it had been a struggle. Some days, the closeness felt more like a détente.

'How about these four?' she asked. 'One for each season.'

She had talent, and it wasn't just in his mind. Some of her work was on display in the bakery/café in town where she used to work, and people bought the framed, signed prints with gratifying regularity. Greg hoped like hell her gift—and her passion for it—would give her something to aim for in the future, something that would fulfill her and make use of her talents. She had a knack for picking the unexpected angle or perspective that turned something ordinary—a tree branch, a window seat, a dock—into something special. She preferred the fine detail over the wider view, showcasing nature's splendor in a single perfect rhododendron blossom. A well-thumbed novel beside a claw-footed tub conveyed a sense of luxury, and panoramic shots of the whole resort showcased the grandeur of the place.

'I'll take that as a yes,' she said to him.

'Your instincts are better than mine when it comes to things like this.'

She nodded and relabeled four of the shots. 'So did you talk to Nina Romano about the inn?'

'Yeah, earlier today.'

'And?'

And he'd done a lousy job explaining himself to the woman. In fact, he didn't know what Nina hated more—him, or the idea of working for him. The fact that he'd bought the Inn at Willow Lake was an affront to her. She acted as though he'd somehow stolen it away from her. 'She's thinking about my offer.' *Right.*

'Well, you'd better make sure she says yes,' Daisy admonished. 'I don't think we can make this work without her.'

'Thanks for the vote of confidence.'

'Come on, Dad. What do either of us know about running a hotel?'

He could have pointed out that he'd built a thriving landscape architecture business in Manhattan. And despite his education and expertise, despite the fact that he didn't have a clue what he was doing when it came to hotels, he had learned that hard work and common sense went a long way. Yet he reminded himself why he was doing this. Making the firm a success had carried a cost he'd never anticipated. Lucrative didn't always mean successful. He had been so consumed by work that, without his even noticing it, years passed and he woke up one day to find himself with two kids who were practically strangers and a marriage that was damaged beyond repair.

As his marriage ended, he had resolved to make a new beginning. He'd pulled his supremely unhappy kids out of their Upper East Side private prep school and moved upstate to Avalon. The Bellamys had long-standing ties to the community. Greg's parents had operated Camp Kioga until their retirement ten years before. They'd held on to the property, and when his marriage raged out of control, the place had been his anchor.

Last summer, with his marriage in its death throes, he had made a desperate move, bringing the kids to Camp Kioga to help Olivia renovate the place for his parents' fiftieth wedding anniversary celebration. He thought he'd seen progress with Max and Daisy by summer's end—his son was no longer obsessed with video games and his daughter had stopped smoking. But when they returned to the city, Daisy had started her senior year in a state of open rebellion and Max had adopted a who-the-hell-cares attitude, wearing it like body armor. Ultimately, when the time came to rebuild his life, he'd decided to do it here, in the riverside town he remembered from the summers of his boyhood.

It was too soon to tell whether or not this was the right move, but he was determined to change his life, engaging in work that revolved around his family. In his former life, he was all about building things for the world. Now he was determined to focus on building a world for his family.

'Your cousin Olivia didn't know anything about running Camp Kioga, and look at her now,' he pointed out. A year ago, Greg's grown niece had also made the move from Manhattan to the mountains. She'd been

47

charged with renovating Camp Kioga, and the project had given her an entirely new direction and a future she'd never expected.

'But Olivia has Connor Davis helping her,' Daisy pointed out. 'He's a contractor. He fixes stuff up for a living.' She sighed romantically. 'Besides, they're, like, the most perfect couple *ever.*'

Greg made no comment. At summer's end, Olivia and Connor were getting married at Camp Kioga, and the event had snowballed into the biggest Bellamy family affair since his parents' anniversary the previous year. Relatives and friends would be coming from all over, many of them planning to stay at the Inn at Willow Lake. He wished Olivia and Connor well, of course, but being regarded as a perfect couple had its drawbacks—like trying to live up to an image that existed in other people's minds. He and Sophie had been called the perfect couple, too, despite the rushed circumstances of their marriage.

He hoped Olivia would have better luck than he had.

Daisy shifted uncomfortably in her chair, folding her arms across her stomach. 'So I wanted to ask you something, Dad.'

'Sure, anything.' But of course, inwardly, he braced himself, wondering, Now what?

'Classes start in a few weeks, and I thought . . .' Her voice trailed off and she got up, rubbing the small of her back. She turned, and the evening light from the window crisply outlined the incongruous curve of her belly.

And with that movement, Greg saw his daughter as though through a fragmented glass. The illusion that she was still his little girl fell to pieces. Even now that he'd had months to get used to the idea, the sight of her extremely pregnant silhouette still sometimes shocked him. She was a bundle of contradictions. The untimely ripeness of her form looked wrong with her still-soft, vaguely childlike features. She had painted her nails a vivid red-black and wore ripped jeans and a top that draped over the arc of her belly. She was a little girl, teenager and grown woman all in one, and she regarded him with a need and trust Greg wasn't sure he deserved. She was his *kid*. And at thirty-eight, he hardly felt ready to be a grandfather.

Cut it out, he warned himself. He simply didn't have a choice in the matter. Regrets and what-ifs were not an option, not at this point. 'You thought what?' he prompted.

'Could you be my coach?' she asked. 'For the childbirth classes, you know, and for the hospital.'

Her coach? The guy who stands by her in the delivery room? No, thought Greg, fighting a sick premonition. No way. Not in a million years would he be that guy, witnessing his child having a child of her own.

'My doctor said it should be somebody I

trust and feel safe with.' She paused, bit her lip, and her expression was one he'd seen a thousand times through the years. 'That's you, right?' she said.

'But I'm . . . a guy,' he said lamely. A scared, freaking-out guy who didn't trust himself to stay conscious in the delivery room or come through in an emergency. A guy who would rather have a root canal than see his daughter give birth. That seemed wrong on so many levels, he didn't know where to begin.

'What about your mother?' he asked, his mouth working ahead of his brain, as usual.

Daisy's expression froze, and although she would not appreciate knowing it, she looked just like Sophie. They both had that regal, withering ice-queen manner, able to belittle or intimidate with a razor-sharp glance.

'What about her?' Daisy asked. 'The classes go on for six weeks. You think she's going to put her life on hold and camp out in Avalon for six weeks?'

Sophie lived in The Hague, where she was a lawyer at the International Criminal Court. She came back to the States once a month to see the kids. After the divorce, Sophie had insisted that Daisy and Max live with her. Both kids, traumatized by the breakup of their family, had returned after just a couple of weeks, demanding to stay with Greg. He didn't fool himself into thinking he was the preferred parent. It was just that the life he offered here

50

in the States was a better fit for his two lost, hurting kids. So now Sophie had to make do with the visits, with phone calls and email. The situation was sad and awkward, and Greg couldn't tell if the kids had forgiven her or not. He figured his job was to stay neutral on the issue.

Daisy made a lofty gesture around the house. 'Will Mom live with us? Yeah, she'd love that.'

'I own a hotel,' Greg pointed out. 'We could put her in the Guinevere suite.' Like many of Avalon's local establishments, the Inn at Willow Lake had an Arthurian theme with rooms named after characters from the old legend.

'Guinevere. Wasn't she the one who cheated on her husband with his best friend?' Daisy asked archly.

'That was never proven. The French added it later.' Greg felt a strange and unjustified sense of solidarity with his ex. It was probably because of Daisy's situation—unmarried and pregnant, with the monumental struggle of single motherhood ahead of her. Despite his differences with Sophie, he shared with her the sense that Daisy was going to need all the support and compassion they could offer. 'I'm sure she'd be honored to be your coach.'

'And you wouldn't?'

'Honey, of course I would. But I'm . . .' *Damn.* 'It would be . . .' He paused, got up and

51

paced the room, searching for the right word to describe attending your teenage daughter giving birth to your grandchild. 'Weird,' he concluded. And that was putting it mildly.

'Listen, it's just classes. You learn about the process and signs to watch for, and what to do when things start happening. And in the delivery room, everything is all draped, and you can just deal with me from the neck up. Maybe, um, hold my hand and talk to me, give me ice chips, stuff like that. It didn't look like that big a deal in the video the doctor gave me to watch.'

'That's assuming everything goes according to the video.'

'Okay, fine,' she said. 'Whatever. A birth coach is optional, anyway.'

'Right, like I'm going to let you do this on your own.' Greg stuck his thumbs in his back pockets and stood at the window, looking out but seeing only memories of his own child being born. He hadn't been there for Daisy's birth, of course, thanks to the way Sophie had manipulated the situation. But he'd been present for Max. He remembered the long night, the glare of lights, the pain and the terror and the joy. God, it was yesterday.

Then he turned back to Daisy, his daughter—his heart. 'I'll do it.'

'Do what?' asked Max, coming in from the kitchen, trailing shoelaces and backpack straps in his wake. He was eating again. Of course he

52

was. It had been a half hour since dinner. Max, who had the appetite of some hypermetabolic creature in a sci-fi flick, had taken to refueling a couple of times per hour. At the moment, he was eating a Pop-Tart, stone cold out of the wrapper.

'I'm going to be your sister's birth coach,' he said. 'What do you think of that?'

'I think you're out of your freaking mind,' Max said with a shudder.

'Gosh, and I was going to invite you, too, Max,' Daisy said. 'Having you there, holding my hand, would have meant so much to me.'

'It would mean you finally lost what's left of your marbles. *Geez.*' He shuddered again.

Greg ground his teeth. Despite the fact that she was pregnant, she still bickered like a third grader with her brother. Although it took some restraint, Greg knew it was best not to intervene when the two of them went at it. The bickering usually played itself out and sometimes even seemed to relieve tension, oddly enough.

With an older brother and two older sisters, he understood the dynamics of siblings. The main thing was to stand back and let the fur fly. He found this surprisingly easy to do, zoning out while they picked at each other about everything from the way Max ate a Pop-Tart to their cousin Olivia's upcoming wedding, in which Daisy was to be a bridesmaid, Max an usher.

'You know you're going to have to take ballroom dancing lessons,' Daisy told her brother with a satisfied smirk.

'Better than birthing lessons,' he shot back. 'You'll be, like, the world's largest bridesmaid.'

'And you'll be, like, the world's dorkiest uncle. Weird Uncle Max. I'm going to teach the baby to call you that.'

Greg figured if these kids could survive each other, they could survive anything. He left them to battle it out and went to his study to check email. There was a message from Brooke with a noncommittal subject line— thanks for today . . .

He didn't even need to click on it in order to guess the rest of the message: . . . let's be sure we never do it again sometime. She probably wouldn't be that blunt, but he'd belatedly figured out that Brooke Harlow's interest in him was as a client, not a boyfriend. That was his conclusion after today, anyway. After the boating fiasco, she'd been all too eager to bug out with the lame-ass bank president in tow.

The encounter today with Nina had caused his confidence to falter. What the hell was he getting himself into? No. Greg was happy enough with the transaction. He did realize it could be a disaster—long hours, a challenge around every corner. Then again, it could be the second chance he needed for his family— an enterprise that kept him close to home, the kids engaged in family life, not avoiding it. He

54

practically flinched as he remembered the end of his marriage, when he and Sophie had given up pretending for the sake of the children, who saw straight through them, anyway. Their unhappiness was like a disease that infected the whole family. They'd engaged in battles of bitter recriminations that usually ended in slammed doors, the four of them hiding from each other. Ultimately, Greg and Sophie attempted a trial separation. There was a sense of relief, sure, but the separation opened a whole new set of troubles.

Greg blamed himself for not seeing how troubled Daisy was by the divorce. If he had, maybe Daisy never would have gone to that weekend party on Long Island, and she never would've gotten pregnant. Well, not so soon, anyway.

He'd spent his entire marriage waiting for disaster and then reacting to it. He was determined to change now. Buying the inn felt right, and he was focused on making it happen.

The soft doorbell sound of an incoming email distracted him. He glanced at the screen and then did a double-take when he saw who it was from—Nina Romano. The subject line read We need to talk.

Well, he thought. *Well.*

*      *      *

Nina looked at her best friend, Jenny, and then

back at the computer screen. 'I just hit Send. I can't believe I just hit Send.'

'That's the best way for him to get the message.'

'But I changed my mind.' Nina swiveled back to glare at the screen. She wished there was some way to dive through the digital ether and snatch back her message.

She and Jenny were in Nina's office. It wasn't properly an office but a small nook in her bedroom where the computer sat on a card table. Everything about the house was small, including the rent check she gave her uncle Giulio every month. She'd lived in the modest, cluttered house since Sonnet was little, trying to balance school and work and motherhood. She was blessed with a supportive family, but ultimately wanted to go it alone. She thought again about the offer from Greg Bellamy. *No way.*

'All you said was that you wanted to talk further about the inn,' Jenny insisted, 'It's not like you made a lifetime commitment.'

Nina's chest hurt and she realized she'd been holding her breath. She let it out in a burst of air. 'He'll see it as a sign of weakness. He'll think I'm wavering.'

'You *are* wavering,' Jenny pointed out. 'And that's a good thing. It shows you have an open mind about the situation.'

'I can't believe you didn't tell me this was happening while I was away.'

56

'I didn't know. Even if I did, it would have been completely pointless to ruin your trip with Sonnet.'

She was right. It would've ruined the trip, her cherished mother-daughter time. 'Sorry,' she said. 'It wasn't your job to keep me informed. He's probably already looking for someone else. I bet he won't even call.'

The phone on the desk rang, and both women jumped. Nina grabbed the handset and checked the caller ID screen. The name *Bellamy, G* winked back at her.

'Oh, God. It's him.'

'So pick up,' Jenny suggested.

'No way. I'd rather die.'

'Then I'll do it.' Jenny grabbed the phone.

Nina made a lunge for it, but missed.

Jenny clicked the talk button. 'Romano residence. This is Jenny McKnight speaking. Oh, hey, Greg.'

Nina collapsed on the floor in a heap of helplessness.

'I'm fine, thanks,' Jenny said pleasantly. 'Rourke, too,' she added.

Of course she was fine, thought Nina. She was married to the love of her life, and she had just found a publisher for the book she'd written, a memoir about growing up in a Polish-American bakery. Of course she was freaking fine.

She chatted pleasantly with Greg about his kids, who also happened to be her first cousins, though she hadn't known them very long. Although Jenny was related to the Bellamys, the situation had come to light only in the past year. Jenny had grown up never knowing who her father was. Only last summer did she discover that there had been a tragic love affair between her mother, Mariska, and her father—Philip Bellamy—who happened to be Greg's older brother. So that made Greg her uncle. They'd met just recently, but now, hearing Jenny chat so easily with him, Nina wondered if that blood tie actually counted for something.

'Yes, she's here,' Jenny said.

The traitor. Nina nearly came out of her skin. With nonverbal Italian-American eloquence, she asked Jenny, *Do you want to die today?*

'But she can't come to the phone right now. I'll make sure she returns your call. That's a promise.'

Jenny hung up the phone, seemingly unperturbed by Nina's fury. 'Good news,' she said. 'He hasn't found anyone else yet.'

'How do you know? Did he say anything?'

'Of course he didn't say anything. It's none of my business.'

'Then how do you know he hasn't moved on to his next victim?'

'If you don't believe me, call him yourself.' Jenny held out the phone.

Nina shrank from it. 'I need a drink.'

'I can help with that.' Jenny led the way to the kitchen with the familiarity of a best friend. She went straight to the cupboard and found a bottle of sweet red wine. 'This will be perfect with the biscotti I brought from the bakery,' she said. Although the Sky River Bakery had decidedly Polish roots, there were a number of Italian selections on the menu as well, including cantuccini biscotti that were admittedly better than anything a Romano woman had ever baked. Dunked in the sweet dark wine, they made Nina forget her troubles for approximately twenty-nine seconds.

'So what did he sound like?' she asked Jenny.

'You already spoke to him today, right?'

'No, I mean did he sound conciliatory? Pissed?'

'He sounded like a Bellamy—you know, Manhattan prep school, Ivy League college and all that.' Jenny emulated the accent perfectly, then laughed at herself. 'Sometimes I still can't believe I'm related to those people.' The lighthearted reference belied the ordeal Jenny had gone through as she discovered her ties to the Bellamy family.

'They haven't changed who you are,' Nina reminded her, 'and that's a good thing. Remember how the two of us used to make fun of the summer people when we were growing up?' As girls, she and Jenny would observe the summer vacationers who escaped the city for the cool relief of Willow Lake. They used to discuss the ridiculousness of the girls' tennis whites and straight, silky hair, and that the kids were looked after by servants. The one thing neither Nina nor Jenny ever acknowledged, however, was the fact that their ridicule was rooted in envy.

'Don't turn this thing with Greg into a feud,' Jenny warned her.

'I was mayor of this town for four years,' Nina said. 'I'm good at feuds.'

'It would put me in an awkward position,' Jenny pointed out. 'I'd have to take your side, and then everything would be all awkward with Philip.'

Even though he was Jenny's father, she called him Philip, keeping a slightly formal distance between them. Nina felt a flash of pity for her friend, knowing from having watched Sonnet how hard it was to grow up without a father. Nina herself came from a large, loud family. She'd grown up way too fast, as it turned out, but that wasn't her family's fault.

She tried to imagine what it had been like for Jenny to wake up one day and discover this whole new side of herself. It would be like Nina finding out she had royal blood.

She'd made certain her own daughter knew who her father was as soon as Sonnet was old enough to understand. There was no veil of secrecy, no confusion. Nina had tried to raise Sonnet to be secure in the knowledge that she was loved and wanted; even though her parents weren't together, she had a mother and father who adored her.

He damned well better adore her, Nina thought. He had plenty of lost time to make up for. Sharply focused on his career in the military, Laurence Jeffries had not played a large part in Sonnet's life. Although he paid child support and came once a year to see Sonnet, that was the extent of their relationship. Now, on the brink of adulthood, Sonnet wanted to know more about her father. She'd seized the opportunity of the summer internship.

'Anyway,' Nina said, 'I don't want things to be awkward between you and Philip because of me.'

'They're already awkward enough, but we're dealing with it. We have no choice, what with Olivia's wedding coming up. Which brings me to the actual reason for my visit.' Jenny unzipped the garment bag she'd brought along and, with exaggerated drama, ducked into the bedroom with it.

'The bridesmaid gowns just came in today,' she called through the door. 'I wanted you to be the first to see my dress.' She stepped out on tiptoe to simulate high heels, and held her hair up off her neck. Nina gasped aloud. The dress was exquisite—a long fall of lilac silk charmeuse. Looking at her friend in the wispy dream of a dress, Nina felt an unexpected jolt of emotion.

Jenny was quick to notice. 'Don't go getting all misty-eyed on me.'

'I can't help it. You look like Cinderella.'

'Hey, in the Bellamy family, I *am* Cinderella. So you like the dress?'

'I love the dress.'

'Me, too. Olivia has exquisite taste.' Olivia Bellamy, the bride, was Philip's daughter, too. As her newly discovered half-sister, Jenny would be the matron of honor. Jenny was just starting to learn what it was like to be a Bellamy. The wedding was a full-blown family affair and already the talk of Avalon.

Nina blinked and cleared her throat. 'Remember when we were little, and we had our weddings all planned out?'

Jenny laughed. 'Totally. I'd still have the notebooks where we wrote down all our plans, except they were lost in the fire.' She had lost virtually everything she owned in a house fire the previous winter. The way she had rebuilt her life and moved ahead was an inspiration to Nina.

'We were supposed to marry in a double ceremony,' Nina recalled, reliving the memories. She and Jenny used to sit on Jenny's chenille-covered bed, discussing their weddings.

'Yep, a double ceremony with Rourke and Joey. Best friends marrying best friends. It was all so nice and neat, wasn't it?' There was a soft note in Jenny's voice, a wistful affection for the girls they had been, and regret for all that had happened since they'd dreamed those dreams.

'The music was going to be the greatest hits of Bon Jovi and Heart,' Nina recalled. 'And the dresses—good lord, we drew so many versions. Yards of metallic fuchsia with puffy sleeves. And bridal gowns that were not of this world.' She laughed, remembering how they had planned out every last detail, from the vows they would recite—an e. e. cummings poem, what else?—to the menu at the reception—macaroni and cheese, barbecued chicken and Sky River Bakery donuts. After dual honeymoons—Hawaii, of course—they would buy houses next door to each other. Nina would run the Inn at Willow Lake while Jenny wrote the Great American Novel.

'I hadn't thought about that in years,' Nina said. 'We had some imagination, didn't we?' If she tried very hard, she was able to remember the kid she had been, before everything had happened. She'd been so full of hopes and dreams, and all her goals seemed completely and utterly reachable. 'Nothing went according to plan for either of us, did it?' she added.

Jenny smiled and fluffed out the hem of her dress. 'I never could have planned for anything this good. And you could say the same. You ended up with Sonnet, after all, which is the equivalent of winning the amazing-daughter lottery.'

Nina couldn't dispute that. 'Does it bug you at all that Olivia's getting the big formal wedding?' she asked her friend.

'Lord, no.' Jenny waved a hand dismissively. 'Philip offered—did I tell you that? He said he'd pay for any wedding I asked for.' She grinned. 'Lucky for him, all I wanted was a quick trip down the aisle with a minimum of fuss, and a honeymoon in St. Croix. And I have to tell you, it was perfect for Rourke and me. And I'm sure you remember, I had a great dress.'

'I'll never forget that dress,' Nina assured her. Jane Bellamy, Jenny's new grandmother, had insisted on taking Jenny to Henri Bendel's on Fifth Avenue, where they picked out a cocktail-length couture gown. 'No one in the history of Avalon will forget that dress, are you kidding? You and Rourke are a great couple. Olivia is going to have the greatest maid of honor—'

'Matron of honor, please.'

'Sure. You'll look like a million.' Then Nina, to her dismay, recognized what she was feeling—a tug of envy. She caught herself thinking that Jenny should be Nina's matron of honor, not Olivia's. This was ridiculous, though. In order to have a matron of honor, she would need to be a bride, which was the last thing on her mind. There was a lot Nina wanted now that she was single and her nest

64

was empty. Getting married surely wasn't one of them. Not anytime soon. But falling in love? Who didn't want that? Unfortunately, you couldn't make it happen the way you made a wedding happen, by hiring a planner and picking out china patterns.

Jenny presented her back. 'Here, unzip me. And let's get back to talking about this thing with Greg.'

'There is no thing with Greg.' The zipper snagged. Nina gently teased it away from the delicate fabric.

'He wants you to be his partner at the inn. I'd call that a thing.'

'He wants to suck me dry and then push me aside.'

'Greg's not like that. He really does need help getting the place back up and running, and he's smart enough to know you're perfect for the job.'

'I just don't get it. There are a hundred business opportunities in Avalon. A hundred and twelve last time I checked—and I did check.' She knew what was out there. When she was mayor, one of Nina's priorities had been to dedicate a page of the city's website to local business opportunities to attract investment. 'Why does he have to pick the one thing I want?'

Jenny pulled on her T-shirt. 'The two of you want the same thing. Maybe it's a sign.'

'Right.'

'I don't know why you're so upset by this. You were willing to run the place on behalf of the bank. Greg is offering you virtually the same deal, only he wants to pay you a much bigger salary. Better benefits.'

'It's completely different. The bank would have sold me the place as soon as I could qualify for a loan. Greg took that off the table.'

'Did you tell him that?'

'What, and make myself seem even more pathetic? No, thank you.'

'Nina, be honest with me, with yourself. Did you really think the bank's asset division was going to wait for you to qualify for a small business administration loan?'

Like most government programs, the SBA moved with leaden slowness. Nina had been told that the process could take months, even a year. 'Mr. Bailey would have waited. I'm sure he assumed his successor would have, as well. Her name's Brooke Harlow and I think Greg's dating her. Cozy, huh?'

'Don't jump to conclusions. This is a safer bet for you, anyway,' Jenny said reasonably. 'Maybe you'll hate it and want to get out. Maybe Greg will hate it, and he'll be the one to get out.'

'Suppose it turns out to be perfect for both of us? Then we'd end up plotting to kill each other.'

'Or making a permanent merger.' Jenny wriggled her eyebrows.

'Don't even.'

'Why not? Olivia filled me in on him. He's her youngest uncle—twelve years younger than Philip, so that makes him . . . thirty-eight. He's single. He's a Bellamy. He's a catch.'

'He's got a half-grown boy and a grandbaby on the way.' Not that Nina had anything against pregnant teenagers. She herself was a member of that club.

'A big family is a blessing,' Jenny pointed out. 'You of all people know that, Miss middle-child-of-nine.'

Nina didn't contradict her, even though she could've come up with a thousand objections. She understood that Jenny had endured a particularly lonely childhood. Her father had been a mystery. Her mother had simply taken off, leaving Jenny to be raised by her grandparents in the quiet, neat-as-a-pin house on Maple Street.

'Maybe so,' Nina said. 'But then again, there's something to be said for being completely on my own. I've never done it before. I need to be on my own for the first time in my life. I want to figure out who I am when I'm not somebody's daughter or Sonnet's mom.'

'I understand. You deserve a chance to do that. I'm sure Greg will understand, too. He made you a business proposition, not a marriage proposal.'

'Yeah, heaven forbid I should get one of

those.'

'Hey, you're the one who said she wants a single life.' Jenny smiled and said, 'Come on, Nina. This could be a great opportunity for you.'

'Oh, man, you're doing it.'

'Doing what?'

'That mysterious wisdom-of-the-married thing. I can't stand that.'

'I'm not doing anything of the sort.'

'You are, too. Look at you. You're so . . . so *happy*.'

'And your point is?'

'That just because being married makes *you* happy doesn't mean it's what *I* need.'

'I know. What you need is to be running the Inn at Willow Lake. That's what this whole discussion is about.'

'Fine. You know what? Maybe you're right. Greg has no idea what he's taking on. I do. He won't last the summer—you mark my words.'

'You're not thinking of scheming against him, are you?' asked Jenny.

'I won't need to. He'll fail on his own.'

'With you in charge?' Jenny eyed her skeptically.

'See, that's the dilemma.' Nina finished her wine and poured another glass. 'It's crazy. One way or another, Greg Bellamy has been a thorn in my side ever since we were kids.'

## Part Two

### Then

The Galahad Chamber is named for Sir Galahad of legend, known for his purity and gallantry. Located high in the main lodge, the room pays tribute to the natural surroundings of the inn, appointed with a hand-crafted birchwood bed frame—topped by birdhouses— antler lamps and antique prints by pre-Raphaelite painter Dante Gabriel Rossetti.

Fresh flowers are provided in every room. A penny and an aspirin tablet dropped in the water will keep the flowers fresh longer. The copper acts as a fungicide and aspirin provides acidic properties to the water. Noted florist, author and social reformer Constance Spry reminds us, 'When creating a floral arrangement, always allow some space between the flowers to prevent a crowded effect. One should leave room for the butterflies.'

# FOUR

Nina blamed all her troubles on a boy named Greg Bellamy. It was irrational for a lot of reasons, not the least of which was the fact that he didn't know she existed. That was maybe the main trouble of all.

The first day she met him, she had driven up to Camp Kioga with her best friend, Jenny Majesky. Once a bungalow colony for rich families from the city, it was now a tony summer camp for their children. Not that Nina was going to camp or anything. *As if.*

No, she was heading up the lakeshore road to the historic, exclusive summer camp in a bakery truck. The truck belonged to Jenny's grandparents and the girls were helping with a delivery. Jenny's grandpa let them play the radio as loud as they wanted, being as he was hard of hearing, and Metallica and a delicious breeze rushed over them with equal strength. As the van lumbered through the rustic archway that marked the entrance, Nina inhaled the green scent of the woods and tried to imagine what it would be like to actually be a camper here. Boring, that's what, she thought defensively. Yet it seemed too good to be true, an entire summer away, with a cabin full of friends. She would never know, of course. Families like hers didn't send their kids to camp.

Besides, she reminded herself, summer camp was for people who had too much money and not enough imagination. This was what Pop said, anyway—people didn't know how to take their own kids on vacation these days so they packed them off to summer camp. Of course, Nina and all eight of her brothers and sisters knew this was Pop's way of making everybody feel better. The Romano family could barely afford shoes, let alone a vacation. Pop was a civics teacher at Avalon High, a career he loved. But with nine kids, a teacher had to stretch his salary thin. Very thin.

Each summer, Pop got involved in politics. He worked as a volunteer for local candidates—Democrats, of course— campaigning passionately and tirelessly for candidates he believed in. Some people criticized Pop for this. They said with that many kids, he ought to be out mowing lawns or digging ditches in the summer to earn extra money, but Pop was unapologetic. He truly believed the best thing he could do for his family was to try to change the world for the better by supporting candidates who shared his ideals.

Nina's oldest brother, Carmine, said Pop could accomplish the same thing if he would learn to use a condom.

When Nina's mother wasn't having babies— or nursing them or changing diapers—she worked during the summer as a cook up at Camp Kioga. She said she didn't mind the work. It was something she could do in her sleep—cook for a ton of people. Getting paid to do it was a bonus. At the summer camp, she prepared three squares a day for kids who probably had no clue what it was like to wear the same pair of shoes until they pinched, or to beg your sister not to write her name on her backpack because you knew it would be yours the following year, or to pay for your school lunch with the shameful blue coupons, handing them over furtively and praying the kid behind you didn't notice.

Nina had a summer job, too, at the Inn at Willow Lake, where she cleaned rooms and made beds. To most people, it didn't sound like much, but Nina liked working there. Unlike home, it was quiet and serene, and after you cleaned something, it actually stayed clean for a while instead of getting immediately trashed by grubby brothers or messy sisters. And sometimes, a guest might even leave her a tip, a crisp five-dollar bill in an envelope marked Housekeeping.

Jenny nudged Nina out of her reverie. 'Let's get going,' she said.

Jenny's grandfather went into the giant industrial kitchen of the camp where Nina's mother worked. The girls hurried through their chores so they could go exploring. Even though Pop had nothing good to say about summer camp, Nina thought it was beautiful beyond all imagination, a wonderland of lush forests and grassy meadows, rock-strewn streams and the glittering lake. The main pavilion, where the campers were just finishing lunch, was a bare-timbered Adirondack-style lodge that housed a vast dining hall.

'There they are,' Jenny said, scanning the groups of campers from the stairway leading down to the kitchen. The different age groups were seated at long tables, raising a clatter of dishes and utensils, chatter and laughter. Jenny homed right in on the twelve-to-fourteens. 'Isn't he amazing?' she whispered in a smitten voice.

Nina couldn't speak, although every cell in her body said *yes*. He was impossibly tall, with perfect posture, sandy hair and a killer smile. He wore navy blue camp shorts and a gray T-shirt stenciled Counselor.

Jenny saw where Nina was looking and gave her an elbow nudge. 'Not him, ninny,' she said. 'That's Greg Bellamy. He's old, like eighteen or something.' She pointed at the younger group. 'I meant him.' Her adoring gaze settled on one of the campers, a quiet, lanky boy studying his compass.

'Oh . . .' Nina said, 'him.' She studied the object of Jenny's enraptured affection, a golden boy named Rourke McKnight. Jenny had first met him two summers ago, and she'd convinced herself that they shared some grand destiny. Destiny, schmestiny, thought Nina.

A smaller dark-haired boy went to sit by Rourke. 'Joey Santini,' Jenny said on a fluttering sigh. 'They're best friends. I don't know which one's cuter.'

I do, thought Nina. Her gaze kept straying to the older boy. Greg Bellamy. The name played itself over and over in her head with full symphonic sound. Greg Bellamy. First of all, the name Bellamy was a clue that he was special. In these parts, being a Bellamy was like being a Kennedy in Boston. People knew who you were, and who your 'people' were. You had this aura of prestige and privilege, whether you'd earned it or not.

'Hey, you two,' Nina's mom called from the kitchen. 'Lunch is just ending. Go on up and grab something to eat.'

Jenny hung shyly back, hovering between the kitchen and dining hall.

'Bashfulness is a waste of time,' Nina murmured. In her family, people got lost if they didn't speak up and make their preferences known. She grabbed Jenny by the arm and drew her into the dining room. At the buffet, they helped themselves to sandwiches and drinks. Taking care not to slosh the lemonade from the glass on her tray, Nina made a beeline for Greg Bellamy. He was perusing the desserts table, laden with a rich assortment from the Majeskys' bakery—lemon bars and peach shortcake, walnut brownies and slices of pie. There was one piece of cherry pie left. If there was anything that could make Nina forget a cute boy, it was cherry pie from the Sky River Bakery.

She reached for the plate. At the same moment, so did someone on the other side of the serving table—Greg Bellamy. She looked up and met his eyes. His Bon-Jovi-blue eyes.

He winked at her. 'Looks like we're both after the same thing.'

Usually when a guy winked at a girl it was totally cheesy. Not with Greg Bellamy. When he winked, it nearly made her knees buckle.

'Sorry,' she said, tossing back her thick dark hair. 'It's mine. I saw it first.' Wink or no wink, she wasn't backing down.

He laughed, his voice like melted chocolate. 'I like a girl who knows what she wants.'

She beamed at him. He liked her. He'd said so aloud. 'I'm Nina,' she said.

'Greg. So are you a visitor?' He studied her as though she was the only person in the crowded dining hall.

'That's right.' It wasn't a lie. She simply omitted the information that she was the underage daughter of the camp cook. Fleetingly she wondered if that would change his opinion of her. Of course it would, she admitted to herself. It was the whole reason such things as 'social class' existed right here in the good old US of A. At Camp Kioga, the lines were sharply drawn: the nobs versus the

76

slobs.

But if she stayed anonymous, the lines went away.

She could feel a keen interest in the touch of Greg's gaze, and it made her stand up straighter. Nina had always looked older than her age, a combination of dark, vivid features and early development. Though she flaunted this fact with pride, her confidence was merely a cover for the fact that she had always felt slightly different. Not radically so, but just a little, because she was a year older than the rest of the kids in her grade.

The reason for her being behind in school was humiliating. It wasn't because she was a slow learner or had flunked an early grade. It was because her mother had forgotten to enroll her in kindergarten at the proper age. *Forgotten.* People smiled and nodded their heads when they heard the story of how Vicki Romano had neglected to send her middle child to school. It was completely understandable. The woman had nine kids, and had given birth to the final two—undersized, sickly twin boys—just a few weeks before Nina was to start kindergarten. The entire family was focused on the fact that the tiny twin boys were fighting for their lives while Vicki battled a postpartum infection. The last thing on anyone's mind was quiet, well-behaved, five-year-old Nina. No one remembered that she was supposed to be in school until it was too late to catch up. She had to wait until the following year.

The anecdote was a family favorite, with an all's-well-that-ends-well conclusion. The tiny twins—Donny and Vincent—were rowdy Little League players now and Nina was in the same class as her best friend. It had all worked out for the best.

Except the experience had a more profound effect on Nina than anyone could know. She always felt slightly out of step, off-kilter. She also transformed herself from the quiet, undemanding middle child into someone who figured out what she wanted and then went for it, every time.

Mr. Blue-Eyes Bellamy was still holding on to the edge of the plate. Her plate of cherry pie.

'So you gonna let go?' she challenged.

'Let's split it.' Without waiting for permission, he tugged it from her grasp. He neatly divided the piece of pie into two portions, put one on a clean plate and offered it to her.

'Gee, thanks,' she said, but didn't take the plate.

'You're welcome.' He either missed or ignored her irony. He was a Bellamy, she reminded herself. He had a stunning sense of droit du seigneur, a term she knew from the historical romance novels she was addicted to.

'You're used to getting your way,' she

78

commented, taking the divided pie from him. She felt a little thrill as she talked to him. Flirting had always come naturally to her—unlike school.

Because she was older than everyone else in her grade, Nina had the dubious honor of being the first at a lot of things. She'd been the first to grow boobs and get her period. The first to turn boy-crazy. It had hit her like a speeding train last year. Before her very eyes, boys—other than her brothers—had turned from loud, smelly, supremely annoying creatures into objects of strange and compelling urges. The boys in her grade still acted like children, but those a few years older seemed to share the same urges that bothered and distracted Nina. At the end of the school year, she sneaked into a high school dance and made out with Shane Gilmore, a junior, until one of her uncles—a biology teacher and chaperone—had noticed her and sent her home to be grounded for weeks.

It was easy to give her parents the slip, and she did so at will. Sometimes she even drove her older sister's ancient Grand Marquis. She had taken it to the drive-in movie at Coxsackie, where she'd let Byron Johnson, a senior, feel her up. Unfortunately, her brother Carmine had spotted her. He hadn't told on her, of course, but he beat the crap out of Byron and promised to break his kneecaps if he ever came near her again.

Now, with Greg Bellamy, Nina forgot all those other flirtations. This was the guy. The prize. The one she knew she'd write about in her diary and dream about at night. The one who made her want to go further than second base. A lot further.

'So, Nina, are you busy tonight?' Greg asked her.

'Depends,' she said playfully. 'What did you have in mind?'

He stared straight at her mouth when he said, 'Everything.'

She felt as though she'd caught on fire from the inside out. 'Sounds good to me.'

'Excuse me.' Something very tall and very shapely sidled up to Greg. It was another camp counselor, looking like a Bond girl in camp clothes. 'Oh, good,' she said, helping herself to Greg's plate of pie. 'You saved me a piece.' She aimed a dazzling smile straight at him. 'Thank you, Greggy. I owe you one.'

Greggy? thought Nina. Greggy? Okay, I'm going to barf.

'Binkie, this is Nina,' he said.

The towering bombshell turned, offering the kind of smile that could freeze an enemy at twenty paces. 'Nina. Now, where have I heard that name before? Oh, yes. You must be Mrs. Romano's little girl.'

Nina was watching Greg, not Binkie. It was kind of amazing to see her image being dismantled before her very eyes.

'You know, Mrs. Romano,' Binkie reminded him. 'The camp cook.'

In the space of a few seconds, Greg went from flirting and making a date with Nina to staring at her as though she had sprouted horns and a tail.

'Right,' he said, turning red to the tips of his ears. 'I need to get back to work.' He glared at Nina. 'See you around, kid.'

Binkie offered a chilly smile. 'Nice to meet you, honey.'

Nina stood unmoving, having been put in her place so decisively that she felt as though she'd been rooted to the spot forever. Everything was boiling inside her—thwarted lust, resentment, yearning, shame and injured pride.

'You coming?' Jenny asked, returning from what had probably been a more age-appropriate conversation with Rourke and Joey. She seemed oblivious to Nina's turmoil. 'Gramp's ready to head back to town.'

'Sure,' Nina heard herself say. She thought Greg Bellamy might be watching her as she left the dining hall. She refused to look back, though. He was a mistake she was only too happy to leave behind.

As she was beating a retreat, she was horrified to feel the hot press of tears threatening to spill. Fighting back, she paused, pretending to study the bulletin board, a patchwork of announcements for the camp staff. Someone had lost a pair of sunglasses. Someone else had two tickets to the new hit musical *Miss Saigon*, for sale. Everything was a blur, but then a bright yellow flier resolved itself before her eyes. Welcome Cadets! Community Mixer at Avalon Meadows Country Club. Each year, the new crop of West Point cadets was treated to a pre-enlistment party, their final hurrah before stepping into the rarified world of rigors that was the United States Military Academy. 18 and Over Required.

At the bottom of the flier was a fringe of phone numbers for the RSVP. Nina already knew one appointee—Laurence Jeffries, from Kingston. She'd flirted with him at football and baseball games, and he had no clue how old she was. He'd be the one to get her into the country club. She defiantly ripped off an RSVP number and stuck it in her pocket.

She glanced over her shoulder at Greg Bellamy. If he'd been nicer to her, she'd still be in the dining hall, eating pie. So really, if she got in trouble, it would all be Greg's fault.

*    *    *

Nina never had any trouble passing herself off as an eighteen-year-old. She and her sisters all looked alike. At church and catechism, people always mixed them up. On any given Sunday, Nina had been called Loretta, Giuliana, Maria and even Vicki—their mother. Nina had learned everything she knew from her pretty, popular sisters. She eavesdropped on their giggling conversations about boys and sex. She'd sat with them late at night, listening to them dissect their dates, moment by moment. Thanks to her sisters, Nina knew how to crash a party, how to flirt with a boy, how to French kiss and what safe sex was.

The West Point reception was scheduled for a Sunday night. Nina planned to wait until Maria was in the shower. Then she would go to her sister's wallet and help herself to the driver's license.

That morning, as everyone was running around, getting ready for church, she told her parents the usual story—her friend Jenny was having a sleepover—though she probably didn't need to bother. Everyone was preoccupied, and her father was organizing yet another fund-raiser for a candidate.

'Isn't it frustrating to see Pop raise all that money for someone else?' Nina asked her mother as they all tumbled out of the van at St. Mary's. Pop had leaped out first to join a group of local businessmen in front of the church. Carmine was left to play parking valet with the lumbering van, which had once been an airport shuttle. Their dad had bought it for a song. It was the only car that fit them all.

'I mean,' Nina continued, 'he's raising money to buy radio ads and we can't even afford to get Anthony's teeth straightened.'

Ma only smiled when Nina said stuff like that. 'This is your dad's passion. It's what he believes in.'

'What about what you believe in, Ma? Don't you believe in getting a new winter coat more than once a decade, or paying the light bill without going into debt?'

'I believe in your father,' Ma said serenely. And boy, did she ever. Giorgio Romano could do no wrong in her eyes. To be fair, Pop was just as crazy about Ma. He went to high mass with her every Sunday and sat there without blinking as she unhesitatingly placed ten percent of their weekly income in the collection basket, because Ma believed in tithing.

At a young age, Nina decided that men who followed their passion were of limited interest to her. She did, however, harbor a passion of her own, and it was for boys. Even in church, she caught herself checking out the boys. The altar boys, for Pete's sake, who used to look so dorky in their red robes and white surplices. Now they looked impossibly sexy to her, with their Adam's apples and big, squarish hands, dress shoes peeping out from beneath their robes. Nina had heard the term *boy-crazy* before; now she understood what it meant. They *did* make her crazy, in the sense that they totally distracted her from everything but thoughts of making out, all day and all night

84

long.

As everyone lurched forward to kneel after the Lamb of God, she glanced over her shoulder at Jenny, a few rows back with her grandparents. The three of them looked so neat and self-contained, not like the whispering, rustling, unwieldy Romano bunch. But Jenny didn't notice Nina trying to get her attention. As she often did, Jenny looked as though she was a million miles away.

Nina turned her eyes to the front and tried to keep her mind blank through the Canon of the mass. It was always a great internal debate with her, deciding whether or not to go for communion. Catholics took their communion very seriously. No wonder you were supposed to unload all your sins beforehand. Supposedly, the sacrament was reserved for people whose souls were spotless, who had emerged from the confessional as squeaky clean as an athlete stepping out of a postgame shower.

Nina did go to confession—and often. Only yesterday, in a voice rough with shame, she'd told the ominous presence on the other side of the screen about shirking her chores, lying to Sister Immaculata about her catechism homework, having impure thoughts about altar boys. And even that was a lie, come to think of it. Her thoughts were *very* pure, indeed. Pure lust.

Sure, she'd done her penance, reciting Our

Fathers and Hail Marys until her knees grew numb, but afterward she went right back to her sinful ways. This very moment, she was sitting before God and thinking about how she was going to the party at the country club tonight to find a boy to make out with.

'"Lord, I am not worthy to receive you,"' she recited along with the congregation, '"but only say the word, and I shall be healed."'

This did not help her decide whether or not to partake of communion. She weighed the pros and cons in her mind: If you just sat there like a bump on a pickle, everyone would know for sure you were a sinner and a slacker for failing to do your penance after confession. If you jumped up and went for it, people would figure you were lying or insincere, because no kid was free of sin, except maybe Jenny. Nina wished there was some designation for the in-between people who weren't perfect but tried to be. Strivers, you could call them. Shouldn't there be some reward for people who strove to be good, even though they fell short most of the time?

Lines were forming along the aisles in preparation for communion. Nina had resigned herself to staying put, letting friends and family speculate about what heinous stain on her soul was keeping her from Holy Communion. Then she saw that Father Reilly's right-hand attendant, the boy designated to hold the chalice of hosts, was Grady Fitzgerald. A year ago, Grady Fitzgerald had been scrawny, pimply and dull. Now he was tall and cute, right down to the peach fuzz mustache on his upper lip. And he kept looking at Nina in a certain way. She was sure of it.

This had to be a sign. She was meant to go to communion. She shot to her feet and took her place in line. Each step brought her closer to Grady. When it was her turn, she was supposed to tip back her head and delicately open her mouth as the priest said, 'The body of Christ.'

Instead, she kept her eyes open and glued to Grady. 'Amen,' she whispered huskily, feeling the insubstantial wafer dissolve on her tongue. She returned to her place, where she was supposed to kneel and contemplate the ecstasy of the miracle. Instead she knelt, closed her eyes and pressed her hands to her forehead, realizing she had hit a new low. She had used the sacrament of communion as a chance to flirt with a cute boy.

She was going to hell for certain.

After mass, as the congregation filed out of the church, Father Reilly made a beeline for her and she braced herself. This was it, then. The jig was up. He was going to expose her as a liar and a fraud.

'Miss Nina Romano,' he said in full view of her parents. 'A word with you.'

'Yes, Father?' Nina's stomach churned. She

87

was going to barf, right here, right now.

'The way you were at communion today . . .'

*No, don't say it. I'm sorry. I didn't meant to—*

'It was quite something, that bold look and loud "Amen."'

'Father, I—'

'I wish more young people had your conviction. Your fervor. Well done.'

Oh. *Oh.* 'Thank you, Father.' Nina lifted her chin, squared her shoulders.

As her parents beamed at her with pride, Nina packed away a life lesson. In every situation, people tended to see what they wanted to see.

## FIVE

Nina found herself swimming in a sea of boys, and it wasn't even a dream. She was surrounded by ninety percent men. She was wide awake, in the ballroom of the Avalon Meadows Country Club, attending the annual salute to West Point's incoming class of cadets. The founder of the country club was a West Point alum, and the large, lavish party had become a tradition. Some of the appointees drove for hours to get there. The following week, basic training would begin for the cadets, so this was their farewell to fancy food and music, girls and partying and long hair.

88

Soon they would have their heads shaved, their uniforms pressed and their every moment scheduled for them. No wonder they were all acting a little wild.

So many boys, Nina thought, bedazzled, so little time. Maybe she would go to West Point for college. Fat chance, she reminded herself. You had to be a brainiac and have perfect grades and play a sport. Nina had none of the above—not the smarts, not the grades and certainly not the sport. Her only athletic activity was outrunning Sr. Immaculata when cutting class.

Her date was Laurence Jeffries, and she'd walked into the country club on his arm, hiding her terror that any second someone would recognize her and rat her out. But there was almost no chance someone would recognize her at the country club tonight. Carmine didn't work here anymore, and as far as she knew, no Romano had ever belonged to Avalon Meadows. Golf and tennis and martinis on the patio were for WASPy types who sent their one-point-seven kids to prep school and summer camp. This only made her deception all the more delicious.

When the festivities first started, she thought she'd made a mistake coming here. There were boring tributes to the appointees— 'Those who dare to serve our country, blah blah blah . . .'—and no alcoholic beverages, because the new recruits were all underage,

89

in the seventeen-to nineteen-year-old range. Nina was contemplating finding Laurence Jeffries and slipping away immediately. But everything changed when the adults headed into the cocktail lounge, the lights dimmed and a hired DJ took over. That was when the sea of boys flooded the dance floor, surrounding Nina like a testosterone forest. A bottle of something sticky-sweet appeared, and they passed it around until it was gone. Nina was fairly new to drinking, but she gamely swigged down the strawberry-flavored Ripple. It made everything seem easier and funnier. It made her a better dancer, for sure.

Nina knew some girls would be intimidated by being in the midst of so many guys, especially guys like this—football captains and wrestling champions, the elite from high schools across America. Not Nina, though. She knew the truth about boys. No matter how smart and athletic, they were all just a mass of hormone-driven urges.

She felt like the belle of the ball, dancing with one guy after another. One of them told her that all fifty states were represented in the class.

Laurence was the perfect date, and perfectly clueless about her true age. She'd first met him last fall, when his football team came to town and defeated the Avalon Knights. Most of the town hadn't taken the loss well, but Nina couldn't care less. Laurence was the quarterback, he was super-hot and he believed she was a senior, like him. In the spring, she'd been delighted to learn he was the pitcher for his school's baseball team, and they took up their flirtation again. They'd made out under the bleachers before, so technically, this was their second date.

He had wanted to pick her up at her house, but she'd made an elaborate excuse and convinced him to meet her at the club. Now he appeared before her like a pagan god, tall and broad-shouldered, his lean, ebony face beautifully chiseled. Even the reflected light from the revolving fixture on the ceiling seemed to highlight his importance, illuminating him from behind, like a rock star. He was by far the best-looking guy in the room, and the best dancer. Nina happily took him as her partner. Over the gut-deep thump of 'Get It Started' by M.C. Hammer, they got to know each other better. He was just seventeen and was leaving home for the first time. She was lying about her age and had sneaked out for probably the hundredth time, but she didn't tell him this.

They danced closer and closer, until they were touching, and Nina was on fire, as if he was a match striking to life against her. Maybe this was it, she thought. Maybe tonight was the night. And why not? He was the perfect guy to be her first—kind, handsome and honorable. Nina had eavesdropped on her older sisters enough to know these were the sort of qualities you didn't find every day in a guy. She'd be nuts to turn him down.

After a while, he bent down and said, 'Let's go outside,' and led her by the hand to the terrace overlooking the golf course. She tipped back her head, welcoming the faint breeze over her face and neck.

'It's so hot tonight,' she murmured, feeling wicked and powerful and filled with a crazy need to touch and be touched.

'Thirsty?' He held out a bottle of Snapple. 'It's spiked with vodka.'

'I'm cool with that.' Boldly she tipped back her head and drank half of it, forcing herself not to gag on the sharp taste.

They walked together down to the darkened golf course and left their shoes at the edge of the eighteenth green. The perfectly groomed grass felt like a cool carpet beneath their bare feet. A hush of luxury and privilege seemed to pervade the atmosphere.

Laurence chuckled appreciatively. 'We're not in Kansas anymore,' he said.

'How do you mean?'

He explained that he grew up in public housing—a hulking project on the south end in a part of town you didn't see in Hudson Valley tourist brochures. He'd been raised by a single mother who worked for the welfare department. 'Demographically speaking, I'm the kid most likely to be doing time by now.'

'And look at you,' she said. 'You're a star. You're going to West Point. In four years, you'll be an officer.'

'It doesn't even seem real.' He grabbed her and kissed her then, and it was an amazing kiss, sweet and sexy at the same time. 'You don't seem real, either,' he said.

'Maybe I'm not,' she said. 'Maybe it's all a dream.' She looked back at the brightly lit clubhouse. The ballroom was dark, flashing with the occasional strobe light. In the opposite wing, the dining room glowed golden, filled with genteel people ordering things Nina had learned about by reading fancy magazines, like Steak Diane and mashed potatoes with truffle oil. She could easily pick out the six members of the Bellamy family, who were known to dine at 'the club' every Sunday evening in summer. There were Mr. and Mrs. Bellamy and their four grown kids— Philip was the eldest, followed by two sisters in the middle, and finally there was Greg. Impossibly good-looking in khakis and a crisp Oxford cloth shirt, a tie worn slightly loose at the throat, he exuded an easy charm, looking completely relaxed, as though posing for a country-club brochure.

'. . . come here often?' Laurence was asking her.

'Sure,' she lied breezily. 'We've been members for years.'

Holding hands, they strolled to the middle

93

of the fairway, and Nina was consumed by a curious certainty—she was going to go all the way with this boy. They both wanted it. She could tell. The knowledge and the anticipation breathed from their skin.

He turned to her and bent down and kissed her, and she felt herself lighting up with a burning need. She silently reviewed all the information she had from her sisters. Sex was natural, it was fun with the right guy . . . but a girl should never leave safety up to the guy. Nina had a tri-fold pack of condoms in her purse. She was fully, embarrassingly prepared to whip them out if necessary.

The starlit night surrounded them with magic. Then Nina heard a quiet popping sound, followed by a staccato hiss. A slap of cold water hit them.

'Hey,' she yelled.

'The sprinklers just turned on.' Laurence grabbed her hand and they tried running for cover, but the sprinklers had sprouted everywhere, forming a gauntlet of arching fountains along the fairway. By the time they escaped the spraying water, they were completely drenched. Ducking the sprinklers, they made their way to a gazebo between two fairways.

Nina got the giggles, and couldn't stop until Laurence kissed her again. These were new kisses, imbued with a searing intimacy, almost a desperation. It was a relief when he stepped

94

back and peeled off her soaking wet dress, spreading it across a privet hedge. She needed this, needed to be close to him, skin-to-skin with nothing between them, nothing at all.

He laid his blazer on the deck of the gazebo and they sank down together, spellbound, intoxicated, consumed by urgency. He paused to grope in his pocket, coming up with a condom, which made Nina weak with relief. Thank goodness he'd spared her the embarrassment.

So this was it, then. Here and now, in the shadowy gazebo with the sprinkler system hissing all around them, the veil of secrecy was swept aside. She wrapped her arms around him and dropped her head back, opening herself to him, and then they kissed and fit themselves together, and it was more incredible than she ever could have imagined. More uncomfortable and awkward, too, but with a sweetness that brought tears to her eyes. And quicker. Laurence almost instantly made a surprised, strangled sound, and then shuddered, covering her like a blanket. Then they both lay still, their hearts beating as one, their bodies still joined together.

After a while, he drew back. 'You all right?' he whispered.

She was intrigued, feeling as though she teetered on the edge of something big. 'I'm all right.'

'I'm sorry,' he said. 'I shouldn't have—'

'Hush. I wanted to. Maybe we can have another go at it.'

'I only brought one condom and—oh, shit.'

He wasn't as experienced as he seemed. Somehow, the condom hadn't gone where it was supposed to go. 'Damn,' he said. 'I'm sorry. I swear, I don't have a disease or anything—'

'Me neither.' Suddenly embarrassed, Nina jumped up and struggled into her wet clothes. The issue of the failed condom put an end to the evening's romance.

Laurence must have felt the same way as he shook out his clothes and put them on. 'Hey, I feel bad,' he said. 'I didn't mean to hurt you.'

'Nothing's hurt, but I'd better go,' she said, suddenly eager to get away. 'My car's at the far end of the parking lot.' Another lie. She'd brought her bike.

Carrying their shoes in their hands, they crossed the parking lot. 'Tell me your phone number,' Laurence said. 'I'll call you.'

She was tempted, but only momentarily. The kind of lies she was telling tonight couldn't be sustained for long. 'I don't think so.'

'You're probably right.' Relief rang clearly in his voice.

'And you're awfully quick to agree with me.' She was only half teasing.

'Look, I think you're really something, but I got to think of the future. I'm a kid from the projects. If this doesn't work out for me, well, let's just say the options aren't good. I better stick with the academy. As soon as I start, I take an oath of honor.'

'And I'm, like, this huge stain on your oath.'

'No, but—'

'It's all right,' she said. 'I'm not going to cause any trouble for you, and that's a promise.'

'You're no trouble, girl.'

Just then, a shadow loomed over them.

She stopped walking and looked up. Uh-oh. Maybe Laurence had spoken too soon. 'Greg Bellamy,' she said with forced brightness. 'Fancy meeting you here.'

\*       \*       \*

Greg stood over the fallen cadet, wondering if he'd broken anything. It had all happened so fast. One minute he was getting a sweater from the car for his sister. The next, he was driving his fist into some cadet's jaw. The guy was gigantic, but Greg had the element of surprise. Shock was more like it. Shock had cut off the oxygen to his brain, causing him to lose the ability to judge whether or not he was right to clean the guy's clock.

One thing he knew for certain, he definitely had a problem with a West Point cadet banging Mrs. Romano's underage daughter. Greg had met her that one time up at the camp, but he couldn't remember her name.

That didn't matter. What mattered was that she was still a kid. Yet there was no mistaking that just-got-laid look of these two—the damp clothes buttoned crooked, grass in their hair, the sheepish, sated expressions on both their faces.

The girl's face changed instantly, sharpening with accusation as she glared at Greg. 'He's hurt,' she said. 'You had no right—'

'I had no right?' Now, that pissed him off. He gave a disgusted laugh.

On the ground, the cadet moved his jaw from side to side. Okay, thought Greg, so at least he hadn't done anything permanent to the guy. He wasn't sure he was relieved by that or not. He nudged the guy with the toe of his shoe. 'Get up,' he said.

The guy frowned, blinked in confusion until he spotted the girl. 'Nina? What's going on? Who the hell is this?'

Greg made a mental note of the girl's name. Then, treating the guy like a recalcitrant camper, he said, 'Party's over, pal. So get your ass up and go back inside.'

'Laurence, I'm really sorry,' the girl— Nina—said in a small, horrified voice.

She was sorry. *Sorry.* Greg rounded on her. 'Do you have a ride home?' he demanded.

She hung her head, turned away from Laurence and mumbled, 'I rode my bike.'

He almost laughed. A bike. She'd ridden a damn bike to the country club to get laid.

'It's pitch-black outside,' he said. 'Were you planning to find your way home by radar?'

The guy called Laurence climbed to his feet. Damn, he was tall. And still a little dazed. Or drunk. Or both. 'Nina?' he asked again.

'Shut up,' Greg snapped, ready to be done with the whole drama, and eager to send the guy on his way before he decided to fight back. 'Get back inside, now, and pray I don't report you. I'm taking her home.'

'Are not,' Nina snapped back, then grabbed Laurence's hand. 'He's not taking me anywhere.'

Greg ignored her and glared at Laurence. 'She's fourteen, you moron. What the hell were you thinking?'

Laurence dropped her hand as though it was a red-hot coal. He even stepped back, hands up, palms facing out, as though Greg had a gun pointed at him. 'Shit—'

'Fifteen,' she said defiantly. 'I just turned fifteen last month.'

The guy's panic was genuine. He truly hadn't known, the same as Greg hadn't known that day in the dining hall. Until someone had clued him in, Greg, too, had been fooled by her impossibly curvy body, her smoldering eyes that pretended to know things she had no clue about, her full lips that made reckless promises to morons like this one.

'Go back inside,' he repeated. 'Like I said, the party's over.'

The guy took a step back. 'I'm sorry,' he told Nina. 'I didn't know, I— Girl, you should have been straight with me.'

'I said,' Greg reminded him, 'it's over.'

'Laurence, no,' Nina protested. 'This . . . this *person* has no idea what he's talking about.'

The cadet offered a wordless look of helpless regret, then turned and hurried back to the clubhouse. Nina started after him. Greg grabbed her arm and held her back.

'Let go of me,' she said. 'I have five brothers, and I know how to defend myself.'

Greg relinquished her. 'How many of those brothers would approve of what you're doing here?'

'None of your business.' She began to stomp toward the clubhouse, which was still bubbling over with golden light and music, as though nothing had happened.

'You go after that kid now,' Greg called to her, 'and you'll end his chances at West Point before he even starts.'

She was young, but she was far from stupid. She stopped walking and turned to him, and he could see the understanding rise in her eyes. An incident like this—fraternizing with an underage girl—was more than enough to get a guy dismissed or worse. Reluctant acceptance softened her face for a moment. Then, with a haughty sniff, she marched past him, grabbing a bicycle from a rack at the edge of the parking lot. The thing didn't even have a light, just a cracked reflector on the rear fender.

'Hey,' he said, 'you're not riding that home.'

'Watch me.' She threw her dancing shoes into the basket and expertly pushed off, swinging her leg up and over the back. The skirts of her party dress fluttered around her bare legs.

Being a camp counselor had taught Greg a few things about catching kids who were trying to escape. He charged, grabbing the back of the seat, pulling her to a halt. She stood on the pedals, putting up a fierce resistance, but to no avail. Greg refused to let go of the bike until she surrendered to him with a surly glare.

'I'm driving you home,' he told her.

'The hell you are,' she shot back.

He saw her weighing her options and making a silent calculation, balancing her need for defiance and rebellion against the consequences he promised. Greg recognized the struggle. Just a few years older than her, he vividly recalled the raging clash of urges in a teenager. Hell, he still had those urges himself.

'You do not want to know how bad this can get,' he warned her.

He could tell the moment she resigned herself to common sense. Her shoulders slumped in defeat as she dismounted the bike. Greg let out the breath he didn't know he was holding. He didn't want her to see how relieved he felt. He hadn't been eager to get her in trouble. He just wanted her home, safe.

And, okay, when he thought about the fact that someone had been banging her, he also felt an undertone of envy, which shamed him. This girl was trouble. He didn't know why he felt so protective of her. It was just that she was so young, so foolish. Somebody had to look out for her.

Now he had a dilemma, though. Driving her back to town could take ten minutes; returning to the country club—another ten. His parents were going to wonder where the heck he'd gone. He could tell Nina to wait right here while he went inside to explain, but he knew she'd seize the chance to bolt. He'd have to risk his parents' displeasure, because the idea of keeping this underage pretty-baby from pedaling home through the dark night was more compelling.

He slung her bike into the trunk of his car and held open the passenger-side door. 'Get in.'

'I'll get the seat wet. It might ruin the upholstery.'

'Don't worry about the seat, just get in.'

Nina gave an elaborate shrug. 'I guess you Bellamys don't worry about ruining things.'

Greg was startled by the resentment in her voice. 'Us Bellamys? So I take it you're acquainted with my family.'

She sniffed. 'I know your type. Spoiled. Bossy. Interfering. Who needs you?'

He wondered why she had such a chip on

102

her shoulder about his family. She probably just had a chip on her shoulder, period. Unconcerned, he got behind the wheel and peeled out, the trunk lid banging on the bike.

'You could have broken his jaw. Why are you so mad? Are you some kind of racist who can't handle seeing him with a white girl?'

'With you being underage, I don't care what color he is. He's got no business messing around with you.'

'In case you haven't noticed, I'm not a kid. I know what I'm doing. And FYI, Laurence Jeffries is seventeen. So we're not that different at all.'

Great, they were both kids. 'You're light years apart. You're a schoolgirl and he's about to go into the army.'

'I can quit school at sixteen without parental permission,' she pointed out.

'Good plan. That'll get you far.'

'I'm just saying.' She sulked a little. 'So is your family, like, going to kill you for disappearing?'

Probably. 'You don't need to worry about that.'

'They were all, like, "it's time we talked about your future, son," weren't they?' she persisted. 'I bet that's what they like to do when they take you to the club.' Switching gears, she moved on. 'What are your sisters' names?'

'Peg and Joyce.'

'And your brother is Philip. He looks a lot older than you.'

'He is. He's got a wife and kid but they stayed in the city this weekend.'

'You're an uncle, then,' she said. 'Uncle Greg.'

She switched gears yet again with another nosy question. 'Do you have a girlfriend?'

He wanted to tell her it was none of her business, but he didn't. Just the thought of Sophie chafed at an old wound. He and Sophie Lindstrom had met in Econ 101 last September and he'd been a total goner. From her Nordic beauty to her prowess at Scrabble to her startling hunger in bed, she had fascinated and mesmerized him.

'She took a semester abroad,' he told Nina.

'Ha. That means she dumped you.'

She was annoyingly perceptive, he'd give her that. 'Where to?' he asked, determined to drop the subject of Sophie.

'Just let me off at the corner of Maple and Vine. And you don't have to do this, you know. I've lived here all my life. I know my way around.'

'If you're so smart, you wouldn't be sneaking around with guys who are too old for you.'

'Screw you,' she said.

He decided not to react, since he knew that was exactly what she wanted. Mercifully, she didn't try to provoke him again, but turned

104

her attention out the window. The road outlined the lakeshore, and it was mostly dark, an unspoiled wilderness. They passed an occasional cottage or cabin with lights winking, but the dwellings were sparse. Most of the lakeshore was a protected wilderness, and no further development would be permitted. The few places along the shore had gone in prior to the 1932 protection agreement.

They drove by the Inn at Willow Lake, somewhat shabby but popular with tourists because of its idyllic location. A quaint roadside sign marked the entrance, and Nina turned her head to stare at it as they passed.

Greg sensed her sinking mood. He wasn't sure how, but he could feel it dragging at him, pulling all the air out of the car. And he felt responsible for her, in a way, as though he ought to process this with her. 'Listen, I probably shouldn't say anything—'

'Then don't.'

'—but I'm going to, anyway. There's no reason for you to be running around with guys who only want one thing from you.'

'Oh, God. I am so not listening to this.'

She was trapped, though. A captive audience. He eased up on the accelerator. 'I don't pretend to know anything about you, but guys like that, well, they're not real complicated.' In fact, they were all exactly the same, letting a certain male appendage do all their thinking for them. Greg was well aware of this. There was something about women that seemed to suck the brain cells dry, turning a guy into a hopeless life-support system for an erection. And a girl like Nina—well, certain parts of him didn't care about her age.

Trying to explain all this to her would be futile. There was no way he could tell her these things without sounding completely stupid. Besides, it was hypocritical. Because the only difference between him and the West Point kid was that Greg knew how old she was.

Still, he felt as though he should say something. Because one of these days, she was going to . . . He didn't let himself finish the thought.

'So anyway, it's plain old common sense,' he told her. 'You're better off hanging around people your own age.'

She snapped, 'Right. Because boys my age are such delightful company.'

He had no answer for that. Greg had kids that age in his counseling group at Kioga this year, and he certainly couldn't vouch for their social appeal. 'You're one of them,' he pointed out. 'You're in the same peer group.'

'Yeah, lucky me.' She turned to stare out the window, her party dress pulled over her drawn-up knees. Then he realized her tough-girl demeanor had crumpled. He heard a tragic sniffle, saw her hand sneak up to surreptitiously wipe a tear.

'Hey, I didn't mean to hurt your feelings,' he

said.

'So is that some sort of a bonus, or what?'

There were few things more daunting to Greg than a crying girl. It was with some relief that he pulled over at the corner of Maple and Vine, went around and held the door for her. She sat unmoving, her arms still looped around her knees. A car trolled past. In one of the houses behind him, a porch light switched on.

He felt a surge of panic. This might look bad, Nina Romano getting out of his car. He quickly turned and went to pull her bicycle from the trunk. She got out, but seemed to be in no hurry to go home.

'It's after ten,' he reminded her. 'Maybe you should run along.'

'Don't worry about my curfew,' she said. 'There are nine kids in my family. I'm right in the middle. Sneaking in and out has never been a problem.'

Nine kids, Greg marveled. His own family felt big with four. Nine was . . . a team. 'So,' he said, attempting a joking tone, 'stay out of trouble and have a nice life. I don't think the two are mutually exclusive.'

She wasn't fooled by his lame attempt to lighten the moment. She seemed to understand as well as he did that something had happened during the drive into town, something mysterious and important and impossible. She gazed steadily up at him and

107

he felt as if he was drowning. He wished he didn't know anything about her, not her age, her last name, or the fact that she cried when he told her to respect herself.

He was glad he held the bicycle between them because otherwise, he might prove to be as stupid as a cadet named Laurence Jeffries. She was that attractive. And no, she didn't look her age.

An extremely knowing smile curved her full lips. 'What are you thinking, Greg?'

'If you were older, this could . . . turn into something.' He blurted it out, just like that. No thought, just words. Girls like Nina Romano were apparently a leading cause of brain damage in guys.

'Someday soon, I will be older,' she reminded him with a soft promise in her voice.

'Then maybe someday, it'll turn into something.'

She laughed a little. 'Right. Like you'd really wait for me.'

'You never know,' Greg said, leaving the bicycle in her hands. He got in the car and put it in gear. She stood there, looking so beautiful that his eyes ached. Don't say anything else, he admonished himself. It didn't work. He offered her his heart in a smile. 'I just might surprise you.'

*Part Three*

*Now*

Since 2005, the town of Avalon has been the home of its very own independent baseball team, the Hornets, a member of the Can-Am League. Independent baseball leagues are known for a high quality of play and fierce competition. A baseball game on a warm, clear night is one of the chief pleasures of summer. General admission tickets are six dollars, available from the inn concierge. In baseball, as in life, every day brings a new opportunity.

# SIX

Greg pulled into the ball field parking lot just as Little League practice was winding down. From a distance, it was an idyllic scene, the surrounding forestland rising up into the hills, the golden light of late afternoon slanting over the green diamond, dotted with laughing, chattering kids shouting to each other as they gathered their things. Greg wondered if anything could be as good as it looked, or if that was just wishful thinking. Then he picked out Max, sitting by himself on the bench in the dugout. Great, he thought. His kid was benched again.

There was no torture quite so searing as seeing your kid in emotional pain. It was torture because it made Greg feel helpless. This wasn't the kind of hurt you could fix with an ice pack or a Band-Aid. This injury was invisible, particularly when it came to Max, who tended to keep things hidden.

Greg sat in the truck for a minute, dissuading himself from interfering. Popping off at the mouth to the coach would do Max no good at all. The kid needed to learn to fight his own battles, and for all Greg knew, Max was sitting out by choice. Or worse, he was sitting out because once again, the kid had blown his temper. It wouldn't be the first time.

111

Through no fault of his own, Max had been at the tail end of all the drama surrounding the divorce, the move from the city, Sophie's job in Europe, Daisy's pregnancy. Max was swept along in the maelstrom, adapting to school and a new town with an easygoing aplomb that masked emotions he refused to discuss with Greg, Sophie or his therapist. Every once in a while, he blew his stack, giving Greg a glimpse of the rage the boy couldn't quite keep in. Greg had the idea that putting Max on a team might give him an outlet. Max had always been physical, a good athlete, obsessed with hockey in the winter and baseball in the summer. He'd been a star on his team in the city. Here in Avalon, he had a chance to shine.

Or not, Greg thought, waiting in the truck while the team gathered for the post-practice meeting with Coach Broadbent.

Greg's phone rang—*please be her*—and he snatched it up, eagerly checking the caller ID. But no. It was his lawyer, and Greg let it go to voice mail. He frowned, ticked off that Nina still hadn't called him. He hoped like hell she would say yes to his proposal, but he wasn't going to beg her. In the meantime, he stayed busy, mindful of his commitment to integrate work and family.

Neither was going well.

Six of the guest rooms were still under construction and would need refurnishing in the style of the period. The caretaker's house,

112

where he lived with his kids, was still a jumble of moving boxes and unmatched furniture. The boathouse and dock both needed work, too. On the upside, he'd assembled what was beginning to resemble a staff. An information technology consultant had set up a hospitality system that Daisy immediately mastered, even personalizing the software with her photography. The website was up and running, and it was with a sense of surreal amazement that they watched the inquiries and reservations flow into the inbox. However, having a staff, a slick site and system wouldn't mean a thing until the general manager was in place to orchestrate everything.

Nina Romano wasn't the only game in town, he told himself. Or out of town, for that matter. The business consultant Greg had hired offered to send experienced candidates for his consideration. But Nina was the only one he wanted. She was the perfect fit. When it came to running an intimate luxury hotel, it was all about getting the right people. Nina was exactly right. He had a feeling about her. She had an air of confidence and a depth of experience no one else could match. The trouble was, she wanted to work there on her terms, and Greg had beaten her to it. Now it was up to him to persuade her that they could both benefit and so far, he'd done a lousy job of it.

Coach Broadbent finished his meeting with

the players and Greg got out of the truck. 'Max!' he yelled and waved at his son.

Max sprang into action, shouldering his duffel bag and water bottle and sprinting toward the parking lot.

'Hey, buddy. How was practice?'

'Fine,' said Max.

'Okay, I asked for that. Let me rephrase. Tell me everything you did at practice.'

Max put his things in the back of the truck. 'Just the usual stuff.'

Greg noticed that his practice uniform—gray knickers, navy shirt and white cap—were just as clean as they'd been when Max put them on. The kid hadn't even broken a sweat. 'You were on the bench when I drove up.'

'Was I?'

'You want me to have a word with Coach?'

'Da-ad.' Max stretched the word into two syllables. 'I can handle Coach, okay?'

'That's what I thought.' Greg studied his son. Sandy-haired and freckle-faced, he had the kind of smile that covered a myriad of issues.

'But handle it,' he said. 'There's no need for you to waste a whole practice on the bench.'

'I wasn't—' Max cut himself off and got in the truck. 'Can we go now? I'm starving.'

Classic avoidance, Greg observed. This was what Max did—turned away from trouble, keeping things bottled up. Later in the summer, Max was going to Holland,

114

accompanied by Sophie's parents, the Lindstroms. Later, Max and his mother would return to Avalon in time for the wedding. Max didn't like the plan. He didn't like the idea that he had to travel thirty-five hundred miles to be with his mother, but he had no choice. And that, Greg suspected, was the reason for his bottled-up feelings.

'Hey, Max—'

'I'm done, okay? I don't want to talk about it anymore.'

'Which is why we should probably talk about it.'

'*Dad.* Starving here.'

Greg decided to let it go for now. When sitting on a bench, a boy could conjure up a lot of things in his mind, but sometimes it was better just to back off. 'Now that,' he said, 'I can do something about.'

'What, you figured out how to cook?'

'Smart-ass. I can cook.' Greg was trying. At first, only grilling felt right. He'd figured out a way to grill every meal, not even balking at things like peaches, which he served over ice cream. As time went on, he progressed to boxed meals that came with clear instructions. 'I'm not doing the cooking tonight, though.'

'Are we going out with Brooke?' A look that was both comical and disturbing animated Max's face. The kid had a thing for Brooke Harlow, that was for sure.

'No, we're not going out with Brooke. We're

going up to Camp Kioga.'

'Yes.' The word hissed from him like air from a balloon.

'I figured you'd like that.' Greg relaxed during the ten-mile drive through the Catskills wilderness. The camp was on the opposite end of the lake, far from town. Greg's niece Olivia's massive project of transforming the property from a defunct summer camp into an all-inclusive family resort that would be open year-round had been going on for nearly a year, but they were yet another year away from completion. Still, Olivia's dedication to it was inspiring, and the way she'd embraced the project had played no small part in Greg's decision to take over the Inn at Willow Lake. Building something tangible, making it work—that was the way to launch a new life and watch it grow.

Although the camp was under construction, its bunkhouses, cabins and main pavilion were still habitable. Two more of Greg's grown nieces had arrived to help with the wedding preparations, and the barbecue was in their honor. Greg's parents and his older brother Philip were there as well. When he and Max arrived, everyone was gathered on the deck of the pavilion, laughing and talking while music drifted from the outdoor speakers. Daisy was there already, having driven herself earlier. The sight of her, seated at a table so her pregnancy wasn't visible, laughing and

116

drinking lemonade with her older cousins, caused Greg to feel a clutch of regret.

Knock it off, he told himself. Not being okay with her pregnancy was simply not an option. He'd had months to get used to the idea, and he needed to put these twinges behind him.

Max took the stairs two at a time, in a hurry to see everyone. Carrying a bottle of wine and a six-pack—his contribution to the barbecue—Greg watched everyone surround Max, enfolding him in a cocoon of relatives. In the Bellamy family, Max was the youngest son of the youngest son. He would be the last of his generation to come of age. His aunts, uncles and cousins seemed to cherish his youth, wanting to keep him young for as long as possible. Greg had no trouble with this. He already had one kid who had grown up too fast. Max's favorite member of the Bellamy family was Olivia's dog, a little mutt called Barkis. Within minutes, the two of them were on the floor, playing tug-of-war with an old stuffed toy.

The gathering included Olivia and Connor, the bride and groom-to-be, and an assortment of cousins and friends. Olivia was just ten years younger than Greg, but he hadn't spared much attention for his niece when she was growing up; he'd been too busy for that. He vaguely remembered some awkward years for Olivia—braces, frizzy hair, glasses, a weight problem. At some point she'd morphed into this lovely woman, filled with confidence and glowing with happiness.

Stranger things had happened, Greg thought, his gaze focusing on Rourke McKnight. Avalon's chief of police, off duty at the moment, had been the ultimate confirmed bachelor—until last winter, when he was snowed in with Jenny Majesky, Nina's best friend. People liked to joke that the chief of police had married her because she owned the Sky River Bakery and he was addicted to her unbelievable, ecstasy-inducing doughnuts, but Greg knew the story was a lot more complicated than that. Relationships always were, whether they succeeded or failed. Greg resolved to talk to Jenny later, try to see if she'd give him some insight as to what Nina was thinking.

During dinner, he let himself relax and, with a wave of gratitude, enjoyed the company of his family. Simply by being present, being who they were, they had helped him survive the breakup of his marriage. He watched the nieces and Daisy mapping out the wedding ceremony with the precision of battle commanders. Olivia, ever-organized, brought out actual diagrams, moving the desserts aside to spread them out on the table.

'So after Jenny—my matron of honor— all the girl cousins will come in order by age,' Olivia was saying. 'Is that okay?'

'You're the bride,' Jenny said. 'You don't

118

need to ask.'

Daisy nodded. 'I'll be last—but not least.' She patted her belly. Her cousins responded with genuine affection. They seemed happy about the baby, which didn't exactly allay his own panic, but it seemed to please Daisy.

'Julian Gastineaux is going to be the best man,' Olivia told Daisy. 'He's coming from California next week. I figured you'd want to know.'

Greg watched his daughter's face bloom like a rose. Not a good sign. Connor Davis's brother Julian was the same age as Daisy. She'd met him last summer, when both of them were working here at Camp Kioga. Julian was the kind of kid whose very name made girls blush. He was tall, good-looking, biracial and incredibly cocky. With dreadlocks, a pierced ear and at least one visible tattoo, the kid was a wild card for sure. He'd worked at Camp Kioga the summer before, and since they were the same age, they hung out a lot. Greg remembered him as an adrenaline junkie, obsessed with heights and dangerous speeds.

Now, however, Greg was forced to admit that Julian was not the ultimate risk-taker. Daisy was. Last summer, she'd been a high-school girl, flirting with a boy from California. A year later, she was about to become a mother. Yet judging by her blooming face, he figured she wasn't quite ready to leave romance behind. Greg reminded himself to quit worrying. These days, Daisy had bigger concerns than flirting with the brother of the groom.

As the conversation shifted to the guest list, Greg noticed Jenny edge away. She went to stand at the railing of the deck, looking out across the lake. She hadn't grown up like those girls, a product of private schools and privilege. It didn't seem to bother her, but he suspected all the talk of people she didn't know bored her.

Which gave him the perfect opportunity to pick her brain about Nina Romano. He grabbed a chilled bottle of Chardonnay and went to refill her glass.

'Thanks,' she said with a smile. 'Nice night.'

Greg surveyed the gathering and for a moment he flashed on the old days, when the camp was in operation. He wondered if those times were really as good as he remembered, or if nostalgia gave everything a rosy tinge. 'You doing all right?' he asked.

'I like getting to know Philip's side of the family, different as they are from my own.'

'We feel the same way about you,' Greg assured her. 'Not that you're different, but that we like getting to know you.'

'Does that mean I should start calling you Uncle Greg?'

'Only if you want to make me feel like a geezer. Seriously, I'm glad you and my brother

120

found each other last year. It's been a good year for him, too. He's like a different person. He used to be this buttoned-down, intense, even angsty guy. Now look at him.'

Philip seemed years younger, in shorts and a golf shirt, his longish hair windblown. A new sense of contentment showed in Philip's face and the way he held himself, at ease in the world. He seemed to be smiling from the inside out. That was how happiness worked—from the inside out. That was why truly happy people shone, even when they weren't actively smiling. He had two new women in his life—his daughter Jenny, whom he'd met for the first time last summer. And Laura Tuttle, who ran the bakery in town. They were old friends whose friendship was becoming something more. Standing at his side, Laura was a quiet but adoring presence. She and Philip were proof of something Greg hadn't quite believed in—until now. Not only could you survive a divorce, sometimes second and even third chances were given. They were unexpected blessings you had to hold on to before you missed out.

Greg wondered if that kind of optimism made him an idiot. After his marriage ended, he expected to be jaded about love. Instead, for no reason that made any sense at all, he felt more hopeful than he had in years.

Jenny regarded her father with affection. 'Love does that. It changes you. Makes you more comfortable in the world.' She turned back to Greg. 'So about Nina,' she said, then laughed at the expression on his face.

'What about Nina?'

'Isn't that why you cornered me? To ask me about her?'

Greg grinned. 'Busted. I want her,' he said, then flushed as he realized how that sounded—Freudian slip. 'I need her,' he amended. Oops. Also Freudian.

'Some women wait their whole lives to hear a guy say that,' Jenny remarked.

'For the inn, I mean. She's the piece I'm missing at the inn. I can't think of anyone else who has her history with the place, her management skills and her depth of knowledge.'

'Have you told her that?'

'She hasn't given me a chance. I met with a resort management consultant from the city, and it just felt all wrong. There's a reason the bank chose Nina to run the place. I don't know of anyone who would do a better job.'

'Then make sure she doesn't turn you down,' Jenny said simply.

'That's the idea. I don't know what more I can offer to make her say yes.' Greg wondered about the expression on Jenny's face, but she offered no further insight. Hell, in his former life, he'd hired and fired people on a daily basis. He wondered why, in this case, it mattered so much.

*     *     *

'So have you made up your mind, Mom? Are you going to take the job at the inn?' Sonnet asked. Although Nina's daughter was an ocean away, her voice sounded crystal clear over their internet phone service. Nina tried to picture Sonnet in the Belgian village where she was spending the summer, calling from the cobblestone town square while watching locals and SHAPE personnel going about their business. The regular calls helped make her absence bearable for Nina.

'Every time I think I know what I want to do, I think of some reason why I shouldn't,' Nina confessed. 'I've been over and over it in my mind. I've tried to think up all kinds of alternatives and there isn't one that feels right. There's only one Inn at Willow Lake. I've always wanted it. You know that.'

'So take the deal. You'd have a job you've always wanted—one with serious money attached. A killer place to live.'

'A boss with two kids and no idea how to run the place.'

'Then he'll hand it all over to you, which is what you wanted in the first place. What's the problem?'

Nina smiled. She took pride in the way her daughter was turning out—mature beyond her years, as practical and blunt as Nina herself.

Then the smile faded as Nina realized that she'd asked herself the same question many times over the past week—*What's the problem?* Ultimately, she had to admit that, while her job at the inn would essentially be the same one she had imagined for herself, Greg had changed everything. Rather than working toward a goal—buying the inn—she would just be . . . working. For Nina, that wasn't enough. Besides, Greg seemed to have some idealized vision of a family business, while she was looking forward to total independence for the first time in her life. Their expectations simply didn't mesh.

Could she outlast him? That had been her initial thought. She certainly ought to try. However, that carried a risk of its own. If Greg didn't make a go of this, he might well sell the place to someone else.

'See, you can't even come up with an objection,' Sonnet pointed out. 'And I'd better go. I've got a movie date for a midnight showing.'

Nina sat straight up in her chair. 'Like a *date* date?'

'Wouldn't you like to know?'

'As a matter of fact, I would. Does Laurence—'

'Chill, Mom. A group of us is going to the cinema on the base. Laurence says it's fine, and he's way pickier than you.'

'I'm totally picky,' Nina objected.

124

'Yes, but Laurence practically does a background check on everyone I meet, and he's got the resources of the U.S. Army at his disposal.'

'Good for him.' Nina glanced at the clock. 'I'd better go, too. There's a Hornets game tonight—they're playing the New Haven County Cutters.'

'Do you know how cool it is that you brought a baseball team to Avalon?'

'It's very cool,' Nina said without modesty. 'My legacy as mayor.' Or so she hoped. She'd left office shadowed by scandal but now, in the bright light of summer, she hoped her greatest achievement would shine through. The Avalon Hornets were back for their second season. Negotiating with the club had taken an incredible amount of political maneuvering and deal-making, not to mention many sleepless nights, but it was worth the effort.

'Angela was skeptical when I first told her. She didn't think Avalon was big enough to have a professional baseball team. I told her about independent baseball and the Can-Am League, showed her the website and everything. She seemed shocked to discover there's something she *doesn't* know.'

Hearing that Laurence's wife was skeptical didn't surprise Nina in the least. 'So other than her being a skeptic and a know-it-all, how are you and Angela getting along?'

'Okay,' Sonnet said. 'I'm so busy with work

that we don't spend that much time together.'

'You rat,' Nina said. 'You like her.'

'You got a problem with that?'

'I do. I'm ashamed that I do. She's just so perfect. And I'm just so . . . not.'

Sonnet laughed. 'Perfect? I'll be sure to pass that on to her daughters. Layla just pierced her eyebrow and Kara wants to run away and join the circus, or something.'

Nina felt a wave of gratitude for her daughter. Sometimes they acted more like best friends than mother and daughter. Sometimes Nina wondered who was raising who. 'I love you, kiddo. You always say the right thing.'

'Maybe I'm always right. And I really do think it's the coolest that you brought the Hornets to Avalon.'

'I always felt guilty, taking so much time away from you while I was making that deal.'

'You can quit that right now,' Sonnet objected. 'It's a professional baseball team, Mom, and it's all your doing. Every time I tell people that, they're like, "she did not." And I'm like, she totally did, single-handedly.'

'It wasn't single-handed, not by any stretch. In fact, the guys I'm going to the game with were instrumental in helping me. Wayne Dobbs and Darryl McNab.'

'And hotties to boot,' Sonnet teased.

Nina chuckled. Wayne and Darryl had been the president and treasurer of the Avalon Booster Club, and the two men had shared

126

her vision of bringing a minor league team to town. 'They had what I needed at the time—a giant budget.'

'I was raised by a romantic,' Sonnet said. 'Don't get in trouble, Mom.'

'With Darryl and Wayne? That would be a stretch.'

Sonnet said, 'Oh, and I meant to tell you, I've been IMing with Daisy. Olivia's going to send you an invitation to the wedding.'

A Bellamy wedding. At Camp Kioga. Nina would rather have her teeth drilled. 'I don't do well at weddings. I never have.'

\*     \*     \*

On the way home from Camp Kioga, Greg's gaze was drawn to a pale glow on the horizon at the west edge of town. He made a snap decision. At a junction at the end of the river road, he turned off, wending his way along a gravel road leading to a broad field flooded with white stadium lights.

'Hey, cool,' Max said. 'We can catch the end of the game.'

Greg handed his phone to Max. 'Do me a favor,' he said. 'Call your sister and tell her we'll be a little late.'

Although Greg knew it was a good idea to take his kid to baseball games, he kept forgetting to do it. He told himself to no longer be the guy who was too busy working or being preoccupied or miserable to go to a game with Max. Starting now.

The bleachers, though only six deep, were full of spectators. With their team colors, face paint and war whoops, they showed major league enthusiasm for their minor league team. The concession stand was doing a brisk business, and the smells of popcorn and hot dogs filled the air. The ball field organ music was canned, but the announcer called out plays with expert, rapid-fire delivery. Some families were making a night of it, with blankets spread on the grass outside the field, people eating and laughing, passing half-asleep babies and toddlers back and forth between them.

Although he'd just finished dinner, Max claimed he was hungry again. Greg provisioned him with a red-and-white-striped box of popcorn and a neon-colored drink called a Blue Crush. As they made their way to the bleachers, Greg saw that it was the bottom of the seventh, score three to two, the visiting team in the lead. The Hornets were at bat, and a few minutes later, they made their third out and players jogged to the outfield.

A spot appeared for Greg and Max on the bottom row of the bench. Greg murmured his thanks, then realized the person who had made room for him was a woman. Thirty-ish, attractive. No wedding band. A pleasant smile and a less-than-pleasant cindery smell of cigarettes. And an expression that telegraphed the message that she was available.

Greg was fast developing a sixth sense about women. He knew when they were checking him out, and could feel the cindery woman's attention wafting toward him. Pretending not to notice, he chatted with Max, who appeared to know more about the Hornets than Greg did. 'The general manager is a guy named Dino Carminucci,' Max was saying with the kind of authority Greg wished he would apply to his schoolwork. 'Used to be a field manager in Duluth, but he grew up right here in Avalon. He's had two league championships in the past five years. And the Hornets, their record's not so hot because they're new, but they got a hot new pitcher this season—Bo Crutcher, out of Texas.' He pointed out a long, lanky guy peeling a jacket off his left shoulder and loping out to the mound.

The hometown crowd cheered as the outfield assembled, then jeered when the batter from New Haven stepped up to the plate. The first pitch confirmed Max's information. It flew like a speeding bullet, but was so wild that shouts of 'Ball one' came from the rival team's spectators well before the ump confirmed it.

'It's okay, Crutch. You got it,' someone shouted.

That voice. The sound of it was like a smack on the head. Greg immediately swiveled around. And yes, she was there. Nina Romano, flanked by a pair of guys in backward-facing baseball caps, drinking beer and cheering on the team. She caught him staring at her and offered a wave of acknowledgment and an uncertain smile he couldn't quite read. Feeling awkward, he turned his attention back to the game.

Or pretended to. His mind was now on fire. He wasn't sure why the sight of Nina with two men bothered him so much. Maybe because she was supposed to be home, perhaps pacing the floors as she decided to take him up on his offer.

Right, he told himself. She'd probably already made up her mind to turn him down and hadn't bothered to tell him. Maybe she was going to throw in her lot with Dumb and Dumber, whoever the hell her escorts were.

While Greg stewed, he barely noticed the woman next to him inching closer until her shoulder touched his. 'Excuse me,' she said.

He simply nodded and shifted, hoping his body language would tell her what he didn't want to say aloud. The lanky pitcher got it together enough to rack up a couple of strikes.

One of Nina's escorts cupped his hands around his mouth and blasted like a foghorn. 'Get him out,' he brayed. 'Finish him off. He's *over.*'

The umpire called the third strike. 'Yeah, baby!' shouted the guy as the crowd of Hornets fans erupted. 'Stick a fork in him—he's done.

He's outta there. He's *gone.'*

Shut up, thought Greg. Just shut up.

The two teams held each other scoreless to the end, and in the bottom of the last inning, the Hornets scored two runs. The Avalon fans went apeshit, and for a moment, even Greg felt it, a happiness. This was why people loved baseball, why they would always love baseball, for this quick adrenaline rush of joy. Yet he knew the feeling was as fleeting as a woman's smile.

He turned to catch Nina's eye, but she and the two guys had gone to the dugout. Surrounded by players vying for her attention, she didn't give Greg another glance.

Then she surprised him by breaking away from the group and approaching him and Max. 'So, you're baseball fans,' she remarked.

'Yeah. Max is in Little League this summer.'

'Jerry Broadbent's team?' She smiled.

Damn, did she have to know every guy in town or just every other guy?

Max nodded.

She stroked her chin like a detective. 'That's the same look my younger brothers wore when they came home from baseball practice with Broadbent.'

Max regarded her with interest. 'Did Coach hate them, too?'

'Coach doesn't hate anybody. He's just a bit intense sometimes.' She let out a laugh. 'Naw, he probably hated them. They're identical

131

twins, and they tended to play pranks, which made him doubly mad. I think they were both on the team for several weeks before he realized there were two of them.'

'Yeah?'

She nodded. 'One summer, they needed a break from Coach. Went off the team. They took up sailing instead.'

His eyes widened. 'They quit the team?'

'Sure. It's a game. Not school. To my way of thinking, if it's not fun, why do it?'

'Because Max isn't a quitter,' Greg interjected. 'Are you, Max?' He caught Nina's eye. 'He's always played sports. It's good for him physically, and a kid in sports learns things, like persistence pays.'

'There's a difference between persistence and beating your head against the wall.' She grinned at Max.

For a few seconds, Max's mood lifted. 'That's right.'

Greg and Nina locked gazes for a moment, and he sensed the conversation's undercurrent. He decided to bring it to the surface. 'So I've been waiting to hear from you about my proposition.'

'I know.'

'And?'

'And—'

'Hey, darlin'.' The team pitcher showed up, sweaty but triumphant over their win.

'Bo, this is Greg Bellamy and his son Max.'

Nina stepped back. 'Bo Crutcher, our star pitcher.'

Damn, she did know every guy in town. That's it, Greg decided. If he didn't hear from her tomorrow, he was moving on.

'Let's go, buddy,' he said to Max. On the way back to the car, they walked past a young family, the husband short and a little paunchy, balding prematurely. Yet as the man watched his wife playing with their two kids on the blanket, he had that funny look Jenny had mentioned earlier. *Love does that.*

Greg realized Max was watching them, too, and the kid had no game face when it came to what he was feeling.

They got in the car, and Max said, 'I hate the divorce. It sucks.'

Greg was at a loss, taken aback by his son's comment. Should he let Max talk, question him, try to divert his attention—what? 'Yeah, it sucks,' he said, opting for honesty.

'Then why did you let it happen?' Max demanded. 'You told Nina I'm not a quitter, like that's something to be proud of. But you quit on Mom.'

'It wasn't just—' Greg stopped himself from objecting *It wasn't just me* . . . That didn't matter to Max, and maybe Greg was wrong. Had he single-handedly ruined his marriage, and could he have single-handedly saved it? Had he tried hard enough? 'I can't explain why,' he said. 'I'm sorry, Max.'

133

'Everything reminds me of the way things used to be,' Max said. 'Birthdays and Christmases, the four of us laughing all the time, feeling happy, like regular people. Now I think that was all a lie. Or that it turned into a lie because you guys split up.'

'It wasn't a lie,' Dad said. 'The love—the happiness—that was real.'

'Then why didn't it last?'

Why, why, why? 'Lots of reasons. Mainly, we changed. Your mom and I, we turned into different people. It's a cliché, but the truth is, we grew apart and didn't realize it until it was too late.'

'Too late for what? Why didn't you fix it? You made us all go to therapy over the divorce. Why didn't you work that hard on your marriage?'

'Good question, and I don't have an answer.' Or maybe Greg did, but it wasn't something he'd say to his son. The fact was, Greg and Sophie had never been right for one another. The only thing that was perfect between them was the fact that they'd made a baby—Daisy, a golden child who had lit their world, obliterating the dark corners where the truth of their incompatibility lurked, banishing it. And a few years later, Max came along, another light, burning even brighter. Burning away doubts and darkness, causing a temporary blindness he mistook for happiness.

Greg hated that the divorce had hurt his

134

kids, hated that he couldn't give Max the answers he sought. Everything he came up with sounded like an empty platitude. 'Son, I want you to believe me when I say things will get better. Here's the truth—you don't get one shot at happiness. You get a lot of shots. Second chances are everywhere. Sometimes the second chance works out even better than the first, because you learn from your mistakes. Trust me on this.'

'Right.' Max lapsed into grumpy silence. After a few minutes, he said, 'I don't even get it, Dad. I totally don't see why people get married in the first place, if they're only going to grow apart.'

'You don't go into a marriage thinking that way. It's hard to explain.' Greg turned at the sign for the inn. 'You do what you need to do, and hope for the best.'

# Part Four

## *Then*

The Guinevere Suite is the favorite choice of honeymooners and anniversary couples. Located in the belvedere tower, it is a luxurious and private oasis featuring a queen-size canopy bed draped with white tulle. A beveled-glass picture window frames stunning views of the lake. The bathroom, with a claw-footed spa tub large enough for two, is stocked with scented candles, soaps and lotions.

The bed linens are perfumed with lavender, an aromatic herb with a distinctive and soothing scent. A sachet of dried lavender buds, placed under the pillow, is said to be an effective aid for insomnia. To infuse bed linens with the scent, toss them into the clothes dryer along with a sachet of lavender.

## SEVEN

Greg kept an eye on Nina Romano, making sure she didn't pull any more stunts like sneaking into a cadet ball. What was it he'd said to her when he'd driven her home? 'I might surprise you.' Man, he never should have said that. Their age difference might not matter at all when they were older, but at the moment, it was an impenetrable wall between them. She was still a kid, he told himself. End of story.

It was the day after closing at the summer camp. The kids were all gone for the season, and all that was left was to close the place up until next year. Nina was helping her mother bring equipment out of the kitchen to hose down. Greg was supposed to be draining hot water heaters in all the cabins and bunkhouses, but he kept getting distracted by her and getting pissed all over again about that dumb-ass cadet at the country club.

He spotted some of the other counselors checking her out and had to threaten them to back off. He'd heard she had several brothers. Where the hell were they when she needed them?

For her part, Nina acted as though he didn't exist. Maybe she didn't see him. Or maybe she was embarrassed by the whole incident with

139

the cadet.

'Surprise.' At the main pavilion, Sophie Lindstrom got out of the van driven by Terry Davis, the head of maintenance. Her smile was both dazzling and uncertain. Given the bitterness of their parting after Christmas, Greg could easily understand her uncertainty.

He believed he and Sophie had been in love. They'd met in econ class the past fall. Over the course of the semester, they had gone from flirting to dating to sleeping together to imagining a future together. Sophie was perfect for him. She was smart, funny, kind, beautiful and ambitious. She came from a Seattle family of lawyers, diplomats and department-store magnates. Greg couldn't wait until Christmas, to bring her home and introduce her to his family.

It never happened, though. For reasons that weren't clear to Greg, their relationship turned turbulent and painful. Sophie had informed him that since they would both be spending the ensuing semester abroad in different countries, they shouldn't allow themselves to be held back by 'emotional ties,' whatever the hell that meant.

As Nina Romano had so aptly put it that night in the car, Sophie had dumped him. Greg hadn't seen or spoken with her since that painful conversation before Christmas break. Yet now here she was. He had no idea what that meant—or how to greet her. He had to reorient himself. He'd anticipated helping the camp workers and his parents with the final chores—clearing out cabins, removing all the perishables from the kitchen and dining hall, securing the boats and sports equipment— and then heading back to the city, ready for the next year of college. He certainly hadn't expected a visit from his old flame—and first love.

'Surprise is right,' he said. Stiff with self-consciousness, he briefly hugged Sophie. They bumped awkwardly, no longer knowing how to fit themselves together, though the action had once been so effortless. She felt different in every way. Even her smell was different. And he could swear she was bigger . . . damn. Had she gotten a boob job?

He let her go and stepped back. They'd been apart for months; they didn't know each other anymore. He didn't know what to say, either. He was debating between 'Good to see you' and 'I thought we were broken up' when she reached back into the passenger side. Poker-faced, Terry Davis went to the back of the van to get her bags.

Great, she had bags, he thought. Clearly she was planning to stick around, at least overnight.

'How did you know where to find me? And why didn't you call first?' he asked, catching himself checking out her butt as she reached inside the vehicle. He always liked her butt,

141

and today it looked particularly fine. Maybe she'd put on a little weight during her studies in Japan. It looked good on her.

'Your roommate told me where you'd be. And I decided not to call first because I didn't want to chicken out,' she said over her shoulder, and then she emerged from the van, straightened up and turned.

For several seconds, Greg stared at her in complete and utter incomprehension. In her hands, she held two gray plastic handles that were attached to some sort of hooded basket. In the basket was a wad of pale, soft-looking blankets.

No, he thought. Just . . . *no.* It roared through his head, a denial so powerful that he couldn't even hear Sophie speaking. He could see her lips moving, but not one word penetrated the frantic howl inside his head.

Okay, he thought. Deep breath. He forced himself to focus.

'. . . that look on your face,' Sophie was saying. 'That's the other reason I didn't call first.' She paused briefly to thank Mr. Davis for the lift in the van, then turned back to Greg. 'Is there someplace we can go to . . . '

'Over here.' He grabbed her wheeled suitcase, picking it up over the bumpy path that led down to the dock in front of the main pavilion. In the wake of the campers' departure, it was deserted. Evening was descending, and a warm breeze rippled the surface of the water.

But now the placid beauty of the evening meant nothing to him. He didn't care about the sheet of light upon the lake, or the gentle lapping of the water at the dock's pilings. It was just someplace to go, a secluded spot to freak out as everything he thought about his life was turned upside down, or inside out, or into something he didn't recognize.

With painstaking care, Sophie set down the podlike carrier.

Greg still couldn't speak. He kept his eyes on Sophie—if he didn't look at it, he didn't have to acknowledge it, and then it wouldn't be real. It wouldn't be happening.

She was staring at him with relentless steadiness. 'When we broke up last Christmas, I didn't know I was pregnant,' she said. 'I swear I didn't. I thought—I just assumed—I was coming down with something, a stomach bug or flu. It never occurred to me . . .' She looked away, cleared her throat. 'There was a lot of stress. I had finals to deal with, and you and I weren't getting along.'

Understatement. By the end of their relationship, being together was like peeling the skin off a blister. The knowledge that they'd be on separate continents during their semesters abroad—he in Granada, Spain, and she in Nagoya, Japan—turned out to be the ideal way to heal from the hurt. Greg assumed he and Sophie would return in the fall as cordial strangers. One by one, memories would fall away. They would forget things about each other—the names of childhood pets, favorite colors, the song that had been playing the first time they made love. Eventually they would forget what they'd once been to each other, or if they did remember, then the memories wouldn't hurt.

Now he realized nothing was over between them. Something was just beginning. He still couldn't look at the bundle of blankets in the carrier seat. But neither could he ignore it any longer. 'So it's mine,' he said. It wasn't a question. Sophie might be a secret-keeper, but she wasn't a liar. And she wouldn't have subjected herself to the pain of coming here if she hadn't been a hundred percent certain of what she was doing.

'*It* is a girl,' she stated, and Greg nearly cringed, remembering that acid tone Sophie was so good at. She'd always had the unique ability of making him feel about three inches tall. 'And yes,' Sophie went on, 'she's your daughter. I came to tell you on my own, because I want us to figure out what to do without anyone interfering.'

'By "anyone," I assume you mean your parents,' Greg supplied. Both Anders and Kirsten Lindstrom were partners in one of Seattle's most prestigious law firms. And this was classic Sophie. Simply by bringing up the subject, a particular pressure was applied. 'So they're your backup plan, right? I mean, if I try to deny any responsibility? Which goes to show you, they don't know me at all. Maybe that goes for you, too.'

To his surprise, Sophie looked close to tears, her face blurred by vulnerability. 'Oh, Greg. I wish I'd told you sooner, but I was just so scared.'

A sound came from the baby carrier. It was a sleepy mew, almost inaudibly soft, yet it thundered in Greg's ears. Sophie seemed to be transformed by the tiny sound. Her soft uncertainty firmed into pure pride as she said, 'Her name is Daisy.'

Greg felt a jolt, followed by a rush of feeling he couldn't explain. Suddenly it wasn't an 'it' but a girl. His daughter. And she had a name—Daisy.

With awkward, wooden movements he hunkered down beside the carrier seat. He couldn't figure out how to move the accordion-pleated hood back, so Sophie bent and did it for him. The golden light of evening fell across the bundle inside. With one finger, a shaking hand, Greg moved the soft blanket aside, and finally the bundle took on human form. He found himself unable to breathe as he looked down at her, at a fragile, tiny child, sound asleep like a creature in a fairy tale. He stared at the round, perfect face, the impossibly little fist tucked beside a slightly flushed cheek. The baby's face flickered in sleep, then softened and resettled.

And just like that, the world shifted. Greg's chest felt as though it was about to burst. From a place in his heart he didn't know he had, he started to love the tiny child. The love crashed over him, as unexpected and intense as a sudden storm, the kind that leaves the landscape forever changed. And then he looked up at Sophie and he knew he'd damn well better figure out how to love her, too.

## *EIGHT*

Summer at Camp Kioga ended with an unexpected wedding, and Nina found herself inordinately intrigued by the development. Mrs. Romano and Mrs. Majesky catered the small family affair, which briefly turned the Bellamy family and Camp Kioga into a whirlwind. A few of Sophie Lindstrom's friends and family came all the way from Seattle, staying at the Inn at Willow Lake, which was how Nina learned the scoop about the wedding. After working at the inn, she had mastered the art of listening in on strangers' conversations without seeming to.

Sophie's friends were sophisticated and well-traveled, yet they couldn't seem to avoid complaining about the plumbing, the lack of air-conditioning and the overwhelming dearth of entertainment in the small town of Avalon. Sophie's guests came in pairs, like creatures to Noah's ark. Two best friends, Lucy Rosetta and Miranda Sweeney, two parents—no siblings—and two sets of grandparents. That was it. Oh, and the baby. That little nest of pink blankets was the reason for all the flurry.

Small families intrigued Nina. They always seemed so quiet, so polite and reserved. She watched them at one of the round tables in the breakfast room, passing the cream and sharing sections of the paper, talking softly to one another.

How different that was from the Romano household. First off, they never went out to breakfast. Who could afford it? Breakfast at Nina's house was always a mad scramble—people fighting over the next piece of toast or the last glass of juice, the feeding frenzy followed by a frantic hunt for keys, sports equipment, schoolbooks or train cards, culminating in a stampede toward the door. In the aftermath, the kitchen resembled a town that had been pillaged by angry hordes.

Small families were so subdued, you could hear the clink of china and silver. You could hear mothers saying, 'Don't fidget, dear' or 'Please pass the salt.'

On the morning of the Bellamy wedding, a brilliant last-hurrah-of-summer day, Nina was working in the dining room of the inn. Unlike most kids who hated their crappy summer jobs at the car wash or municipal pool, Nina loved working at the Inn at Willow Lake. Though somewhat shabby, it was still genteel and peaceful. Nina loved welcoming guests, making them comfortable in their haven on the shores of idyllic Willow Lake.

Today, though, she had to leave right after breakfast. Her mother had recruited her and Jenny to help with the wedding. After the ceremony, there would be a dinner at the main pavilion of Camp Kioga, and Nina's mom was in charge of the food.

She and Jenny rode in the Sky River Bakery van, along with the magnificent tiered wedding cake Mrs. Majesky had just finished with touches of gold leaf and silver nonpareil beads. Jenny was subdued, because her main reasons for visiting Camp Kioga—namely two of the boys who went to camp there—were gone for the summer. She knew she wouldn't be seeing them until next year.

Nina was subdued, too, and she had an upset stomach, but she didn't attribute it to being lovesick, like Jenny. The sugary smell inside the van, combined with the winding road up to the camp, didn't help. She wished she hadn't skipped breakfast. Usually the staff at the inn was allowed to help themselves to breakfast, but this morning the idea of eating anything made her want to hurl. Plus, she had to pee really bad, and as soon as they got to the pavilion, she had to bolt for the ladies'

148

room.

For the rest of the day, she kept too busy to focus on her upset stomach. At the last minute, Greg's two sisters and his brother showed up, followed by some of Greg's college buddies, and the gathering began to seem like an actual party. She and Jenny helped in the kitchen, and when the guests arrived for the reception, the girls kept the buffet tables filled with the feast prepared by Mrs. Romano. A band was playing and by sunset, the dancing began. Nina kept sneaking glances at Greg Bellamy, though he didn't seem to notice her. He and Sophie—whoa, his *wife*—were all caught up in the festivities. According to gossip, the two of them had been college sweethearts. They'd broken up months ago, and then Sophie just showed up out of the blue with a new baby, and all of a sudden, they were madly in love again.

No wonder Greg simply looked straight through Nina when she passed by with a platter of chicken cacciatore. He probably didn't even remember that flower-scented summer night when he'd given her a ride home from the country club, when he'd said, 'Maybe someday . . . I just might surprise you . . .'

Embarrassingly enough, Nina had relived that night over and over—the night she'd lost her virginity to a West Point cadet. But the part she remembered most vividly, the part she replayed again and again in her head, had less

149

to do with Laurence Jeffries, and more with Greg Bellamy. Which was really dumb because he clearly didn't think of her at all. He was totally immersed in Sophie and the little baby she'd brought to him.

At one point during the evening, she found herself standing against the wall, trying to figure out how to adjust her bra without seeming too obvious. Maybe she was going through some developmental change, because all her bras felt too tight lately. She set her serving tray on a stand and tried, discreetly, to pull at the elastic through her blouse.

'Is that for me?' someone asked.

Nina came to attention like a soldier. Oh, crap. Greg Bellamy. 'What?' she asked, then realized he was looking at the tray, not her. 'Yes, sure.' She picked up the tray of champagne flutes.

He looked directly at her, yet she was suddenly tongue-tied. What did you say to a guy who was completely, a zillion percent unavailable?

'Uh, hi,' she said. Oh, brilliant, Nina.

He barely glanced at her. 'Hi,' he replied, then seemed to be at a loss. He helped himself to a champagne flute from the serving tray she held and drank it down without pausing.

Wonderful, she thought. He didn't even remember her. She was hired help, no more distinctive than wallpaper. Of course, that was the whole point—she, Jenny and the others working the wedding wore black trousers, sensible black shoes and crisp white shirts, hair neatly pulled back into a ponytail. Still, she thought, setting the tray on a rack for the busboy. *Still.*

A group of Greg's college friends surrounded him and started teasing him about being the first of their number to get married. 'Here's to you, buddy,' a red-faced frat boy said, 'may you boldly go where none of us has gone before.'

'Yeah, right into the arms of the little woman,' another guy said. 'Hear that? It's the sound of the trap slamming shut and the key turning.'

They all laughed as though this was something hilarious. As though teasing him about being trapped like a rat was a good thing to do at his wedding reception. She saw him slam back three more flutes of champagne, one right after another. She was no expert on newlyweds, but she was pretty sure they weren't supposed to drink themselves into oblivion on their wedding day, because it tended to affect the wedding night. After his fourth glass of champagne, he stalked away, his body language exuding anger. He appeared to be heading for the restroom at the top of the stairs. Instead, at a side door, he paused and looked around, then slipped out.

Now Nina was on a mission. What was this guy up to? She edged over to the door and saw that it gave access to an outside stairway leading down to an enclosed walkway and the dock. She stepped out, unseen, and saw him stop on the walkway, which was lined with a display of painted oars and other memorabilia the campers had made over the summer. As she watched, Greg drew back his fist and slammed it into the wall. The Sheetrock gave way with a dull cracking sound. He uttered a swear word even her brothers refused to say, and a cloud of gypsum powder erupted around him.

Nina didn't hesitate. She skimmed down the steps and hurried over to him just as he was drawing back his fist for another blow. 'Hey,' she said in a stage whisper. 'Hey, cut it out.'

He whirled toward her, his rage seeming to lash out through the darkness. Nina didn't flinch. She was a Romano. She had brothers. A pissed-off guy didn't intimidate her. 'I said, cut that out.'

To her surprise, his shoulders slumped as the fight went out of him. 'Who the hell're you?' he muttered, trying to peer at her in the darkness.

She bit back a sarcastic remark. Of course he wouldn't recognize her, not here in the dark, under these circumstances. She took a linen towel from the waistband of her pants. 'You need to straighten up, pal. Hold out your hand.'

She took it gently in her own, trying not to

152

feel his warm strength, or to hear the despair in the ragged breaths he took. 'Be still, okay?'

'Sure. Whatever.'

She gingerly dabbed away the blood where the skin had broken. 'Not the smartest thing to do on your wedding night,' she said.

'This is not supposed to be my wedding night.'

'Maybe you should have thought of that before.' She cleaned up his hand, then lightly brushed the plaster dust from his sleeve.

'Before what? Jesus, she shows up out of nowhere with a baby. What the hell else could I do?'

'Did you really just ask me that? Please tell me you didn't ask me that.'

He shoved his splayed hand through his hair. 'I do love her. I *have* to. I love them both.' He was muttering under his breath now, as though trying to convince himself that he'd done the right thing. 'They're my life, now. Maybe not the life I'd imagined, but so the hell what?'

'Fine, so here's what you can do.' She took his arm and towed him toward the stairs. 'You can quit whining. You can man up and be with the girl you just married. That's what you can do.'

He stopped and held himself very stiff. For a moment, she thought he was going to balk. Then he looked at her, his face unreadable in the darkness. 'Nina.' He chuckled without humor at her gasp of surprise. 'I do know who you are. I've filed you under "no longer an option."'

He was drunk, she reminded herself. He wouldn't remember this conversation. 'Go on,' she urged. 'Get a cup of coffee. Go back to your wedding.'

She stood in the darkness and watched him head back to the party. Although he took the stairs two at a time, full of purpose, she realized he probably understood that tonight would not be the hardest night of his marriage. Far from it. Tonight was just the beginning, and that was likely the reason he'd freaked out. He was trapped, neatly and completely. She'd heard people talk about such things before, girls getting pregnant in order to hedge their bets. Had the bride gotten pregnant on purpose, in order to marry a Bellamy? Nina had no idea. If she had, she was in for a rude awakening, maybe not tomorrow, but one day.

None of your business, Nina scolded herself. She couldn't believe how out of sorts she was feeling, yet she wasn't quite able to put her finger on the cause. Standing there in the darkness of a beautiful autumn night, she felt a sudden rise of queasiness. The smells of the lake and the drying leaves and exhaust from the parking lot mingled in a particularly unpleasant way.

Almost too late, Nina realized she was about to puke. She looked wildly around.

The restrooms were just inside the door. She lunged for the stairs and made it, just barely. The ladies' room was empty, a small mercy, she thought as she lost the meager contents of her stomach.

Instead of feeling better, she was plagued by a fresh wave of nausea. She blotted her face with tissue, then leaned against the stall door, letting the metal chill her sweating forehead, waiting to make sure she wasn't going to puke again. Fatigue rolled over her in a wave. Lately, it seemed, she was constantly tired.

She heard the door to the outer lounge open and close. 'So how crazy is this,' said someone. 'Here I am, taking a break from my wedding reception to nurse my baby.'

'It's not crazy at all, Sophie,' said someone else. 'It's a blessing.'

Nina made extra noise coming out of the stall so they would know they weren't alone. Sophie, the bride, and her best friend Miranda, were seated in the adjacent lounge, which was furnished simply with rustic benches and a mirrored vanity.

Nina turned on the water at the sink extra hard to make certain they knew she wasn't eavesdropping on purpose. Nevertheless, she overheard a snippet: '. . . nobody. Just the help.'

Yeah, that's me, Nina thought bitterly, waiting for the water to warm up. Nobody. Just the help. The help, who had been on her feet

155

for like five hours waiting on Sophie and her friends.

She knew the kind of people these girls were—society nobs who treated drivers and housekeepers like nonentities, pieces of furniture you could say anything in front of. She and her friends had that fake-earnest, West Coast way of acting like your best friend while not really giving a shit about you. Greg Bellamy could have her, and good riddance.

In the mirror over the sink she could see their reflection through the doorway to the lounge. Sophie had peeled down the bodice of her wedding dress and was holding a little pink-wrapped bundle to her breast.

'I think it's incredible,' Miranda said in admiration. 'You've got it all—the guy, the baby and everything.'

'Remind me of how incredible it is at two in the morning, when I have to do a night feeding,' Sophie said.

Poor little rich girl, Nina thought, rinsing out her mouth at the sink. Cry me a river.

Miranda lowered her voice, but still Nina could hear. 'All right, so spill. Did you plan this?'

Nina had been about to leave. Now she grabbed a paper towel and dampened it, taking her time as she blotted her face. She couldn't help herself; she strained her ears to hear.

'What do you take me for?' Sophie asked.

'Hester Prynne? I didn't even realize I was pregnant for weeks and weeks. I just felt sick and nauseous and constantly tired. I thought maybe I had a bug, or maybe an allergy to Japanese cuisine, and couldn't keep any food down. Then I was worried that I had a bladder infection because I had to pee all the time. Pregnancy never even crossed my mind. Finally the thing that tipped me off was that my boobs changed. Got, you know, bigger and . . . kind of sore and tender.'

Nina's hand trembled as she brought it to her chest, felt the elastic of her bra binding her. Was she different, there? Sore? She kept thinking she'd just slept wrong.

'That was when I started trying to remember if I'd missed a period,' Sophie confessed to her friend. 'Turns out I'd missed, like, two . . . .'

Nina dropped her hand and stood frozen, the warm water pouring over her fingers. She was trying to remember, too. Ohmygod, she thought. Oh god oh god oh god.

\*     \*     \*

Nina never spoke to Greg again. She assumed he had forgotten her. He'd never really known her in the first place, and probably wouldn't recognize her if he tripped over her.

And as for Nina, she had neither the time nor the emotional energy to spare for someone who occupied such a minor part of her life.

157

Her life changed on the day of the Bellamy wedding, though it had nothing to do with the Bellamys. Or the wedding. That was the day Nina realized she was pregnant. In a state of horrified shock, she had denied it for as long as she could, hiding it from everyone but herself.

Or so she thought. One morning in autumn, her mother shooed everyone off to school early. As Nina gathered her things in her backpack, the house seemed almost preternaturally quiet. She could actually hear a radio playing; it was set to her father's beloved NPR morning news.

Frowning, Nina went to the window and looked out across the leaf-strewn yard. 'Hey, Pop left without me,' she said. One of the few—very few—perks of having a dad who was a teacher was that they didn't have to take a bus to school. She and her older brothers and sisters caught a ride with their dad.

'I told them to go on ahead,' Ma said.

For the first time, Nina noticed that her mother was wearing something other than her usual mom clothes—jeans and a sweatshirt, slip-on sneakers. This morning, Ma had on a skirt and sweater set, and low-heeled pumps.

Nina felt a curl of inner dread. Something—besides the obvious—wasn't right. 'What's going on?'

Leaning forward into the hall mirror, Ma put on lipstick and closed her pocketbook with

158

a decisive snap. 'I called the school and said you'd be coming in late today. I'm taking you to the doctor.'

'I'm not sick,' Nina blurted out.

Ma only nodded. It was funny, how she was a naturally quiet woman. It was easy to mistake her for loud, because she was always yelling. Not by choice, though. She yelled simply because it was the only way to be heard. She much preferred to speak softly.

'I know you're not sick,' she said. Very, very quietly. 'We're going to Dr. Osborne.'

Oh. Dr. Osborne was a women's doctor.

Nina hugged her backpack against her chest. 'Ma—'

'It's time,' her mother said. 'Probably past time.'

Nina didn't know what else to say. In a very small corner of her mind, she felt an eddy of relief. At last, her secret was out. She'd contemplated telling Jenny or one of her sisters, but she could never find the words. Fear and guilt sealed her lips and fused her jaw. Now her mother was forcing the issue.

Marching in front of her mother like a prisoner of war, she went to the car and got in. Like everything else that belonged to the Romanos, the car was shabby and outdated and practical rather than stylish—a Ford Taurus. Nina sometimes wondered if her mother ever fantasized about owning an Alfa Romeo or even a Cadillac, something with just a bit of style. Today, though, such thoughts failed to distract her.

They rode in silence for a while. Nina looked out the window at the scenery going by, trying with all her might to let the world outside push through her nervousness and terror. Avalon was at its most beautiful in the fall, when autumn was flaming its last hurrah. The sugar maples painted the hills with burning pink and orange and amber. People raked leaves into piles in front of their neat clapboard houses. The shops of Main Street had mums and asters in the window boxes. She knew everyone in town, all the family-owned businesses—Zuzu's Petals Boutique, the Camelot Bookstore, the Majeskys' Sky River Bakery, Palmquist Jewelry. And everyone knew the Romano family. Her dad was the most popular teacher at the high school, winning 'Teacher of the Year' more frequently than anyone else on the faculty. Once, he'd won for the whole state. They were known as a 'good' family with 'nice' kids. In a town like this, that designation meant something. So many kids got caught stealing beer through the back door of Wegmans, smashing mailboxes along River Road or climbing the water tower. Not the Romanos. Everyone admired the relatively well-behaved Romano kids.

They weren't exactly altar boys and Girl Scouts, but they stayed in school, played sports and held down after-school jobs. You'd never find one of them being escorted home in the back of a squad car. It was well-known around town that the Romanos would never have a big, fancy house or new car or a vacation to Florida. They'd never attend private college or join a country club. But that had never seemed important, because as a family, they had something money couldn't buy—'good' kids who were the envy of everyone in town.

Until now. Until Nina had managed to get herself in a fix so bad that even her mother was mad at her.

She twisted her hands in her lap and gave up trying to concentrate on the world outside. 'I'm sorry, Ma,' she said.

Her mother kept her eyes on the road. 'We'll figure this out.'

That made Nina feel worse than ever. She wanted to hear, 'I forgive you,' but that wasn't what Ma had said. 'We'll figure this out' sounded difficult and painful.

When you were in high school and having a baby, that was pretty much all you could expect—for it to be difficult and painful.

'How did you know, Ma?' Nina couldn't help herself. She had to know. She'd been so careful.

'You can't hide a pregnancy from someone who's been pregnant ten times.'

'Ten?'

'Seven regular pregnancies, one set of twins plus two miscarriages.'

161

'I never knew about the miscarriages.' I should be so lucky, Nina thought, and then felt a shiver of remorse. It was probably a sin to hope for such a thing.

'There's no point in dwelling on things that will never be.'

'Does Pop know? About me, I mean.'

'Not yet.'

'Ma, I'm so scared to tell him. I was scared to tell you both, and that's why I didn't say anything.'

'Nina, we're not monsters.'

'I know. I just . . . the thing that was so scary was the thought of disappointing you.'

'Honey, you don't need to be afraid. And don't worry about your dad.'

'Will I have to go away?' asked Nina.

Ma turned to glance at her. 'Where did you get that idea?'

'It was something I read in a magazine at catechism.'

Ma looked back at the road. 'These days, girls in your position don't go away. They go on TV talk shows.'

Nina didn't know what to say to that. She couldn't tell if her mother was being sarcastic or what. They rode along in silence for a while. The dazzling beauty of the autumn colors against the clear blue sky was hurtful, somehow. She couldn't figure out why, but the sight made her eyes tear up. She kept her gaze trained out the window until they arrived at the doctor's office, a white Victorian mansion that had been converted into a professional building. Her mother parked and turned off the car, but made no move to get out.

'Were you forced?' The question came out of nowhere, on a rasp of pain.

At first, Nina didn't quite comprehend. Then it dawned on her what her mother was asking, and Nina wanted to cry all over again. It didn't occur to her until this very minute how much this was hurting her mother. Ma had probably been suffering for days, wondering if some guy had raped her daughter.

But instead of bursting into tears, Nina gave a short laugh. 'No, Ma. I wasn't forced. I assure you, I was a willing participant. Swear to God.' For some reason, her mother's question made the situation very real to her. She was having a baby. A real live baby. Just for a second, she felt a genuine pride of accomplishment. After being mediocre at everything all her life, she would be first at something. Then the feeling was quickly doused by icy, soul-shriveling terror. A *baby*. What on earth was she going to do with a baby?

Ma flexed her hands on the steering wheel and let out an audible sigh. 'Then . . . have you told the boy yet?'

The boy. Laurence Jeffries. She hadn't spoken to him since that night, and she assumed he never wanted to see her again. Why would he, after Greg Bellamy and his big mouth blurted out her true age? And honestly, Nina couldn't blame Laurence. According to the Legal Eagle—a radio talk-show host who answered anonymous questions on the air— there could be dire consequences for a shiny new West Point cadet if this ever got out. Nina had phoned in every day until he finally answered her question on the air—this could turn out to be a life-altering decision, not just for her but for Laurence.

His training at West Point and the possibility of a big military career would be over. There could be criminal charges because of her age, even though he, too, had been a minor, just seventeen, when it happened. His life, along with Nina's, would be forever altered. Cadets were forbidden to marry—not that she would want that—and having a baby out of wedlock was grounds for dismissal and severe discipline, as well.

Nina didn't actually give a hoot about Laurence Jeffries's future, yet the extent of her power over him frightened her. In a single moment, she could completely change his life, the same way the pregnancy was changing hers, the same way she'd watched Sophie Lindstrom change Greg Bellamy's life. If Nina decided to speak up, then within a matter of hours, Laurence would no longer be in training at the most elite military academy in the world.

He'd be just another punk from the projects with nothing but a high school diploma under his belt. He'd have no military career, no elite education. High-paying, prestigious firms were not known for hiring guys like Laurence, that was a fact.

She had made him a promise that night—she wouldn't cause him any trouble. Of course, neither of them had foreseen an unwanted pregnancy. That didn't change her mind, though. She kept remembering Greg Bellamy, putting his fist through a wall at his own wedding. No, getting together because of a baby was a bad idea.

'I'm not telling him,' she said to her mother. 'Not anytime soon, that's for sure.'

'You have to. He's part of this—'

'For, like, five minutes, he was,' Nina said, pretty much summing up her entire relationship with Laurence Jeffries.

## Part Five

### Now

The Inn at Willow Lake was originally
built for railroad baron Thaddeus
Morton. Legend has it that Morton
designed the main entryway himself, with
a rising sun fanlight over the door, so his
new bride could see the sun rise even on
a cloudy day.

When the sun shines through the
transom, the crystal edges of the bevels
create an ever-changing array of delicate
rainbows in the front hall, splashing
color across the ceiling, walls and floor.
The refraction and dispersion of light is,
of course, enhanced when each pane of
glass is kept spotless.

To make a streakless window cleaner,
put a tablespoon each of white vinegar
and rubbing alcohol in a spray bottle with
water. Add a drop of clove oil for a fresh
scent.

# NINE

Nina took a deep breath and squared her shoulders. Standing on the brick-paved path, she regarded the entryway of the Inn at Willow Lake with a mixture of yearning and trepidation. The double doors had beveled glass panes in an art deco design, and a fanlight over the top in the shape of a rising sun. In front of the door, a workman on a ladder was painting a coat of primer on the ceiling of the porch, while another, in a mask and goggles, was smoothing the floor planks with a power sander. All this busy renovation was supposed to take place under her watch. According to Jenny, and even Sonnet, she could still take charge here. She simply had to wrap her mind around the idea that Greg Bellamy now owned the place.

*Simply.* There was nothing simple about this. Of course, that didn't mean she should shrink from the challenge. She'd thought about what to do until her head felt ready to explode. She'd talked it over with anyone who would listen. Ultimately, she'd realized that there was no solution, only compromise. She'd been in city government. She could do compromise.

The guy on the ladder spotted her and started to climb down. 'Wait a minute, miss,' he said. 'I'll move this.'

'No need,' she said, easily ducking under the ladder.

'That's supposed to be bad luck,' the painter said.

'I make my own luck,' Nina said, and opened the door to the lobby.

Inside, the place was a hive of activity as well. Workers in shirts with the Davis Construction logo were busy plastering, priming, painting. An electrician was installing a light fixture above the mantel. The lobby was taking on the look of a luxurious old-fashioned salon, its tall ceilings bordered by ornate crown moulding, the fireplace marble clean and bright, the window casements newly refinished.

She spotted Greg bent over a table mounted on two sawhorses, studying some kind of construction diagram. He had a pencil behind each ear, a tool belt slung low on his hips and a look of total absorption on his face. He's in this for keeps, thought Nina. She sensed that from him, and grew irritated. *This is my dream*, she wanted to tell him. *Not yours.* Yet as she looked around the big, empty room, she could see evidence of his touch in the restored details—the parquet floor and wainscoting, the fresh coat of paint on the walls and the bright white plasterwork. Would she have chosen that particular dove-gray color for the walls, the deep brown stain for the floor?

As she crossed the salon, the whine of a saw

170

filled the air, and she had to wave to get his attention. He looked up at her, his face lit with a smile of welcome, and her heart skipped a beat.

'I've decided,' she said. Because of the noise, she had to stand very close to him in order to be heard. He was so much taller than her that she had to tip her head back in order to look him in the eye. As she did so, she felt a little unbalanced, as though she teetered on some precipice. Maybe she did, and they both seemed to know this. Courage, she told herself. You're doing the right thing.

She swallowed hard, moistened her lips and said, 'I accept.'

Despite the chaos of the renovation erupting all around them, she had the strange sensation that she and Greg were completely alone, an island of two. A grin spread slowly across his face, its effect on her devastating. She tried to act as though guys like this smiled at her every day, but he probably saw right through her. Ever since her ill-fated days as a boy-crazy teen, she'd been a sucker for a pretty face. He wiped his plaster-dusted hand on his painter's pants and held it out to her. 'Great,' he said. 'Excellent, Nina. You won't be sorry.'

We'll see about that, she thought, motioning him through the French doors that connected the lobby to the sunroom, where it was quieter, with the windows open to dispel the harsh odor of new varnish. She fully expected him to discover exactly how hard it was to run a business and raise a family as a single parent. He might not even last the summer. Yet the renovations done so far, and the fact that he wasn't afraid to roll up his sleeves and work, surprised her. His sturdy self-confidence didn't, though. Wiping his hands on a bandana from his back pocket, he added, 'Man, you really know how to keep a guy in suspense.'

'I wasn't doing that on purpose,' she said. 'That's not me, Greg. I'm not being manipulative.'

'Hey, take it easy.' He laughed aloud. 'I wasn't accusing you of anything.'

Nina flushed. After four years of city council meetings, she was hypersensitive. 'I'm just saying, I didn't treat this decision lightly.'

'Never thought you did. And for what it's worth, I didn't offer it lightly.'

'I'm ready to start right away,' she said, her manner businesslike. 'I can move in tonight. I've got all my stuff in back of my brother's truck.'

Confusion clouded his face. 'Move in.'

'The boathouse,' she reminded him, indicating the envelope containing the contract. 'It's part of our agreement. I'm going to have to be on-premise if you expect me to do this right.'

'And you want to live in the boathouse.' He frowned, and she thought he was getting ready to object.

Say one word, she thought, just one word, and I'm out of here.

Instead, he led the way through a side door and started walking along the gravel path that sloped down toward the lake. A grounds crew was hard at work, pruning and hauling things by the wheel barrowful. 'You'd better check it out before you make up your mind to move in.'

She caught herself checking out something else. The painter's pants fit him perfectly, sitting low on his hips and outlining a butt that was—

'. . . might want to give it some serious thought,' Greg was saying.

Shoring up her willpower, Nina yanked her attention back to the conversation. She did so by reminding herself that he was the adversary—her boss. No matter how good he looked in a pair of well-worn work pants.

As he led the way across the rolling slope of the lawn to the boathouse, she had to admit that she was impressed by the work done on the property so far. And, okay, she was impressed by him. Initially, she expected him to be all lord-of-the-manor, sitting on the porch with a mint julep while the hired help whipped the place into shape. Instead, it appeared that Greg had dived right in, working along with the contractor's guys as he tackled everything from landscaping to plaster moulding. On the far side of the property, Max was on the driveway of the owner's house,

173

shooting baskets.

'We've got most of the common areas and six of the guest rooms good to go,' Greg was telling her. 'The grand opening . . . I'll need to know what you think.'

What she thought was that she wanted this to be her project. And although he seemed eager to sweep her into the process, she didn't forget who was in charge here. She tamped back her resentment. It was unproductive. One thing she knew for certain was the futility of focusing on unproductive things.

They reached the boathouse, which was set off by itself, surrounded on three sides by an emerald apron of lawn and a fringe of sugar maples, and on the other side, of course, by Willow Lake itself.

Nina had always thought there was something magical about this place, as though its timber and stone walls held old, delicious secrets. Situated perfectly between water and sky, the boathouse felt detached from the everyday world. Its narrow upper deck projected out over the lake, and Nina remembered that it was so quiet there, she could hear the fish jump.

She and Greg walked around the outside first. Three of the water-level boat slips were empty. One was occupied by a vintage Chris Craft runabout made of mahogany. It was in remarkably good condition, gleaming with a recent polish.

174

'It was my father's,' Greg explained. 'As a kid, he spent every summer on Willow Lake. We put the boat in as soon as I took possession of this place.'

And with those words—*It was my father's*—it struck her. She wasn't the only one who had a history here, whose emotional ties held it close to her heart. 'It's beautiful,' she said. 'What's that other one?'

'A catboat. I want to teach Max to sail.'

Nina fumbled over the thought that Greg would be raising his family here on the premises. Kids, curfews, rules, school hours—that phase of her life was over, yet Greg was smack in the middle of it all. Not my problem, she thought. Much as Nina had loved raising Sonnet, she had to admit she was happy it was him and not her, juggling everything.

'. . . boat lifts need to be repaired,' Greg was saying, completely unaware of her hesitation. 'I'll need to get a welder in to fix these. Or I suppose I could do it myself.'

'Welding? Is this something you learned at Harvard?'

'If that's meant as a dig, forget it. I'm in too good a mood to let anything tick me off, even your smart mouth.'

'I do not have—'

'So. Let's take a look at your new digs.'

He unlocked the door and held it open. The hinges let out a rusty squeal. She paused, suddenly finding herself standing too close

175

to him—again. He smelled of plaster and sweat, and for some reason, she found herself inordinately attracted by that. This was problematic on so many levels that she nearly turned and fled. Then she reminded herself— she was taking a step toward her dream. He was just a minor hurdle. And, like Jenny said, he was taking all the financial risk here.

She stepped over the threshold and into her new home. A musty odor of disuse hung in the air. Nina opened a few windows, stirring a lonely sigh from the brittle lace curtains. The floors creaked and the plumbing groaned when she turned on a faucet, which spewed liquid rust. Cobwebs hung from the rafters. Storage boxes cluttered the floor.

The place was a nightmare. But when she opened the storm shutters and faced the view out the windows, all the flaws of the place fell away. She pictured herself living here, so close to the lake she could hear the water lap at the shore.

'It used to be my favorite place on the property,' she explained. 'When I worked here as a teenager, I used to save it for last, so I could end the day right there, looking out at the lake. It was . . . a way to find just a few minutes of peace and quiet before heading home.'

He lifted one side of his mouth in a half smile. 'I never knew it was possible to find peace and quiet at work.'

'Sometimes work is less chaotic than being at home. Sonnet and I lived with my folks back then because I was working and going to school. And don't get me wrong—I was incredibly grateful for the support, but life was pretty . . . chaotic.' She could still remember the nonstop noise and activity of the Romano household, the unceasing demands of a toddler. The boathouse had been her oasis, a place where she could think and dream, even for just a short while.

She stood and surveyed the property, the placid lake, the dock and the storybook architecture. She inhaled the air, sweet with the promise of summer. *I'm back*, she thought. *Finally.*

## TEN

Daisy felt like crap. She was tired of feeling like crap, tired of people telling her it was normal to feel like crap in the final trimester of pregnancy. In the old-fashioned parlor of the house where she now lived with her brother and father, she shifted restlessly on the sofa and contemplated her ankles. At least, they used to be ankles. Now they were as swollen and unattractive as the rest of her.

So okay, she thought, flipping through one of her many pregnancy books, nobody said this was supposed to be fun. What could possibly be fun about gaining forty pounds, having to pee every five minutes, waking up in the middle of the night to find your belly alive with a squirming, elbowing, hiccupping, growing baby?

Everybody was constantly reminding Daisy not to compare herself to other people. Ha, like she could avoid that. Everyone she knew had moved on after high school, or planned to very soon. Some of her friends, like Sonnet Romano, were traveling. Others had already found jobs and places to live.

Daisy was grateful for her supportive family. How could she not be? She was glad her father had found something to be excited about—the inn. She didn't mind helping out, either. Photography was her passion, and it was great that she could do something useful with it.

The trouble was, she was at a phase in her life where she didn't want to do anything useful. She wanted to explore and dream and be irresponsible. Which, at this point, was no longer an option.

She wondered if genetics had anything to do with her predicament. She was upholding a family tradition. She'd been born out of wedlock. Her parents had married, but look how that had worked out. Daisy wasn't going to make that mistake. It wasn't genetics, she concluded. It was her own dumb choices.

She listened to the clothes dryer in the

utility room, tossing around a load of washing, its rhythm oddly soothing. She smoothed her hand over the mound of her belly. The good news was, she was getting so big that pretty soon, she wouldn't even be able to see her swollen ankles. Talk about feeling lucky.

Restless, she put away the pregnancy book—did she really need that image in her head of the mucus plug?—and went to the screened window facing the lake. She thought about the uncountable ways her life had changed since she'd visited Willow Lake last summer. Back then, she'd been in full-on rebellion mode, furious at her parents over the divorce and determined to make them pay. Her stupidity had backfired, which in retrospect was no surprise. She was the one bearing the consequences now.

Her mom had begged her to move to The Hague. She'd promised the best care to be found for Daisy and the baby, as much support as she could offer. Daisy had refused; her anger at her mother ran too deep. So here she was, in this beautiful place, with her future hanging in the balance. It was pretty surreal, living at the owner's residence of the old inn. It was like a mansion in a movie, with all the grounds and outbuildings. From the window of the house, Daisy spotted her dad with Nina Romano on the deck of the boathouse on the opposite end of the property. They appeared to be having some kind of intense conversation.

Sonnet, Nina's daughter, was Daisy's first and best friend here in Avalon. As for Nina, she had always been a bit of a mystery. Now that Sonnet was headed off to college, Daisy expected to see her slow down, maybe write a memoir or take up a hobby. Instead, Nina was plunging right straight into something new. A business, with Daisy's dad.

Daisy wasn't sure how she felt about that. She admired Nina, and it was somewhat reassuring to know Nina, too, had been a young single mom and everything had worked out okay for her. Daisy liked Nina, but at the same time, felt intimidated by her. Nina was the single mom everyone admired—hardworking, determined, and so successful that she'd been written up in a magazine, as the youngest town mayor in the state. There was something about Nina that made Daisy feel inadequate.

When it came to her dad, Daisy didn't exactly feel inadequate, but helpless. As in, she didn't know how to help him. He seemed to spend every day hurting and lost, which most people didn't realize because he did such a good job covering it up. Daisy knew he was totally consumed by guilt about the divorce. He blamed himself for letting his marriage fail. He'd been so busy with work and launching his own firm that he'd blown off his family. Now he was trying to make a new start—

small town, family business, the whole bit. But he was still sad all the time. Still hurting and really, really lonely. He was the youngest of the four Bellamys, and, according to Daisy's grandmother, the happy-go-lucky one. Maybe that was the reason he hated being by himself.

Daisy often thought about going it alone with the baby, as so many single mothers did these days. A part of her yearned for independence. Then she would remember how lonely her dad was, and the idea of leaving him just seemed cruel.

A knock at the door distracted her. Probably one of the workmen. With all the refurbishing going on at the main inn, there were workers all over the place, measuring and fixing things, asking questions and sometimes even checking something with Daisy, as though she had the answer. Didn't they know she was clueless about everything? She wasn't even sure she'd loaded the dryer correctly.

Her flip-flops slapping against her heels, she went and opened the door.

'Hey, Daisy.'

She stood there, frozen, staring at her visitor. It was Julian Gastineaux, a guy she'd met last summer. Back when she was just a high school girl. That felt like a lifetime ago. She'd changed so much, she was surprised he recognized her.

Julian was pretty much the hottest guy ever to draw breath. A year later, this was still the case. He was tall and slim, African-American on his father's side, with his Caucasian mother's light eyes and a smile all his own, the kind of smile that made a girl hear some kind of theme song in her head.

Daisy heard it now, a delightful twinkling of acoustic guitar that stirred her from her frozen state. She couldn't help but smile back, and just for a second, she felt like her old self again—young, flirty, carefree, like any other girl her age.

'Julian,' she said, lifting up on tiptoe to give him a hug. And of course, that shattered the illusion of normalcy because in between them was a belly the size of a Volkswagen. Yet she was way beyond feeling self-conscious about her pregnancy. She'd found that people either accepted her, or not, and there wasn't anything she could do to change anyone's attitude. 'Come on in,' she said, stepping back and holding open the door. 'I knew you were coming for your brother's wedding, but I didn't expect to see you so soon.'

'Connor gave me a job again this summer. I need to save up for college.'

'He must've prepared you for me,' she said, 'because you're being totally cool.'

'Yeah, he told me. And I'm always cool, you know that.'

It was true. If he hadn't figured out how to take things in stride, Julian probably would have imploded a long time ago. His

182

background couldn't be more different from hers; a lot of it was a dark nightmare. He'd been raised by his dad, a professor at Tulane—a rocket scientist, in fact. When Julian was a boy, his dad had been killed. Julian had to go live with his mom—she was also Connor Davis's mom—an aspiring actress who took the concept of neglect to new depths. She made Daisy's mother look like Mary Poppins.

The surprising thing about Julian was that he wasn't totally destroyed by his situation the way most kids would be. He sailed through school, acing all his classes seemingly without effort. If there was anything odd about him, any personal flaw, it was his craving for taking physical risks. While lots of kids in his situation drifted beyond the fringe, his drug of choice was adrenaline. Anything involving dangerous heights and speed appealed to him. As Daisy recalled, his most exultant moment last summer had occurred when he scaled the most difficult rock climb in the Shawangunks, up the river in New Paltz.

His life was radically different from Daisy's. Before moving to Avalon, she had attended a Manhattan school so exclusive that people were known to put their unborn children on the admissions waiting lists. Julian, by contrast, had bounced around in his mother's wake, finishing high school in Chino, California, where he probably would have ended up working at some crappy job and surfing on the weekends, except Julian had an ace in the hole—his brother Connor, who believed in him. Thanks to her dad, Daisy was learning what a powerful thing that was—to have just one person who totally believed in you and trusted you. It made you feel as if you could do anything.

'So you're going to be the best man,' she said.

He spread his arms like a showman. 'That's what they tell me.'

No kidding, she thought. Those shoulders. Those cheekbones. The theme song tingled in her ears again. 'You know, if somebody had predicted last summer that my cousin and your brother would be getting married, I would've thought they were insane.'

He nodded. 'Me, too.'

Olivia was the quintessential Manhattanite and Connor a small-town working man. But together, they made the perfect couple.

'I suppose you could say stranger things have happened,' she said.

'You want to talk about it?'

There was no need to explain what *it* was—not just the elephant in the room, but something even bigger than that. She sank down on the sofa, pulled her shapeless jersey shirt down over her belly. Since she'd revealed her condition last winter to her father in tearful defiance, she'd done plenty of talking—

184

to her family, to her co-workers at the Sky River Bakery where she used to have an after-school job, to teachers, counselors and doctors. She had talked until she was exhausted, and certain things didn't change. She was still pregnant, still confused, still indecisive.

'It's pretty much what it looks like,' she said. 'I screwed up. I can't even say it was an accident.'

Feeling flustered, she grabbed a shirt she'd been mending for Max. Somehow, her brother had managed to lose three of the buttons, so she had to sew on all new ones. Keeping her hands busy helped her organize her thoughts. She was terrible at sewing, and the thread kept knotting up, but she doggedly kept at it.

'It's a boy, by the way,' she said. 'Due right around the time of the wedding. I'm a bridesmaid, but Olivia's prepared for me not to make it that day. If, you know, he decides to come early.'

Julian nodded, steepled his fingers together. 'That's pretty outrageous.'

'You have no idea.'

'I think I do. It happened to a lot of girls at my school. There was a day care center right on campus.' Julian cleared his throat. 'Uh, so, are you . . . with the baby's father?'

At that, she laughed. 'You can't know how absurd that would be. He's a guy from my old school in the city. Logan O'Donnell. The last time I saw him, he was dancing on a table after

185

snorting about a thousand dollars worth of cocaine.'

'So what does he think of—' Julian made a nonverbal gesture '—all this?'

'I haven't told him yet. I will, though,' Daisy assured him. What she didn't tell Julian was that Logan had kind of freaked out after that weekend. Every time he saw her, he was all, 'I seriously love you, let's stay together,' but she figured that was what any guy said when he was trying to get laid. She told him she didn't want to see him anymore, blocked him from IMing, e-mailing and texting her.

According to her friends back in the city, Logan's folks had sent him to a very private, very expensive therapeutic boarding school for the remainder of his senior year to deal with his drug problem.

She finished sewing on the buttons. They were crooked, but at least they were attached. 'It's just that, before I tell Logan what happened, I need to get everything in order.' Get control of everything, she silently amended. She was, after all, her mother's daughter. 'See, I don't really want anything from him. But one day, the baby will want to know. I've decided to write him a letter. My mom says I should get it notarized and send it registered, so he'll know it's from me and I'll know he's got it. I haven't written it yet, though. It's hard to know what to say.'

'Don't rush it,' Julian said. 'It'll come.'

186

His laid-back attitude made her smile. Thank goodness he wasn't like some of the girls Daisy hung out with who thought she was crazy not to try to get Logan to pay her a fortune in child support, which was the last thing she wanted. Daisy suspected that would never cross Julian's mind. This was what she liked—well, one of the many things she liked—about him. He was easygoing, completely nonjudgmental, and he *got* her. Even sitting here, feeling as though she'd been pregnant for eleven years, she didn't have to pretend.

She heard the clothes dryer turn off and went to empty it, talking the whole time. Methodically folding towels and clothes, she filled him in on the rest of her life. She'd graduated from Avalon High and recently stopped working at the bakery in order to focus on getting ready for the baby. She was still pursuing her passion for photography, and in fact, she was in charge of all the artwork for the brochures and website for the Inn at Willow Lake.

'What about you?' she asked Julian, setting the towels in a lopsided tower. Folding laundry was one of the few domestic chores she had mastered.

'I've been accepted into the Air Force ROTC in college. Then I'll go into pilot training and eventually, TPS—Test Pilot School.'

'I've heard that's pretty much the most

dangerous thing there is,' she said.

'Only if I'm not careful. I'm going to be careful.'

'And it's going to be hard,' she said.

He looked at her pointedly, his gaze unabashedly outlining her stomach. 'Not as hard as that. Being scared isn't always a bad thing. Makes you careful. I guess with a little baby, that's about the most important thing.'

'Maybe it is,' she said, 'but jeez. I've never taken care of anything in my life. Not a dog or a hamster. Not a philodendron or an African violet.'

He looked at the pile of folded laundry, the shirt she'd just mended. 'Right.'

'I still haven't closed the door on all my options,' she said faintly, her voice a breath of confession. 'Once the baby comes, that is. Sometimes I think about what it would be like to give the baby away. Sometimes I think it wouldn't be so horrible.'

'You wouldn't be the first to think that.'

Daisy had spent many hours imagining different lives for herself. She could be this young single mom, devoting her life to raising her child, much like Nina Romano had. Or she could give the baby to a family that desperately wanted him. After that, she'd resume her life, going to school or work, whatever she wanted.

'I wish I could figure out the right thing to do,' she said to Julian.

'There's more than one right thing,' he said

188

matter-of-factly. 'My mother would have given me up for adoption if my father hadn't stepped up to raise me. Sometimes I think about what my life would've been like if I'd had two regular parents.'

'News flash. There's no such thing as a regular parent, genius.' Daisy's counselor had urged her to explore the option, to educate herself. She learned that adoptive families tended to offer a wonderful future to the children who came into their lives. One phone call, and meetings could be set up with couples, and singles, of every sort—young, mature, straight, gay, wealthy, modest . . . There was no end to the families who wanted to open their hearts and their homes to a newborn.

'Yeah, my dad wasn't perfect, but I wouldn't have traded him for the world,' Julian said.

Daisy felt the bittersweet sentiment radiating from him. Somehow, he'd made peace with his loss. 'And speaking of that, Mr. Brainiac, where are you planning on going to college?'

'Cornell. I start in the fall.'

Her heart lifted. 'Ithaca isn't that far from here.'

'That was definitely a consideration,' he admitted. 'My brother and I were separated, growing up. I'll finally get to see more of Connor.' He paused, looked straight at her. 'And you.'

189

She blushed. It was funny how she could still want to flirt when she was as big as a house. Then she forced herself to be realistic. 'Cornell's like, the hardest school there is. You're going to be really busy, hitting the books.' There was also the matter of about five thousand eligible, nonpregnant female students, but Daisy figured he'd find that out on his own.

'What about you?' he asked.

'What about me? Hel*lo*. Gestating here.'

'There's no law that says you can't have a kid and do other stuff, too.'

She motioned him over to the computer and started a slide show of her images. 'I'm taking an online photography class.'

Julian watched the screen appreciatively as the images floated past. 'These are good.'

Daisy had always liked photography. As a little girl, she had captured everything with her point-and-shoot—family members, flowers and trees, people and scenery of the Upper East Side neighborhood where she'd grown up. As she got older, she experimented with different styles and methods. She tended to capture the small but significant details most people overlooked. In Daisy's pictures, a rusty hinge on a barn door told a whole story. She could show an entire season in a raft of autumn leaves floating on the water, a world of pain in her father's face as he bent over his drafting table, working on a design, or the

190

story of her brother's hopes and dreams in the way his grubby hands gripped a baseball bat.

She got out her camera now, inspired to take some shots of Julian. He'd always been a good sport about being her subject. She focused on the sharp lines of his profile, and then a slim-fingered hand resting on the back of the chair as he leaned toward the computer screen. He exuded a peculiar athleticism, a kinetic energy, even when he was at rest. She'd probably never tell him so, but he took her breath away. How could one guy be so beautiful and so damaged at the same time?

The slide show was on random mode, and images from the previous winter came up. She had done a whole series of images of Sonnet Romano. Julian didn't really react, yet through the lens of her camera, Daisy could see the change in him. Sonnet was super-cute. And biracial like Julian, too.

'My best friend,' Daisy explained to him. 'She's spending the summer with her father, but she'll be here for the wedding. I can't wait for you to meet her. You'll probably fall totally in love with her. Everybody does.'

He sat down, leaned back in the chair. 'I'm not everybody. Who's this?' He clicked Pause, freezing the slide show at a starkly beautiful shot of a young man in the snow. It was one of Daisy's best images. The subject had the sort of wintry, Nordic features of a character in an illustrated fairy tale—straight, white-blond hair, sculpted features, eyes of sea-glass blue. He stood in a snow-covered park with bare trees inked in the background. A translucent ribbon of smoke from an unseen cigarette formed an imperfect halo over his head.

'His name is Zach,' she said. 'Zach Alger. Another friend I made when we moved here.' There was so much more she could say, but didn't, because she'd probably start crying. Unlike Sonnet, Zach had not moved on to bigger and better things after graduation.

'Where is he now? Will I meet him?' Julian asked.

She shook her head. 'He kind of . . . got into some trouble and moved away. I think he's working up at the racetrack at Saratoga.'

'What kind of trouble?'

'It's complicated. And it's not Zach's fault. His father had this online gambling thing going, and Zach was the only one who knew. He took some money to cover his dad's debts. Now the dad is in prison and Zach's on his own. It's amazing, what a kid will do for a parent. I'd never make my kid do something like that for me.'

As though on cue, a set of images of Daisy's mother spread across the screen. Sophie Bellamy—she was keeping her married name for professional reasons, she said—was pretty, perfectly groomed and serious. Daisy sensed Julian watching her, not the slide show.

'My mom got this once-in-a-lifetime job

at the International Criminal Court in The Hague. She's been working on a big human rights case.' As always when she thought of her mother, Daisy felt a mixture of love and pride, frustration and anger. Sometimes she just wanted to sit in her mother's lap and cry. Then she felt totally selfish for wanting such a thing. Her mom was working to save helpless children from torture and starvation. Who was Daisy to stand in the way of that?

She grabbed her camera and stood up. 'We need a change of scenery,' she said. 'How about we go outside for a while?'

'Sure.' He got up and held open the door. 'Lead the way. I'm supposed to be replacing a gutter, but I have to wait for the foreman to bring a taller ladder.' He pointed at a rusty gutter hanging from the attic eaves, four storeys up. 'I offered to climb it, but Connor's pretty picky about safety liability.'

'He's got a lot to lose these days,' Daisy reminded him, walking down a gravel path toward the lakefront.

'Who's that?' Julian shaded his eyes toward the boathouse.

'Nina Romano, my friend Sonnet's mom,' Daisy said. She waved, but Nina didn't seem to see her. They continued in silence for a bit, and finally, Daisy unleashed the crucial question. 'So, do you have a girlfriend?'

'Not unless you've changed your mind from last summer.' He grinned at her.

Last summer, he'd made overtures, but she'd been in such a terrible place over her parents' divorce that she hadn't wanted to let anyone get close. Idiot, she thought.

'Very funny,' she grumbled, turning away so he wouldn't see her blush.

'I'm not trying to be funny,' he said. 'I really wanted to go out with you.'

So had a bunch of other guys, she recalled, feeling no pride in the knowledge. She had been the party girl, the easy girl, the one who was always good for a few laughs.

The one who would do anything to get the attention of her unhappy, work-obsessed parents.

'I'm not that girl anymore,' she said quietly.

'You're still you,' Julian reminded her. He could always make her smile.

'And then some,' she said.

She gave him a tour of the property, pointing out the interesting facets of the inn, the pickle-ball and tennis courts, the bowling and croquet green. The crazy-tall structure called a belvedere. From the end of the long dock, they could pick out various local landmarks—the Avalon Boating Club at Blanchard Park, the summer cottages scattered along the shore.

'It's really nice here,' he said.

'Uh-huh. I'm glad my dad decided to buy the place.'

'So you plan to stay here . . . ?' He left the

question open-ended.

'I plan to get from one day to the next as best I can.' Then she decided to be straight with him. 'Also, even though it seems like I'm the one in trouble, my dad and brother are just . . . lost. Something tells me that they need me to stick around.'

'They might surprise you,' Julian said.

Daisy pictured her dad and Max, two guys struggling along. 'Maybe. I'm not going anywhere for the time being, though.' She took some pictures, capturing the glints of light on the water, a family of mallard ducks drifting past. 'What I'd really love,' she confessed, 'is to study photography, and not just online. I'd like to turn professional.'

'Then that's what you should do.'

'Yeah, I'll get right on it.'

He shrugged off her sarcasm. 'The idea will still be there tomorrow, and next year and whenever you decide.'

She nodded. 'It's ironic that I finally figured out something I love and I'm good at right when this happened.' She took a shot of a loon landing in the water, creating a sharp white wake. 'I wish I could rewind my life, you know? Make some better choices.'

'Everybody wishes that.' He shaded his eyes, watching the lake. 'It sure is pretty here.'

'I guess. Sometimes when I think about spending my life right here, I freak out.'

'Nobody's making you stay here.'

She thought about her dad, and Max, and how lost they'd be, just the two of them here alone. Yes, she thought. They are.

## ELEVEN

The day after signing her agreement with Greg Bellamy, Nina arrived with the last of her belongings and a burden of misgivings. She'd lain awake all night, wondering if she'd made the right choice, or if she'd sold out. The entire property was a hive of activity, with workmen crisscrossing the lawn, guys up on ladders, landscapers busy in the gardens. She glanced at the narrow, tall Victorian house at the far edge of the property, where Greg now lived, then tracked her gaze to the boathouse, a few hundred yards away, and hoped it wouldn't be too close for comfort. In the past, whenever she'd pictured herself at the Inn at Willow Lake, that picture hadn't included a divorced man and his two kids and, in a matter of weeks, a grandbaby. Yet her entire adult life had been about making compromises, and this was no different. Maybe she just wasn't meant to have what she wanted on her terms. And maybe that wasn't such a bad thing.

The thought echoed in her mind after she climbed the stairs to the boathouse and found a living, breathing fantasy in motion. Greg was standing on a ladder on the deck, washing the windows. His shirt was off, its hem stuck in the waistband of his pants. The summer sun had painted a golden tan on his shoulders. He wore a Yankees cap turned backward, and each methodical stroke of the squeegee was poetry in motion.

'To what do I owe this honor?' she asked. 'The owner himself, washing my windows?'

He stepped down from the ladder. His chest was glistening with sweat, and she made a concerted effort not to stare. 'I'm paying Connor's workers by the hour,' he said, 'so I don't want to waste their talents on manual labor.'

'Ah. For that I have you, with your degree in architecture.'

'I'll help you with your things.' He crossed the deck, stepping between her and the French doors. For a moment, she found herself mere inches from his tanned, sweaty, glistening chest. A patch of light-colored hair highlighted the center of it. A wild, male smell wafted to her. Rather than being put off, she experienced her usual undeniable, visceral response to him. Her cheeks caught fire and she swallowed hard, feeling trapped between him and the door. 'Um, Greg . . .' She had no idea what to tell him. Thanks for doing the windows?

He pulled open the door and stepped aside with a little flourish.

She ducked her head, pretending to be unaffected by him. 'That's not necessary.'

'No, but it accomplishes a couple of things. It shows I know how to be neighborly—we're going to be neighbors, after all—and the sooner you get moved in, the sooner we can get started.'

'I see. Well, thank you.'

'No problem.' He grabbed his T-shirt and pulled it on. Nina couldn't help feeling the slightest bit disappointed. She eyed him speculatively, trying to figure out why he was being so blatantly sexual one moment, so kind and helpful the next. In general, this was not the way men treated her. The kind ones were rarely helpful, and the helpful ones were rarely kind.

'Thanks,' Nina said again. The ensuing silence felt awkward, so she added, 'So how did you and Max like the game the other night?'

'We're both baseball fans. Max, especially. Hockey in the winter, baseball in the summer. I signed him up for Little League.'

'Is he liking that?'

A guarded look suddenly shuttered his eyes. 'Sure,' he said.

'Well, I'm glad you came out for the game.'

'You seemed . . . busy.'

Good lord, did he think she was romantic with Darryl or Wayne? Or both of them? The idea made her laugh aloud. 'Right,' she said.

He went to the kitchen sink, took off the baseball cap and washed up, splashing water over his face and head, drying off with what seemed like half a roll of paper towels. 'Tell me where to start helping you move in, boss,' he said.

'The boxes, I guess,' she said, still in the grip of a highly inappropriate attraction. And it only got more intense from there. A curious air of intimacy seemed to hover between them as he helped her move in. Nina had spent the previous day cleaning and airing out the place, and early this morning, two of her brothers had set up her queen-size bed, aiming it toward the broad picture window in the bedroom. This was part of her dream—waking up to Willow Lake every morning.

Now, as she and Greg unboxed her things—linens and keepsakes, lamps and books—she felt completely torn between attraction and contention. She hadn't asked for his help, but he'd dived right in. Helping her move allowed him to dig into her life, to discover the things that were important to her. Shouldn't she resent that? Did she? If not, why not?

He opened a large box containing framed pictures and memorabilia. Nina caught her breath, mentally sifting through the contents of the box. Was there anything too personal, anything she didn't want him to see?

'Hey, Greg.' Her voice sounded hollow in the sparsely furnished space. 'Um, about this

199

. . . arrangement. I really think we should set up some boundaries here.'

He laughed, which was not the response she'd expected. 'What kind of boundaries, Nina? To keep you in, or to keep me out?'

'Seriously,' she said. 'When people work together, they need boundaries.'

'All right. You got it. Boundaries. I guess you'll let me know if I've strayed over the line. Of course, that means you'll have to explain where the line is.'

She sensed an undercurrent of anger beneath his humor, and was alarmed to realize that made him more interesting to her than ever. 'It's something to talk about,' she said. 'Where to draw the line. I mean, I'm grateful that you're helping me move in.'

'But you don't want to see my sweaty chest while I'm doing it.'

'It's not that—'

'So you do want to see my sweaty chest.'

*Yes.*

'No.' She folded her arms across her middle. 'Listen, neither of us was born yesterday. We both know how to be professional in business. That's all I meant.'

'Done,' he said. 'I'll leave my shirt on.'

'So will I,' she said. 'Now, I'd better get to work.'

'All work and no play,' he said.

'That's me.' Good lord, was he hinting at some kind of friends-with-benefits scenario?

No, he couldn't be. She shied away from the idea and went back to work. While she was trying to recall what she'd packed in the box he'd just opened, he pulled out a framed photo that had been wrapped in a tea towel. The shot depicted Nina in her fifteenth summer—just weeks before everything had happened. Maybe that was why she liked the picture. She was still so young and innocent in it. She and Jenny were sitting on the city dock in town, their arms around each other, their faces full of possibility.

'You were a cute kid,' he commented.

Nina bit her lip. She glanced at him, then back at the photograph. Who knew that within weeks of that photo, she would have careless sex with a West Point appointee and wind up in trouble?

'You don't even remember me, do you?' she asked Greg, thinking of that pivotal summer.

'Remember you from what?'

God, was he pretending ignorance? Or protecting . . . what? Her? Himself?

'From the past,' she said. 'Our paths crossed several times. My mom used to work in the kitchen of Camp Kioga in the summer. I used to go up there all the time.' She didn't remind him about his wedding. He might be her adversary, but she wasn't going to play dirty.

'And you think I don't remember you,' he stated.

'I figured you'd say something if you had.'

201

Nina tried not to dwell on all those times she'd fantasized about him and it turned out he wasn't even thinking of her. She tried to feel insulted. Instead, she simply felt wistful.

'Christ, Nina, you know I remember,' he said with sudden intensity. 'You know damn well I remember it all, including that night at the country club. I can safely say that West Point cadet is the only guy I ever hit over a girl.'

Oh. Crap. That was one detail she wished he'd forgotten. 'Sorry. Since you didn't say anything, I assumed . . .' She didn't know what she assumed. For some reason, she was having a hard time being coherent when she was around him.

'Just because I had other stuff going on in my life doesn't mean I have amnesia.'

'Me, neither,' she admitted. It was a relief, in a way, to have it out in the open.

'One thing I remember is staying right here at the Inn at Willow Lake,' he said. 'We'd come up for a family reunion. The kids were little, and my wife didn't want to stay up at Camp Kioga. I guess it was a bit too rustic for her. Sophie was worried that if something happened, we wouldn't be able to get help fast enough.' Greg shook his head. 'We stayed less than a week, because that's all the time we had to spare. I was busy with my firm and Sophie was putting in long hours practicing law. I wish I'd taken things slower. I lost whole years of

202

my life back then, and never even noticed.'

'Does it help to look back with all these regrets?' she asked.

'Not at all.'

'Then don't do it, Greg. Look ahead.' She bent down and unwrapped a collage of matted prints, smiling at the images, most of them of Sonnet at different ages. 'The nice thing about the past is that you get to choose the memories you keep close to your heart. The rest, you can just move on from them.'

His smile faded and he lowered his voice. 'Thanks, Nina.'

'Don't thank me.'

'Why not?'

'I didn't do anything.' She bit her lip and busied herself looking for picture-hanging wire. She turned to ask him to pass her a hammer, and saw him staring out the window. His daughter, Daisy, was seated in an Adirondack chair, facing the lake. Despite all the bustling activity around her, she looked very much alone.

As if he felt Nina watching him, Greg seemed to give himself a mental shake. 'Sorry. Just checking up on Daisy.'

'Don't apologize for that.'

'I wasn't. It's just frustrating, you know, trying to talk to her. Half the time, I'm walking on eggshells around her.'

'Try not to take it personally. Even the most talkative kids in the world tend to give their

203

parents the silent treatment.' Nina paused, then added, 'Maybe she's trying to protect you.'

'From what?'

She didn't want to point out that Greg, like many suddenly single guys, had an air of vulnerability about him. 'Some people say expecting a baby can bring out a woman's protective instincts. It might just be her nature, though. Or the way she was raised. Protecting those you love isn't a bad thing.'

'Agreed.' He studied her with a curious expression on his face.

For no reason she could name, Nina felt a beat of sympathy and in the next moment, tried to deny it. Don't bring me your problems, she thought.

The irony was, it was already too late. She hadn't even spent one night on the premises, yet she felt as though their lives were twining together in ways she hadn't anticipated. She should have known better, should have realized it simply wasn't in her nature to ignore Greg's concerns. As mayor, she used to take on the problems of a whole town. No wonder she felt compelled.

\*　　　\*　　　\*

Thoughts about Daisy took Nina back to her own youth. Although Nina's situation had brought on all the expected reactions—

shame and worry and sorrow—it also brought out Nina's inner resources. Perversely, after being a mediocre student in school, she found something she was good at—teenage pregnancy.

Instead of letting it defeat her, she had set about to prove her independence. The baby was the motivation she needed to finally do well in school. She went from pulling a C average to making A's and B's in all her classes. She got herself elected to student council because she wanted a say in how the on-campus day-care program was run. She went dutifully to all her doctor appointments, memorizing a thousand aspects of fetal development and self-care during gestation. She listened with hard-won patience to Father Reilly, who admonished her to give the baby up for adoption, though she knew that would never happen. In the first place, she would need consent from the baby's father, and she didn't want to go there. In the second place, she felt an almost spiritual sense of possession over this child. She had never been in love, but she knew this was love in its purest form, and she would never let it go. But she gave serious attention to the school guidance counselor, Mrs. Jarvis, who talked about budgets and schedules and the frighteningly awesome responsibility of being in charge of another human being.

Despite the fact that she had flourished,

Nina still suffered the pain of the incredible sacrifices she'd made, missing out on dating and dances, the senior trip, graduating with her class. The senior trip had been to Washington, D.C., which was why it had been so important for Nina to take Sonnet there.

Nina had tried not to listen to the gossip and ignored the speculation about who had fathered her child. She refused to give credence to the naysayers who loved to explain how difficult raising a child was, even for grown-ups who were married. For a teenager alone, it was impossible, or so people said.

But for Nina, this baby became a goal, a mission, something that gave shape and purpose to her life. Sure, she felt a twinge when she saw her friends all heading off to school dances or the movies, but she powered through the moments of regret by teaching herself something useful, like how to chart a baby's immunization schedule. She put together a crib all by herself. She learned to install a car seat even before she could legally drive. She studied finance and social policy because suddenly these things mattered to her. She was bringing a child into the world, so she wanted the world to be better than it was.

Nina tried to explain these things to Greg now, wanting to reassure him. And why, she asked herself, did she want to reassure him? Because, in spite of their situation, she caught herself liking him.

206

'I suspect Daisy's going through something similar,' Nina concluded. 'Certain things never change. She's seen all her friends go off to college or work or travel, while she's still living at home.'

'There's no reasonable alternative for her right now,' he said.

'I know, but she might be feeling restless. I know I did. My family was supportive from day one. They would have done anything for me, but that only made me more determined to make it on my own.' She suspected Greg wasn't ready to hear that his daughter might not agree with him about living at home. She went to the fridge and found two bottles of water. Handing him one, she said, 'I have a suggestion for you, and I mean this in the best possible way. Give Daisy your trust.'

'I do, I—'

'You say so, but in the meantime, you're making all these contingency plans for when she fails. You've given her a roof over her head, a job, and I'm sure she appreciates that, but she also needs to live her own life. Having Sonnet made me a better person. You have to believe Daisy's baby will have that same impact on her. Sonnet was the whole reason I eventually became town mayor.'

'To make Avalon a better place to raise her.'

'Exactly. It all started before she was born, when I heard Blanchard Park had cut its budget to eliminate playground equipment. I took my complaint straight to the city council and Mayor McKittrick. I'm my father's daughter, after all, and he's the consummate activist. And then again, I'm also my mother's daughter—I offered a practical solution, a way to fund the playground.'

Despite the fact that she'd probably looked absurd—five foot nothing with a stomach out to here—she had stood at the podium in the city council chambers and made her case with clarity and confidence. At the end of the meeting, her father was beaming with pride, and the mayor offered her a paid internship as well as free tuition to a local community college.

'I knew taking the mayor's offer was the right thing to do. It was a job with a future, and a way to get an education.' By that time, the inn had passed on to the Wellers' nephew, an absentee owner who had never even gone to see the place. She'd still dreamed of owning it one day. But with a baby to look after, her plans had receded like all dreams do, fading into the distance and sinking out of sight.

Some of the local gossips opposed the idea of an unwed mother working for the mayor. They were few in number, though, and easily silenced by those who commended the mayor for giving a hand up to a young person. The people of Avalon weren't cruel when Nina gave birth to a mixed-race baby,

208

either. It was the 1990s, after all, and such things failed to create a ruckus anymore. The baby's appearance did, however, change the speculation about the identity of the father. A number of boys' names were crossed off a number of lists. And a couple of new names were added.

Nina had ignored the whispers. She focused on building a life for herself and her baby. True to everyone's predictions, being a single mother was unimaginably hard sometimes. She still remembered those endless nights when the baby was fussy and had worked herself into her trademark relentless, I-can-outlast-you crying jags. She could still recall helplessly walking the floor, dreading the morning when it would start all over again, only worse, because she was so sleep-deprived.

She decided not to share that with Greg. He'd find out on his own, soon enough, from Daisy.

'While I was working for the city,' she explained, 'I got my associate's degree and eventually a bachelor's from SUNY New Paltz.'

'People say you were the best mayor the town's ever had.'

'Depends on who you ask.'

'Baseball fans, mainly,' he said with a chuckle.

He had a sexy laugh. She wondered if he knew that.

'So Sonnet's father . . .' Greg began.

'What about Sonnet's father?'

'Baseball fan?'

She knew he was probing. Which was fine; she had nothing to hide. 'I wouldn't know.'

'Daisy still hasn't contacted the baby's father,' he said, blurting it out like something painful he wanted to get rid of.

'It's natural to put off things that are hard,' Nina said. 'I didn't tell Laurence about Sonnet until she was three.'

Greg looked stunned. 'You didn't?'

'I had my reasons.'

'So what made you decide to tell him?'

Nina busied herself, stacking empty moving boxes by the door. She didn't want him to see the look of irony on her face. Although he didn't know it, the impetus for her telling Laurence was Greg himself.

## Part Six

### Then

The Inn at Willow Lake takes pride in preserving and maintaining its own private lakeshore beach. Guests will find a natural wonderland of native plants and wildlife. Keep your eyes peeled for plants like marsh marigold, spicebush— the home of the spicebush swallowtail— and hobblebush, which offers spring blossoms, summer berries and fall color. Wildlife abounds at Willow Lake—blue heron, box turtle, river otter, beaver and deer are commonly spotted. You might even see a rare resident moose.

The shoreline is made for strolling, sitting, splashing in the shallows or just watching the scenery and dreaming. Guests of the inn come from all over, as far away as Japan or as close as New York City. You never know who you might meet along the shore some bright, sunny day—an old friend, a new acquaintance or someone you just want to reconnect with.

## TWELVE

When Sonnet was nearly three, Nina moved into a small clapboard house in town, rented from one of her uncles. Her parents had protested—it was too soon, she was too young, Sonnet needed watching—but Nina knew it was time. Past time. She had a job and was going to school. It was enough, more than enough, that her parents were Sonnet's babysitters.

There was something both satisfying and lonely about living on her own. She felt grown-up and utterly alone at the same time.

One summer morning, as she was finishing a paper for her macroeconomics class, Nina looked down at Sonnet, who played quietly at her feet. The little girl had learned to keep boredom and restlessness at bay. When had that happened? Nina wondered. Where was her fussy baby?

Then it hit Nina—Sonnet wasn't a baby anymore, and Nina had pretty much missed the transition. Despite the fact that she'd spent endless nights pacing the floor with a crying baby, or cramming for exams, or catching up on work, time had shot by in a blur. It made Nina a little sad, so she picked up Sonnet and swung her around. 'I finished my paper and you've been really good,' she said. 'Let's do something fun.'

'Let's go see Nona.' Sonnet's grandmother was the little girl's favorite person in the world, bar none.

'Nona's working today at Camp Kioga,' Nina explained, 'just like she does every summer.' Her mother claimed to enjoy the work and there was no doubt that the Bellamys paid her well. Still, Nina wished that just once, Ma would take a rest. But of course, Ma would say the usual—'In this family, the women work. It's who we are.'

'What about the men, Ma?' Nina sometimes asked.

'The men? They dream.'

'I guess somebody's gotta do it.'

Sonnet's face collapsed into a mask of tragedy. 'Nona,' she rumbled.

Nina glanced at the clock. 'Tell you what. I'll take you swimming at the lake.'

That did the trick. Sonnet clapped her hands with glee.

Through the years, the Inn at Willow Lake had lost none of its magic for Nina. Although she no longer worked there, the manager knew and liked her, and she had an open invitation to use its beach, a broad smile of sand at the lakeshore. Despite its slightly shabby air of gentility, the place still attracted summer visitors who enjoyed the slow pace and seclusion of the inn. Nina believed that people came for the chance to experience

Baby or no baby, she intended to pass that test. She wanted—needed—all the credit she could get.

When the baby was born, Nina didn't experience that sacred moment of spirituality some women claimed to have. She didn't feel a sudden oneness with the universe or depth of bonding with the earth or humankind or whatever. The only thing in her head was the structure of the sonnet, so she figured that was what she should name the baby.

'My kid's name is Daisy,' Greg told her, seeming to expand with pride. 'Isn't she great?'

As though she'd heard him, Daisy looked up, favoring him with a smile as bright as her namesake, and waved both her hands. 'Let's go, Daddy-O,' she said.

'You got it, Daisy-O,' he replied. 'Nice talking to you,' he said to Nina, stuffing the camera into a big plastic tote bag. He walked down to the water's edge, peeling off his shirt one-armed and tossing it aside to reveal a tanned, muscular physique. He caught the little girl's hand in his and they ran together into the water.

Nina watched them for a moment, feeling a peculiar sense of unease. She couldn't quite put her finger on the reason. Greg Bellamy was nothing to her—not a friend or old flame, certainly not a crush. He was just some guy whose life tended to intersect with hers at the odd moment, a moment that dissipated like a soap bubble, colorful and glistening and fragile, and then . . . gone. They were strangers. It was better they stay that way.

Someone else was watching Greg Bellamy and little Daisy, too—Sonnet. She had a pensive expression on her face, with an unspoken wish sparkling clearly in her eyes.

Nina felt a stab of guilt, because Sonnet didn't know her father. And there was no denying that a father's love was special. Just watching how strong and sure a man was with his child, remembering what Pop meant to all his kids—Nina couldn't refuse to see the truth. No matter what she gave her little girl, Nina would never be able to replicate for Sonnet the experience of having a father. And as she got older, Sonnet was beginning to ask. She saw other kids with daddies and wondered where hers was. Nina knew the time had come. She would keep no secrets from her daughter.

*Part Seven*

*Now*

Each room at the inn is furnished with painstakingly-selected period pieces. The Scribe's Chamber is a cozy room accented with restored picture trim, exposed gables, a washstand sink and private bath. Situated on the west side of the house, this chamber enjoys the last sun of the day and has a view of the willow trees along the lakeshore. The room features a tall antique rice bed covered with a time-worn quilt, and pillows in delicately embroidered covers. Designed for solitary contemplation, this room has a small writing desk and oval-back chair that once belonged to American author James Fenimore Cooper.

The Inn at Willow Lake avoids the use of commercial furniture polishes containing petroleum products and other neurotoxic solvents. A much more pleasing preparation is easily created by combining jojoba oil—available at most drugstores—with lemon oil and a squeeze of lemon juice.

## THIRTEEN

Greg and Nina started arguing as soon as they pulled out of the parking lot in his truck. 'We're going to New Paltz,' he said. 'It's closer.'

'But there's a warehouse store in Rhinebeck. It's one-stop shopping.'

'Not for what I have in mind,' he said, dialing the steering wheel toward Route 28. 'You just hired an assistant. Walter can get the supplies.'

'But—'

'Besides, I'm driving.' He didn't fail to notice the way she dressed, even for a day of work-related errands. She had on a gauzy red cotton dress that showed off her cleavage, bare legs and sandals. He wondered if she dressed this way for him, or if this was just her style. Doesn't matter, he thought. Three weeks into their partnership, he had no complaints about working with Nina, even when she argued with him, which was most of the time. She was a far cry from the humorless, pocket-protector-wearing stiffs at his firm in the city. Despite the dress and the cleavage, she was the hardest-working woman he'd ever met. She'd jumped into her job with both feet, and was totally focused on the grand reopening.

Unaware that he was checking her out, she

scowled at a handwritten list of things to do. 'Not only do we need to get supplies. We're supposed to go to the quarry in Marbletown to arrange a delivery of pavers and gravel.'

'And landscaping rock,' he reminded her. 'Don't forget that.'

'We'll never get all this done today,' she said.

'Who says we have to?'

'No one says. Heck, it's your business. You can keep the place closed for renovations for as long as you want. I don't care.'

'Yes, you do.'

'I do not,' she said.

Greg knew he could end the current argument with a brief explanation. He'd delegated most of the items on the list to Walter and Anita, their two newest hires. Meanwhile, Olivia had set up an appointment for him to see an antiques broker to select pieces in bulk at a discount. Greg decided to keep Nina in suspense a while longer. He was having way too much fun getting on her nerves.

'You do. I can tell,' he said. Having fun being in business—that was a new one on him. Before Nina, he hadn't even realized it was possible. She had the unique ability to make him want to act dumb and immature, and he drew a curious sort of relief from that. It was safe to behave this way around her, because in all the other areas of his life, he didn't have

226

that liberty. With his kids especially, he felt an enormous, often crushing pressure to behave responsibly and maturely at all times. With Nina, he could tease and let the pressure off.

'You hired me to do a job,' she said, 'and now you're not letting me do it.'

'Sure, I am. We're just not doing it your way, and that bugs the shit out of you.'

'No, it doesn't.' She thrust up her chin defensively.

'Then why are we fighting about it?'

'You call this a fight?' She laughed. 'This isn't a fight. Believe me, you'll *know* when it's a fight.'

'I'll look forward to that. So if you're not fighting with me, you're . . . what? Arguing?'

'I'm asserting my opinion and you're ignoring it. Listen, you claim you want a business partner. So treat me like a partner, not some flunky. This "my way or the highway" tactic just doesn't fly with me.'

'Tell you what. You dictate your list to Walter and have him pick up everything this afternoon.' He passed her his mobile phone.

She took it, but didn't dial. 'You and I should split up. You can go do your errands in New Paltz and I'll get everything from the price club.'

*Split up.* No way, he thought. 'What can I say? I'm flattered that you trust me to pick out furniture for the guest rooms.' From the corner of his eye, he saw her stiffen with surprise.

'*That's* why you're going to New Paltz? To buy—'

He played his ace. 'Vintage fixtures and furniture, linens . . .' He wracked his brain, trying to remember Olivia's instructions. There were a half-dozen rooms left to furnish, and she'd given him strict orders to stick with an authentic period look. 'Accessories and wall art,' he concluded, remembering her specific words.

'I thought you were going to the quarry to look at hardscape supplies—gravel and rock,' she said.

'You should have asked. Then I would've told you I also have an appointment with a wholesale antiques broker.' He glanced over at her and saw that she'd taken the bait, and it was having the desired effect. Pure, unbridled lust shone in her eyes. It was an indisputable fact that no woman could resist wholesale antiques. 'So,' he prompted. 'What do you say?'

'I surrender,' she said. 'We'll both go.'

Did she speak a little too quickly? Why did he sense a whir of suspicion, barely detectable but unsettling all the same, tickling at the back of his mind? As she made the call to Walter, Greg decided not to care. In general, a woman's heart was as mysterious as an undiscovered country. However, there was one thing he knew with complete and total certainty. When it came to decorating decisions, no woman ever born would allow a man to make them. Nina was no exception.

Trying not to act too cocky, he twiddled the dial of the radio, stopping at the sound of Led Zeppelin, with its almost-sexual thumping beat and piercing vocals. He could see Nina trying not to wince. Tooling along with the windows down, the stereo blazing on a perfect blue-sky day—it was a rare break for him. Just for these fleeting moments, he didn't let himself worry about the kids.

'You're in a good mood,' Nina said suspiciously when he parked at the antique warehouse, which was actually a converted barn. She climbed out of the truck before he could get the door for her, thus depriving him of a view of her bare legs.

'You say that like it's a bad thing.'

'It's not.'

'I'm always in a good mood,' he said. 'It's kind of pointless not to be.' Greg found that if he stood close enough to her, his height allowed him a killer view of her cleavage.

She caught him staring—probably with six kinds of lust written on his face—and said, 'Cut that out.'

'Cut what out?'

'You're looking down my dress.'

'I'm looking at the clipboard.' He indicated her scribbled notes and lists.

She hugged it to her chest. 'I've never met a

229

guy who actually liked shopping for antiques.'

'I don't.'

'Then why—'

'You figure it out.' He left her to wonder and went inside to introduce himself to the broker. Honestly, he didn't exactly relish the prospect of picking out furniture. However, it had to be done. They had several rooms to finish and he was glad to have Nina along to do the choosing.

Like most women, she had a gift for it. Greg looked around and saw nothing but secondhand stuff, yet she seemed to regard the huge, barnlike warehouse as a treasure trove of furniture, vintage linens, even a hand-loomed wool rug. In one shadowy corner of the barn, she spotted an Adirondack-style bed made of birch logs, and a lamp with a hand-stitched shade. In short order, she had picked out beds, washstands, benches and occasional tables, lamps and linens and throw pillows.

Her face was flushed with triumph. 'What else? More accessories?'

Greg didn't want to feel completely redundant, so he picked up something and handed it to her. 'What about this?'

'It's a tin bait box,' she said.

'That's right.' It was humble and old-fashioned, a painted can with a hand crank on the side and the directions, 'Half a turn, and there's your worm.'

She beamed at him. 'It's brilliant.'

He wasn't sure what knocked him out more—her dazzling smile, or the fact that she deemed a tin bait box 'brilliant.'

'Cool,' he said, then spotted a framed picture leaning against a wall. 'We should get this, too.' It was one of those iconic Maxfield Parrish prints—a portrait of a muse at sunset, staring dreamily across a glowing, otherworldly landscape.

Nina clearly didn't like it as much as she did the bait box, though she nodded her approval. 'Guests will like that.'

'But you don't.'

'It's a bit predictable. That's a good thing, though. People like a touch of the familiar when they're away from home.'

He eyed a picture of a group of cigar-smoking dogs dressed as humans, sitting around a card table.

'Don't even think about it,' she said.

'Come on, Martha Stewart,' he said after settling with the broker and arranging for delivery. He drove just a few blocks, then turned into a parking lot.

'Now what?' she asked.

'What's it look like?'

'Matt's Mattress Ranch?'

'We're getting all new. And you and I are picking them out.'

'But—'

'No buts. I'm not leaving the decision to anyone else. If people don't get a good night's sleep, we'll never see them again, so we can't leave this to anyone else.' He dared her to disagree with him.

'Good plan,' she said, getting out of the car.

He wished she would let him do things like get car doors for her. For one thing, it gave him a chance to check out her legs. For another, he just liked it. He liked *her*.

His assistant had made an appointment, and Matt himself greeted them. He was a friendly sort with a comb-over and a string tie, Greg figured in keeping with the ranch theme. 'Howdy, folks. Welcome to Matt's Mattress Ranch. We've been expecting you.'

'Um, howdy,' Greg said.

'Opal,' Matt called to his assistant, 'bring Mr. and Mrs. Bellamy something to drink.'

'Oh!' Nina's cheeks reddened. 'We're not—'

'Mr. and Mrs.,' Greg finished for her. 'This is Nina Romano. We'd like to place a wholesale order.'

Opal brought chilled bottles of water, and Matt invited them to check out the showroom, inviting them to try any of his wares.

'Hear that, Mrs. Bellamy?' Greg teased, leaning down to whisper in her ear.

'Shut up,' she said, focusing on the hunt. She paused at several models, pressing her flattened palm down, dismissing each in turn.

'This is going to be the one,' she said, stepping out of her sandals.

'Are you kidding me?' he asked, eying the

cushy mattress topper. 'Way too much fluff.'

'Some people like fluff.' She lay down on the mattress.

For a second, he couldn't do anything but stare at her bare feet and legs. She looked different—unbearably sexy—lying down.

'Greg,' she prodded him. 'This is it. Try it.'

He lay down next to her, sinking into the mattress until they rolled together, almost touching. Then he reacted like any revved-up teenage boy and hoped like hell she wouldn't notice. 'Oh, okay,' he said. 'I get it.'

'Told you so.' She started to sit up.

He held her there. He wished he could hold her there forever.

She turned to him, pillowing her head on her arm. 'Let's place our order, then.'

'In a minute.'

Her lips twitched, and he could tell she was trying not to smile. 'Some guys will try anything to get a girl in bed.'

'I'll try anything to get *you* in bed. There's a difference.'

That shut her up, but only for a moment. 'I'm leaving,' she said, getting up and slipping on her sandals. 'You coming?'

Not today, he thought. With pained reluctance, he extricated himself from the fantasy and got up. 'Whatever you say, boss. Come on. I'll buy you lunch.'

'We don't have time for lunch.'

She was as contrary as she was sexy. 'Fine,'

233

he said. 'I'll get something for me and you can sit there and worry about staying on schedule.'

'As if.' She brushed past him and marched outside, leading the way to the Starlight Diner, located across the street.

*　　　*　　　*

Nina was trying to figure out if she was having a good day or a bad day. She was having far too much fun with Greg Bellamy. Even picking out mattresses was a kind of wicked fun she hadn't experienced in . . . probably ever. That was good, but it was also bad. Every time she was with him, she found it difficult to focus on business. He was just so . . . distracting. That was why she hadn't wanted to stop for lunch with him. She knew she'd be distracted.

She was right. He looked boyishly handsome in cargo shorts, a Hawaiian shirt and boating shoes. Yet with the antiques dealer, he'd been all business, negotiating fairly and getting exactly what he wanted. Delivered. She'd expected him to be some spoiled, overeducated guy from the city, but every day, he surprised her.

Concentrate, Nina reminded herself. Stick to business. Over grilled cheese sandwiches and coleslaw, they went over the plan to get everything done in time for the grand opening on Independence Day weekend. Nina sipped her cherry Coke, frowning at her notes. 'I don't see how we'll get it all done in time.'

'We have no choice.'

'True. Every room is booked for all three nights, some of them longer. There's one couple coming from Chicago for a whole week.'

'Every room? I thought there was one left.'

'Last confirmation came in this morning,' she said. 'I had an e-mail report from the reservations service.'

He leaned back in the Naugahyde booth and clasped his hands behind his head. 'Fantastic, Nina. The contest was a great idea,' he said, placing a fat manila envelope on the table. 'We were flooded with entries.'

She didn't tell him that she'd long had a grand opening planned out in her mind. In order to build a mailing list, they had offered a free stay at the inn to the winner of a random drawing. All the entries went straight to a database to use in their marketing.

He grinned at her. 'You're as good at this as I knew you'd be.'

Nina felt a flush rising in her cheeks. Something—she didn't want to name it— pulsed between them. 'Yeah?'

He cleared his throat, pulled his gaze away.

'So. I appreciate the vote of confidence.' Nina was embarrassed by herself. It was as if she was thirteen again, starry-eyed and clueless. She busied herself with the clipboard, now cluttered with even more notes.

'Listen, I know this isn't the arrangement you were expecting,' Greg said. 'You're being a good sport about this.'

She got the feeling he'd been working up to telling her this. 'Of course I am.'

'Seriously. I realize you wanted to go it alone, and now you've got me and my kids in the mix.'

Nina didn't respond to that. By now, life should have taught her not to plan anything, because there always seemed to be a detour down the road. She found herself in a very strange position. Greg had what she wanted—the inn. She ought to resent him, but perversely, she felt an insane attraction to him.

She sorted through the rest of the mail they'd picked up at the post office earlier. 'I'm glad the contest was a hit, but Daisy gets the credit for so many bookings,' Nina stated. 'Her photographs made the brochure and website irresistible.'

'You think?'

'Absolutely.'

'I'm glad to hear you say that about her. She gives me plenty to worry about. Nice to be reminded that sometimes, she's an amazing kid.'

His comment touched a soft spot in Nina. How well she remembered Sonnet's ups and downs. And how she missed them. 'Every kid comes with her own unique set of worries.'

He nodded. 'I find new ones every day.'

The cocksure Greg Bellamy was taking a break, she observed. There was something vulnerable about him now, and he didn't seem like a business partner or a rival or anything but a worried parent.

'Max is having problems that I never anticipated. Sometimes I'm amazed at all the anger he has bottled up. I asked myself, did I sacrifice my kid's happiness? Should I have stuck it out with Sophie, worked harder—'

'News flash, Greg. Kids have anger and issues and problems no matter what. You can blame the divorce if you want, but you might need to rethink that. Living in a house where people are unhappy is toxic. It's a slow poison. You can't hide things from your kids. They see everything. And even if they're not old enough to understand, they know unhappiness when they see it, no matter how hard you try to hide it. So I'm just saying, don't beat yourself up over the divorce. Give him a stable, loving home and hope for the best. And if he wants to quit baseball, for god's sake let him quit baseball. There's no shame in letting him see that sometimes the right thing to do is cut your losses and move on.'

'Are you speaking from experience?'

'With eight siblings, I've had a front row seat at every possible family quarrel. I'm the only one in my family who never married. I didn't even date while Sonnet was growing up. It just seemed too complicated.'

237

'So now that she's away . . . '

'I've got options,' she said. She didn't want him to think she was trying to get him to ask her out, so she changed the subject. 'And that's pretty much all I have to say about that. How's Daisy doing?'

'She asked me to be her birth coach,' he said. Then he looked amazed, as though someone else had spoken the obviously unplanned words.

Hold on, Nina thought. This was supposed to be a business arrangement yet here they were, talking about his kids. She needed to figure out how to avoid these topics, how not to care about the heartbreaking expression on his face—a combination of love, terror, commitment and uncertainty.

Yet it was not the sort of conversational leap you could avoid. She moved aside her glass and studied his face, wondering what to say, how to react. *What about your ex?* She nearly asked the question aloud, although it was none of her business. Still, Nina found herself wondering about Daisy's mother. If this had been Sonnet, wild horses couldn't keep Nina from her side. But every family was unique, she reminded herself. Each had its own distinctive emotional landscape, its own geography.

'So, um, how do you feel about that?' she asked Greg, suspecting he hadn't broached the topic because he wanted her opinion, but because he simply needed to talk.

'It just feels crazy. I mean, how can I not go crazy when my own daughter's asking me to be her birth coach? I have no idea what I'm doing. My worst problem used to be making a deadline at work, getting Max to do his vocabulary homework or convincing Daisy not to dye her hair blue. That all seems trivial now that I have to go to class to learn about prolapsed cords and demand feeding.' He flashed a look that had a curious effect on Nina. 'Sorry, I didn't mean to go on.'

She cleared her throat. 'What did you do when Max was born? You must have been there for his birth.'

'I was, but this is different. This is my daughter. I feel guilty as hell, you know? I'm the one who let her go away to Long Island that weekend with her friends—'

'Oh, no,' she said, 'you are not going there. It's no one's fault. You can blame whatever you want, but everybody knows there are few things quite so powerful as a teenager's sex drive. No high school girl asks to get pregnant. So just move on from all the blame and the guilt.'

'I thought I had. I don't know what to tell her besides the fact that I love her and want only the best for her.'

'Have you told her that?' Nina asked.

'Yeah, of course.'

'I mean, have you really told her like you

239

mean it, or was it just something you said?'

'Of course I meant it.'

'But you definitely have a preference about how you wish she'd handle this.' She couldn't help remembering the way her family had been—hurt and scared and angry and so deeply disappointed in her. And she remembered her reaction, the utter determination to prove herself. She had no doubt Greg's daughter was going through the same things. 'I know you don't want to hear it, but Daisy will handle things herself, in her own way. She'll probably go off on her own and—'

'She's not going anywhere.'

'Well, guess what, Greg? It's not up to you. Every single member of my family wanted to help me. I had a chance to work at my brother's car lot, or as a teacher's aide for my dad, or at my sister's salon . . . I was so grateful that they cared but ultimately, I had to go my own way. Daisy might, too.'

'She loves the inn.'

'She loves you,' Nina corrected him. 'But don't be surprised if she tells you she needs to find her own life.'

'What do you mean, find her own life? She's staying right here.'

'Is that what she wants?'

'Of course that's what she wants.'

'Have you asked her?'

'I don't need to ask her. I know what's best for Daisy.'

'If you say so.' Nina definitely wanted to drop the subject. In the first place, this was not her business and she was definitely not comfortable in the role of Greg's adviser when it came to his daughter. In the second place, she knew something he was refusing to see. Daisy didn't want to spend her life, and not even the next year or two, working at the Inn at Willow Lake. Nina wasn't about to say that to Greg, though. It wasn't her place. She didn't want it to be her place.

'I still think of Daisy as a little kid,' he confessed. 'I can still picture her with her hair in pigtails, skipping rope or showing me a loose tooth. Her whole childhood went by at the speed of light, and suddenly she's about to have a kid of her own. And I'm not ready for her to stop being *my* kid.'

Though her heart ached for him, Nina knew that wouldn't help. 'She won't ever stop,' she said, thinking about her own father. 'When I told Pop I was pregnant, he blazed through the whole spectrum of emotional reactions— shock, rage, grief, disappointment . . .' Even now, Nina could feel the sadness echo through her. 'Disappointment was the worst for me. I remember thinking that I'd ruined everything, that Pop and I would never be the same.'

'Great,' he said.

Nina took a deep breath. 'No, hear me out,' she said. 'You know, I suppose I could tell you everything will be fine, but honestly, there'll be

241

plenty of occasions when everything is *not* fine. There will be times when Daisy will fall apart and the baby won't stop crying and things are going to seem so far from fine that you'll probably feel like putting your fist through a wall.'

He started to say something, but she held up a hand to stop him. 'I'm trying to explain to you that you're going to be all right, you and Daisy both. Trust me on this. When Sonnet was born, Pop fell in love with her the second he held her in his arms. All of a sudden, he wasn't thinking about what people would say, or how I was going to deal with everything or what sort of life I'd give my child. He just loved her, and knew somehow that would be enough. And to this day, they have a special bond, my pop and Sonnet. She brings him . . . I don't know. Some kind of quiet joy he doesn't get from any of his kids. So what I hope you'll remember is that even after things fall apart, they fit back together eventually, and you somehow get to the other side of whatever crisis you're facing, and you're smiling again. It's a baby, Greg, not a ball and chain. Sonnet and I were there. Me, having a baby alone, my folks crazy with worry about whether or not we'd be all right. I'm not saying it was easy. But I don't regret one single second of it.'

He was a listener, she'd give him that. He had this way of listening with every cell of his body—eyes, face, posture—that blew her

242

away. He nodded, seemingly clear on just what he was agreeing to. 'Every once in a while, I feel excited at the prospect of having another little kid around the house. One that calls me Gramps before I've even turned forty.' He shuddered. 'Okay, now I'm scaring myself.'

She knew exactly what he was saying. The irony of the situation struck her. He was living a life Nina had just left behind; he was entering a world of parenting that would consume him with worry, with mirth and frustration, with a spectrum of emotions she clearly remembered. Just hearing him talk about his kids took her back there.

She was supposed to be moving in the other direction. Her active parenting years were done. She was glad to have that phase behind her. At least, that was what she told herself.

Watching him, thinking of what lay ahead for him and his family, she didn't feel pity. What she felt instead surprised her—envy.

No. That couldn't be right. No sane person would envy his situation. Here he was, about to become a grandfather before he was done being a father. There was nothing enviable in that. And yet . . . and yet . . .

'I guess the thing that freaks me out is the thought of seeing Daisy dealing with a kind of pain I can't do anything about,' he said.

'Just being there and holding her hand is probably all the help she'll need.'

'She's had to go to the emergency room

three times in her life, and I wasn't there for any of them. I have no idea how I'll be in an emergency.'

'Chances are, there won't be an emergency. And if there is—does anyone know? We might think we do, but until the situation arises, you can never really predict. Maybe you're too focused on the delivery room stuff. That's just a small part of it. Doesn't the whole process involve classes spread out over weeks?'

He nodded. 'I'm going to be okay with this. I have to be. Also, uh, sorry about bringing this up. I shouldn't have dumped it on you.'

'Don't worry about it.'

'I didn't expect you to tell me these things. I know some of them are . . . pretty personal.'

She felt her cheeks heat. The way he was staring at her now was a little scary. He looked as though he was about to explode. She'd probably offended him. *Here's how I screwed up; maybe Daisy can screw up better.* She swallowed, not sure how to respond. He made her feel unsettled and . . . exposed. He made it impossible not to care about him. 'I just wanted to let you know, good things will come of this.'

'I'm counting on it.' His smile was as sexy and slow as a caress.

Nina grabbed the plastic-coated menu. 'Are you having dessert?'

'That's the best part.' They perused the selections, and Greg spoke up again. 'You

244

know what else has been bugging me?'

'I have no idea,' she said faintly.

'The kid who fathered Daisy's baby isn't someone she wants in her life. He needs to be told, though, he and his family.'

'Yes,' she agreed, and a faraway memory nudged its way into her mind. 'Yes, he does.'

'You understand, I have zero compassion for the little rat bastard. I don't give a shit— or even half a shit—about him. But then I think . . . I remember . . . What if Sophie had never told me about Daisy? What if I'd never had a chance to be a father to her? What if, someday, this baby needs a dad the way Daisy needs me? I can't even get my mind around that.'

The waitress brought dessert—a big wedge of berry pie for Greg, a dish of melon sorbet for Nina.

'Don't get me wrong, I don't want her to marry some guy just because of the baby,' he said. 'A person can only pretend for so long, but eventually the misery catches up with you. I mean, her—Daisy.'

Nina suspected that Greg had just told her the story of his marriage in a nutshell. 'Maybe you should explain this to Daisy.'

'No. That wouldn't be fair. She needs to make up her own mind.'

'She'll have an easier time doing that if you tell her from the heart what you think.'

'I'm not so sure. Over the past year, dealing

with my daughter has been a roller-coaster ride. Can I ask you something personal?'

She lifted her eyebrows. 'I can't promise I'll answer, but since I just told you my life's story, you might as well ask.'

'What's the story with Sonnet's father? I mean, I know she's with him now, but . . .'

Oh, boy, thought Nina. This was her doing. She'd dived right into the conversation. She should have expected the question. 'Does it matter to you?'

'I just wonder how you handled it. Sonnet's father, I mean.'

She folded her arms on the Formica table and looked at him. 'It's kind of a long story.'

*Part Eight*

## *Then*

Some hotels promise visitors 'no surprises,' but you'll find the Inn at Willow Lake to be a place that is full of them. The walnut-paneled library is lined with bookcases originally brought from Hay-on-Wye, a Welsh town famous for its bookshops. In addition to the surprises found on the shelves, one of the bookcases has a hinged mechanism so that it opens like a door, revealing an intriguing nook behind it.

The library houses a fine collection of books and memorabilia from the early days of Avalon. When an illustrated antique book finally comes apart beyond repair, individual pages can be framed and hung as art prints. While the form changes, the beauty lasts.

# FOURTEEN

There was no ceremony quite so auspicious as graduation from the United States Military Academy. Nina didn't attend, of course, but as she sat in Veterans Memorial Park in West Point, paging nervously through the schedule of activities in the local paper she'd picked up, there appeared to be no end of meetings, receptions, celebrations and galas. And, of course, the ceremony itself. The front of the journal bore the iconic photograph—a thousand hats flung into the air, sailing against the bright blue sky.

Nina and Jenny had driven down with Sonnet, who had napped through the hour-long trip. Never had Nina been so grateful for Jenny's friendship. This promised to be one of the most difficult days of Nina's life, and Jenny insisted on being there to watch Sonnet while Nina met with Laurence. They'd arranged to meet at the local park, which had stately shade trees, manicured grass and a well-equipped playground. As the appointed time drew near, Nina's nerves wound up to the point of physical pain. She was sitting on a bench by the statue of George Washington Goethals, West Point Class of 1880. He had designed and built the Panama Canal, among other things. Nina had read the commemorative plaque at least a dozen times and currently knew way too much about Colonel Goethals.

'Lookit me, Mamma, lookit!' Sonnet yelled, lurching back and forth on a spring horse while Jenny stood by.

'Wow,' Nina called across the playground, 'you're a cowgirl.' She tried not to sound distracted, but what else could she do? This was her last chance to meet with the father of her child before he got orders and was sent to his first command, possibly overseas. She gripped the edge of the bench she was sitting on to keep herself from bolting. Every instinct she had shrieked at her to flee—just grab Sonnet, strap her into the booster seat in the back of her secondhand Ford LTD and run like hell.

No. She schooled herself to stay where she was. She needed to do this, for Sonnet's sake. No child should ever be deprived of her father. She was fast approaching the age where she was starting to wonder, and Nina didn't ever want to lie to her or evade the question.

Restless, Nina couldn't sit still any longer. She got up and walked over to Jenny and Sonnet.

'I can't tell you how much I appreciate this,' Nina said to Jenny.

Jenny gave her hand a quick squeeze, putting on a fake-tragic expression. 'And to think I gave up a whole day of bookkeeping at the bakery for this.' She cast a fond glance at Sonnet. 'She'll thank you one day. She deserves to know who her father is.'

Nina swallowed hard, nodded briefly. 'I . . . um . . . couldn't tell how Laurence felt when I talked to him on the phone. Besides completely shocked, that is. I never really knew him, which is so strange when you think about it, since he completely changed my life.'

'I guess you'll find out what he thinks pretty soon,' Jenny said. 'This is such a gift you are giving Sonnet. At least she'll know. I've spent my life wondering who my father is. Every day I stare into the mirror and try to see him. I look around at men who might have known my mother, and I go crazy wondering. I'll tell you, my mother might have her reasons for walking away from me when I was little, but the one thing I can never get over is the fact that she never told anyone who my father is.'

Only Nina knew how much Jenny had struggled with the pain of that mystery. It was one of the reasons Nina had finally called Laurence Jeffries and requested this meeting. The other reason came from yet another man Nina barely knew—Greg Bellamy. Seeing him with his little daughter at Willow Lake had reminded Nina that, no matter how hard she worked or how much she loved Sonnet, she could never fill the place of a father in her child's life. Sonnet would be just fine without a father. She had strong male influences from Nina's father and brothers, and she seemed

251

to be a naturally sturdy child. Yet Nina didn't want to take advantage of Sonnet's nature. She wanted to answer the questions her daughter hadn't yet asked her, starting now.

The sound of a car door slamming startled Nina.

'Well,' said Jenny with a bright smile. 'Sonnet and I will be over there on the seesaw.' She sent a meaningful look over Nina's shoulder, then hurried away, towing Sonnet by the hand behind her. They joined a laughing, shouting crowd of kids around the jungle gym.

Nina knew what that look meant. She smoothed her suddenly sweaty hands down her sides, and turned to face him.

*Oh, Lord.*

How on earth could this be the shy, awkward boy she'd known so briefly—but so thoroughly—four summers ago?

This was a perfectly groomed man in uniform, striding toward her with single-minded purpose. His posture was flawless, his stride purposeful as he approached her. He was commanding, intimidating, compelling—a handsome, storybook prince come to life.

Pierced by his flinty, intense stare, Nina felt her much-prepared speech evaporate. 'Thanks for coming,' she said.

'Nothing would have kept me from coming.' He stood implacably before her, as stiff and formal as a six-foot GI Joe.

Nina couldn't tell what this overbearing

252

stance was—a facade of self-confidence or a cover for his quaking fear? She could see him scanning the area, his Terminator gaze seeking a target but not finding one, since the distant playground was overrun by kids of all shapes, sizes and colors.

'Where's the child?' The barked question rang like a command, the sort designed to intimidate his inferiors.

Nina laughed briefly, and she could tell from his reaction that he wasn't used to getting this particular response. 'You don't need to do this,' she stated, oddly feeling less threatened now. 'And furthermore, you can't.'

'Can't what?'

'Intimidate me. Or bully me, or whatever it is you're doing.'

'I'm not—'

'I gave birth in an ambulance without anaesthesia. I've raised a kid on my own for three years while holding a job and going to school, so by now, nothing can intimidate me. Certainly not you.'

He glared at her, stone-faced. 'That wasn't my intent.'

He even spoke differently now, in clipped, articulated imperatives. Nina refused to flinch. 'I'm doing this as a courtesy to you and because it's something Sonnet deserves to know about herself. But if you think for one minute I'll tolerate you acting all GI Joe around her, you're dead wrong.'

'But I—'

'At ease, soldier,' she said. 'Or this meeting is over.'

His eyes surrendered first. They turned from flinty to worried. The taut lines of his face softened, and his impeccable posture relaxed the slightest bit. Nina gestured at the swarm of kids. 'My daughter, Sonnet, is over there on the seesaw, with my friend Jenny. I'll introduce you in a minute. But she's so little. You've got to promise—'

'I gave you my word of honor on the phone,' he interrupted.

And of course, a West Point man's word of honor was legendary. She had to trust it. He'd assured her that he would respect the fact that he was a complete stranger to Sonnet. He agreed that she needed to get to know him gradually. At her age, she had only a rudimentary grasp of the concept of *father*. She would have to grow into an understanding. Nina hoped Sonnet would come to know her father as a good man who happened to live far away.

As his gaze settled on Sonnet, his mask fell away. There was a flicker of naked pain, and in those few seconds, Nina saw the bashful boy she remembered, and she could see precisely where Sonnet got her regal beauty. She had her father's high-cut cheekbones and gorgeous black eyes; she even had that physical presence—an athlete at ease in her own skin.

On the phone, Nina had assured Laurence that this meeting was all about Sonnet, about banishing doubts as to her identity for the child's sake. This was not about trapping Laurence or squeezing child support from him. Nina had told him earlier that she would agree to a blood test. But the moment she saw them together, she knew anyone with eyes could see the resemblance.

'She's . . . oh, sweet Jesus.' He paused, cleared his throat. Then he turned to Nina. 'You should've told me about her a long time ago.'

'I thought about doing just that,' Nina said. 'I almost did, many times. But it would have ruined your career at West Point. And for what? I didn't want you to marry me, didn't want your help raising her. I had my family for support. Telling you would have done nothing but derail all your plans for the future.'

He didn't deny it. 'A part of me is grateful for that. But another part . . .' He looked again at Sonnet, and the power of speech seemed to leave him.

Nina refused to apologize. She didn't want either of them to regret something they couldn't change. 'What we need to do is figure this out,' she said, catching Jenny's eye and waving her over. 'Keeping in mind what's best for Sonnet.'

'Of course.' He stood and waited as Jenny and Sonnet approached, hand-in-hand.

255

Laurence was clearly at a loss; he looked as though he was about to salute them. His eyes seemed to devour her, taking in every detail of Sonnet's appearance.

'Don't be scary,' Nina advised, acutely aware that this man had zero experience with children. She'd had time to grow into parenthood; he had mere minutes. 'Just smile and get down on her level and let her come to you.' Then Nina demonstrated, opening her arms to Sonnet. 'Hey, kiddo. Did you have fun on the seesaw?'

'Yep. I went really high,' Sonnet said in her Minnie Mouse voice, launching herself at Nina. Her cotton-candy scent filled Nina, making her smile as it nearly always did.

Jenny quietly introduced herself to Laurence. Then she excused herself and moved away, giving them privacy.

'Baby, I want you to meet . . . my friend,' Nina said cautiously. 'His name is Laurence Jeffries.'

'Hello.' Sonnet pressed herself against Nina, gazing up at the stranger.

'Hi.' Following Nina's advice, he went down on one knee as though genuflecting—or assuming the position to fire a gun. Even so, he was still tall and imposing. 'I'm very glad to meet you, Sonnet.'

'Sonnet Maria Romano,' she said dutifully. Nina had taught her to introduce herself. 'I found a garnet.' She dug in her pocket and held out a stone in her slightly grubby palm. Rough garnets were common in the area, and one of Sonnet's uncles had shown her how to spot them. Though she eagerly held out her prize, she also kept a tight grip on Nina with her other hand.

Nina was proud of her little girl's precocious intelligence and grown-up-sounding speech. Sometimes Nina had to remind herself that Sonnet was too young to understand complicated matters. Despite her sophisticated vocabulary, she couldn't be expected to comprehend the fact that the handsome soldier before her was her father.

'That *is* a garnet,' Laurence said. 'You're lucky to find it.'

'You keep it,' Sonnet said. 'For a present.'

The offering brought the first genuine smile to his face as he put out his hand, palm up. 'I sure will,' he said. 'Thank you, Sonnet. I'll keep it forever. I'll never lose it.'

She beamed at him. 'Okay.'

For a second, her tiny hand disappeared inside his and the three of them were connected—Nina, Sonnet and Laurence, a family of sorts. The thought made Nina dizzy with a sweep of euphoria. Maybe . . .

A car door slammed again, and they all turned. Laurence snapped back into military mode, straight as a steel sword blade. Nina hoisted Sonnet into her arms.

'This is Angela Hancock,' Laurence said as

a beautiful, well-dressed woman joined them. 'Angela, this is Nina and Sonnet Romano.'

She was, in her own way, as scary and self-possessed as he—a tall, graceful Nubian princess to his storybook prince. 'How do you do,' she said.

'Angela's my fiancée,' he continued. 'We're getting married in a week.'

Ah, thought Nina. No wonder the guy was a wreck. It wasn't all about her or even all about Sonnet. She mustered a smile and said, 'Congratulations.'

'Thank you,' Angela said.

Nina set Sonnet down. 'Go play with Jenny on the swings, baby.' As the little girl ran off, Nina turned to Angela. 'I realize this whole situation is awkward. I've explained to Laurence that I don't intend to make any trouble,' she stated. 'I simply want my daughter to know who fathered her.'

'Of course.' Angela had a lovely, resonant voice, like a stage actress. She was remarkably calm and seemed oddly familiar.

Nina suspected Laurence had prepared her as much as possible for the meeting. 'How you and Laurence deal with this is your business. I'm not making any demands.'

'Indeed.'

'I keep thinking we've met.' Nina felt apologetic, which was annoying. She owed no explanation or apology to anyone. 'Have we?'

'Angela's father is the Reverend George

Simon Hancock,' Laurence said, shining with pride. 'She's been with his ministry, so maybe you saw her on TV.'

'Maybe,' Nina said, though she could safely say she had never watched a gospel ministry on TV. Still, she reminded herself to be generous. After all, Nina had Sonnet. So it was only right that Laurence would get someone like Angela—gorgeous, famous and an evangelist's daughter. 'I hope you two will be very happy together,' she said, then faced Laurence. 'I meant what I said, about not wanting anything but for Sonnet to know who you are. What you tell people is up to you.' Although privately, she admitted she would find it very interesting to see him telling the famous Reverend Hancock that he'd had a child with a white woman. 'I thought you might want to write her a letter for her to read when she's old enough to understand. And I guess, if she wants, maybe you'd like to visit her once in a while,' she said. 'That will be enough.'

She saw his hand clench into a fist. It was the hand that held the garnet. He looked over at Sonnet and his eyes swam with tears, but they didn't fall. It must be so painful, Nina thought, holding them in like that.

'It'll never be enough,' he said quietly.

'Yes,' Angela contradicted, tucking her hand into the crook of his arm. 'It will.'

## Part Nine

### Now

Frequent visitors will witness the changing of the seasons. At any given time of year, the ever-changing landscape is adorned in different raiments—the tender buds of spring, the flowers of high summer, extravagant fall foliage or a quiet blanket of snow in winter. King Arthur's Suite is a favorite, with a huge bay window that frames the scenery. The room is furnished with a white iron bed, covered with a handmade cutwork duvet and matching pillow covers. An imposing dresser conceals a dry bar stocked with fine port wine and a selection of single-barrel whiskey.

The bathroom features a deep jetted tub made for a long, quiet soak. To enhance relaxation, add three drops of lavender oil, two drops of frankincense and two drops of petit-grain, a citrusy essential oil, to the bath.

# FIFTEEN

'Are you sure this is the right thing to do, Dad?' Daisy asked, her pen poised over the signature line on her letter to Logan O'Donnell.

Greg felt the churchlike hush of the bank pressing in on him. The antique gothic building's soaring ceilings and marble floors provided a cool refuge from the summer heat, but Greg was sweating from nerves. That, and the suit he was wearing. It just seemed right to wear a suit for the occasion. Daisy had written a letter informing O'Donnell that he was the biological father of her child. She would agree to a DNA test if he requested it. She absolved him of all legal and financial obligation, hoping to avert a custody battle down the road. The kid would be an idiot not to agree to Daisy's terms, which basically let him off scot-free. Of course, he'd already proven he was an idiot, so Greg wasn't sure how O'Donnell would react when he got the news from Daisy.

Greg glanced around, not sure what he was looking for—a sign? Someone to advise him? He wasn't likely to find that here. Shane Gilmore, the bank president, was on his phone in a glass-walled cubicle. Brooke Harlow, the asset manager, was away from her desk. Across the counter, the notary waited, her mouth forming a prune of disapproval as she scanned the letter and filled out a form. She had hair of blue steel and the kind of holier-than-thou judgmental air Greg had come to despise. He was sick of strangers who looked at Daisy and thought the worst.

'Let's have a seat,' he said, guiding her away from the counter. The damned notary could wait until hell froze over, as far as Greg was concerned. Sophie had advised them to notarize the letter and send it by courier, signature required. Daisy sat down on a lobby bench, the papers in her lap.

Greg considered what Nina had told him about her own experience with the father of her child. A young man—even a careless, hormone-driven boy—had to at least be given the information that he'd fathered a child. Nina claimed she had never regretted the way she'd handled Sonnet's father, not telling him until he'd graduated from West Point and gotten engaged to another woman. It was, Greg realized, consistent with Nina's independent nature—a way to insure her role as sole parent to her daughter. Did Daisy want to go it alone? The agony of indecision on her face indicated that she wasn't sure.

She fiddled with the pen. 'Mom said it's my call and no one else's.'

So she and Sophie had been communicating, he reflected. That, at least, showed a bit of progress. 'Your mom's right.'

'What, did you guys, like, talk about it?'

He nodded, perversely pleased that he and Sophie were on the same page for once. They got along fairly well, now that they were an ocean apart and rarely spoke.

They weren't exactly the perfect role models for Daisy's situation, either. As young parents with an unplanned child, they'd done their best, and that had been good enough for a long time, but not forever. When Sophie had presented him with his newborn daughter, he'd felt a love so intense it bled into his feelings for Sophie. Within mere moments, he'd convinced himself—and Sophie—that the marriage was meant to be. They believed they were doing the right thing for the sake of their child.

'Your mom and I both want you to make your own decision,' he said.

'So if I blow it, I don't have anyone to blame but myself.'

'Daisy—'

'I get that, Dad. Believe me, I do.' And with that, something seemed to spur her to action. She marched over to the notary, signed each copy of the form and pushed it across the counter to the steel-haired woman.

Give her hell, Greg thought. His daughter's implacable pride was evident in her posture and the set of her chin as she slid the papers into a long, legal-size envelope.

'Greg.' Brooke Harlow came out of the back office, a polite smile on her face. 'It's nice to see you.'

'Same here,' he said, briefly taking her hand. He hadn't seen her since their not-quite-a-date on the lake, but he hadn't forgotten how attractive she was. Her every hair was slicked into place, and she wore a straight skirt and high heels that showed off her legs. Greg suffered an untimely reminder of how long it had been since he'd gotten laid. Lately it seemed everywhere he turned, he encountered women—smiling, helpful, attractive women. He spotted them in line at the post office, browsing the aisles of the hardware store, using the pumps at the gas station, haunting his dreams. They'd always been there, of course, but deprivation had made him more keenly aware of them. He wondered if they could tell.

'I guess you've been busy,' Brooke said, her tone open-ended. She gave him an unmistakable once-over, focusing on the hand-tailored Brooks Brothers suit he was wearing.

Her manner surprised him. He'd actually written her off based on that first disastrous date. Now she seemed to be telegraphing ask-me-out signals.

'I've been plenty busy, but a guy's got to eat,' he said. 'Maybe we could go to dinner sometime.'

Her face lit up, her eyes bright with a 'mission accomplished' expression. 'That sounds—'

266

'All set, Daddy-O.' Daisy joined them, preceded by her conspicuously big abdomen. 'Hi,' she said, checking out Brooke with just a hint of wariness in her eyes. She claimed it was fine with her if Greg wanted to date, but she had definite opinions about the women he picked. Long-haired bankers in spike heels didn't impress her the way they did Greg.

He introduced them, and Daisy said, 'Hello, Ms. Harlow. I was just getting something notarized.' She patted the thick envelope and smiled, clearly aware of the effect she was having on Brooke.

Brooke's expression was almost comical. Hell, it *was* comical. Greg could see the surprise chasing across her prom-queen features, though she managed to paste on a smile.

Greg didn't say anything. He surveyed the bank lobby and acted as though he didn't feel anyone's scrutiny. He felt it, though, seeping through the layers of his suit like the summer heat. In a town like this, no one got to be anonymous. It was impossible to have secrets. For long, anyway. Within hours, it would be put out there that Daisy Bellamy's situation had come as a shock to the bank's new asset manager.

Brooke cleared her throat. 'It's very nice to meet you,' she said to Daisy. Then she turned to Greg with an apologetic smile. 'I'd better get back to work. It's good to see you, Greg.

267

Good luck with the new property.'

She walked briskly to her office, high heels clicking decisively on the marble floor. Greg watched her go with a twinge of regret.

'I guess I caught her off guard.' Daisy offered him a rueful smile. 'People don't look at you and automatically think, "Grandpa."'

'Yeah, if they did that, I'd shoot myself,' he admitted. 'I was just in the process of asking her to dinner.' He held the door for Daisy and they stepped out into the bright summer day.

'Sorry, Dad.' An awkward silence pulsed between them. This was surely a new family dynamic—the grown daughter coming to realize her father wanted to date. 'I'll wait out here while you go back and talk to her.'

'No, it's fine. I changed my mind.' That was true. The moment he'd seen the way she looked at Daisy, Brooke had lost all her appeal—high heels or no. And honestly, he could understand Brooke's reluctance. She was barely thirty. The idea of dating a man with kids wasn't so outrageous. But the idea of dating a man about to become a grandfather was a bit much for a woman Brooke's age.

Damn. He shouldn't be thinking about dating at all. He had kids to raise and a business to launch and he ought to know better.

Heat blazed up from the sidewalk, and he hastened to peel off his suitcoat and tie. Had he really dressed for work this way every day in the city?

'I mean it, Dad,' Daisy said as they headed for the car. 'I don't want women to run the other way just because of me.'

'If they run the other way because of you, I wouldn't want to date them in the first place,' he insisted, starting the car and blasting the air conditioner.

'Great, you just eliminated about ninety percent of the female population.'

'Thanks a lot.'

'Because of me, not you,' she said. 'I do want you to find someone, Dad. Just not . . . a clone of Mom.'

'Is that what Brooke is, a clone of Mom?'

'Dad. She looks like Mom's younger sister.'

'Your mother doesn't have a sister.'

'But if she did, she'd look like that bank teller.'

'Asset manager.'

'See? That's very Mom-like. Why settle for bank teller when you can be asset manager?'

She knew him and Sophie better than he thought. But then, she'd had a ringside seat, watching her parents as she grew up. He noticed she had slid the envelope under the seat. 'Do you want to mail that?'

'I'll, um, take care of it myself later.'

He didn't push. It was a big step, and he wanted her to take all the time she needed. *Like her mother had.* The thought chilled him. Sophie had certainly taken her time, waiting until after Daisy was born to bring Greg into the loop. Would anything have been different—for him and Sophie, for Daisy—if he'd been with her from the start?

He loosened his collar, and they headed to the printer's to pick up proofs of the inn's new brochures. The artwork and layout evoked another place in time—a simpler, romantic era when the most pressing item on the agenda might be a tee time at Avalon Meadows. There were shots of Willow Lake in full summer glory, a mirror to the blue sky, surrounded by rising layers of woods and mountains. There were catchphrases—'escape and find yourself,' 'relax, renew, reconnect'—and an earnest promise that guests of the inn would enjoy the best in service and comfort. Daisy's photography highlighted every page, and the graphic designer praised her work.

'Where did you study?' she asked.

'High-school photography class,' Daisy said. 'But mostly, I'm self-taught.'

'Do you do freelance work?'

Greg stepped back, letting Daisy and the graphic designer talk and exchange cards. When she'd visited earlier in the summer, Sophie had given Daisy a box of printed business cards. This was something Greg never would have thought of, but now he was glad Sophie had.

As they drove away from the printer's, he said, 'I'm proud of you, Daze. I like it when other people see your talent.'

'I have a lot to learn when it comes to photography,' she said.

Greg waited. He sensed she was leading up to something.

'I wasn't real keen on college, but now I'm thinking I should take some classes. In fact, if I moved to New Paltz, I could go to the state college there.'

'You're not going anywhere,' he said, dismissing the idea. 'New Paltz is miles away.'

'I know where it is, Dad, and no offense, but I'll go where I want.'

He crushed his back teeth together to keep from replying. Then he couldn't help himself. 'I thought we agreed you're staying at home.'

'You agreed, Dad. I said I'd see.'

He clenched his jaw again, and this time, it stuck. He ought to know better than to get sucked into an argument with her. She was staying with him, period. She really didn't have any other options, though he wasn't going to hurt her feelings by pointing that out. She needed his support.

Hell, who was he kidding? His daughter was eighteen. She had a trust fund—all the Bellamy grandchildren did. He was scared shitless that she'd leave, go somewhere he couldn't protect her. Nina had warned him about this. No, not warned him. But she had definitely seen it coming. So she was either eerily tapped in to Daisy's mindset, or maybe the two of them had been talking. Greg dismissed the idea. No way would Nina do that, put ideas about leaving home into Daisy's head.

She angled the A/C vent toward her face. 'There are a lot of things I want to do. I'll just have to find a way to make it work, you know, with the baby.'

He never knew what to say when she spoke of the baby in such concrete terms. To Greg, it was still an abstraction; the idea hadn't quite sunk in that, yes, he was going to be someone's grandfather this summer. Discomfited, he found a radio station they both liked and turned up the volume.

'I'm starved,' Daisy said after a while. To Greg's relief, she seemed oblivious to his turmoil. 'It's time to meet Nina, anyway,' she added.

Greg resisted the urge to accelerate. It was a business meeting, he reminded himself. Yet he couldn't deny that doing business with Nina was a pleasure. Somehow, he had known that would be the case. It was funny. Though he barely knew her at all, he sometimes felt he knew her better than most of the people in his life.

Today they'd chosen to meet at the Sky River Bakery. Nina was there already. She had commandeered an outdoor seat at an enameled steel café table shaded by a broad-brimmed umbrella. She spied them and motioned them over. Greg noticed that Daisy was carrying the envelope from the bank with her, as though she didn't want to leave it in the car.

Connor Davis sat with Nina, both of them bent over his contractor's book, deep in discussion. She and Connor both offered him a brief greeting and scooted their chairs to make room.

As he took a seat next to her, Greg caught her scent—a mingling of sunscreen, shampoo and the glazed donut she was eating. He felt a now-familiar jolt of attraction, strong enough to drive away the echo of Brooke Harlow's high heels. Which was interesting, since Nina seemed to favor shorts and flip-flops, short hair and no makeup. She wasn't his type at all, he reminded himself. Except . . . damn . . . she was.

'Dad.' Daisy nudged his shoulder. '*Dad*. I said, the usual? I'm going inside.'

'Sure. That'd be great,' he said. He didn't realize he had a 'usual.'

As Daisy went in, she passed Olivia, who brought out a pitcher of ice water and some glasses. At her heels trotted the ever-present Barkis. 'Hey, Greg. Don't you look spiffy.' She sat down next to Connor and hugged his arm. 'After we're married, maybe Greg will take you shopping.'

Connor laughed. 'What, I'm not spiffy enough for you?'

'Sure you are. But there's something about a guy in a really good suit . . . '

Nina studied Greg, seeming to notice his clothes for the first time. 'What's the occasion?'

'Daisy and I had a meeting.' He didn't elaborate, conscious of protecting Daisy's privacy. He got the feeling the bank wasn't Nina's favorite place these days, though she'd never told him why.

'Nina, did you get your invitation?' Olivia asked her.

Greg glanced at Connor, who spread his hands. 'What can I say? It's all wedding, all the time.'

Nina and Olivia ignored them. 'I did, thanks,' Nina said. 'It was so nice of you to include me and Sonnet. You didn't have to, though.'

'Nonsense. You're my sister's best friend. I hope you're planning to come. I'd love it if you and your daughter would share the day.'

Nina seemed uncharacteristically awkward, her gaze shifting and her cheeks coloring up. Watching her, it struck Greg that this woman possessed facets he was finding one by one. Maybe he wasn't supposed to be privy to them. Maybe he shouldn't want to be—but he did.

Twirling a lock of hair around her finger, she smiled at Olivia. 'Thank you. I'll send in my RSVP right away.'

'Mission accomplished,' Connor said,

seizing the slightest pause in the conversation. He handed Greg a work binder filled with permits. 'Everything should be in order. The crew will be done by the end of the week.'

'We need to go look at wedding cake designs.' Olivia grabbed her fiancé's hand and pulled him toward the bakery. 'And don't give me that look of desperation. Come on, Barkis.' She patted her thigh.

After they'd gone, Nina explained her strategy for getting more media coverage for the inn. Even though it was fully booked for opening weekend, they both knew promotion was an uphill battle. She showed him the list of places she wanted to send the press kits. She had targeted a range of media, from small, local outlets to the *New York Times*.

As he listened to her pitch, Greg felt the warmth of the summer sun on his back and watched her nibble at her donut. She ate methodically, in tiny bites around the periphery.

'What's that smile?' she asked, eyeing him across the table.

'I just flashed on the way business meetings used to go for me in the city. Baked goods were not involved. Just a lot of caffeine and testosterone.'

'Sounds like you don't miss it.'

'Nope. Can't believe I put up with it all those years.'

'So why did you?'

'That's a good question. I wish I'd asked myself that fifteen years ago. I felt . . . driven,' he admitted. 'Nobody was forcing me to compete that hard, but it was the sort of thing guys in my position did.' It seemed bogus, now that he looked back. There was just something in the air in the city—a keen sense of competition, an urgency. He felt responsible for producing a big income, too, what with the kids, a mortgage and Sophie just starting her law career.

Then a stark realization struck him. Those were all rationalizations. The real reason he'd worked so hard, spending so many long hours at the firm, never slowing down to take a breather—the reason for all that was his own unhappiness. Not that he knew at the time, of course. The competition and chaos of work kept a thick barrier around the truth. But he could see it now, clearly. If he kept busy enough, he didn't have to think about the fact that things were strained with Sophie, that a subtle, simmering discontent flowed deep beneath the surface, so deep that it was possible to overlook, provided he kept himself preoccupied.

'Here you go, Dad.' Daisy returned with a cheese kolache and a glass of lemonade.

'Thanks.'

Daisy studied her fingernails, which were painted a deep red-black. Greg found that he disliked the color intensely.

276

'Great nail polish,' Nina said. 'What's the name of that color?'

'Dark ruby, I think. If you ever need to borrow it, let me know.'

Nina smiled. 'Thanks, I might take you up on that.'

Girl talk, Greg realized. For the first time, it occurred to him that Daisy had been without it for quite some time.

Acting almost shy, she put the envelope on the table. 'So this is it,' she said to Nina. 'It's the letter for Logan.'

Greg was startled to hear her bring it up with Nina. Clearly, the two of them had discussed it already. So much for Daisy's privacy.

Nina glanced from Daisy to Greg and back to Daisy. 'How do you feel about it?'

'All right, I guess. Glad I got it over with. I have no idea how he's going to react.'

Greg was torn between annoyance—this was a family affair, after all—and gratitude, since he figured he needed all the help he could get. Most of the time with Daisy, he had no idea what the hell he was doing. Sometimes he felt so alone that he panicked, so knowing Nina was in the loop calmed him. Nina herself had walked this path, and she seemed comfortable sharing her experience with Daisy.

'Anyway, thanks for hearing me out,' Daisy said. 'Hey, Dad, can I take the car, and you get a ride back to the inn with Nina? I, uh, I kind of have a . . . well, not a date, exactly, but I asked Julian if I could get some shots of him at the Shawangunks.'

The rock-climbing mecca was legendary, and Julian Gastineaux had quickly become her favorite subject to photograph. For some reason, Greg felt an impulse to glance at Nina, to see what she would say to the request. Then he caught himself. 'You're not planning to climb any rocks.'

'Dad.'

'Okay, okay.' He dug in his pocket for the keys. 'I don't mind. Be back before dark.'

'Thanks, Dad. See you, Nina.'

After Daisy left, Greg looked across the table at Nina. 'So you and she have been talking about . . . her situation.'

'We have. I hope you don't think I'm meddling. Actually, I *am* meddling.'

'I noticed.'

'Only I prefer to think of it as being a good friend, a confidante. Not a meddler—that's someone with a malicious intent. Daisy knows I can relate to her situation, which is why I think she trusts me.'

He stared down at his hands for a moment. 'So when you told Sonnet's father . . . '

'Awkward,' she said. 'Discovering the existence of Sonnet had to be a blow to Laurence. He built his life with military strategy, and he was masterful at it, creating a big future for himself. His marriage to Angela Hancock might have been a love match, but it was strategic as well. They became the perfect D.C. power couple—young, brilliant, educated, African-American, dedicated to serving their country. Their girls are perfect, too—private school, every advantage. He goes up a notch every year, it seems. The sky's the limit. Although there's that one little blooper from his past.'

'Sonnet.'

'Yes. I figured he'd run the other way once I told him about her. But to his credit, he didn't do that. After I told him, he paid child support, and he sent me a letter to give her when I thought she was old enough to understand. He said I could read it first, and I did, to make sure it wouldn't upset her. When Sonnet was eight years old, I gave her the letter. She disappeared into her room with it and came out an hour later asking if she could make a long-distance phone call. Ever since, he's been open with her and involved in a marginal level in her life. One thing he did— something I never asked for—was start a fund for her education. He did it right away, from the first moment he knew about her.'

'So telling him was the right thing to do.'

'For Sonnet. And this boy Daisy was with— maybe he'll step up, but even if he doesn't, she'll be all right.'

'I know,' he said, letting go of his irritation.

'And I know the future's going to be hard as hell for her, so having people she can talk to helps. Dammit.' He raked a hand through his hair, telling himself to quit babbling. 'There are just so many ways to screw this up. Damn. It's . . . we do it again and again in an endless stream. You'd think we'd learn, or at least keep our kids from messing up.'

'That's not the way it works, and you know it.'

'I do know. I'll try to take it easier.' He found that he was able to do that around her. Simply sitting here in the sun, feeling the breeze and looking across the table at her filled him with a curious sense of calm pleasure. All right, he thought, studying the way she sipped her iced tea and the shadow of one dark curl, forming a comma on her forehead. Ask her. He'd been thinking about it for days—what it would be like to go out with her. To do something with her that wasn't business-related for once. He'd lain awake night after night, mulling over his options, and finally, last night, a bone-deep sense of loneliness had driven him from his bed. He'd slipped out into the summer night, the warm air busy with crickets and frogs. He looked across the compound and spied a light on in the boathouse. The idea that Nina was up, too, had been instantly compelling. Here was this girl he'd known for years, and finally their lives were intersecting. Why the hell not? he thought.

He straightened up in his seat, cleared his throat. 'So I was wondering—'

'Yes?' She leaned forward, watching him with a peculiar intensity. Her response had come quickly, almost as if she'd been expecting the question. She seemed to realize she'd jumped the gun, and laughed a little. 'Sorry. You were saying?'

'I thought you and I—'

'Yo, Romano. I was hoping I'd run into you here.' A big guy in jeans and work boots came over to the table.

She beamed up at him. 'Hey, Nils. This is Greg Bellamy. He owns the Inn at Willow Lake. Greg—Nils Jensen, from the jewelry store.'

They shook hands, squaring off with their eyes. The guy didn't look much like a jeweler. 'Nice to meet you,' Greg lied.

'Likewise,' Nils lied back. He turned his focus to Nina. 'So are we still on for tonight?'

'Definitely,' she said.

Still on? On for what? Greg told himself not to get bent out of shape. He hadn't even asked her out. And Nina was his partner, not his girlfriend. Still, he disliked the proprietary way Jensen firmed up his plans for some kind of date with her, then departed with a Paul Bunyon swagger.

She didn't offer to fill in the blanks after Jensen left. Instead, she turned her attention

281

back to her agenda. 'Okay,' she said, 'so I made a timeline of everything that needs to be done before we open. Here's your copy.' She presented it to him with a flourish. 'Oh, and did you get the boat lift fixed?'

'There's a part that needs welding.' He grabbed the list and crammed it into his pocket without looking at it. 'It'll get it done.'

Seemingly oblivious to his irritation, she finished eating all the glaze off the donut and left its carcass. 'Thanks. So . . . were you going to ask me something?'

Right, he thought. 'What? No.'

'Oh. I thought, before Nils showed up, you were going to ask me something.'

'Totally forgot,' he said. 'It must not have been important.'

'Must not,' she agreed. 'You ready? I'm parked down the street.'

Nina's car was like everything else about her—small, cheerful and cute. She drove a Fiat the color of a buttercup, with the radio set on his favorite station—coincidence, he told himself—and the backseat filled with the flotsam and jetsam of a busy person.

'You've got a mobile office back there,' he observed.

'I haven't figured out a filing system yet.'

'Connor had some efficiency expert lay out the office at the inn,' Greg reminded her.

'It's impossible to impose one person's system on another.'

Greg didn't argue. He suspected there was a deeper reason she hadn't inhabited the office of the inn yet, but he forced himself to shake off his annoyance. *Focus. It's just business.*

*       *       *

For some reason, Nina felt out of sync with Greg, and she wasn't sure why. Before Nils had stopped by to remind her about bowling league, she'd had the feeling Greg was going to ask her something. Ask her out. Like, on a date.

No, probably not, she corrected herself. That was most likely just wishful thinking. And it was for the best, because if he'd asked her out, then she would have had to make a decision she didn't want to face.

There were supposed to be boundaries in place, to create a distance between her business and personal life. Yet time and again, she was lured to the brink, and not just with Greg. She found herself drawn to his kids, too—soulful Max, and Daisy, who was at a vulnerable spot Nina could totally relate to. Had she stepped over the line, talking to Daisy? She didn't know. Daisy talked to her and Nina listened. And, all right, she couldn't help herself—she sometimes chimed in with an opinion or advice. It just came naturally to her.

She still felt out of sorts later when she and

283

Greg went to work on the attic of the inn. This had been a work-in-progress for days. The attic was a labyrinthine repository of mostly junk that probably hadn't been touched in decades. They'd been sorting through broken furniture, musty books, rusty tools, abandoned toys, spider-infested linens. The vast majority of items went straight to the dump, but every once in a while, they found a small treasure, like a white hobnail vase or a tole-painted tray.

Greg had changed from the gorgeous slacks and dress shirt he'd had on earlier. This was a good thing, she decided. In the obviously expensive hand-tailored clothes, he looked exotic and impossibly attractive. In his more ordinary cargo shorts and T-shirt, he looked . . . well, still attractive, but not scarily so. 'Trash or treasure?' he asked her, holding up a moth-eaten lampshade.

'Trash,' she said. 'The more we sort through, the more ruthless I'm getting about what to keep and what to toss.'

'Ditto,' he said, adding the item to the discard pile. 'And this?'

'What is it?'

'Not sure.' He turned it over in his hands. 'I think it might be a whetstone. It was in a crate with . . . hello.' He bent and emerged with a large, rusty blade, posing with arms akimbo. 'Check it out.'

'Very *Pirates of the Caribbean*,' she

observed.

'It's a machete,' he said. 'There's an ax, too, and . . . whoa. I think I found the family arsenal.' Waving a flurry of dust out of his face, he lifted the top off another crate. 'These are old black-powder shotguns and supplies. We're definitely keeping these.'

'My thoughts exactly,' said Nina.

'I'm glad we're on the same page.' He carefully placed the guns and machete back in their crates.

He didn't seem to realize she was being facetious. She turned her attention to a box of books. The antique volumes would go nicely in the guest rooms and library, adding to the ambiance. She read their quaint titles aloud— '*Dogs and All About Them, The Bedside Esquire, The Housekeeper's Companion* . . . ah, *The Hygiene of Marriage.* Fascinating.'

'That is *not* going in a guest room,' Greg said.

'We don't want our guests' marriages to be hygienic?'

'We don't want them thinking about that,' he said.

An old photograph fell from the dog book. Undated, it appeared to be from the 1920s, judging by the people's clothing. It showed what appeared to be a family and three Labrador retrievers. The people were stiffly posed, though the middle dog had moved its head, creating a blur in the middle of the photograph. The imperfection somehow humanized the picture. She handed it to Greg. 'Look at that. Ghosts in the attic.'

He admired the picture and put it on the 'keeper' pile. 'Are you bothered by ghosts?'

'Not at all. Maybe hinting that the inn is haunted would be good for business. This place has a history, and I'm glad it's not going to be turned into condos or something.' The words just came out of her. She ducked her head, abashed by the rush of sentiment.

'I would never do that,' he said.

She set aside the hygiene book. 'If you don't mind, I'll save this for Sonnet. It's good for a laugh.'

'I guess you miss her a lot,' he said.

'More than I ever expected.'

'You must be pretty proud of your daughter,' he said.

That wasn't envy she heard in his voice, was it? 'Are you kidding?' Nina said with a burst of honesty. 'Every day, I wonder what I did to deserve that girl.' It was true. Like all kids, Sonnet had challenged Nina growing up, but at heart, she was a loving daughter with talent to spare—valedictorian of her class, a scholarship winner and now she was spending the summer in Europe. 'I miss her so much, though,' she admitted.

'Ironic, huh? Yours left the nest and mine is getting ready to hatch.'

She paused, studied his face, filtered by the

dusty light through a dormer window. 'Scary.'

'Yeah.'

Nina felt a moment of connection with him, and wondered if it was just her. She suspected that if she pushed, just a little, she could find out. But did she want to? 'I have a feeling they're both going to be fine,' she said, letting the moment ease past, unacknowledged. 'Absolutely fine.'

'I hope you're right.'

'That's why you pay me the big bucks.' She felt a beat of nervousness, of hesitation. Not because of the way she was feeling about Greg, but about something else she needed to get out of the way. 'Quick question for you. Suppose Sonnet pays a visit to The Hague.'

The Hague was in Holland, a two-hour train ride from Brussels. It was the seat of various world courts, including the International Court of Justice and the International Criminal Court. It was also where Greg's ex, Sophie, lived and worked.

He stacked the discarded books in an old crate. 'And your question is . . .'

'I just wanted you to know. Daisy told Sonnet to call her mother when she hits town. Sonnet's going to go and see her.'

'Sophie's my ex, not a national monument. I hope Sonnet will do more than see her. I'm sure Sophie will show your daughter some incredible things. It's a great idea for Sonnet to take advantage of that.'

'All right. I wanted to make sure you're cool with it.'

'Not my call,' he said. 'But for what it's worth, I'm cool with it.' He carried the crate to the top of the stairs, setting it down hard enough to raise a cloud of dust.

Uh-huh, thought Nina.

He wiped his hands on his shorts. 'And Sophie'll show your daughter around better than a native, I guarantee it.'

'That's good,' Nina said. 'I felt a little funny, bringing it up.'

'It's okay. Listen, I think I can level with you, since we're friends.'

'Right. Friends.'

'Sophie and I were married for seventeen years. That's a huge chunk of my life—there's a whole history between us. I won't lie and tell you it was one long span of unrelieved misery. We had good times, raised two kids.'

'I know. About the kids, that is. They're great.' The good times, she'd have to take his word for.

'Sophie and I married under . . . difficult circumstances,' he added.

'I know,' she said again. Did he remember talking to her at his wedding reception, putting his fist through a wall?

'It wasn't something we planned,' he went on. 'It was something we did for Daisy, and it worked for a long time because we both tried so damned hard. Ultimately, Sophie and I grew apart. Neither of us noticed it happening at first, but we were focused on our careers and stopped paying enough attention to us.'

Nina felt a blush rise in her face. 'And you're telling me this because . . .?'

He laughed. 'I have no idea. Sorry.'

His easy laughter and the unavoidable spike of attraction she felt toward him left her unsettled. 'I need to get going,' she said, knowing she'd need to hurry through her shower if she was going to be ready on time.

'That's right, you're going out with—what's his name?'

'Nils.' Nina was surprised by Greg's sudden tenseness. 'I don't mean to ditch you, but—'

'Don't worry about me. You gave me a list, remember?'

Her list of things to do. 'Look, if you need me to stay—'

'I said, don't worry.' He waved her away. 'I'll be fine.'


## SIXTEEN

'You're a lot better bowler than I thought you'd be,' Nils told Nina as he drove her home from the Fast Lanes.

'Really?' Nina glanced over at him. 'I'm way out of practice. Haven't been in years.'

'I'd never know from that score.'

A group of them had gone bowling, a regular occurrence among her friends around town. It was something Nina rarely had time to do until lately. It was fun getting together with some of her old gang, but it seemed strange, too. These were people she'd known forever. They were her age, but she felt as though she was in an entirely different place than they were. Her daughter was about to start college while most women her age were newlyweds or new moms, trading stories of home decorating, precocious toddlers and scary bouts of croup. Fortunately, a number of her friends were single, Nils included. He wasn't bad-looking. He'd been pleasant all evening, polite and funny.

'Maybe I got lucky tonight,' she said.

He chuckled, easing the car around a curve in the road. 'Maybe so.' He turned at the sign marking the inn, freshly painted and illuminated on both sides, welcoming visitors. The limbs of the sugar maples along the drive had been pruned recently, the surface of the road regraded. With the grand reopening nearly upon them, she found herself checking out the place with a critical eye. Even after 10:00 p.m., it needed to look inviting.

Gaslights lined the walkways of the property and coach-style sconces illuminated the main entrance and porch. There were lights on in the guest room windows. Overall, the property promised retreat and respite. The guests would never know how much thought went into every detail, nor would they know she and Greg had argued about each one, or so it seemed.

She turned to thank Nils for the evening, but he was already getting out and coming around to get the door for her.

'I'll walk you to your place,' he said.

'Oh! All right. It's this way.' It was a date, she reminded herself. A freaking date. She'd spent an hour bathing, buffing and getting ready. This was supposed to happen—the guy was supposed to walk her to her door and she was supposed to invite him up.

She remarked on the balmy warmth of the evening. They admired the silvery path of the moon's reflection on the lake. There was a moment, at a turn in the path, when Nils's hand brushed against hers and she felt the gentle trap of his fingers.

Just go with it, she told herself. See what happens. She reminded herself that a first date was supposed to be a little awkward, a little nerve-racking. She was supposed to be at least mildly thrilled that he'd taken her hand. Instead, all she could think about was the fact that he wasn't—

'Hey,' said Nils. 'What's that?'

In the lower part of the boathouse, a blinding shower of sparks erupted. Nina yanked her hand from Nils's and stopped to stare. 'My God, is the place on fire?' she asked.

291

The moment the words were out of her mouth, she and Nils broke into a run, then skidded to a halt when they reached the boat storage area. It wasn't a fire; the fount of sparks was flowing from the flame of a welder's torch. 'Greg?' Nina yelled. 'What are you doing?' At least, she thought it was Greg. Who else would be out here working at this time of night?

She called his name louder, and he straightened up. His face was obscured by a clear safety shield and he wore a pair of fireproof gloves. If this was a horror movie, this would be the moment the serial killer would lunge, snuffing them both.

Instead, he raised his shield and gave her a boyish grin. 'Hey, Nina.' His gaze flicked to Nils and seemed to chill the slightest bit. 'Neil, is it?' he said.

'Nils.'

'Oh, yeah. Sorry. Nils. How's it going?' Greg didn't wait for an answer. 'I'm working on the boat lift.'

'I can see that,' she said. She'd been pestering him to fix it for days. Interesting that he would finally tackle it now. 'Greg, it's ten o'clock at night.'

'I know. I thought I'd be finished before you got back. Didn't want to bother you with all the noise.'

Uh-huh. A likely story. She turned pointedly to Nils. 'Would you like to come up?'

292

Greg fired up his blow torch again with a blue *whoosh* of flame.

'I'd better be going,' Nils said, taking a step back. 'Take care, Nina.'

What about the handholding? she wanted to demand. Instead, she was too startled to do anything but mutter a good-night.

He didn't bother with a token 'I'll call you.' Maybe the sight of a large man with a blow torch was a little off-putting.

'Thanks a million,' she said to Greg, raising her voice above the hissing torch.

'That's okay,' he said, lowering the face shield. 'I'm just about finished here.'

'Indeed you are,' she said, and stomped up the stairs to her place.

\*       \*       \*

The disruption of her date with Nils was one thing. Nina gave Greg the benefit of the doubt—she *had* been nagging him about the boat lift and he *had* fixed it. With opening day nearly upon them, they'd both been working crazy hours. However, a couple of days later, when she went on a picnic with Marty Lewis and then got home to find Greg using the whetstone to sharpen a machete, an ax and a hatchet, she strongly suspected she was starting to see a pattern. After her third date, a movie with Noah Shepherd, the local veterinarian, she was sure of it. Greg greeted her and Noah on the front porch of the main building. He was surrounded by weapons. Nina recognized the antique guns they'd found in the attic.

'Black powder rifles,' he explained jovially. 'They might be collector's items. I was going to see if any of these was operational.'

Noah looked at his mobile phone. 'Got a foaling this weekend. I'd better go check on my patient.'

Nina offered a smile. She suspected the phone's screen was blank. 'Sure, Noah.' He was wildly good-looking in a dark, brooding, Heathcliffian sort of way. He was also down-to-earth and unpretentious, yet much too quiet and circumspect for her, she'd discovered during a strained stop for coffee after the movie. Nina supposed, if she gave it her best effort, she could get him talking. But at this point in her life, she wanted a date, not a project.

Still, she resented the decision being taken away from her by Greg. She gave Noah a hug—it was like hugging a slab of granite—and murmured a good-night.

As he hurried toward his car, she swung back to Greg. 'Congratulations. You're three for three. Maybe even four for four, if we count Shane Gilmore.'

'What do you mean, count him?'

'Technically, it could be traced back to you, since the reason I got so mad at Shane was because the inn was sold to you.'

'Okay, I'm really not following you now.'

She watched the swing of headlights across the parking lot as Noah Shepherd drove away. 'I think that might be a record, even for you. He didn't bother even telling me goodbye.'

Greg smiled at her, all boyish innocence. 'What do you mean, "record"?'

All through Sonnet's growing-up years, Nina had hardly dated at all. Now she was trying to go for it, putting herself out there for the first time in her life. Some were acquaintances she'd known for years. With Noah Shepherd, she had done the asking. He was that good-looking. But so far, the only chemistry she'd experienced was the volatile flare of Greg's black powder. There was something seriously wrong with this picture. To her horror, Nina nearly choked on a ball of tears in her throat. Praying he didn't notice, she turned on her heel and marched down the path to the boathouse. She didn't go home, though. She was too restless for that. She veered toward the dock, pacing its planks in frustration.

Greg followed a minute later. 'I couldn't get any of them to work.'

That was probably for the best. She was in no mood to be anywhere near operational firearms. She took a deep breath, forcing anger to evaporate her tears. 'You're doing this on purpose,' she accused, swinging around to face him.

295

The moon shone from behind him, forming a silver halo around his head. 'Doing what?'

'As if you didn't know. You're not my guardian. I don't need you to wait up for me every time I go out.'

'I'm not waiting up for you,' he said. 'I'm just . . . up.'

'And you just happen to be cleaning guns or sharpening knives or welding something when I get home with my date.'

He chuckled. 'That's totally planned.'

She was taken aback by the admission. She'd been prepared to argue with him. 'Totally planned,' she echoed. 'You mean you intended to be scary?'

'Hell, yes.'

'I don't get it.'

He closed the distance between them, cupped his hands around her upper arms and pulled her against him. The sudden movement stole her breath, and she stared up at him with wide eyes.

A crazy yearning filled her up, and she flashed on all the times in her life that she had imagined this—being in Greg Bellamy's arms. There was a soft shock of recognition, and then he was kissing her, and this was something she'd imagined, too, though the reality was nothing like her dreams. It was so much better that she felt herself grow dizzy with sensation, as if she was being taken somewhere, far away. There was nothing particularly gentle about his touch, yet she had never felt so cherished. His kiss was rough, too, with urgency, with possession—yet she'd never found a kiss more thrilling. It made her forget every other time she'd ever kissed a guy.

This had never happened to her before. She'd never been transported in a man's embrace, and it was like finding the missing piece to an unfinished puzzle. All too soon, it was over and he let her go, stepping back so quickly that she found herself wondering if that amazing kiss had actually happened.

'You're a smart woman, Nina,' he said, heading back to the path. 'You'll figure it out.'

For a few seconds, she was stunned speechless. Then, finally, she found her voice and hurried after him. 'Just a damn minute,' she said. 'You can't do something like that and simply walk away.'

'Agreed,' he said, without even slowing his pace. 'I could sling you over my shoulder like a caveman, take you upstairs and ravish you.'

All of which had an undeniable, devastating appeal to her. Shaken, she said, 'How politically correct of you.'

'You think I care about political correctness?' He didn't seem to want an answer; he gave an angry bark of laughter and kept walking.

'I don't know what you care about, Greg. You're giving me way too much credit,' she said. 'Maybe you think I'm a mind reader, but

I can't figure you out.' She was furious with . . . what? Resentment? Frustrated longing? She could point the finger at him if she liked. She could say he'd ruined her evening more than once. But the sad fact was, her dates were ruined long before the seemingly inevitable, absurd encounters with Greg. Not by him, but by her, with her inability to start with a basic attraction and deepen it into a relationship. She'd never been able to do that with a man, ever. And it wasn't Greg's fault. All he did was hold up a mirror. All he did was kiss her, forcing her to know she'd never come close to knowing what it was like to love a man.

She grabbed his arm, feeling tension hardening his muscles. 'Would you please explain to me what you think is happening here? What you *want* to happen?'

He took a deep breath, and anger glinted in his eyes. 'Look, if we do this—if the evening goes the way I wish like hell it would go—it's going to change things between us. Everything will be different. I don't know about you, but I wouldn't mind a change.'

His candor and intensity nearly undid her. She was still on fire from his kiss. Yet he was offering her a chance to choose. She could keep things as they were, or change everything—right here, right now. He'd opened the door for her to declare that yes, she wanted this, too. Although he didn't know it, she had wanted this practically from the first moment they'd met, years ago. A moment he probably didn't even remember.

The temptation was almost more than she could bear. A daring little voice inside her whispered, why not try it with him, see where it went?

Because the stakes were too high with Greg. He wasn't some guy taking her bowling or to the movies. He was the guy she worked for. The guy she knew she wouldn't be able to survive losing—so it was safer to simply back away.

She had to wrestle to find her willpower, and finally forced herself to brush past him. 'Good night, Greg. I'll see you in the morning.'

\*       \*       \*

'Wait a minute. Let me get this straight.' Jenny studied Nina's face. They were in Zuzu's Petals, shopping for a dress for Nina to wear on opening day at the inn. 'He propositioned you?'

'He was pretty explicit, assuming ravish means what I think it means,' Nina admitted.

'He said ravish? Do people even say ravish anymore?'

'People said ravish last night.'

Jenny gave a pleased little shiver. 'And here I thought it was something that only happened in old-fashioned Gothic novels. So how was it?'

Nina laughed. 'You're kidding, right? You think I went for it?'

Jenny's eyes widened. 'You mean, you didn't?'

'I'm not getting involved with Greg Bellamy. Not even if I get to discover the meaning of ravish with him. He's the enemy,' she reminded Jenny.

'Because he bought the Inn at Willow Lake.'

'Exactly.' She took an apple-green dress from the rack and held it under her chin.

Jenny took the dress and put it back. 'I think it's good he did that. He's taking on all the risk. It's no picnic, owning a business.'

Jenny would know, reflected Nina. She'd been co-owner and then sole owner of the Sky River Bakery ever since she was a teenager. She endured hard times and uncertainty, knowing she had no safety net.

'I realize that,' Nina said. 'But he took away my chance to succeed, along with my risk of failure.'

'You know what I think? I think the ownership of the inn has nothing to do with it. I think what you're really worried about is falling for Greg.'

'Falling for—' Nina gave a little bark of disbelief. 'And why should I worry about that? He's the last person I want to fall for. For that matter, why should I fall for anyone? I've been going on dates, having the adolescence I missed out on.'

'And how's that working for you?'

'Very funny, Doctor Phil.'

Jenny handed her a form-fitting dress in peach jersey. 'Believe me—and you know this better than I do—adolescence isn't all it's cracked up to be.' She grabbed a few more dresses and marched Nina into the dressing room.

'Greg's got kids,' Nina said, changing into one of the dresses. 'And a grandbaby soon.'

'Do you have anything against kids and grandkids?'

'No. But I'm done with that.'

Jenny lifted one eyebrow. 'You did a fabulous job with Sonnet. You could easily do it again.'

'Easily? Yeah, right. Half the time, I was scared to death I was doing something wrong. It was like being on a tightrope over a swamp full of alligators. Why would I sign on for more?'

'Because you're good with alligators.'

'This is a big leap from talking about dating him to talking about forever,' Nina said. She stepped out and posed in front of the mirror. She had to admit, Jenny had a good eye. The dress was a winner, businesslike without being boring.

'Could you date him with no commitment?'

'I work with him, end of story.'

'Sounds as if you've made up your mind, then.'

Nina ended up buying the peach dress with a three-quarter-sleeve sweater. Jenny beamed at her. 'You'll be dazzling.'

'It's the inn that needs to dazzle.'

'You seem nervous to me,' Jenny observed. 'You always twirl your hair around your finger when you're nervous.'

Nina lowered her hand. 'Do I? I suppose I am nervous. When you think about it, a grand opening is all about being accepted or rejected. And I've never been good with rejection.'

'Is that why you never go on second dates? Is that why you don't want to consider dating Greg?'

Nina started to twirl her hair again, but caught herself. 'Cut it out. All this shopping made me hungry.'

They walked down the block to the bakery. It was mid-afternoon, and the place wasn't busy. As they were helping themselves to kolaches, Laura Tuttle came backward through the swinging doors, wheeling a cart with a lofty wedding cake on it. 'Another day, another cake,' she said.

'That one is stunning,' Nina said. When she and Jenny were little, they used to watch, mesmerized, as Laura created fondant icing, sugar-dough flowers and leaves, turning humble ingredients into magnificent confections of culinary architecture. Naturally in planning their fantasy weddings, Nina and Jenny had debated long and hard about the cake, arguing tradition versus innovation. As adults, neither had had a cake after all, what with Jenny stealing off to St. Croix in the middle of winter to get married, and Nina not marrying at all.

'Thanks,' Laura said. 'The old broad's learning some new tricks.'

'Don't be calling yourself an old broad,' Jenny said. She turned to Nina. 'She's dating my father, you know. She's dating Philip Bellamy.'

'Nonsense,' Laura scolded. 'We're just two friends catching up on old times.'

'Yeah,' Jenny said with a wink. 'Sure.'

'Aren't happily married people annoying?' Nina said to Laura.

'Tell me about it.' Laura rolled her eyes.

Yet Nina didn't fail to notice the blush that lit Laura's cheeks. She didn't pry, though. Especially not in front of Jenny. Philip Bellamy and Jenny were not your typical father and daughter. The two of them were still finding their way toward one another.

'I wish you'd let yourself go for it,' Jenny said to Laura. 'You and Philip have known each other since you were teenagers. Is it possible to know someone that long and still not be sure?'

Oh, yes, Nina conceded. Definitely. It was possible to live a whole alternative life.

Jenny gazed in admiration at the wedding cake. 'I knew I was meant to be with Rourke the minute I saw him, and we were just kids. It's just crazy that it took us so long to wake up and figure it out.'

'Some people are lucky enough to find what they're looking for the first time around,' Laura said. 'Others . . .'

Her voice trailed off, but Nina recalled something Greg had said to her. 'Life gives you lots of chances to screw up.'

'Which means you have just as many chances to get it right,' Jenny reminded her.

## SEVENTEEN

'You're nervous.' Greg's statement was decidedly accusatory.

'Don't be silly,' Nina assured him. 'I'm not the least bit nervous.'

He stared pointedly at her finger, twirling a curl of hair at the nape of her neck. Good lord. Was she that obvious?

'Right,' he said. 'Not nervous. Got it.'

'So I'm nervous. Whatever. So sue me.'

On the official opening day at the inn, everything was finally ready—painted, freshened, furnished, buffed and polished. Flower arrangements from a local grower graced the tables and fireplace mantels. Becky Murray, a local musician, was playing the harp like a seraphim. The muted notes shimmered through the salon, creating an air of elegance and luxury. The staff was discreetly going about their duties. Bone-china trays of treats from the Sky River Bakery had been set out on an antique table, along with a silver samovar of iced tea. Nina and Greg were ready at the registration desk while the housekeeping and support staff were nearly invisible in the background. Everyone was awaiting the arrival of the first guests. Some waited with more nervousness than others.

Part of the reason for her nerves was standing next to her in a gorgeously tailored sport coat—not too formal, but dressy enough to show this day meant something to him. He smelled of some delicious cologne and seemed so at ease in the luxurious setting, while Nina was having second thoughts about her new sundress. She was having second thoughts about everything. Ever since he'd kissed her, she felt as though aliens had possessed her body. She was no longer in control. All Greg had to do was walk into the room and her panties fell off. She fantasized about him constantly. Once, to her horror, she'd caught herself unconsciously doodling his name on hotel stationery.

To his credit, he was a gentleman about the encounter. He hadn't said anything, hadn't pushed the issue. Nina tried to put it behind her. She kept telling herself it was no big deal. He'd kissed her, and she'd brushed him off—

305

not because she didn't like him but because she liked him too much. He'd claimed he wanted their relationship to change, but he hadn't said what he expected it to change into. Nina figured they were better off leaving that stone unturned.

Greg seemed mercifully oblivious to her thoughts. 'Everything is going to be fine. Better than fine. Today's going to be a kick in the ass.'

'I know that's what I look for when I go on vacation,' she murmured. Yet when he smiled at her, she felt that now-familiar melting sensation, and knew he was right—everything *would* be fine. His supreme self-confidence was infectious. People were going to walk through that door, take one look at this tall, smiling, incredibly handsome man and know they'd chosen the right spot for their holiday. How could they not?

'Welcome to Fantasy Island,' she murmured in a fake Spanish accent.

'What's that?'

'Um, nothing.' Nina had initially expected this whole process to be hard for him. She'd expected him to wave a white flag of surrender, declaring that he'd made a terrible mistake, that he didn't want the inn after all. Now she conceded that he'd done a fantastic job with the place. He had a natural air of calm and the respect of everyone who worked for him—including her. Somehow, he had orchestrated the opening of the Inn at Willow Lake with amazing precision.

This was problematic. He was supposed to fail and go away.

There was still a lot of summer left, she reminded herself. Plenty of opportunities for Greg to learn he didn't belong here, that he was better off designing golf courses or mall layouts. The arriving guests could very well change everything. People were fickle, unreasonable, hard to please. They'd wear him down by summer's end. She could afford to be pleased for him—for them all—today.

She glanced at the card Sonnet had sent her—*Good luck, Mom*—that Nina had propped on the desk under the reception counter, and her nervousness slipped away. The card depicted a romanticized drawing of Casteau, the little town of cobblestone streets and ancient churches where Sonnet now lived with her father and his family.

'I guess you miss her a lot,' Greg said.

She nodded, startled by his scrutiny. 'It feels a little funny that she's not here for this. She's been present for every big moment of my life, even my high school graduation. Then there was college graduation, my swearing-in as mayor, everything.' Nina sighed and touched the card.

'So this is a big moment for you,' he said.

'Absolutely.' Why pretend otherwise?

For some reason that made him smile. 'Me,

307

too.'

A sound drifted through the open window—the thud of car doors slamming, and voices approaching. Greg squared his shoulders as the first guests came through the door. 'Welcome to the Inn at Willow Lake,' he said.

They were the Morgans, a couple from the city, an effusive woman named Sadie and her husband Nate, who was quiet and indulgent. Nina checked them in and Walter showed them to their room. Within the next couple of hours, they welcomed a variety of guests—a dating pair from Buffalo who had won the Web-based promotional contest for a free stay. There was a young woman named Kimberly Van Dorn, traveling alone, who was so stunningly gorgeous that Nina stopped what she was doing to stare. Not that Kimberly Van Dorn noticed, of course. She saved all her attention for Greg, managing to slip certain key facts into the conversation—she had attended Camp Kioga as a girl, and she was newly divorced.

Greg took it in stride, assuring Ms. Van Dorn that her stay would be relaxing, a chance to escape the everyday demands of life.

She barely looked old enough to have been married for any amount of time. She was tall as an Amazon, with Katharine Hepburn cheekbones and a swimsuit-model figure, cascades of red hair, and—probably most attractive of all to the men present—she drove a fancy sports car and had brought along a set of golf clubs. Amazing. Here was every man's fantasy all in one shiny, revved-up package.

Yet Greg treated her the same as any other guest as he handed her a room key and sent her and her designer luggage off with Walter.

'Welcome to the Inn at Willow Lake,' he said to the next party of guests.

'Gayle, hi.' Nina was happy to see a familiar face. Gayle had been her assistant when she was mayor. She turned to Greg. 'This is Gayle Wright, and her husband, Adam.'

'We own the Windy Ridge Flower Farm.' Gayle surveyed the salon. 'The flowers look fantastic in here.'

Nina had ordered weekly service from Gayle and Adam. Gayle was a genius at arrangements. Instead of the usual jungle of flowers in a giant urn, she'd created single-variety arrangements in clear vases, grouping them on pedestals of varying heights around the salon. 'You get the credit for that,' Nina assured her.

Gayle beamed. 'I wish the kids—'

'No, you don't,' Adam interrupted, then addressed Nina. 'This is the first time we'll both be away from them overnight.'

'All three of them are at my mother's,' Gayle said.

'And they're fine,' Adam assured her.

Nina observed them, feeling a peculiar warmth build inside her heart. She'd gone all through school with Gayle, a quiet, heavyset girl with lanky brown hair and horn-rimmed glasses. As an adult, Gayle had changed very little, yet when she was with her husband, she glowed from within. Being in love really did make a person beautiful. It was a magical phenomenon in that way. When you looked at a couple like Gayle and Adam, you saw something that was invisible, yet as tangible and real as the earth itself. That was the way love was supposed to be. That was what Nina wanted for Sonnet one day. Okay, it was what she wanted for herself. Maybe she was crazy for still believing it was possible.

It was the inn, she thought, and this romantic atmosphere they had worked so hard to achieve. Good lord, it was working, even on her.

'Is this a special occasion for you guys?' she asked.

A light flickered and dimmed in Gayle's eyes. She pressed her lips together, nodded. Her hand found her husband's. 'Adam's National Guard unit is being deployed.' Her voice wavered over the announcement. 'He's leaving next week.'

Nina felt a chill touch her spine, but she kept her smile in place. 'We'll make this weekend extra special for you,' she promised. The chill lingered as she watched them go, and it occurred to Nina that even true love had its down side—the hurt that came from separation, the fear of danger.

As the Wrights made their way to their room, Greg was already speaking with the next couple—Jack Daly and Sarah Moon, from Chicago. They were young and prosperous-looking, perhaps a little subdued.

'Any special occasion for you?' Greg asked.

The couple exchanged a smile, tinged with irony. Jack was slender and attractive, with close-cropped hair and the spare, athletic look reminiscent of Lance Armstrong. 'Yeah, actually, it is,' he said, but he didn't elaborate; he scooped the keys off the desk and headed for the stairs.

His wife, Sarah Moon, finished signing the registry book with a flourish. She had a quiet beauty that radiated from her smile, which she used to deflect her husband's brusqueness. 'I'm glad we're staying a whole week,' she said. 'We need the time.'

Nina and Greg exchanged a glance as the couple headed for their lakeview suite. 'I wonder what that was all about,' she murmured.

'None of our business,' he reminded her.

She sniffed. 'You're no fun.'

He laughed softly. 'I'm tons of fun. You just haven't given me a chance yet.'

'A chance at what?'

'Don't pretend you don't know.' The phone rang, and he answered it, never taking his eyes off her.

311

Saved by the bell. She pretended to forget their conversation as she busied herself with other things, and stayed busy the rest of the afternoon and well into the evening. She enjoyed every minute of it, as she'd known she would. She liked orchestrating the guests, making sure they had not just everything they needed, but things they didn't know they wanted—like a crisp linen mat on the floor by the bed at turndown time, accompanied by a soft pair of spa scuffs.

By the time they had everyone checked in and finished up for the night, it was nearly 10:00 p.m.

'Wow,' said Greg, looking around the salon. 'That was amazing.'

'Good amazing or bad amazing?' she asked.

'Just . . . amazing.'

She grabbed her bag from a cabinet under the counter. 'And just think, you get to do it all over again tomorrow.'

'I can't wait.'

'Good night, Greg.' She made a hasty exit, not eager to linger with him in the dim, flower-decked salon. She walked alone down the lighted path to the boathouse. Out on the dock, a couple stood holding each other in an embrace while a silver mist of moonlight played upon the water. There was something compelling about the way they clung to each other, and Nina looked away, loathe to intrude on their privacy. She smiled, because that was

312

exactly what she wanted for the guests of the inn—romantic moments of searing intimacy, a chance for people to connect or renew bonds that had grown weak or ragged with the demands of everyday life.

Yet on the heels of Nina's satisfaction came a peculiar restlessness. She stole one more look at the couple on the dock. They were kissing now, lost in each other. And without warning, Nina was pierced by a loneliness so deep that she shook with it.

Snap out of it, she chided herself, climbing the stairs to her place. Not everyone got to fall in love. And that wasn't such a bad thing. Love tended to complicate matters and so often, it ended badly. It wasn't something she wanted or needed in her life at this point. She'd done just fine without it for a very long time.

At this hour, she didn't feel just fine. She wasn't sure what she felt like. She wasn't hungry, although she'd skipped dinner. It was too late to call Jenny and talk about her day. In Belgium, it was not quite dawn, and Sonnet would probably be sound asleep.

Within minutes, the phone rang, and Nina snatched it up. Problems with the guests already? 'This is Nina,' she said in a clipped voice.

'Hey, Mom.'

'Sonnet! Good lord, what are you doing up at this hour?'

'I got up especially to call you, see how

313

things went today.'

Nina smiled and wandered out to the deck. 'It was great, honey. I wish you'd been there.'

'Me, too. So, how's it going with Mr. Bellamy?'

Nina's grip tightened on the handset. Did Sonnet know? 'Never mind me,' she said. 'You're in Europe. Let's talk about that.'

'Whoa, you totally evaded my question. Nice, Mom.'

'I didn't evade. I simply don't want to bore you.'

'So are you getting along?' Sonnet persisted.

Yes.

'Is he driving you nuts?'

Yes.

'Are you—'

'It's business, all right? His business, and I work for him. The inn had its grand opening and everything went really well.' She saw the flash of a camera in the distance. Looking across the lawn, she spotted Daisy, easily picking her out by her very pregnant silhouette, outlined by the path lights. Daisy was with a tall, long-haired boy, walking down by the lakeshore, taking pictures. 'Daisy has a new friend,' she told Sonnet, welcoming the diversion. 'He's Connor Davis's younger brother.'

'Way ahead of you, Mom,' Sonnet said. 'Daisy already e-mailed me pictures. He's a complete hottie but Daisy claims they're just

314

friends. For the time being, anyway.'

Nina watched them for a moment, their shadows fused into one that lay huge upon the sloping lawn. Their heads were inclined together as they talked. 'Just friends,' she agreed. That was all they could be, under the circumstances. Watching them, she remembered being young and pregnant, missing out on the chance to date and stay out late and do stupid, irresponsible things. By the age of fifteen, she'd done more than her share.

'Mom?' Sonnet prodded. 'You got quiet on me there.'

'Oh. Sorry. Bad connection. How was Wiesbaden?'

'Incredible. Except Kara and Layla whined the whole time we were at the castle, because they were bored.' When Sonnet spoke of her two younger half sisters, her tone changed to one of exasperation. 'I swear, sometimes I just want to smack them.'

'In my family, we just went ahead and did that.'

'Did it work?'

'Temporarily.'

'Then I might have to try it.'

Nina laughed. 'But other than that, everything's okay?'

'Totally.'

'I mentioned to Greg that you'll be seeing Daisy's mom when you go to The Hague. I figured he should know. He's fine with it, of course. Even encouraged you to contact her. Although that doesn't matter. What matters is you—'

'Mom.'

'I mean, she's the obvious person to show you around, since she's a local there, and works at the ICC—'

'You're babbling.'

'Oh. Sorry. Long day, I guess. I'm keyed up.'

'I don't blame you. I'm excited for you. And I miss you. I miss home.'

'Everybody misses you.' She felt a squeezing sensation in her chest. Of everything in Nina's life, Sonnet was her one true thing. Without her, there was nothing to mask Nina's desperate loneliness.

'But I need to go now.'

'I know, honey. I can't believe you got up so early just to call me. You're the best.'

'I just wanted to be the first to say congrats again on the opening. I'll see you before you know it,' Sonnet said.

'Can't wait.' Nina turned off the phone and sighed, leaning against the railing of the deck. The hotel grounds were empty now. Daisy and Julian had gone somewhere else. In the silence following the phone call, she felt a tug of yearning for her daughter. Sonnet was coming back for the Bellamy wedding. Nina couldn't wait to see her again, and she refused to think about the fact that Sonnet would be leaving for college right after the wedding.

She took a deep breath of the sweet night air and reminded herself that she had to get up early tomorrow. She ought to go to bed. Wandering inside, she discovered that she was too restless, so she opted for putting a Tony Bennett CD on the stereo and pouring a glass of wine. Then she wandered back outside, drawn by the cool stillness of the night. Sipping her wine, she swayed gently to 'Because of You,' drifting softly through the screen door. This was more like it, she thought, feeling her nerves uncoil, massaged by the music and the wine. She didn't need anyone or anything except this—a pleasantly cheesy song, a glass of merlot, a little peace and quiet to savor the victory of a day that had gone well.

The quiet lasted maybe thirty seconds. Then she heard footsteps on the stairs. The motion-activated security light flickered on.

'Greg,' she said, feeling a hard-to-deny quiver of reaction. 'What's the matter?'

'Nothing,' he said, stepping onto the deck.

'Daisy?' she asked, unconvinced that 'nothing' had brought him here.

'She and Julian are on the computer, working with some pictures she took.'

They stood awkwardly for a moment. Tony Bennett warbled 'Love Look Away.' Nina had no idea what to make of this visit. Nothing was the matter, and he'd come to see her. He glanced at her wineglass. 'Drinking alone?'

'I think today warrants a glass of wine. And

I was just on the phone with Sonnet.'

'I'm not sure that counts.' He glanced around. 'You look pretty alone to me.'

She scowled at him. 'You don't have to rub it in.'

'I'm not. I'm alone, too,' he pointed out.

She nodded. 'So have you heard from Max? How was his trip to Holland?' Accompanied by his grandparents, he'd gone to see his mother. Nina sensed that Greg had mixed feelings about his son being away, because she had been experiencing the same thing with Sonnet, all summer long. On the one hand, the freedom from moment-to-moment responsibility was exhilarating; on the other hand, the child's absence left a hollow spot where doubts had a way of flourishing.

'His trip was fine, and we talk every day,' he said. 'We talk, but I have no idea how he's doing. He says he didn't mind the overseas flight. Sophie's parents are great with him.'

'How long will he be away?'

'A couple of weeks. I hate to see him miss his Little League practices and games, but I guess it's more important for him to spend time with his mother.'

It was, she knew, the age-old dilemma of a divorced couple. She didn't envy him.

'Max seems to handle this well enough, but there are definitely times when I know he's completely messed up about the divorce and I feel like shit.' Greg's candor was disarming.

'He is a typical kid,' she assured him. 'Everybody has their ups and downs.' It sounded like an empty platitude, though. For a child of divorce, life could be complicated. For Max, visiting his mother entailed an intricate journey and precise scheduling, a lining up of helpful adult relatives.

'When we first split,' Greg said, 'Sophie thought both kids would move overseas with her. She had a school all picked out, a house . . . but they had trouble right away and the kids begged to live in the States. They chose this town, this life. I don't pretend it was me personally. Given the way things worked out for Daisy, I sort of wish—'

'Don't,' Nina advised. 'That's completely pointless.'

'I just hate the thought that I've made a mistake, let them down. Max has kind of gotten lost in all the drama about Daisy. In a lot of ways, he's a typical kid—all boy, all mischief, all the time. Some days, he seems happy, having this idyllic small-town boyhood—the lake, the ball field, the family summer camp up the road. Other days, he acts as though being here is torture.'

'Which is why you should be fine with letting him visit his mother.'

'Yeah, good point.'

'So listen, can I get you—'

'I hope you don't mind—'

They both spoke at once, then both stopped.

Greg laughed. 'After today, I was just too wired to sit still, so I thought I'd pay you a visit.'

She was ridiculously pleased to hear it. 'I admit, I'm a bit keyed up, too. Would you like a glass of wine? Or I have beer.' She bit her lip. Beer was so unsophisticated. She shouldn't have mentioned it. She always felt so outclassed by Greg. She wondered if he noticed.

'Thanks. A beer would be great.'

She hurried inside and opened a longneck bottle of microbrew. At least it was a boutique beer. 'Would you like a glass?' she called.

'Straight from the bottle's fine.'

Nina Romano, what the heck are you doing? she asked herself. Then she stifled the little voice in her head. She brought him the beer, angled her wineglass in his direction. 'To a great start for the inn.'

'I'll drink to that,' he said. 'We did great today, both of us.'

Nina felt an odd tension between pleasure and disappointment. 'So all the hard work was worth it.'

'Yep.'

'You didn't ever feel like giving up?'

'Before the place opened? No way,' he said.

'Suppose you get tired of all the work and hassle.'

He gave a soft, velvety chuckle, which she found far too appealing. 'Not an option,' he said simply, and took another swig of beer.

'What, you expect me to pick up my toys and go home? I'm not a quitter. I had every advantage growing up but it didn't spoil me. I like to work. I don't shy away from things just because they're hard. And you worked damn hard for this place. Why would you expect me to bail?'

Observing him these past few weeks, she recognized that giving up was not his way. He was hard-wired for success, no matter what he did. Maybe that was why he took his divorce so hard, she speculated. Maybe one day, she'd ask him about that. No, she thought. That was far too personal. This—her relationship with Greg—was about the inn, a business enterprise. She reminded herself to focus on that. She imagined their guests comfortably ensconced in rooms where she'd sweated every detail, from the fresh rose in the bud vase at the bedside table to the thick terry robes and shea butter soaps. In their advertising literature, they promised 'uncommon luxury,' and Nina meant to give it to them.

'Well,' he said, finishing his beer, 'I'd better get going.'

'See you tomorrow.'

'Yeah, listen, about tomorrow night—I thought maybe we could go to dinner.'

'You mean like a date?' Nina was incredulous. She thought their kiss had been a fluke. A crazy impulse. She thought they'd gotten past it and moved on.

'No. I mean, yeah. A date, whatever. A date between friends.'

'I can't date you, Greg,' she said, surprised at the sharpness of the regret she felt.

'Why not?'

The regret deepened. She wondered if it was possible to forget about business and rivalry, forget the fact that he was a Bellamy and simply enjoy his company.

'I just . . . can't,' she said. 'It's a bad idea, any way you look at it. We talked about this before.'

'No, we didn't. I kissed you and you spent the next week pretending it didn't happen and refusing to talk about it.'

Ouch, she thought. 'All right, suppose we hit it off. Suppose we want to keep seeing each other.'

'Then it will be really easy,' he assured her, 'since we both live on the premises.'

She shuddered—with excitement? Nervousness? She couldn't be sure. 'Think about it. How much would it suck to work together after we've broken up?'

At that, he laughed aloud. 'We're not even dating and you've already got us broken up.'

'I just like to think things through to their logical conclusion.'

'And the logical conclusion to the two of us dating is that eventually we'll wind up at each other's throats.'

'Are you making fun of me?'

'Nah. Just trying to figure out the way your mind works.'

No one had ever bothered to do that before. She wasn't sure she liked it. She was in danger of letting Greg own her heart as well as her career. And because she had always taken care of herself, the idea of giving so much to a man scared her.

'Tell you what,' he said. 'How about we go to dinner tomorrow and just see how it turns out.'

'Maybe I already have a date,' she said suddenly.

Though it was too dark to see his face, she could see his shoulders stiffen. 'Maybe you do? What, did you just remember it?'

Actually, it was a standing offer—Nils had said there would always be a lane for her at the bowling alley on couples night.

'I do,' she said decisively. 'I've got a date.'

'You could've told me that when I brought it up and spared us this whole conversation.'

'You caught me off guard,' she admitted.

'Right,' he said, heading toward the stairs. 'You're never off guard, Nina.'


## EIGHTEEN

Running the inn was everything Nina expected it to be—exciting, frustrating, challenging,

323

rewarding. It was also as close to her dream as she had ever been. She loved the ever-changing array of visitors, from an elderly couple who remembered their courtship days here to newlyweds on a honeymoon. She also appreciated that the work kept her as busy as she cared to be, certainly too busy to be preoccupied with thoughts of Greg Bellamy. For whole days at a time, she managed to coexist with him while avoiding any further discussion of personal matters.

At breakfast, Sarah Moon had requested some maps and an area guide. Spying Sarah and her husband, Jack, on the lawn overlooking the lake, Nina decided to deliver them in person.

They were an incredibly good-looking couple. Jack seemed filled with a brash, almost cocky, self-confidence. Sarah was lovely and quiet, a dreamy sort who didn't—at least on the surface—seem like a match for her husband. Maybe they complemented each other, Nina speculated. She seemed to have discovered in herself an inordinate interest in couples, and she refused to ponder the reason for that.

Jack was dressed for tennis and talking on a mobile phone while Sarah relaxed in an Adirondack chair, drawing or writing in an oversize spiral-bound book. Nina handed her the brochures and maps of Ulster County and the Catskills Wilderness. 'I highlighted a few

324

suggestions,' she said.

Sarah beamed at her. 'That's so nice of you. We're really enjoying our stay.'

Jack had moved away to continue his phone conversation. To Nina, it seemed borderline rude, but Sarah smiled indulgently. 'He never stops. Just can't seem to get away from work, poor guy.'

'Is he some kind of doctor?' Nina asked. She figured saving humanity was worth a few minutes of a man's vacation.

'Building contractor,' Sarah said. 'He's doing this luxury-home development outside Chicago called Shamrock Downs. Equestrian community—it's a real juggling act, dealing with all the subcontractors.'

A few minutes later, he flipped his phone shut and offered a smile that made Nina blink. His long-lashed eyes were as bright as the sky. 'Sorry. Had to take that call.'

All right, so he was *that* guy, Nina conceded. The hunky, charismatic guy who knew how to use his assets to advantage. Even she was going soft, watching him turn on the charm.

'Maps,' Sarah said, waving them at him. 'We can go to a state park or a flea market or . . . wow, are we really that close to the original Woodstock?'

'The one and only,' Nina assured her. 'There's not much to see, but the town's fun.'

'We'll go this afternoon if you want,' Jack said. 'I've got a tennis match set up this

325

morning. Right now, in fact.'

He'd paired himself with another guest. Kimberly Van Dorn stood at the top of the lawn, waving at him. In crisp tennis whites, she looked like the embodiment of every man's dream and every woman's nightmare—long, silky red hair caught in a high ponytail, big boobs, supermodel legs.

Nina glanced nervously at Sarah, but she smiled up at her husband with a complete lack of concern about his choice of tennis partner. 'Have fun—but don't overdo.'

'I always overdo,' he said with a grin. 'Isn't that the point?'

She laughed. 'Sure, Ace. Give the poor woman a drubbing.'

He loped toward Kimberly like an obedient Doberman. Sarah was absorbed in her book again, sketching studiously with a Pantone marker. Nina was impressed by Sarah's ease with the situation. Either the marriage was so solid, she didn't care who her husband played tennis with, or she was clueless.

'You're not into tennis?' Nina asked.

'Athletics isn't my thing. Jack lives for sports, though. I'm just so happy to see him doing something he loves . . . He can play with Paris Hilton, for all I care.'

'Oh, I didn't mean—'

'I know you didn't.' Sarah laughed again. 'It's probably hard to believe, but not so long ago, we weren't sure Jack would even be

326

around to play tennis at all.' She paused, then said, 'The fact is, he just finished treatment for cancer.'

'I'm so sorry—I didn't know.'

'He'd be delighted to hear that. He hated looking like a patient.'

Nina turned to watch him holding open the gate to the tennis court. 'He definitely doesn't look like a patient.'

Sarah beamed at him. 'This is our first vacation since before he was diagnosed. We came here to get to know one another again, post-treatment. Away from all the hospitals and labs and doctor visits.' Her smile was a thousand watts strong. 'We really want to reconnect as a couple.'

So why was the husband off playing tennis? Nina didn't allow herself to ask. This was simply further proof that she wasn't cut out for relationships. She tended to read them all wrong.

'You picked a beautiful place to reconnect,' she said, indicating the brochures. She directed Sarah to the most scenic drives and the best shopping in the area. 'In Phoenicia, you don't want to miss the Mystery Spot— the most amazing collection of antiques and ephemera I've ever seen. If you like going out to breakfast, try the pancakes there, at Sweet Sue's. However, I'm biased toward Avalon. There's plenty to do right here. Be sure to hit the Camelot Bookstore. The Apple Tree Inn is best for fine dining. And the Sky River Bakery is probably the best in the state—maybe the whole country.'

'Thanks. You're a walking chamber of commerce.'

'I was the mayor for four years,' Nina explained. 'Assistant to the mayor before that.'

'You're kidding. That's really impressive.'

'It's a small town with a salary to match,' Nina said. 'People weren't exactly beating a path to the door of the mayor's office. But it was a stable job, and I needed that while my daughter was in high school.'

Sarah gave a short laugh. 'Now I'm completely intrigued. You have a daughter in high school?'

'Not anymore. She graduated in May.'

'You look like you're just out of high school.'

'Sonnet's off to college at the end of summer, and I'm facing an empty nest.' Nina wondered if saying so would ever get easier. 'It's not that I'm not completely happy for her. She's all about study and travel. She's living a life I never did.'

'What, the travel? The studies? You could be doing that now. It's not too late.'

'The funny thing is, I didn't have to go anywhere in order to figure out that the life I want is right here.'

'Well, you're lucky. Sometimes people feel like strangers in their own lives.'

Nina suspected Sarah was directing the comment at herself. 'Can I see what you're drawing?'

Sarah turned the sketchbook toward her.

Nina was impressed. The pictures were cartoons, but somehow Sarah had managed to express an array of human emotions through the stylized, comical figures. 'Ever read a comic strip called "Just Breathe" with Lulu and Shirl?' Sarah asked.

'Lulu and Shirl? They're in the *Avalon Troubadour* every day.' The characters were a quirky mother and daughter, a long-time divorcee and a younger woman whose marriage was teetering on the verge of failure. 'You mean you're the creator of Lulu and Shirl? I've never met a cartoonist before.'

'I told Jack I didn't care where we went for our getaway, but it had to be in a place where the local paper carried my strip. I found the Inn at Willow Lake on the web in a search for romantic hotels. Romantic hotels in towns where "Just Breathe" is available. That definitely narrowed down the options. The website is beautiful, by the way.'

'I think so, too,' Nina agreed. 'The photography was all done by the owner's daughter.'

'She's very talented.'

'She'll be thrilled to hear that, especially from a fellow artist.' Nina made a mental note to pass on the compliment. She knew from experience that a girl in Daisy's position needed all the positive reinforcement she could get.

'So are you working on your comic strip?' Nina asked Sarah.

'Sort of. I'm doing some preplanning for a future storyline, so it doesn't feel like work.' She flipped a page of the sketchbook and turned it toward Nina again. The character known as Shirl was studying a pregnancy-test stick, a cross-eyed look of intense concentration and hope on her face.

'I'm praying life will imitate art,' Sarah explained. 'Jack and I both want children so badly, and . . . well, the sooner the better. After his illness, it hit me that the future's so uncertain. We shouldn't put off something we want. Now, hold still and I'll make a sketch for you.'

'Really? Thanks.' Nina thought about Sarah's unquestioning devotion to her husband. Maybe this was Nina's trouble with relationships. She wanted everything just so. She not only wanted those long-lashed eyes, she wanted them trained on her and her alone. She probably wanted something—someone— who didn't exist. Maybe it was better that way. If she wanted someone who didn't exist, she wouldn't waste her time looking.

Which was one of the more pathetic notions she'd had. She was supposed to be living the single life, dating, being carefree, going out with friends.

Watching Sarah draw, Nina wondered what it would be like to yearn for a child with such fervor. Although Nina had the unasked-for gift of a daughter, she didn't know what it was like to hope and plan and ache for a baby.

Sarah Moon was a reminder to Nina that life's journey could include overwhelming hardships, and that love wasn't always easy. Sometimes there were terrible things like a cancer diagnosis or infertility. Still, it was clear that facing trouble with someone you love made the burdens bearable and the joys sweeter. Too bad her husband was an ass, Nina thought. Then she felt guilty for her cynicism.

Sarah finished the sketch. Even though it was a caricature, it made Nina look smart and good-humored, and she felt guilty for her critical thoughts about Sarah's husband. 'This is fantastic,' she said. 'And you put the inn in the background. It's a wonderful keepsake, Sarah.'

'Then I insist that you keep it.' She signed it with a flourish and ripped it out of the book.

'I'm getting this framed,' Nina promised her.

Sarah gathered up the maps and area guides. 'I'm flattered. And I'm glad we found this place. This feels like another world.'

'I've always thought so. It's always felt like *my* world.'

'So have you lived here long?' she asked.

331

'Every minute of my life—so far. I don't ever want to live anywhere else.'

'Well, I don't blame you. I woke up this morning and thought to myself, what a great place to get pregnant. And then of course, Jack was gone on his morning run, so I don't think he had the same thought.'

'I can safely say, no guy in the history of the world ever had that thought,' Nina assured her.

## NINETEEN

Daisy was taking photographs of Camp Kioga. It didn't even feel like an actual job, yet it was. Olivia and Connor had been so impressed with her portfolio of pictures of the Inn at Willow Lake that they'd hired her to photograph the camp. Within the next year, they planned to reopen the place as a family resort. Her job was to capture its wild splendor, covering two hundred acres of pristine lakeshore wilderness, with networks of trails through mountains and streams.

Julian had accompanied her, carrying the big duffel bag of gear she needed for the shoot. They had walked up a path to Meerskill Falls, which sprang from the depths of the mountain, crashing down to a fern-fringed pool. She took close-ups of the dewy rhododendron blossoms, made a long exposure of the flume pouring down past the rocks and framed a wide-angle shot of the old concrete bridge that spanned the waterfall.

The full summer foliage obscured the trail leading to the top of the mountain and the myriad caves gouged into the striated rock. They were ice caves, so cold in their depths that they never thawed. Last winter, she and her friends had made a sinister discovery in one of the caves, evidence of an old, old tragedy. Even now, in the lush heat of summer, she felt a chill at the memory of it.

'You all right?' Julian asked.

Daisy gave herself a mental shake. 'Sure. I'm done here.' She straightened up. The motion caused a sharp twinge in the small of her back.

'Really all right?' Julian asked again.

'Yeah. I'm so tired of being pregnant, sometimes I just want to scream.'

'So go ahead and scream.'

'It won't help. Believe me, I've tried it.' She put the lens cap back on the camera. 'Sorry, I'm whining. Just tired, I guess.' They headed down the trail together. Julian had been such a good friend to her this summer, just as he had the summer before. Did he know how much she'd learned from him, about being self-reliant and in control? Did he realize that even though she was massively pregnant, she still had a crush on him? She wasn't going to do anything about it, though. The friendship meant too much to her, and trying to turn it into something more, especially at this point in her life, would probably cause her to lose him entirely.

She couldn't afford that. With Sonnet gone for the summer, she needed someone to talk to, someone she trusted. 'I've decided,' she said after a while. 'You know, the thing we talked about before.'

'You want to move away.'

She nodded. 'Not right now. But . . . soon. Maybe when the baby's a few months old. I haven't told my parents yet.'

'Why not?'

'Oh, boy. If you knew my dad, you'd know why.'

'He's not going to want you to go.'

'Exactly. See, I never meant to stick around after high school. I mean, how lame is that, living at home?'

'Not lame at all, with what you have going on.'

'Maybe so, but I need to know I've got somewhere to go with my life instead of mooching off my dad indefinitely.'

'So do you have a plan?'

'Kind of.'

'He's not going to like "kind of." He's going to want specifics.'

'He's not going to like anything except his plan, but at least I'm starting to feel okay about going off on my own. Until recently, I was afraid to leave. Not so much for my sake, but for my dad's. He seemed so lost after the divorce. I was afraid if I left, too, he and Max would . . . I don't know, just shrivel up and blow away. Figuratively speaking. I mean, it's not like I'm the center of their universe or anything, but since my mom left, I've felt like I needed to be there for them.'

'What's changed?'

'My dad doesn't need me the way he used to. I think he's dating Nina,' she said.

'Oookay,' Julian said.

'No, listen, it's important. I can tell they've liked each other for a while. I think now they're more than friends. A lot more.' She hadn't noticed precisely when it had started, but it was becoming very clear that her father and Nina Romano were more than friends. Like, way more. They were trying not to be obvious about it, yet when they were together, her dad was different. Happier and more animated. And the way he dressed lately was a tip-off, too. Sure, he'd always known how to dress for business, but he fussed over his hair now. Last time they'd gone shopping, he'd spent a full five minutes picking out an antiperspirant. Some days, his belt and shoes even matched.

Daisy's initial reaction had been surprisingly positive. Prior to this, he'd gone out with a few different women, and Daisy had always found it strange and unsettling. Yet the idea of him with Nina sat well with her, maybe because she was best friends with Sonnet and had always liked Nina. Maybe because Nina was someone Daisy could talk with about the baby—about anything, come to think of it. And definitely because Nina had been a single mom and her life didn't completely suck. Daisy needed to know things would work out for her. When she looked at Nina, she could see a way for that to happen.

So far, her dad hadn't said a word about liking Nina. Daisy wondered what he was waiting for. Maybe he needed a nudge. Maybe he needed to hear from Daisy that she was in favor of Nina, that she trusted her and even shared confidences with her.

'I don't get it,' Julian said. 'Your dad's got a girlfriend so that means you get to take off?'

'I'm just saying, if he's with Nina, I won't worry so much.'

'You can do that anyway.'

Daisy felt a wave of relief. Of all the people in the world, Julian would understand. He knew exactly what it was like to be a kid, worrying about your parent. 'Thanks for listening,' she said, taking his arm, hugging herself against him. It was a dumb thing to do, touching him like that. She let go, suddenly self-conscious. 'Um, sorry about—'

'Don't be sorry,' he said. 'I'm not.'

'Seriously?'

'Seriously.'

Well, now. Wasn't that an unexpected reaction?

'You're looking at me funny,' he said. 'Like you don't trust me.'

'I totally trust you. I'm just surprised you're able to look past . . .' Embarrassed, she let her voice trail off.

'What, you being pregnant?' he asked, cutting right to the chase.

'Well, yeah. I guess.'

'You're not going to be that way forever.'

'But I'm going to have a child forever.' In her more optimistic moments, Daisy pictured herself as the young hot mom, toting a baby around like the latest fashion accessory, as though she were a character on a TV show. Of course, the classes she'd been attending were more reality-based, preparing her for night feedings, safety precautions and diaper rash.

They drove back to the inn, a companionable silence mellowing the atmosphere. As they got out and retrieved her camera gear from the trunk, Daisy said, 'I finally sent the papers. To Logan, I mean. Actually, I left a message on his voice mail and finally sent the letter by courier, signature required. So I know for a fact that he got them—this morning, actually.'

'Then it's done,' Julian said. 'That's good. You can move on.'

'Uh-huh. Except for one itty-bitty detail.

Logan has to acknowledge that he got my letter and agree that he doesn't need to be involved. Once he does that, I'll feel a lot better.'

'You're letting him off easy.'

'I don't think he should be punished.' She didn't want Logan to have a stake in the child they'd made. If he had no obligations, he'd have no parental rights, as if Logan O'Donnell would even want that.

They took her gear into the house, then went to the kitchen and helped themselves to lemonade. Daisy was standing at the sink when a low-slung BMW Z4 convertible came growling into the parking lot. The icy glass she was holding slipped from her fingers, shattering into the sink.

'Hey, you all right?' Julian asked.

Daisy nodded, wiped her hands on a tea towel. 'I'll clean that up later,' she said. 'I, um, I think I've got a visitor.' She went outside, feeling suddenly afraid, but she covered her weakness with defiance.

Julian frowned at the tall, flame-haired guy striding straight at her. 'Who the hell—'

'That's Logan,' she said.

'Who the hell is this, your bodyguard?' Logan demanded, glaring at Julian.

Julian glared back. 'Does she need one?' He assumed a protective stance, angling himself to the side and slightly in front of Daisy. All the harshness of his rough upbringing shone on his face.

Logan took a step toward him. 'You don't want to threaten me,' he warned. His eyes were narrowed, his body taut. He looked dangerous in his own way, cold and angry.

'And you don't want to take me on, white boy.'

'Give me a break,' Daisy said in exasperation. 'Back off, both of you.'

It was an interesting contrast, to say the least. The kid from nowhere and the heir to a shipping fortune. Julian had survived by his wits and his fists, and was good at using both. Logan, on the other hand, was raised by a small, skilled army of nannies, tutors, coaches and the fine faculty of Manhattan's Dalton School. He had trophies for rugby, hockey and wrestling, and as Daisy recalled, he loved violent competition.

She put her hand on Julian's arm. 'It's all right,' she assured him. 'Really. I need to talk to him, okay?'

Julian aimed a flinty-eyed glare at Logan. 'I'll be around.' He deliberately brushed against Logan's shoulder as he made an unhurried turn and sauntered away.

Daisy saw Logan's hand curl into a fist, and she took hold of his arm. 'Don't even,' she muttered under her breath, holding on until he relaxed. She took her hand away and faced him, more self-conscious than she'd felt in ages. After being gossiped about, poked, prodded, weighed and measured by doctors, she didn't think she could be made to feel self-conscious.

She was wrong. She looked at Logan and felt as though someone had set her on fire.

Not someone. Logan. He was burning a hole in her with his glare. He tossed aside the courier envelope, not looking to see where it landed. 'You couldn't have called?' he demanded. 'It never occurred to you to let me in on your plans? Or—God forbid—give me a say?'

'I think this is the part where you call me a slut and question the baby's paternity.'

'We can skip that part,' he said.

She lifted her eyebrows. This was unexpected. 'We can?'

'You think I don't know you, Daisy,' he said. 'Well, you're wrong. We've known each other since Miss Deering's class in kindergarten.' He lowered his voice to a husky rasp. 'You were never as bad as you wanted people to think.'

Of all the things he might have said to her, she couldn't have anticipated this. People thought she was promiscuous but that was an illusion. Logan was the only boy she'd ever been with. 'Logan—'

'I guess that doesn't matter one way or another now,' he broke in. 'My parents want the paternity test, of course. I don't need it to know the truth. I just need your word, and I have that.'

'Were they . . . were your folks . . . did they go ballistic?'

He laughed without humor. 'What do you think?'

'Ballistic,' she said. 'Your dad, for sure.' Mr. O'Donnell was a big, blustery hard-drinking man with a temper to match his red hair. Mrs. O'Donnell was quiet, maybe even timid, though tireless when it came to mothering her children. She'd always been at the school, volunteering in the library or lunch room. Not that her presence had kept Logan in line.

'Good guess,' he said, then eyed her with slightly less hostility. 'Yours?'

'They were great, after the initial shock. Too great, maybe. In a way, it would have been kind of comforting if they'd grounded me.' She touched her hard, distended stomach. 'Then I figured they probably realized they didn't have to. I'm already grounded for life.'

Anguish flickered in his eyes. 'Why did you wait so long? For all I knew, you'd gone to another planet. After that weekend on Long Island, I never saw you again.'

Calling it 'that weekend on Long Island' was, of course, code for getting high and being careless about birth control. They'd been beyond stupid, something they'd probably both known at the time. Yet she hadn't cared. She'd been so crazy, so messed up about the divorce, and not knowing what she wanted to do with herself. Her mom had just announced

341

that they were moving to The Hague. Daisy had an epic battle with her and then took off to someone's weekend house. She hadn't been thinking. She'd been one big ball of hurt, and she'd found that getting drunk and high with Logan made her forget.

She cleared her throat, made herself look at him. 'I, um, I thought it would be better if we didn't see each other again.'

'Better for who?' he demanded. 'I told you I loved you that weekend. I said I wanted us to go to the same college, to stay together, and you said—'

'I know what I said.' There had been a lot of drinking that weekend. A lot of partying. 'So listen, I'm not a big believer in long-term relationships. My parents got married because of me. I'm sure they had good intentions, but ultimately, we all fell apart.' She knew even as she spoke that she was oversimplifying the situation. Her family had been happy for a long time. The slow erosion to divorce had not been one endless torture session.

'And yet you're committed to having a baby,' he pointed out. 'I'd call that long-term.'

'That's different.'

'Oh. Tell me about it.' He jabbed his thumbs into his back pockets and paced in agitation. 'It took me months to get over you,' he said. 'And I never did quite make it, but at least I'd quit thinking of you every single minute of every damn day. I'd progressed to every other minute. But I still—even now—wake up each morning and remember every damn thing about you, like what it sounds like when you laugh, and how you hold your camera, and what your hair feels like, and the look on your face when a song you like comes on the radio. And then you hit me with this.' He gestured in fury at the envelope with the legal document in it. 'I'm not going to back off, by the way,' he informed her.

Daisy's mouth went dry. 'You have to.'

He laughed bitterly. 'Right.'

'I mean, it's more than fair. I said you don't owe me—or the baby or anyone—a thing. You're under no obligation—'

'Yeah, well, suppose I want to be obligated?' he asked. 'We're talking about a baby. A person. Someone who's completely innocent. What were you planning to tell the kid—sorry, you don't get to have a father?' Before she could answer, he said, 'Well, guess what? I'm not on board with that.'

She wondered what he was getting at. 'What do you want, Logan? Do you want to have this baby with me?'

Putting it so bluntly seemed to help her cause. The expression on his face told her everything she needed to know. 'Yeah, I thought so,' she said. 'Go home, Logan. Go back to the city. Go to college. You don't want to be here with me, doing this, pretending you care.'

He glared at her. 'Don't tell me what I want or don't want. This is a child we made. We're both responsible for it.'

'Him,' she said before she could stop herself. 'It's a boy.'

The slightest of smiles twitched across his lips. 'Yeah?'

She nodded. 'I'd like to call him Emile.'

'After the book by Rousseau,' he said, 'the one we were studying in AP French.'

She caught her breath. 'I can't believe you remembered that.'

'You'd be surprised what I remember,' he said. There was no softness or sentiment in his voice, but anger—and maybe hurt. 'I remember reorganizing my entire class schedule just so we could have AP French together and the same lunch. I remember standing in line overnight to get us tickets to the Rolling Stones. I remember—'

'Quit it,' she snapped. 'You didn't even want people to know we were hooking up,' she said. 'That's what I remember, that you were ashamed of me.'

'That's not the reason, and you know it.'

'Do I?' She was mystified. She'd never figured it out. She assumed his declarations of love came from a place of drunken sentiment and adolescent horniness, and she'd dismissed his claims out of hand. They'd both been seventeen, spoiled and stupid.

'I was never ashamed,' he said. 'That's not it

344

at all.'

'Then what?'

'I didn't want you to get a reputation,' he said.

She burst out laughing. It was just so . . . so outlandish and . . . unlikely. Logan O'Donnell, concerned about her reputation. In what alternate universe would such a thing be so? 'Yeah, well, thanks for that,' she said. 'It worked out real well for me.'

'You don't believe me.'

'Of course I don't believe you.'

'Then give me a chance to prove myself. Let me help with this . . . this . . .' He gestured at her belly. 'My feelings for you . . . they just felt . . . private. I didn't want anybody in on it. Didn't want anyone to tell us we were too young, give us all the reasons it wouldn't work out . . . but as it happened, the ultimate skeptic was you.'

'We acted like a couple of dumb kids. We weren't the first and we won't be the last. I'm dealing with this the best way I know how, okay?'

'No,' he said, stone-faced. 'Not okay. I'm going to open a trust account for the baby. I want regular visitation—'

'Logan, don't. I tried to make this as uncomplicated as possible. There's nothing I want or need from you.'

'This isn't about you. It's about the—about Emile.'

It sounded so strange to hear him refer to the baby by name.

'And by the way,' he added, 'I'm not so sure about that name for a boy. People aren't going to know how to pronounce it and I don't want anyone calling him "Emily."'

'So what about Jean Jacques, like the author?'

'Yeah, that'd be great, two weird names instead of just one. Do you know how tired he'll get of telling everyone how to pronounce and spell his name?'

Good point, Daisy thought. 'His middle name is going to be Charles, after my grandfather. Maybe I'll call him Charlie.'

'Better. Way better.' Logan nodded. He used to smile and laugh so much more. Daisy was still pretty shocked to see him. What were the chances? she wondered. Every other boy in this situation would be grateful to be absolved of all responsibility, under the circumstances. Logan seemed to be the one guy who wanted to step up. What a mess.

'Do your parents know any of this?' she asked.

'They wanted me to agree to your terms, put it behind me and move on with my life.'

'Because they know that's the way things ought to be.'

'It's not their decision.' He grabbed both her hands, held them tight. 'Let's not screw this up, Daisy.'

His touch felt . . . different. More assured, somehow. 'What, you don't think things are already screwed up?'

He kept hold of her hands. 'You know where I went last winter, right?' There was something haunted and fragile in his eyes, and this was new. She used to look into his eyes and see nothing but laughter and mischief.

'To a boarding school, for rehab. That's what I heard, anyway.'

'It's no secret. It totally sucked, but even while it was sucking, I learned a lot, including the fact that I need to take responsibility for things I've done, not run from them.'

'So the baby and I are, what, part of your twelve-step program?' She tried to pull her hands from his.

He held on. 'You're part of me. Part of my life. I'm asking for a chance, Daisy. A chance to show you I can be good for you and for the baby. We're too young, yeah, and we're going to make mistakes, but who doesn't make mistakes?'

Parents who aren't around for their kids, thought Daisy. If they weren't around, they didn't mess up. And there was something to be said for that. She looked down at their joined hands, then into Logan's face. He was the boy she'd gone crazy over in high school, yes. But someone else lived behind those eyes now.

A stranger.

The father of her child.

347

# TWENTY

Nina sat in her office adjacent to the salon of the inn, studying her bank statement with a feeling of incredulity. For the first time in her life, she didn't cringe at the sight of the bottom line. She not only had enough to cover her expenses; there was actually a surplus. Greg had promised that she'd be well-compensated, and he'd delivered on that promise. Still, this was not what she'd planned, not for herself or for the inn. Once again, life had thrown her a curveball. She had become that most pathetic of creatures, the woman with a crush on her boss. She'd been trying to deny it, but she'd never been good at self-deception. Her worst moments were when the two of them worked side by side, planning or supervising; they made such a good team, it was hard to avoid being drawn to him.

She slammed the file shut and put it away. She had a choice. She didn't have to be that woman. She'd just have to make peace with the fact that this was a job. Not her life. Not her future.

Through the open window, she saw Max riding his bike home from Little League practice. He was back from visiting his mother, and he'd returned an angry, unhappy boy.

Not your concern, she told herself as she

348

watched him nearly crash his bike, leaping off at the last moment and letting it clatter to the ground. His duffel bag of gear was flung away. Max picked up the bat and swung it violently.

Oh, boy, thought Nina, hurrying outside. As she approached Max, calling his name, she felt a chill, despite the heat of the day.

She reminded herself again of the vow she'd made—the line she'd drawn. She wouldn't let herself be pulled into this family. It wasn't in her job description.

But when she studied Max's tormented face, something inside her melted. He was at that irresistible stage a boy went through, teetering back and forth between childhood and adolescence. He had a child's soft, round cheeks, and the long, coltish limbs and big feet of a kid on the verge of a major growth spurt.

He didn't hear her. He was too busy pounding everything in sight with his baseball bat. His chest heaved with ragged exertion and his eyes blazed with fury. His team jersey was torn and stained, his sweat-soaked cap askew. His red face was slick with tears or sweat— probably both.

There was nothing quite so volatile as a young boy in a rage. They were such an awkward mingling of urges, both adult and childish. In a boy Max's age there was almost a wildness, as though he was on the verge of exploding beyond control.

'Max,' she said again, shouting now, looking

349

over her shoulder to make sure none of the guests was watching.

He turned on her, the bat drawn fiercely back, his eyes on fire. She kept her distance. The bat went flying; it grazed low-hanging limbs and startled birds into flight before landing with a *thud* some yards away.

'Bad day at Little League practice?' she asked.

He glared, the fury rolling off him in nearly visible waves. 'How'd you guess?'

She shrugged. 'Just lucky. What's going on?'

'Nothing,' he said.

He was trembling, a volcano about to blow. She waited.

'I quit the team.'

Nina merely nodded. 'Your prerogative. It's only a game.' She knew this was less about the team than about his parents and how he felt about himself. But then again, in a town like this, to a kid like this, baseball was everything. She could see the heartbreak in his eyes. He loved baseball. The only time he sat still was when a game was on. His bedroom was a virtual gallery of memorabilia, pennants and game programs. He owned and had memorized the stats on hundreds of baseball cards. 'You want to talk about it?' she prompted.

'No.' He stared at the ground. 'You're not my mother.'

'Well, guess what? I don't want to be your

mother. And that's lucky for you because if I was, you'd be doing hard time for ruining this expensive equipment. Now, if there's something you want to talk about—'

'All people ever want to do is talk,' he snapped, practically yelling. 'My dad and sister. My mom's the worst. It's just talk, talk, talk.' He gave his duffel bag a kick. 'I take that back. Dr. Barnes is the worst.' Max picked up a baseball and hurled it wildly into the trees. The kid had quite an arm.

Dr. Barnes was the family counselor Max saw every week. 'Why's he the worst?' Nina asked.

'He keeps wanting me to work on my issues and find appropriate strategies for managing strong emotions,' Max mimicked as he lobbed another ball.

'So how are you doing with that?' Nina asked.

He glared at her.

'Why'd you quit the team?'

'Because Coach Broadbent is a dick.'

She knew Jerry Broadbent. Max's assessment was not far off the mark. Still . . . 'With a mouth like that, no wonder he's giving you a hard time. Did Coach tell you you're off the team?'

'I suck at baseball,' Max burst out. 'I'm the worst one on the team.'

'I don't get it. You're strong and fast. You can throw. You know the game better than any kid I've ever met. You're a good athlete, Max.'

'Yeah, tell that to Broadbent.'

'You practice constantly with your dad.'

'That's not the same as actually being on the field. I hate getting yelled at every freaking minute.'

'Let me get this straight. You love the game but you're bad at playing it.' The expression on his face confirmed it. 'If you love something, then you find a way to enjoy it. Don't let your coach or teammates take that away from you. What does your father think?'

'He doesn't give a sh—a darn,' Max said.

'Somehow, that doesn't sound like your dad.'

Max shrugged. 'I spent the last two games on the bench. Since I'm not playing, I might as well quit.'

Watching him, Nina felt that most fiery and elemental of emotions—maternal outrage. No, she was not his mother, but he moved her, this boy trying so hard to be brave and not disappoint his father. And Broadbent. He was older than dirt. Older than rock itself. And apparently he was just as disagreeable now as he'd been with her brothers. Nina was itching to pick up the phone and let him have it. A woman would suffer all the hurts in the world when they were aimed at her. But a child in distress turned her into a bear. Wait, she told herself. Wait.

'Max, how are you at bats, stats and water?'

352

Another shrug. 'I don't know. It's not like it's hard or anything.'

She sensed a lot more to the situation than he was telling her. She knew perfectly well there was nothing wrong with his athleticism or skills. This was a different issue. Max's father was preoccupied with Daisy. Max had just returned from a less-than-happy visit with his mother. Nina suspected he'd opened the vent at practice.

She glanced at her watch. She had thirty things to do in the next twenty minutes; she didn't have time for this. Then she looked at the fragile set of Max's chin and heard herself say, 'Let's go. There's someone I want you to meet.' She didn't mean to reward Max for having a tantrum, but he needed to see how a real team worked, that it wasn't driven by rage.

He scowled and balked, and she reminded herself of that lengthy to-do list. 'Now, Max,' she said, and she could tell the sharpness in her voice startled him into compliance. He followed her to the car.

As she drove, a familiar stirring of sentiment passed through her. Max made her feel like a mother. She couldn't help herself. He roused that fierce, protective instinct in her and it felt good and clean and right, even though she told herself she was beyond it and didn't want to feel it.

They drove in silence to the ball fields at the edge of town. In the gravel parking lot,

353

she stopped, shut off the car and turned to watch Max's face, a mixture of caution and eagerness.

'Come on, I want you to meet Dino.'

'Dino Carminucci? Get out.'

Nina couldn't help smiling. His mood was so mercurial. 'Let's go,' she said.

'You know him?' Max asked, incredulous. 'Like, personally? I can't believe you know him.'

Dino was, in actuality, the biggest political favor of her career. Thanks to something her father had done twenty years before, Dino had brought his team to town. Nina was about to call in another favor. She stopped and turned to Max. 'Listen, I want you to know, it's not okay for you to lose your temper like you did today. Everybody gets mad, but throwing things isn't the answer. You could hurt someone, or yourself, or you could break something, and that's not okay.'

His face was soft with remorse, but he maintained eye contact. 'You're right.'

'I'm just making sure you know, this is not a reward for you having a tantrum.'

'Who had a tantrum?' asked Dino, coming from the dugout. 'I bet it was just a bit of excess energy.' This was his gift, his instant understanding of a boy on fire. She knew Max was in good hands.

354

# Part Ten

## Then

The town of Avalon is known for its civic pride, which is rooted deep in its history. When the nearby city of Kingston was burned by British troops during the American Revolution, Avalon opened its gates to the fleeing refugees, offering a safe haven from the invaders. Today, visitors are more likely to find their heroes at the ball fields.

'Since baseball time is measured only in outs,' Roger Angell once wrote in the *New Yorker*, 'all you have to do is succeed utterly; keep hitting, keep the rally alive, and you have defeated time. You remain forever young.'

# TWENTY-ONE

'Mayor Romano?'

The secretary's voice crackled from the intercom speaker on Nina's desk. Nina almost jumped out of her skin, not because there was anything scary about the voice, but because she'd been immersed deep in concentration. The latest audit of city finances was not a pretty sight, and it was driving her crazy, because she and the city council had done everything they could think of to improve the bottom line. Somewhere, there was a leak, and no one could seem to find it. By the middle of her term as mayor, she had discovered innumerable ways for things to go wrong.

She took a deep breath to clear her head, then depressed the intercom button. 'Yes, Gayle?'

'You have a visitor—your father.'

'Oh!' Nina shot up, primping her hair. 'Send him in.'

Seconds later, the door swung open, and there was Pop. 'I'm kind of early,' he said. 'Hope you don't mind.'

She closed the spreadsheet program on her computer. 'I don't mind. I just need to grab a couple of things,' she said, hastily stuffing some printed reports and correspondence into a huge wicker tote bag. Then she flipped open a compact, checked her hair. Some of her detractors had dubbed her Avalon's 'hippie' mayor, which was a complete crock, but it made her hypersensitive about the way she dressed and wore her hair. She hadn't met Dino Carminucci in person yet and didn't know what he was expecting. She'd opted for a knee-length beige dress and low-heeled pumps. No one who wore pumps could be called a hippie. 'Do I look okay?' she asked her father.

He gave her the ear-to-ear smile that had won over students at Avalon High for the past thirty years. 'You look like a million bucks. I couldn't be prouder.'

'I've waited a long time to hear you say that to me, Pop.'

'What, that I'm proud? Are you kidding? I'm proud of all my kids. You, especially. You and Sonnet both. Maybe I don't tell you every day, but there you go. I'm proud. I always have been.'

'Thanks. I'm just feeling a bit nervous about the meeting today. This is a huge commitment for the city to make. A huge risk.'

'Since when are you afraid of risk and commitment?' he asked.

'Since I've been in charge of a whole city, that's when.'

'There's a reason you're in charge. People trust you.'

True, that was her reputation. She was Nina

the doer. Nina the reliable one. Nina the little engine that could. Nobody knew about the other Nina, the one who sometimes woke up in the middle of the night, her heart aching for something she'd never had.

They walked out of city hall and got in her father's car. It was a silver Prius hybrid, which he'd bought when the twins went away to college. 'My empty-nest-mobile,' he told Nina as she put on her seat belt. 'Man, I couldn't wait to get a car that didn't look like an airport shuttle.'

'So how do you like it?' she asked.

'It's a funny thing. I like it all right, but the empty nest, it's not all it's cracked up to be. I miss my crazy, loud houseful of kids.'

She nodded. Now that Sonnet was zooming through high school, on track for early graduation, Nina could relate to his feelings. Much as she was looking forward to a new phase of her life after Sonnet left home, she was also bracing herself for a kind of loneliness she'd never felt before.

The meeting was going to take place at the Apple Tree Inn, a riverside B&B near Avalon's much-photographed covered bridge. Mr. Carminucci was staying there. She wished she could recommend the Inn at Willow Lake to visitors, but that place, though close to her heart, had seen better days.

'I'm looking forward to this,' her father said. 'Haven't seen Dino since we were in college.'

That was the way deals like this worked, Nina had learned. They were all about connections and past relationships.

'You know,' she said, 'when I took office, I had all these big plans and goals for the city. I had no idea how hard it was to get something done, even the smallest step. I kept thinking that once I get my shot, everything will fall into place. I was determined to turn Avalon into the best little town in Ulster County. In the whole state. What if my only legacy as mayor is that I brought a baseball team to town?'

'You kidding?' Her father regarded her with raised eyebrows. 'It's huge, and you know it. You pull this off, and people will always remember you for turning this place into a baseball town.' He held open the door for her. 'Just remember, win or lose, I meant what I said earlier, girlie. I couldn't be prouder.'

As she stepped into the beautiful—but overdecorated—salon of the Apple Tree Inn, Nina felt just a pinch of regret.

Something must have showed on her face. 'What's the matter?' her father asked.

He knew her well. 'I do like being mayor,' she said. 'I love this town and I don't mind working for it. But deep down, I always pictured myself working in a place like this.'

'You're not going to be mayor forever,' he reminded her.

'But I am for the time being,' she said, fixing

a smile on her face. 'Come on, Pop. Introduce me to your friend.'

## Part Eleven

### Now

You won't find any conventions going on at the Inn at Willow Lake. You won't find anything that interferes with the tranquility and comfort of the guests. What you will find is a warm welcome, a quiet place to reflect, a beautiful spot to renew a bond with someone you love and memories to last a lifetime. See you down at the dock . . . .

## TWENTY-TWO

Greg was with Daisy and Max, standing at the edge of the lake, just after sundown. They'd walked down, hoping for a breeze off the water, but the night was still. And hot, probably the hottest night of the year. Daisy was focusing her small, portable telescope, trying to get an image of the surface of the moon. Max was throwing stones, trying to skip one after the other. They dropped into the water with a deep gulping sound.

There were moments, like now, when Greg didn't know what to say to his kids, how to talk to them. When he asked them how they were doing, they gave him pat answers that revealed nothing. Daisy was understandably tense and short-tempered. Max hadn't been himself ever since he got back from visiting his mother. Greg didn't blame Sophie for the boy's mood, though. Max had been having a hard time all summer.

Stooping down, he picked up more stones to throw. 'I like it better at Camp Kioga,' he said. 'Remember last summer, when we slept in the cabins and had bonfires?'

'You did nothing but whine last summer,' Daisy reminded him. 'You kept wanting your Xbox—'

'And you were whining about no cell phone

365

signal.'

'And here's a shock,' Greg put in, 'the world didn't come to an end. Let's make a fire on the beach.'

'It's too hot for a fire. It's too hot for anything.'

'We could go swimming,' Greg said.

'Yeah, if Shamu here goes in the lake, it'll probably cause a flood.' Max snickered.

'Shut up, moron.'

'You shut up.'

'You—'

'How about this? How about we go get something cold to drink? I'll teach you to play Texas Hold 'Em.'

They didn't exactly bowl him over with their enthusiasm, but they agreed to give it a shot. The three of them sat around a wicker table on the front porch with a fan blowing softly. Daisy played a few hands, clearly already familiar with the game, but she started yawning and shifting in her seat.

'You all right?' Greg asked.

'Yes,' she said. 'And you don't need to ask me that every five minutes.'

'Sorry.' He reminded himself not to take her testiness personally.

'It's all right. I'm tired, though. I'm going to bed,' Daisy said.

'We're still playing,' Max objected. 'It'll be boring with just two players.'

Daisy gestured in the direction of the

366

boathouse. 'Go get Nina. I bet she'd play.' Her mood had suddenly swung to bright and cheerful.

Greg shook his head. In fact, he'd like nothing better than to go get Nina, but he was determined to keep his distance.

'I like Nina,' Daisy went on, still cheerful enough that Greg wondered what she was getting at. 'I think it's awesome that she's managing the inn. She's being totally cool about working here, all things considered.'

'What things considered?' asked Greg.

'Well, what with her wanting to own the place—' She stopped, studied him for a second. 'You didn't know? Sonnet told me ages ago, so I just assumed . . . Dad, you didn't know? It was always this big plan she had, for when Sonnet went to college and Nina finished her term being mayor.'

Finally, Greg understood why Nina had been so furious with him. No wonder.

'I like her, too,' Max said, making little stacks of his poker chips. 'Especially after today.'

'What happened today?'

Max continued stacking the chips, concentrating hard on making the ridged edges match up precisely. 'I quit the team,' he said. 'No more Little League for me.'

\*　　　\*　　　\*

367

Hot. A wave of heat arrived in late summer, like the final push of an army before surrender. Temperatures hovered in the nineties, which was fairly unbearable around Avalon. It was Nina's night off, but she didn't have any plans. Her house was a mess, but she didn't feel like cleaning it. She'd always been a reluctant housekeeper. Now that Sonnet was gone, Nina had unleashed her inner slob. When the weather was this hot, no one should have to do housework.

She was restless and sweaty. Even with the windows open and fans blowing, the place was stifling. She fixed herself a bowl of cereal and stood out on the deck, watching the stars hover in the summer sky. Finally, she couldn't stand it anymore, so she put on a bathing suit and went for a swim, all by herself, in the dark. As she sank beneath the surface, she thought about how a dip in the lake on a summer night used to feel when she was younger—cool and liberating and vaguely illicit. She floated on her back and looked up at the stars.

Once again, she was alone. She liked being alone. She didn't have to be if she didn't want. She had options. Bo Crutcher, the Hornets' star pitcher, had invited her on a date tonight. Well, he hadn't called it a date, but he'd asked her if she wanted to go to the Hilltop Tavern later. Bo was fun—maybe too much fun—and for a moment Nina had been tempted. Lord knew, he was attractive enough, tall and athletic and dripping with Texas charm, drinking beer after beer until he was mellow and prone to saying romantic things he didn't mean. It wouldn't be fair to him, though. She'd be lousy company, because try as she might, she couldn't stop thinking about Greg Bellamy.

Telling herself to snap out of it, she dove beneath the surface and came up for air. She lingered in the chilly water, studying the way the moon's reflection painted a long, silvery path upon the water. And the bone-deep sense of loneliness made her change her mind—maybe she would go to the Hilltop Tavern after all, shoot some pool or throw some darts. Determined to shake off her mood, she went upstairs and quickly showered, singing along with the radio. She'd just twisted a towel on her head when she heard a knock at the door.

Muttering a curse, she pulled on a Hornets jersey and dug in a drawer for a pair of undies. No luck—all her underwear was in the laundry basket in the living room, waiting to be folded and put away. The knock sounded again, loud and urgent. Grabbing a pair of cutoffs, she opted to go commando.

As she walked through the house, she frowned at the clutter. Her inner slob hadn't been expecting company. There was a basket of half-folded laundry, a sinkful of dishes she hadn't yet tackled, a stack of unopened mail, dust bunnies scattering in the wake of her bare feet. Holding the turban on her head with one hand, she flipped on the porch light with the other. On the opposite side of the screen door stood Greg Bellamy.

'I just had an interesting talk with my kids,' he said, and his tone was not particularly polite. 'Can I come in?'

Nina froze. Ordinarily the sight of a guy who looked like this, asking to come in, occurred only in the realm of fantasy, especially since she'd all but given up on dating. At first she'd tried blaming it on Greg but ultimately—and only to herself—she conceded that going out with other guys wasn't working for her.

So here was Greg, who made dating everyone else so pointless, asking to come in.

Without a word, she stepped aside, held the door and then closed it behind him.

'I don't suppose it occurred to you to check with me before telling Max to quit his team and go to work for the Hornets,' Greg said.

Oh. Oops. 'Nope,' she admitted. She didn't think she'd actually told Max to quit—but she hadn't told him not to, either.

'He's not even your kid.'

'I think maybe I was aware of that. And you're right, Greg. I should have checked with you—or better yet, let you handle the situation.' The expression on his face made her smile; she couldn't help herself. 'What, did you think I was going to get defensive on you?'

'Well, yeah. Yeah, I did.'

370

She didn't tell him that Max had misled her deliberately into thinking Greg already knew about the situation. That was something Max would need to address with Greg. 'I don't get defensive when I know I'm wrong,' she explained. 'I'm not making excuses for myself, but the fact is, I never had a partner in raising a child. I got used to making decisions on my own. The notion of consulting with someone else—this whole partnership thing—is an alien concept to me.'

'We're business partners. When it comes to the inn, it's all fair game. But when it comes to my kids—'

'Back off?' She bit her lip. There was so much she could say, so much she saw when she looked at Greg and his kids . . . The thing she feared was happening. She was being drawn to this family. Not just to Greg but to Max and Daisy, too. Not your business, she reminded herself. 'All right,' she said. 'I'll back off.'

He seemed surprised by her concession. 'Uh, okay.'

'But I need a little clarification here. Which is it, Greg? When it comes to your kids, do you want my opinion or not? Or only when it's convenient for you?'

'Hey, I didn't ask—'

'Yes,' she said, 'you did ask. Maybe not about Max's Little League team, but about other things, and you know it.' She unfurled the towel from her head, furtively studying him. Despite the heat, he looked perfectly comfortable in a Hawaiian shirt and khaki shorts. Why did he have to be so damn . . . so . . . everything?

She tried not to feel self-conscious about her place. It was hard, though, not to wish she'd taken a few minutes to do the dishes, straighten the stack of half-read books on the coffee table, fold the clothes she'd taken out of the dryer—oops—two days ago.

Yet Greg stayed focused on her. He seemed to be at a loss.

'Let me guess,' she said. 'You came here spoiling for a fight and I conceded and now you don't know what to do with all that excess energy.'

He shrugged his shoulders. 'Something like that.'

'I really am sorry about Max,' she said. 'I can vouch for Dino Carminucci and Bo Crutcher. I can vouch for everyone on the team. Max'll learn a lot from them—not just their bad habits. It took me three years to convince the team to pick Avalon, and I got to know several of them really well.'

Greg nodded, his jaw flexing. 'I don't know how I missed it,' he said. 'How did I miss seeing how unhappy my own kid was with his team? I mean, I knew he had his ups and downs, but I didn't realize he was ready to quit. That's why I was spoiling for a fight. I'm pissed at myself.'

'Kids can hide the whole world from their parents if they want. You know that.' She paused, studied his taut shoulders and flexing hands. 'Have a seat, Greg.'

He frowned. 'It's your night off. I figured you'd be going out.'

'And yet that didn't stop you from coming to see me.'

'I'll leave if you—'

'I just invited you to sit down. What can I get you to drink? The usual?'

'I have a usual?'

'Summer Ale Microbrew.'

She went to the fridge, pulled out a bottle and grabbed a bag of pretzels from the counter. When she turned, she nearly bumped into him. 'You're supposed to be sitting down.'

Keeping his eyes on her face, he opened the beer and took a sip. 'Let's both sit.'

They went to the sofa. She tried to be nonchalant as she moved a stack of books and the laundry basket, making room for both of them. A song she loved by the Dixie Chicks drifted from the stereo, sad yet beautiful and wise and soothing. Nina turned to him, drawing one knee up to her chest. 'What are we doing, Greg?'

'Not sure. All I know is if you go out with one more guy, I'll probably explode.'

Candid of him. 'So I should spend my night off by myself to keep you from exploding.'

'No. You should spend your night off with

me.'

'That might cause *me* to explode,' she said with equal candor.

'I've been known to have that effect on women.'

She tossed a pillow at him. 'I thought you came here to talk about Max.'

'We did. We talked about Max. I said I was pissed about what happened and you explained and now we need to move on to the fact that you never told me you had plans for the inn.'

Her face heated, and it wasn't from the night air. He knew. How had he found out? 'I don't know what you're talking about.'

'Daisy told me tonight. She heard it from Sonnet—the reason you were so pissed that I bought the place from the bank was that you wanted it.' He took a long drink of his beer and set the bottle aside.

She bristled. 'So what if I did?'

'You might have said something.'

'What, and make myself even more pathetic than I already was?'

'Nina, you were never pathetic.'

Yes, she thought. I was. She'd been naive, too, thinking the world would wait for her to buy the inn herself. Had she really thought no one would come along? Why had she left this to chance? Why had she failed to safeguard her plan?

'You should have told me,' Greg said.

'Would you have changed your mind?'

'I doubt it.'

'Then there's nothing to discuss. I always dreamed of having the inn. Once you bought this place, I had to find another dream.'

'And did you?'

'I'm . . . still looking.'

He studied her oversized baseball jersey, which looked like something straight out of Li'l Abner. Her hair was still damp, spiky and unkempt. She tried not to feel self-conscious about her bare feet, the chipped pink polish on her toenails. 'I don't want to talk about this anymore.'

'All right. Change of subject. So you want to go out tonight? Maybe find a place with air-conditioning?'

She shook her head. This, like all her dealings with men, was not going well. She was too awkward, too blunt, too forward, definitely too much of a slob. Besides, first dates were supposed to take place in an elegant setting, with scented candles and soft music surrounding the gauzy, golden-hued couple. She was supposed to have spent three hours primping and pampering herself. A plunge in the lake didn't count.

And the food. There was supposed to be champagne and something light and sophisticated to eat, like vichyssoise or sushi, not beer and pretzels.

'Come on, Nina, what do you say?' Greg

375

asked. 'Is it a date?'

'Everything about this is wrong,' she blurted out.

He stared at her. 'You're right. You're absolutely right.' He slammed back the beer and stood up. 'Glad we cleared that up about Max. Thanks for the beer. See you around.'

He left so quickly that she was still sitting there, mouth agape. 'Unbelievable,' she muttered, getting up and taking the bottles into the kitchen. She told herself there was no reason in the world to feel hurt—and yet she did. But why? She'd run him off and then felt hurt when he was gone, even though he was simply doing what she'd asked him to do.

No, wait. He was supposed to understand the meaning behind *Everything about this is wrong*. He wasn't supposed to agree with her and leave. He was supposed to stay and . . . and what?

She rinsed the beer bottles and placed them in the overflowing recycling bin, then stood at the sink, staring down at the dishes she hadn't bothered washing. A cereal bowl and spoon, the lonely remains of a dinner consumed alone.

The sight of it pushed some button and Nina melted from the inside out. She'd never been much of a crier, but now she found herself overwhelmed with emotion—the painful kind. Greg was able to walk away from her at the drop of a hat. It wasn't fair. She'd

376

finally met someone she could really fall for, and he was all wrong for her. Not only that, he didn't care about her. He was all too ready to flirt with her and then turn away, walk out. It was only a game to him. He had no idea how this was tearing her up. The sobs spasmed through her body and the tears burned her cheeks. It was not a release for Nina. It was not a 'good cry,' the kind that made her feel cleansed and emotionally healthy. It was a moment of hurt and despair so profound that she nearly didn't hear the phone ring.

She decided to ignore it. She didn't fall apart and cry very often; a single mother didn't have that luxury. She wasn't going to let herself be interrupted.

Then she couldn't help herself. She checked the caller ID. It read *Bellamy, G* and his number.

Oh, God. If she picked up, he'd hear the grief in her voice. He might even question her about it or worse, realize he was the cause of it. Then again, if she didn't pick up, he'd know she was avoiding him and realize she was devastated, which might mean he'd come back, and then he'd see what a mess she was—

'Hello.' She snatched up the phone on the ninth ring.

'Nina, it's Greg.'

'Yes?' She paused, swallowed hard, tried to sound normal. 'Did you forget something?'

'Boy, did I.' He chuckled. 'I forgot the

most basic rule of dating. Don't show up unannounced.'

'We're not dating.'

'I know. My bad.'

'Greg—'

'That's why I'm calling. I was wondering if you'd like to go out with me.'

'What?'

'Go out. With me. You know, on an actual date. I owe you the courtesy of a formal invitation for our first official date. A first date should be special, in case we end up together, so when our grandkids ask us what our first date was like, we don't have to tell them it was a night of sweaty sex on a sofa— not that there's anything wrong with sweaty sex on a sofa. Personally, I find it a turn-on but I wanted to ask you—'

'No.' The tears welled in her eyes again; his attempt at humor hurt. Everything hurt. 'I'm not going anywhere with you, Greg. But, um, thank you.'

'That's not the answer I was looking for,' he said.

'It's the only one I have for you.' She was shaking with the effort to control her voice. She paced the room as she spoke, struggling with her emotions. She hated being in this position. Hated the fact that it was torture to hold back her emotions and keep herself from wanting the impossible.

He was saying something else, but she

didn't let herself listen. "'Bye, Greg,' she said quietly, and turned off the phone. As she set it in its cradle, she was still shaking. Get a grip, she told herself. It was actually good that they'd gotten this out in the open, this doomed attraction. It clarified for her exactly what she needed to do, so really, she should be grateful.

Except she didn't feel grateful. She felt empty, bereft. And lonelier than she ever had in her life. And whose fault was that? She'd just run him off. It was time, she told herself, to face facts. Clearly this thing with Greg wasn't working, wasn't ever going to work. She simply had to accept that and move on, even if it meant leaving the Inn at Willow Lake. She just could not stay. The sense of resolve came with a fresh influx of tears. She hated this, hated breaking down and losing control. She felt betrayed by her own emotions.

When she heard the heavy footsteps on the deck outside her door, she froze, too surprised to do anything but stand there as Greg returned to her. He didn't bother knocking but wrenched open the door and strode inside. How Rhett Butler of him, she thought. But still she stood frozen in her old clothes and bare feet, her face burned by tears. And although she found her voice, the words that came out were totally inane. 'I thought you had a new rule about unannounced visits.'

'I lied,' he said and grabbed her as though she'd been about to fall off a cliff. And then he walked her backward into the room, pressed her down on the sofa and kissed her—long, hungry kisses that took her away somewhere, huge and endless makeout kisses that felt more like sex than sex. In those moments she forgot everything. Mostly, she forgot to worry or try to control things. They didn't come up for air for a very long time, and when they did, Nina felt dizzy and helpless, and amazed herself by loving the feeling. 'This wasn't the way I pictured getting together with you,' she blurted out.

'Yeah? Totally flattered. So tell me how you pictured it.'

Busted. She scooted away from him on the sofa. 'I'll do no such thing.'

'Come on. This has been a long time coming.'

She glanced away, hoping he didn't know she'd been crying. 'What do you mean by that?'

'You know what I mean. You think I don't remember all the times we brushed up against each other in the past, but I do. I just pretended not to because it seemed so pointless. I remember your smile the first time we met. I remember what it felt like seeing you with that West Point cadet, knowing what you'd done. I remember watching you with your little daughter. Just because I kept quiet doesn't mean I didn't see and don't remember. It was pointless to talk to you, to let you know

380

you mattered on any level to me. We had different lives. I had a marriage and kids. You had Sonnet and your family and your job. What would be the point of letting you know you mattered to me?'

Nina gaped at him, not bothering to act as though she didn't know what he was talking about.

'It's different now,' he said, pulling her back into his arms. 'I don't have to pretend. I can tell you flat out that you matter to me.' He bent and used his teeth to slip the shirt down her shoulder, kissing her bare skin with searing, single-minded attention. He kissed her again and his hand drifted down, undoing the top button of her cutoffs. He made a hissing sound, as though she'd burned him.

'Something the matter?' she whispered against his mouth.

'You're not wearing any underwear.'

She blushed. 'It's, um, not a habit with me.'

'It should be. Promise you'll always dress this way. I'm begging you. I'll do anything . . .' He kissed her again, long and hungrily.

Men were so easy, she thought. In some ways.

'What turns you on, Nina Romano?' he asked, barely lifting his mouth from hers, very slowly unzipping her shorts.

*Everything.* Fortunately for her, she couldn't remember how to speak, and even if she could, she would not know what to tell him. This was so new to her, this feeling of need and surrender.

'On second thought,' he whispered, his hand disappearing beneath her shirt, 'don't tell me.' And with that, he pressed her back against the sofa cushions, causing the stack of folded clothes to topple in a soft heap. 'I'd rather figure it out on my own.'

\*     \*     \*

When Greg woke up at dawn with Nina in his arms, he didn't say the first words that popped into his mind—*I told you so.* He *knew* the sex would be amazing. He'd had all summer to contemplate and imagine and fantasize. But the fact that she hadn't been wearing underwear . . . good lord. That was the sort of thing a guy didn't even dare wish for. He couldn't believe it had taken so long to get to this point.

She slept as though wrapped in the softest of dreams, breathing lightly, arms and legs entwined with his. Taking care not to wake her, he rubbed his eyes and looked around. At some point in the night, they had migrated into the bedroom, leaving a trail of clothes on the floor. Incongruously, there was a half-empty pint of maple syrup—never let it be said they lacked imagination—and towels leading from the shower to the bed. It had been a long, incredible night, one he would never forget.

382

One he already wanted to repeat, as soon as possible.

Yet at the same time, he felt an insane surge of tenderness for Nina. He liked her. He was starting to love her, and not just for her inventiveness with maple syrup. He liked her independent nature and her fierce loyalty. He liked her passion and her decisiveness, even when she was arguing with him. And he liked—no, this he definitely loved—the way she was during sex, vulnerable and bold at the same time, and the way she slept in his arms.

Easing out of the bed, he left her asleep, pausing to drape a sheet over her. He slipped on his shorts and made his way to the kitchen, quickly picking up condom wrappers along the way.

He checked the time—6:00 a.m. The kids wouldn't be up for a couple of hours. Good. Trying to be quiet, he found the Moka—the only coffeemaker, Nina had once insisted, worth having—and a bag of Lavazza, which was apparently a direct import from Italy. Okay, so she wasn't a neat freak, he thought, shaking yesterday's coffee grounds from the filter. To Greg, that was an asset. Sophie, now, she had been neat in the extreme. So neat, he always got the feeling he was messing up a room just by breathing the air.

Willfully he banished Sophie from his thoughts and lit the flame under the Moka. Then he rummaged in the fridge for something to eat, discovering such unacceptable options as fat-free soy milk, grapes that were well on their way to becoming raisins and a scary wedge of something that resembled a science experiment. He was about to give up when he moved the milk carton aside and spied, in the white Sky River Bakery box—paydirt. A half-dozen sfogliatelle—pastries filled with sweet ricotta. Greg held one clamped between his teeth while he rinsed two cups he found in the sink and poured the coffee, balancing the cups atop the pastry box. Hearing a noise behind him, he straightened up and turned.

Nina stood there, draped in a sheet, staring at him. She resembled a pint-sized goddess, with her short, tousled hair, creamy olive-toned skin and the sheet tucked under her arms. He felt her surprised gaze travel slowly from the pastry in his mouth to his bare chest and the two coffees he held.

'Mmm,' he said, carrying the coffee into the bedroom and motioning her with his head to follow. He set them down and took the pastry out of his mouth. 'Get back in bed,' he ordered around a bite of sfogliatelle. 'I'm bringing you coffee.'

'You are not,' she said from the doorway.

'Too late,' he said, capturing her hand and bringing her to the unmade bed. 'I already did.'

'Greg—'

'Coffee,' he said. 'You take it black, right?'

He passed her a cup and offered the box of pastries. 'Hungry?'

'In a minute.' She propped herself back against the pillows, holding the sheet in place. 'I need to savor this first. This is not something that happens to me every day—some guy bringing me coffee in bed. In fact, I think this is the only time it's happened.'

He clinked his coffee cup to hers. 'But not the last, not if you stick with me.' Crap, he thought as soon as the words were out of his mouth. Not only did that sound cheesy, it also implied a choice to be made. He quickly covered the mistake by leaning across the bed and giving her a long, sweet, good-morning kiss, not letting up until he felt her lips curve into a smile under his. 'You're beautiful, you know,' he said.

She laughed softly and touched her messed-up hair. 'Yeah. I know.'

'Really. I mean it.'

'Okay, whatever. A girl doesn't argue with something like that.' She sipped her coffee, gazing out the window while he gazed at her. She sighed with contentment. 'I love this view,' she said.

For a moment, Greg was sure she'd said, 'I love you,' and even the imagined declaration caused the world to shift. Then he regrouped, realized what she was talking about and laughed at himself.

He turned to look at the lake. The sun

wasn't up yet. There was a thin pink thread on the horizon above the hills, weaving its way down toward the water. A few shadowy puffs of fog gathered here and there on the lake. A deep stillness pervaded the scene. Yet Greg knew the contentment he felt this morning had far less to do with the view out the window than with the woman in the bed behind him. His heart hadn't felt like this since . . . *never.* He had never felt like this. He'd always gone for the Sophies and Brookes of the world. Nina made him feel something. She delved down to the heart of him. Somehow, she managed to find the place he never let anyone touch before.

He turned to her, savoring the sight of her, still slightly groggy but clearly grateful for the coffee. Her eyes seemed misty, a bit unfocused, and her mouth was soft, as though she was about to smile. Unable to resist, he crossed to the bed, slipped beneath the covers. He was mesmerized by a gap in the sheet covering her breasts. 'Hey, Nina—'

'Greg, I—'

They both spoke at once, both hesitated. 'Sorry,' he said. 'Go ahead.'

She set her coffee very deliberately on the nightstand. 'I just thought you should know, this changes things.'

He settled in beside her, propped himself up on his elbow and used his free hand to punctuate the conversation, watching her

386

face as he touched her. 'Good. I'm ready for something different.'

She shivered a little, but didn't push him away. 'So that's what this is, a change of pace to keep you from getting bored?'

He couldn't help smiling. 'Yeah, that's it. Exactly.'

She put her hand over his, stopping his under-the-sheets teasing. 'I can't talk when you do that.'

'My plan is working, then.'

'Are we really not going to talk about this?'

That would be too good to be true, he reflected. But gamely enough, he grew serious. 'That day in the attic, you asked me why I was telling you about my marriage. I wanted you to know I get it. I know what went wrong. And I know how to get it right.'

'It all seems a little fast to me.'

He thought about all the times their lives had crossed paths over the years. 'Not to me.'

'I'm not so good with change,' she admitted.

'Believe me, it's not a bad thing.'

'Depends on what it changes into— something good and strong and fulfilling, or something complicated and messy and sad.'

'You act as though we don't have a choice. Don't get cold feet on me now, Nina. It's too late for that, anyway.' He traced the line of her jaw with his index finger. He wanted to learn every part of her, the geography of her body as well as the secrets of her heart.

She turned to him, her eyes filled with uncertainty. 'What are we doing, Greg?'

'Falling in love.'

'Right. Very funny.'

'I'm not joking. We're falling in love. Tell me you're not feeling it.'

'You can't just—'

'Sure I can, honey. It's happened to me before. I know what it's like. I can identify all the signs. And this is . . . whew. Off-the-charts better than anything I've ever felt before.'

'Well, maybe I'm not that experienced, but I'm sure I'd recognize the feeling when it came along.' She ducked her head as she spoke, as if she didn't want him to see her face.

'You're probably having a tough time admitting it, but my God, Nina. There were moments last night . . .' His body reacted to the memory, and he shifted even closer to her, catching her gasp of surprise with a kiss, tasting her, skimming his hands down her body. 'Even in the dark, with the lights out, some things can't be hidden,' he said.

She shuddered a little as he caressed her, moving close.

Greg didn't really like the direction the conversation had taken. Talking was inadequate in this situation. There were things he needed to tell her, but not with words. He knew of one way to avert the discussion. Several ways, actually. They'd tried only a few the previous night. Maybe this morning, they'd discover a few more.

All, right, Nina, she told herself as she got out
of the car and went to find Jenny and Olivia.
She'd agreed to join them today at Camp
Kioga to help create little parcels of birdseed
for the wedding. Focus, she admonished
herself. Be cool. For God's sake, don't act as if
anything is different.

'Something's different about you,' Jenny
said as Nina walked into the main pavilion.
Jenny had all the materials spread out on a
long table—spools of white satin ribbon, tiny
squares of mesh, a big sack of birdseed.

Nina tried to act nonchalant. Okay, maybe
she was walking a bit gingerly. Maybe she had
a vague, stupidly satisfied look on her face.
She and Greg had spent every night together
for the past week, and very little sleeping had
been accomplished. And—she couldn't lie to
herself—she loved it. She loved every little
ache and twinge of ecstasy she felt as she went
about her business during the day, guarding
her delicious secret. There were moments
when she also felt vulnerable and afraid of
what might happen next, but she kept that a
secret, too.

'I had a hair appointment,' she told Jenny.

'No, that's not it . . . Oh. You got laid.'

'I didn—'

'You did, indeed. And it's about time. So it's Greg, right?'

'What's Greg?' asked Olivia, walking into the room, carrying a basket of more supplies. Her little dog trotted at her heels.

'Nina slept with Greg.'

'It's about time.' Olivia grinned at Jenny. 'She looks pissed.' The dog flopped down at her feet and curled up for a nap.

'She is pissed. She wanted to keep it a secret while she decides whether or not this was a short-lived fling, or if it's the start of something. So she's pissed because we guessed the secret.'

'*You* did, Miss Smarty-Pants. Remind me to steer clear of you when I have a secret.' Despite her words, Olivia regarded Jenny with open affection. Every once in a while, Nina saw the family resemblance in them and was reminded they were both Philip Bellamy's daughters. And right now, they were in cahoots and they were the enemy.

'Can we please not talk about this?' she asked.

'Where's the fun in that?' Jenny asked.

'This is not about fun. This is about . . . God, I don't know what it's about.'

'Sure you do—finally,' Jenny said. 'You've had a crush on Greg forever. And now he likes you back. So where's the problem?'

390

'Everywhere I look,' Nina said. 'I see nothing but trouble ahead.'

'That's not like you,' Jenny said. 'You're the girl with all the solutions. You always have been.'

'Not anymore. I don't know how to do this, how to be this person. It used to be easy when it was just me and Sonnet, you know?' She tried to make a little packet of birdseed, but it kept spilling across the table.

'Easy? Being a single mother is easy?' Jenny carefully placed a scoop of birdseed on a square of mesh and drew up the corners.

'Making my own choices is easy,' Nina clarified. She grabbed a pair of scissors and cut a piece of ribbon, efficiently doing up Jenny's small bundle. 'I didn't have to check with anyone, you know, or take some guy into consideration.'

Jenny smiled. 'I've never known you to shy away from a challenge.'

'I just don't know how to . . . do this,' she admitted, looking at Jenny and Olivia. Love had changed these women, both of them. And she knew things hadn't been easy for either of them. Jenny had lost everything in a fire; Olivia had walked away from a life that wasn't working for her—and each woman had taken a leap of faith. In a way, it seemed that love had actually saved them, given them a new life. A better life. Yet Nina simply couldn't see herself doing such a thing, letting go, taking

391

such a huge risk with her heart. It all seemed impossible. 'Okay, so the falling-in-love bit, I get that. It's really not that hard, especially not with someone like Greg. The thing I don't understand is what makes it last, and how you can escape getting hurt,' she explained. 'And especially with Greg Bellamy. I look at all the complications and it . . . it scares me.'

Olivia and Jenny exchanged a glance. 'It shouldn't,' Jenny said. 'You're already living that life, and you're doing just fine.'

*No*, thought Nina. *I'm not.* Maybe the thing with Greg was just a fling, a one-night stand that went on a little too long.

No. It was something so beautiful that it hurt, something she craved like an addict. Something too fragile and dangerous to last.

'You know what,' she said to the others, 'I'm not going to think about this today. We're getting ready for a wedding, for lord's sake, and worrying about my love life doesn't seem right.'

'I don't mind,' Olivia said. 'But—'

'Here comes the bride,' sang two women, parading into the room, holding a zippered bag. They were Olivia's and Jenny's cousins, named Dare and Francine, Nina recalled. They both had the Bellamy good looks and the sporty, effortless ease of people born to privilege. Behind them came Freddy Delgado, Olivia's best friend and business partner from the city. He was adorable, with fashionable blond-tipped hair and hip-hop clothes that somehow looked just right on him. And he was clearly smitten with Dare, who directed him to stand up on a bench and hold the zippered bag up off the floor.

'It's here,' Francine announced. 'Back from the final alterations.'

Discreetly, Olivia slipped her hand into Jenny's and held fast as Dare unzipped the bag with a flourish. When Freddy reverently drew out the dress and veil, even Nina was affected. It was *that* beautiful, a couture dress of ivory silk with a bodice sewn with crystal beads and gorgeous swags of gossamer tulle.

'It's incredible,' Jenny said. 'It's the prettiest dress ever.'

Olivia laughed with relief and joy. Nina guessed that she'd been concerned about sibling rivalry, but she needn't have. Jenny and Rourke had married quickly and quietly— their choice—and Nina knew Jenny didn't envy her all the fuss and bother. Clearly loving it, Olivia climbed up on the bench beside Freddy and put the veil on her head, while he held the gown against her. Nina was amazed to feel a surge of tender emotion. There was something about the sight of a bride . . . Seeing Olivia standing there, incandescent with joy, embodied a dream Nina had never allowed herself to have.

She watched as the others gathered around, oohing and ahhing over the dress. For no reason other than her own insecurity, she felt like an outsider amidst this group, the hired help as opposed to one of the family. It was that age-old invisible line that had always existed in a town like Avalon—the summer people versus the locals. She knew it was a false division, particularly now, yet her sense of it was keen.

While everyone was talking at once, someone else arrived. Only Nina saw her at first. She was tall and self-possessed, wearing a beige designer suit, big-eyed designer shades and carrying a Chanel bag. Every blond hair was in place and her makeup was perfect, done with a light touch. She might have stepped right off the society pages—resort edition. As recognition dawned on Nina, the world tilted.

'Sophie!' Francine spotted her and gave a little cry of delight. 'You made it! Everyone, Sophie's here.'

The oohing and ahhing shifted from the dress to the new arrival—Sophie Bellamy, Greg's ex-wife. She walked into their midst, smiling, hugging and air-kissing. Jenny and Nina exchanged a glance, then eyed the swinging doors to the kitchen with longing. Jenny shook her head. She was right, Nina conceded. Best to get this over with. Oh, boy, though. The way people were watching, with ill-concealed tension, she knew everyone was braced for drama. Damn it, she thought. Did everyone in the room know about her and

Greg? Oh, God—did Sophie?

'Here's Jenny,' Olivia said, drawing her forward. 'My half sister. And this is Jenny's friend, Nina.'

'Nice to meet you,' Nina said, her smile bright and sincere, a trick she had perfected back in her city-politics days. 'Nina Romano.'

An equally sincere smile greeted her. Clearly, Sophie was no stranger to politics, either. 'It's so good to meet you in person. Sonnet's an absolute joy. When she came to visit me in The Hague, she told me so much about you.'

All right, so she hadn't yet received the memo. Either that, or the woman knew how to give an Oscar-worthy performance. Nina's neck itched, but she resisted the urge to scratch it. She wished she'd taken the time to dress better today. Maybe taken ten seconds and put on a bit of lipstick. Because Sophie was dazzling in a classy, put-together fashion that made Nina feel like a complete slob. 'Thanks,' Nina said. 'And thank you for showing her around The Hague.'

'It was my pleasure, believe me. I only wish my own children would take that kind of interest in the city where I live.'

*Try taking an interest in your own children.* Nina couldn't keep herself from thinking it.

Yet as Sophie turned to exclaim over the wedding gown, Nina had to admire her firm control. She was pleasant and cool, like a

395

breeze off the lake. The sunglasses let in only enough light to show the shape of her eyes. Slowly, she took them off and looked around the dining hall. 'Wow,' she said, 'this certainly brings back memories.'

This was where Sophie's own wedding had taken place—the ceremony out on the deck and the reception right here in the hall, with an ensemble playing on a raised dais in the corner. And a bridegroom who'd had too much to drink and punched a hole in the wall. Since Nina wasn't sure Sophie was talking to her, she didn't reply. She was convinced Sophie didn't remember her from the past. Why would she remember the catering help?

'Olivia, I really appreciate that you included me,' Sophie said.

'Of course I'm going to include you,' Olivia replied.

'I was worried that, with the divorce—'

'Don't give it a thought. I'm honored that you came. And I'm excited for you, you know, about the baby.'

'Excited.' Sophie was cool about this, too. Calm and bemused. The woman was an ice queen. 'Yes, of course.'

'I'd better be going,' Nina said, certain she'd make a fool of herself if she lingered. 'See you around, Sophie. Olivia, the dress is amazing. I'll see you on your big day.'

Jenny walked out with her, exploding in the parking lot. 'Oh. My. God. Can you believe her? How weird was that?'

'Too weird for me.' Nina glanced back over her shoulder. 'I think I'll skip the wedding—'

'Oh, no you don't,' Jenny said. 'Especially not because of that woman.'

'It's Olivia's day.'

'Yes, it is, which is why you're not going to cause a drama by boycotting her wedding.'

'It wouldn't be a boycott. I—'

'Enough. You're coming. And Sophie will be there and so will Greg and it will be fine, because we're all grown-ups, right?'

'Last time I checked.' Nina opened her car door.

Jenny held it ajar. 'Hang on,' she said, studying Nina's face. 'You're a wreck.'

There was no point in denying it, not to Jenny. 'I'm just . . . not used to dealing with something like this.'

Jenny, who had always had the softest of hearts, pulled Nina into a hug. 'Sweetie, you've always been such a stoic. Ever since you were in high school with a new baby. It's all right to be vulnerable every once in a while.'

Nina stepped back, nodded her head. 'That's easier said than done. Over the years, I've gotten so used to being by myself that I don't really know how to do this. You know, I look back and ask myself, do I have regrets? I tell myself that I don't. When you're in the position I was in, you feel like you're on display. Some people vilify you, but others admire you for taking the ultimate responsibility, for sacrificing. You give up things like education and career options and maybe some personal privacy, but those things don't crush you. There's really only one thing that crushes you, and it's this—that you miss out on the one kind of love that makes all the difference, the kind of sweep-you-off-your-feet romance that only comes during certain special times in a person's life. And when you've got a kid and you're struggling to survive, you tend to miss those special moments—they pass you by and you don't even know what you've missed. And I thought that chance was gone for me, that I'd left it behind somewhere in my twenties. That's why Greg is such a surprise. I'm feeling things now that I never felt before. This stuff might be old hat to someone else, but for me, it's a first. That's why I'm so scared.'

Now they were both crying, Nina grabbed a box of Kleenex from her car, offering it to Jenny. 'And if you say one word of this to your sister—'

'I'd never. I only want what I've always wanted for you,' Jenny said. 'Don't talk yourself out of this, Nina. Just because he's complicated doesn't mean he isn't right for you.'

## TWENTY-FOUR

Greg pulled into the hospital annex parking lot, found a spot and turned to Daisy. 'So,' he said. 'Last class before the big event.'

She nodded, but seemed distracted as she levered herself out of the car. Greg suspected it was probably because her mother had asked to accompany them today. Sophie had promised to be present when the baby came, and in order to do so, she had to attend at least one class. As she got out of the backseat, Greg saw the flicker of apprehension in his ex-wife's eyes. Welcome to my world, he thought. Hell, he'd felt that same fright, he felt it every single day. But he knew avoiding it wouldn't make it go away.

As the three of them walked toward the community center adjacent to the hospital, he felt an unexpected sense of detachment. He hadn't known what it would be like when Sophie arrived. He'd braced himself for a storm of hurt, the kind of hurt that burned right through to the soul, which was what he'd felt the final year before the divorce, when it became clear to both of them that the marriage was over. Yet the pain never came. He found himself capable of looking at Sophie and seeing a person he'd once loved but didn't any longer. As the mother of his children, she owned whole chapters of his life, but she didn't own him. They knew each other in ways they'd never know anyone else, and that was all right. He was no longer being civil to her for the sake of the children. It was simply because he had moved on.

When that had happened, he couldn't say. He suspected it had been a gradual process of figuring out who he was when he wasn't part of a couple and moving on from there. And lately, of course, he was distracted by something far more delectable—Nina Romano.

'You look pleased with yourself,' Daisy remarked as they went inside.

'Do I?' Greg hadn't realized he was smiling.

'I guess you're pretty glad this is almost over,' Daisy said, supplying him with an excuse.

'Just, um, looking forward to the next stage,' he said, lying through his teeth as he held open the door for Daisy and her mother. The thought sobered him, even though his mind lingered on Nina. His feelings for her hadn't exploded overnight. They'd been growing for a long time, but in a dark, unacknowledged place. Once he finally cut them loose, they were like a force beyond his control, a forest fire, an obsession.

He thought about her all the damn time, even now, as he and his ex and their pregnant daughter headed for the floor mats in front of the video screen.

Focus, Greg reminded himself. All this was about Daisy. To that end, he introduced Sophie to Barbara Machesky, the childbirth instructor. Barbara was, at first glance, the quintessential, crunchy-granola, Birkenstock-wearing New Age childbirth guru—at least, that was the first impression she projected. Later, her students would discover her no-nonsense, drill-sergeant nature. Still, the contrast between her and Sophie, in her European-designer outfit and beauty-parlor-blond hair, was almost comical, and Greg sensed Sophie's opinion forming.

His ex, he remembered, had a way of instantly sizing people up, passing judgment with the swiftness of a falling guillotine. He had always loved it when she got it wrong, which she was in the process of doing right now, with Barbara. 'Daisy tells me she's learned so much from you,' Sophie said in the tone she used with unsatisfactory schoolteachers and household help.

'You don't say,' Barbara replied. She'd clearly caught the condescension. Her students, Greg included, were completely devoted to her. She inspired confidence in all of them, from the emigrant couple from Korea to Daisy, who was the youngest in the class. 'Take a seat, everyone. We're down a pair today. Randy and Gretchen's little girl was born last Wednesday, and they're all doing fine.'

The news was greeted with murmurs of appreciation. Bonds had formed in the class, which was to be expected, given that they were all about to experience the same life-changing event. It was an interesting enough mix—married transplants from the city, a gay couple and their relentlessly cheerful surrogate, an unhappy pair who seemed grimly determined that the baby would fix their marriage, a tattooed teenager who had so many facial piercings she looked as though she'd fallen headfirst into a tackle box. Randy and Gretchen had been nicknamed the Honeymooners, since they fought and loved with equal ferocity. Sophie took everyone in with a sweeping glance.

Greg had watched his son being born, he'd cried the moment it happened, but a part of him had dwelled in blissful ignorance. Coming here once a week with Daisy was quite a different experience. He found himself focusing on all the things that might go wrong—a compressed cord, abnormal presentation, bleeding, infection . . . His head was filled with all the terrors in the world, and he had to act as though everything was going to be fine.

'Since this is the last class in this cycle, let's review final-stage labor and delivery,' Barbara said, her brisk tone and downstate accent belying her mellow exterior. She put a list up on the screen. 'Let's focus on pushing . . . .'

Greg had a hard time focusing, period, even when Barbara moved on to topics such as bringing the baby home. With each passing day, the idea that Daisy was going to give birth became more and more real to him. The notion of a baby in the house—a new baby boy—was overwhelming.

This is going to be so cool, he thought.

*       *       *

Daisy caught a glimpse of herself in the window of the store where they'd stopped on the way home from class. As always, the image startled her. I'm a linebacker, she thought, studying her pudgy face and neck, her thick legs and ankles under a sundress the size of a circus tent.

'Are you all right, honey?' her mom asked, taking her hand.

*I was until a second ago.* Daisy didn't say so aloud, but damn. It was bad enough looking at all the weight she'd put on. When her mother—her gorgeous, perfect, skinny mother—stood next to her, it made Daisy look like a parade float.

'Sure,' she said. 'Let's go inside.'

She observed her parents acting like polite strangers, and it made her incredibly sad. The thing about this divorce was, there was no villain. Just two people who couldn't live together anymore, no matter what. Although nearly a year had passed since the family had shattered apart, Daisy still felt the occasional sting of pain. Maybe she always would. She still felt pretty bad about the way it had worked out for her mom. Last fall, when all the broken pieces were making a landing, there had been endless discussions—okay, fights—about where Daisy and Max would go and who would be in charge and what was best for the kids. Mom had wanted Max and Daisy with her, of course. Since the mother was almost always the default custodial parent, it was decided that they'd go with her.

But there was a catch. Mom was saving the world. More specifically, she was saving a small principality in southern Africa, prosecuting a warlord for crimes against humanity. People would live or die depending on the outcome of the case. So in order for Mom to continue her work, she had to live in The Hague, home of the International Criminal Court. She'd had a school all picked out for Max and Daisy, an international school any kid should feel privileged to attend. It should have been simple—a divorce, the kids go with Mom. Happened every day.

Disaster. Max had lasted mere days in the hostile environment before total meltdown; Daisy hadn't gone much longer, getting violently ill. Later, of course, they would all figure out that it was the pregnancy. Daisy was still haunted by the look on her mom's face when she and Max said they wanted—needed—to live with their dad and move to Avalon. The Bellamy family had a long, distinguished history in the town. It was a safe place to adjust to the changes in their lives. And Mom, usually such a fighter, spent hours in consultation with their family therapist, and then said she understood. Given the trauma of the divorce, she didn't want to make things worse by forcing her kids to live an ocean away in a world of strangers. But neither could she turn her back on the case to which she'd devoted herself, even though she said she would.

Daisy could still remember the tremor in her mom's voice when she said, 'I'll stay in the States with you guys.' Both Daisy and Max recognized her turmoil.

And both Daisy and Max knew it would never work, their mother trying to turn her back on her mission. Daisy, in a moment of cruelty that still shamed her, did her part by telling Mom it was pointless for her to move back to the States when they wanted to live with their dad, anyway.

So Mom made the transatlantic flight to see them every few weeks, grimly racking up the frequent flyer points. The visits were often strained and forced, weighed down by her mom's guilt, Max's hurt and Daisy's defiance. Max had gone to visit Mom a few times, but not Daisy, although the invitation remained open. Cynically, Daisy figured the fact that her kids went with their dad after the divorce seriously messed with Mom's constant struggle to be perfect—the perfect wife, perfect mother, perfect international jet-setting lawyer saving the world. The thing her mom finally had to accept was that she couldn't be perfect at everything. Just some things.

But that didn't stop her from trying to be the perfect grandmother, which was the primary reason for the current outing.

The store was called New Beginnings, and it billed itself as one-stop shopping for expectant parents. Daisy already had the basics—crib, carseat, carrier—and her cousins had given her a shower worthy of a royal princess, but her mother had insisted on getting the layette. Daisy figured, why the heck not? Her mom was dying to do something, and she was better at shopping than anyone Daisy knew.

Walking between her parents, Daisy felt a brief, false flash of security that took her back to childhood days when things were so much simpler. After her parents had first separated, Daisy had entertained the idea that maybe they'd change their minds, get back together. She knew better now, though. But not Max. He still lived for the fantasy that his parents would reconcile. Pretty soon, Max would know what their mom had figured out a long time ago. A reconciliation was no longer an option.

That train had left the station.

Daisy knew that what she had suspected for a while, what she'd hoped for, had come true. Dad was with Nina. A couple of nights ago, Daisy had gotten up for the hundred-and-seventy-fourth bathroom break and she'd heard a noise. It was her dad, coming in the back door at like 4:00 a.m. He'd told her he heard raccoons in the trash.

Yeah, right.

She saw a salesclerk eyeing the three of them. The clerk was probably trying to figure out what the deal was. Her parents didn't look anything like grandparents-to-be. An observer might think they were adoptive parents, and that Daisy was going to give them her baby.

Such a thing wasn't unheard of. The family-planning counselor encouraged her to explore adoption, including intra-family. Daisy had done so, gamely entertaining the notion for, oh, say, ten seconds before concluding that it wouldn't work. It was one of the few choices in this ordeal that she'd found easy. Early on, she'd contemplated terminating the pregnancy, but she couldn't do it. Then, once she committed to keeping the baby, she was determined to *keep* the baby.

She wished she could experience an indisputable, firm conviction about her future, a feeling so strong she heard music playing in her head, the way girls did in made-for-TV movies. No such luck. Sure, she'd made the decision and she was going to stick by it, but that didn't mean she knew what the hell she was doing.

She'd been trying to figure out a way to tell her parents that Logan O'Donnell had refused to surrender all parental rights. He'd shown up out of the blue, and his reaction to the situation had been completely unexpected. He not only refused to accept her terms, but he'd put forth some terms of his own. Which, of course, she'd refused to consider. So they were at an impasse, and Daisy didn't know what to do. She wasn't ready to discuss any of this with her parents.

There was one topic she needed to talk to them about, though. Her future. Still, she kept putting it off, certain her dad would blow a gasket when he heard what she was planning.

Her mom held up a sailor suit the size of a Cabbage Patch doll. 'What do you think?'

'Adorable,' Daisy said. Maybe it was hormones, but just the sight of baby clothes made her feel all soft and mushy inside.

'So we're liking the sailor theme?' Mom asked.

'Sure,' said Daisy.

Her dad was checking out crib mobiles and seemed sold on the golf-themed model. The tension between her mom and dad hummed like an incoming storm. Daisy felt stretched between them like one of those rubber-armed tug-of-war dolls. Why had she thought coming here together was a good idea?

Because, married or not, they were her parents. They were Emile's grandparents. They'd better get used to the idea.

## TWENTY-FIVE

It was the night before Olivia's wedding, and Nina felt almost giddy with contentment, because Sonnet was home at last. Nina, Sonnet and Daisy sat on the raised deck of the boathouse, drinking iced tea and enjoying the balmy evening. The heat wave had subsided, a small mercy Nina no longer took for granted. She'd been wondering if the torrid heat had anything to do with her borderline-insane feelings for Greg. Now that the temperature had cooled a bit, she realized the weather had nothing to do with it. She was still crazy about him. She'd tried so hard to deny it, to avoid getting attached to a man whose life was complicated.

The trouble was, Nina had discovered that she *liked* complications.

Willfully, she shifted her focus to her daughter. She'd need to say something to Sonnet, and soon. First, though, she had to figure out what to say.

For now, she contented herself with sipping tea and watching the two girls, best friends who reminded her of herself and Jenny Majesky, years ago, two young women who loved and trusted one another. Jet-lagged, Sonnet was struggling to stay awake, stretched out on the chaise longue. Each girl was on the verge of a major life step. Sonnet was about to start college, Daisy about to give birth. Both shone with a combination of youth, foolishness, fear and excitement. Teenagers, Nina reflected, were the idiot savants of the human race, so smart in some ways, completely clueless in others.

'So anyway,' Daisy was saying, 'I can't wait for you to meet him.' She was talking to Sonnet about Julian Gastineaux, one of her favorite topics. 'I know I sent pictures, but in person, he's even more amazing.'

'What did you tell him about me?' Sonnet asked.

'That you're disgustingly perfect but not to hold that against you,' Daisy said.

'Right,' Sonnet said, 'me, perfect.'

'Total prodigy, straight-A student, and look at all the stuff you did on your internship this summer. You're an international woman of mystery.'

Sonnet yawned. 'Not buying it. I sound totally boring.'

'So did you meet any guys?'

'He*llo*, it's a military base. It was swarming with guys. None of them was interested in me, though. They were all looking for girls who were . . . more adventurous, if you know what I mean.' Sonnet had decided during high school that she wasn't going to have premarital sex, an idea Nina heartily endorsed.

'Oh, yeah,' Daisy said. 'I totally know.'

'All righty then,' Nina said with exaggerated brightness, not loving this topic. 'I'll just take these glasses inside, give you girls a bit of privacy.' She went to the kitchen, making a clatter as she washed the glasses at the sink. Sonnet didn't make a big deal of her vow of abstinence, but Nina knew she was quite serious about it. And why not? Seeing the impact premarital sex had had on her own life, Sonnet was determined to follow a different path.

Nina turned on the radio, humming along as she folded clean clothes from the dryer and took a stack to Sonnet's room. It was barely a room, more like a sleeping nook with a window seat that doubled as a twin bed. Unlike Nina, Sonnet liked neatness and order. She had already unpacked, hanging her clothes with a military precision she might have inherited from her father. The gifts she'd brought back were displayed on a shelf—little items of delft china and bits of hand-tatted lace.

The girls were both quiet when Nina went back outside. Daisy looked up at her. 'She's sound asleep. The jet lag finally got to her. Do you think we should try to get her to bed?'

Nina smoothed her hand over Sonnet's

head. 'I'll do it later.'

Daisy's eyes were bright, her energy level high. 'I'm glad she's back.'

'Me, too.' Nina refused to let herself dwell on the fact that Sonnet would be going away again, very soon. 'You must be pretty excited about the wedding,' Nina said.

'I'm pretty excited about lots of things.'

'That's good. You've got plenty to be excited about.' Nina sensed that Daisy was lingering for a reason. 'Everything all right?'

'Sure. I mean, things are a little awkward with my mom around, but that's to be expected. My mom's pretty much a fish out of water here in Avalon, that's for sure.'

'It's a pretty big leap from the capitals of Europe to a town like this. I'm sure your mom will be fine.'

A silence stretched out between them. There were things Nina wanted to ask Daisy, but didn't let herself. She'd already become too tangled up with this family. But she could wait, and listen.

She didn't have to wait long. Daisy said, 'You know, I thought I'd end up staying with my dad forever because he needs me. And I owe him that, I truly do, but I wish I could know he'd be happy without me.'

Nina was startled. This wasn't what she'd expected to hear from Daisy. 'Just to clarify,' she said. 'You *are* talking about your dad.'

'Yeah, who else?'

Nina was touched. Had Sonnet worried about her in this manner? Yet Nina suspected there was a layer of meaning in Daisy's suggestion. 'And I assume you haven't said a word to him about any of this.'

'He'd only tell me that he'll be fine, which is total b.s. Or, it would have been. Before you came along, I was really worried about my dad.'

'What do you mean, "came along"?' Nina asked. 'I've been here all my life.'

'I mean now that I see my dad with you, for the first time in a really long time, I'm not worried about him.'

*With you.* Nina flushed, wondering how much Daisy knew. She decided to play dumb.

'Daisy, I don't want you to get the wrong idea. I work for your dad. It's not necessarily a permanent arrangement.'

'Not yet, anyway,' Daisy said with breezy assurance. 'It's just good to see him so happy. Good for all of us.' Daisy stared at the citronella candle, flickering on the table. 'I don't want my life to be here.' She almost whispered the words. 'I want . . . something different, for myself and the baby, and it's not here. I've wanted for so long to go away, to be on my own, but then I worry about Dad, and I know he would hate that if he knew, but I can't help it. There's this trapped feeling, I wake up at night and I can't breathe. I feel smothered. But then when I see him with you—'

413

'Daisy, don't make a decision based on your dad or anything but you and the baby. Seriously, you can't live your life for other people. You'll be miserable if you do.'

'I've been doing that all summer. I'm not anymore, though, so, thanks for reminding me I need to find my own life.'

'I didn't—'

'I'd better go.' Daisy yawned and stretched. 'Big day tomorrow.'

After she left, Nina covered Sonnet with a light blanket. Then, restless, she stood looking out at the lake, watching the reflection of moonlit clouds breezing past. *When I see him with you . . .* The thing Daisy didn't understand was that Nina didn't want a permanent arrangement with anyone. Did she? She wasn't supposed to. What she was supposed to be doing was finding herself. Following her dreams. Figuring out who she was now that Sonnet was headed to college. At the beginning of summer, she'd known exactly what she wanted—the inn, and a new sense of freedom. Now she had neither, but her life felt rich in ways she'd never imagined.

There was one problem. Something she could barely stand to admit to herself. And the problem was that every time she thought about the future, images of Greg Bellamy crowded into her mind—and her heart. She had spent the entire summer focusing on all the reasons he was wrong for her and ignoring the only thing that mattered.

It was shocking, how quickly she'd gotten used to having him in her life, waiting for him to come to her every night. Now she missed him so badly she shook with it. Even with her daughter home, she missed his arms around her, his easy laugh, the scent of him and the taste of his kisses. She missed everything about him.

And the terrible thing was, she'd never told him what he meant to her. What was she so afraid of? What was she waiting for? The clock chimed, signaling that midnight had passed. She'd better get to bed, too.

Tomorrow would be the perfect day to tell him. It was a wedding day, after all.

\*    \*    \*

On the day of Connor and Olivia's wedding, Greg got ready in one of the old bunkhouses at Camp Kioga. Once the scene of late-night pranks, kitchen raids and ghost stories, it was now the designated dressing room for the groomsmen and ushers. Greg noticed Max struggling with his tux, and went over to help.

'What's up with the studs, anyway?' Max groused, looking down cross-eyed at his pleated white shirt.

'I just think it's cool that they're called studs,' Greg said. 'Yo, Dad. Max needs help with his studs.'

Charles Bellamy looked impeccable as always—slim, silver-haired, with perfect posture and a ready smile for his youngest grandson. 'Never let it be said I've outlived my usefulness,' he said. 'I've done up my share of studs in my time.'

'Totally pointless,' Max said. 'What's wrong with buttons? Or a zipper? Yeah, a shirt with a zipper—now, that makes sense.'

'Young man, I'll have you know these are Dunhill mother-of-pearl studs, exactly the same kind the men wore at my own wedding. That was fifty-one years ago, right here at Camp Kioga.' With nimble fingers that belied his age, Greg's father helped Max with the studs. 'So,' he said, 'how has your summer gone this year?'

Max shrugged with elaborate nonchalance. 'Okay.'

'Just okay?'

'I got a job with the Hornets,' he said, growing animated. 'That's way better than okay.'

'I'd say so. You're a lucky boy, getting to work with a professional baseball team.'

'Yep. Nina got me the job. Nina Romano—she's awesome.'

No shit, thought Greg. He hadn't seen nearly enough of her lately, what with Nina's daughter here, Sophie in town and the wedding in full swing. The inn was booked solid, a good portion of it with wedding guests, and everyone had been so busy, he couldn't find enough hours in the day to steal away with Nina. If he had all the time in the world, he'd spend it with her—talking and laughing and making love. *Being* in love.

Max held out the silk bow tie at arm's length. 'How about we just forget about this?'

'You wish,' said Greg.

Charles was already standing up the starched collar. 'Brace yourself,' he said. 'I'm going in.'

'This is so gay,' Max said.

Greg laughed. 'You think that'll work on this family?'

'These shoes pinch.' He shuffled his feet, clad in gleaming black tuxedo oxfords.

'That won't work, either.'

'I don't see why getting married is such a big deal,' Max grumbled. 'Most people end up divorced, anyway.'

Greg knew Max was trying to provoke a reaction. But this was no time for a big family discussion 'Nice attitude, buddy.'

'It's true,' Max insisted.

Greg felt his father watching him, watching them both. After having to tell his kids about the divorce, telling his parents was the second-worst thing he'd had to do. He'd felt like such a failure that day. He'd been so ashamed. They'd offered support but ultimately, Greg felt responsible for letting the love seep out of his marriage until it was impossible to recapture.

He took the silk tie from his father and looped it around Max's neck so they were face-to-face. 'Look, buddy. No one can predict the future. People fall in love and sometimes it lasts forever, like Nana and Grandpa. Other times, it changes, the way it did for your mom and me. That's no reason to quit hoping for the best, though. That's what a wedding's about, being in love and trying your best to make it work. It's what we want for Connor and Olivia, and it's why we fasten our shirts with studs and wear bow ties.'

'Huh?'

Greg chuckled. 'Just hold still and let me finish.' Afterward, he stepped back, feeling a surge of pride. 'Check out my boy, Dad. He looks like a million bucks.'

He did. Max's hair had been expertly styled by one of his girl cousins, and his face shone from scrubbing. Over the past year, he'd grown tall and strong, poised on the verge of manhood.

'Can I go outside now?' he asked.

'Don't get dirty.' Greg and his father exchanged a glance.

'So when will I meet this "awesome" Nina Romano?' asked Charles.

'She'll be at the wedding and the reception.'

'Who?' asked Philip, looking remarkably like their father as he nudged his way in front of the mirror.

'Nina Romano, Greg's business partner,' said Charles.

Philip leaned into the mirror to loop his bow tie. 'Yeah, she's coming. Greg's crazy about her. He doesn't think anybody knows, but we all do.'

Greg grabbed a fistful of Philip's shirt and hauled him away from the mirror. 'Mouth,' he said. 'Don't you have some fathering-of-the-bride to do?' He elbowed his way in front of his brother to work on his own tie.

'Olivia's with her mother.' Philip put on a pained expression. He'd been divorced for nearly two decades, and his ex still managed to be difficult, a situation that came to a head when Philip learned Jenny was his biological daughter. Greg gave momentary thanks for Sophie, who wasn't difficult at all. She was the same in divorce as she had been in marriage—absent most of the time.

Charles eyed him speculatively. 'I'm looking forward to meeting her.'

Greg carefully looped the long end of the tie, his movements precise and practiced, which was odd, since he hadn't worn a tux in ages. In fact, it was the same damn tux, altered over the years, he'd worn as best man at Philip's wedding and then to his own. Both marriages had failed. Maybe this was a bad-luck tux. 'Am I crazy, thinking I can do this, all over again?'

'Could be. But why would that stop you?'

419

'I don't want to blow it this time, Dad.'

'Take your own advice. Give it your best effort and don't try to predict the future.'

*          *          *

Walking around the camp, past playing fields, wilderness trails and bunkhouses, filled Greg with memories. In the ball court, Max and some other boys had already shed their jackets and were shooting hoops. Greg yelled at him not to mess up his wedding clothes, but then kept walking. He found his thoughts turning to Nina, but the guests hadn't started to arrive yet. Maybe he should go find Sophie. This was, after all, the place where they'd married long ago. He felt curiously detached from the past, and he wondered if it was the same for Sophie. Since she'd come to Avalon for the wedding, he had spent minimal time with her. The wounds of their marriage had scarred over, though they still ached, and neither of them felt eager to test the strength of their healing. All things considered, he and Sophie were doing a passable job of being exes. Certainly they were better at that than they were at being married.

He thought about Max's attitude, voiced earlier. Was that all the boy had seen? Greg hoped like hell Max would remember that there had been periods of happiness, even moments of joy. But gradually, the dynamic

420

had shifted; there was no denying it. No one had wanted to see or speak of it. Ultimately, though, they all saw the shadow of change, sweeping over them like clouds across the sun. When the four of them were together, they hadn't felt like a family, not in the end. The essential connection, tenuous at best, was gone. Sure, there was still love and caring—for the kids. Between Greg and Sophie, there existed a kind of benign respect.

She seemed different, though Greg couldn't say why. She still possessed that formidable Nordic beauty, and when it came to her professional life, she exuded confidence. But when confronted with her kids, she seemed chastened. Maybe even humbled. Whether it was right or not, they had turned from Sophie. Their rejection had cut deep, exposing a hidden vulnerability that used to be cloaked by her steely reserve.

He hadn't asked her how she was doing. Should he? The role of ex-husband didn't come naturally to him. He knew how to be civil, though. If he could start with that, maybe he'd figure it out.

'Hey,' he said, stepping into the bunkhouse. Inside was an explosion of femininity—garment bags and trimming from bouquets, satin ribbon, spray bottles and jars of things designed to primp and tint and lacquer.

Sophie was by herself, in a sleeveless, light blue dress, ironing a matching jacket. She'd

421

always been a master-ironer, able to smooth every surface of any garment, making it look brand-new again. She worked with efficient competence, down to the last detail.

Greg thought of Nina, who had probably never ironed a thing in her life and didn't intend to.

He ran a finger around the inside of his collar, wondering what kind of etiquette governed this situation. Did he owe Sophie any sort of explanation? He stood and watched her, a stranger he knew with searing intimacy. She knew him the same way, and maybe she always had. He remembered the day he'd told her he was going to sell his firm, move from Manhattan to Avalon.

'Of course you are,' was all she'd said, yet in those four little words was a world of understanding. Now that he thought about it, Greg realized those were the words that had officially ended their marriage.

Sophie's response in the wake of divorce had been different. Something in her compelled her to flee. To run away, fast and far, to hide in a crowd of strangers. Maybe she reinvented herself, showed them an entirely different side of her. He didn't know. It wasn't his business. Sophie had been running from trouble and hurt for as long as he'd known her. After their breakup in college, she had gone abroad to study in Japan, neither of them knowing when the decision was made that she was already pregnant with Daisy.

And so the pattern was set. When it came to her personal life, Sophie didn't retreat from trouble; she fled.

'Did you need something, Greg?' she asked.

'I wanted to make sure you're all right.'

She glided the iron over the jacket. 'Why on earth would you even ask?'

'Because I care. For the kids' sake, I do care, Soph, and for the sake of who we used to be to each other. So . . . I'm sorry you're not okay. Is there anything I can do?'

She smiled. 'No, thank you. You've done enough.'

'Hey, Mom, Dad, can I talk to you?' Daisy took a tentative step into the room.

She looked so terribly young at the moment, with her hair in plastic curlers, like a kid playing dress-up. Except she wasn't playing at anything. Everything was for real. For keeps. 'Okay, um, maybe this'll take a little more than a minute,' she added. 'It's probably not the best timing, but it's not easy, finding the two of you together.'

He and Sophie hadn't made it too easy. They'd become masters of avoiding each other.

Daisy looked from him to Sophie, then back at him. 'First of all, I want to tell you both thank you. I haven't actually said that until now—just, thank you. For everything you've given me all my life, and for being so great about the baby. Thank you. I couldn't have asked for more.'

Greg glanced at Sophie. Daisy hadn't spoken kindly to her mother in a long time. Sophie was blinking back tears, although she held her face perfectly impassive.

'Honey, you know we'd do anything for you,' he said.

She nodded. 'I need to tell you something. Dad, I know you thought I'd stay here and work with you at the inn. But I've given it a lot of thought and I've decided to do something else.'

Greg felt a fistlike clenching of his gut. He literally had to bite the inside of his cheek to keep himself from reacting.

Sophie said nothing.

'Did you know anything about this?' he demanded.

'Don't you dare accuse me—'

'Stop it,' Daisy snapped. 'Just for once, will the two of you please listen to me and not get in a fight?'

Greg clenched his jaw and fell silent, his eyes narrowed in suspicion at Sophie. He could feel her waiting to pounce on the opportunity Daisy was offering. Maybe Sophie saw a chance to finally get their daughter to move overseas with her.

No way, he thought. Over my dead body.

'I'm going to be moving out of the house,' Daisy said.

'Daisy, now is not the time—'

'I have to think about my own life. My future. I'm not sure what it is but I know what it's not. It's not here, at the inn. It's the only future I've got, and I don't want to spend it doing something because I think it's expected of me, or because you or anyone else says it's best.'

A hundred objections crowded up into Greg's throat. He clenched his teeth to keep them in, but it was no use. 'Your life is here,' he said.

'Maybe it *is* here,' Daisy said, 'but then again, maybe it's not. The point is, I need to figure it out on my own.'

Greg caught the scent of something burning. 'Soph,' he said.

She snatched up the iron, revealing a brown triangular burned spot in the jacket she'd been working on. She held it up and shook her head. 'Ruined,' she said. 'And, Daisy, you have a beautiful room and nursery at your father's house. Are you saying you don't want that anymore?'

'I'm saying I appreciate everything,' Daisy said hastily, placatingly. 'But I don't want a room. I want a life of my own. I'm not leaving tomorrow, but I *am* leaving. I'll wait until after Christmas and the start of spring semester. I want to get a place of my own, a job to support myself. I want to go to school. I already sent in my application to the college at New Paltz.'

425

Greg couldn't help himself. It was the kind of insane, idealistic plan he might have expected from the old Daisy. 'I don't get it. Christ, I bought the inn, thinking it would be a good, safe place for you to make a life.'

'Maybe you should have checked with me first, Dad,' she snapped at him.

'Maybe you should have checked with me before getting knocked up,' he snapped back. Oh, shit. Had he really said that? He caught the expression on his daughter's face. Yes. He'd really said that. 'Daze, I didn't mean it.'

'I know. Dad, believe me, I know.' She made a face, as though she felt a twinge of pain, and pressed her hand to the small of her back.

'I'm just completely surprised by this. Honey, do you know how hard that's going to be?'

'A lot of things are hard. Golf. Climbing Mount Everest. Giving birth. That doesn't stop people from doing them.'

Greg glared at Sophie. 'Say something, will you?'

She lifted her chin defensively. 'She's a grown woman. I'm not going to tell her what to do.'

'Mom's right,' Daisy said, intervening before things escalated between them. 'I just need to be on my own,' she concluded.

'That's insane,' Greg said. 'You need to be with your family. You've got a baby to support.'

426

'Two words, Dad,' Daisy reminded him. 'Trust fund. Grandpa Bellamy set them up for each of his grandchildren.'

Right, thought Greg. He crushed his teeth together to keep from mouthing off again. He couldn't help it, though. 'You're too young. I'm not letting you do this.'

'Dad, just listen to me. This is my life. My decision. Nina said—'

'Nina?' asked Sophie. 'What's she got to do with you finding your life?'

Greg felt sucker punched. This was not the first time he'd heard those words. Daisy had been talking to Nina. She'd told him this. She'd known it was going to happen. How had she known? 'Nina told you to go off half-cocked like that?'

'I made the decision myself. And it's not half-cocked. It's what I want. I know it's safe to stay here with you, and for a long time, I tried to make myself believe that was the best plan. Then I realized the only reason I was staying was that I thought I needed to be here for you and Max. But I need to go, Dad. For me.' She went and hugged Sophie and then Greg. 'Anyway, that's what I wanted to tell you. Just so you'll know. I'll see you after the ceremony, okay?'

Once she'd left, Greg turned to Sophie. She put up a hand to hold him silent. 'Before you say anything, I want you to know, I had nothing to do with that, nothing whatsoever.'

'I know,' he said, beginning to do a slow burn when he thought of Nina.

Sophie raised her eyebrows. 'You mean everything's not my fault?'

'Soph.'

'Then we're making progress. And maybe nothing will come of this,' she added. 'We shouldn't worry about anything until there's something to worry about.'

There was something to worry about, all right. Their daughter had always been this way, keeping everything in and not making her move until she knew what move to make. Daisy never would have brought the subject up if she hadn't been a hundred percent serious.

### TWENTY-SIX

As they drove along the lakeshore road on the way to the wedding, Nina tried to hide her nervousness. Twice, she caught herself reaching up to twist a lock of hair.

Sonnet, who'd always had a kind of radar for her mother's moods, shot her a glance from the driver's seat. 'Relax, Mom. I didn't forget how to drive while I was in Belgium.'

Nina was relieved Sonnet had mistaken the source of her nervousness. 'I realize that, but you get rusty. Out of practice. That's why I wanted you to drive. To get back in the game.

428

Everything gets better with practice.'

'Dad let me drive a mobylette around the base,' Sonnet said. 'It's kind of like a moped but with a tiny engine, so you can't go very fast.'

Nina's blood chilled. 'You didn't tell me that.'

'Didn't want to worry you.'

'You shouldn't do that,' she said. 'You shouldn't keep things from me to spare me the worry.'

'Mom. You do it to me, all the time. You always have.'

And just like that, Nina realized Sonnet understood her in ways she'd never imagined. No one loved her the way Sonnet did.

'So what was it like, really, being part of a two-parent family?' she asked.

'It was all right. Interesting.'

'In what way?'

'I never saw a marriage up close before. Never quite clued in on the way it worked.'

'What did you think?'

'Dad and Angela . . . they're good together. Not perfect, but they take care of each other.'

Nina was moved by Sonnet's wistful tone. 'That's what I want for you one day.' She wanted her daughter to learn how people loved each other and, yes, how they hurt each other. She wanted Sonnet to figure out how to survive all of it and still be able to hold hands with the same guy after fifty years.

The turnoff to Camp Kioga was marked by a cluster of pearl-white helium balloons. 'It's what I want for you, too, Mom.'

Nina felt a surge of emotion. This thing with Greg was turning her into a leaky faucet. She looked out the window to cover her reaction. As the deep, shadowy forest flickered past, she took a deep breath, blinked fast and tried to regain her equilibrium.

'Mom?' Sonnet prodded.

'That's sweet of you,' Nina said.

They arrived a bit early for the wedding. Camp Kioga was beautifully festooned for the occasion and the parking lot was full. People had waited a long time for Olivia and Connor to get married, and a good many guests were expected. Nina scanned the area for Greg, but didn't see him. She hadn't slept well last night as she tied herself in knots, wondering what she would say to him. He seemed convinced that they were falling in love, making the declaration as easily as if he were giving a weather report. She wasn't so certain, yet she knew she was consumed by her unadmitted obsession with him. All right, she admitted it to herself. She was obsessed with the man. She'd never experienced anything like . . . whatever it was she was having with him. It had exploded into far more than a one-night stand. They'd been together every chance they got. So was it a fling? No, not a fling. A fling was lighthearted, fun and frothy. And finite.

430

She couldn't quite convince herself that the thing with Greg was a fling.

'Affair' sounded too dark and dramatic. Nina didn't have 'affairs.' She dated, and then she moved on. That was what she was supposed to be doing now that her nest was empty, dating and moving on. Instead, she found herself yearning for Greg, wishing the world would go away so she could be with him.

Row upon row of rented chairs had been set up for the guests. There was an aisle leading to a flower-festooned archway over a raised dais. 'I'm glad they don't do that whole "friends of the bride, friends of the groom" thing,' Sonnet said as Max escorted them to their seats.

'I'm glad, too,' Nina said. 'I always thought it was a dumb tradition, plus it was bound to make one of them look more popular than the other.'

'Thanks, Max,' Sonnet said. 'You look like a million bucks. Seriously, you little hottie.'

He blushed to the tips of his ears. 'No talking during the ceremony.'

'And I am *so* dancing with you at the reception,' Sonnet added.

'If you're lucky,' he said.

'I'm always lucky.'

Nina watched him hurry off to help someone else. 'You made him blush,' she said.

'He's twelve, Mom. Everything makes him blush. Daisy said you helped him out a lot this summer. That was nice of you.'

431

'It's easy to be nice to a kid like Max.' She tried not to be too obvious as she looked around. Toward the front, the families gathered. The Bellamys were a handsome bunch, from Charles and Jane, the dignified matriarch and patriarch, to Max, the youngest grandson, already showing promise of the family's heartbreaker good looks. Yet they were only human like everyone else, as evidenced by the subdued mother and father of the bride. Philip Bellamy had been divorced from Pamela Lightsey for many years, yet just for today, they presented a united and loving front. Nina knew the harmony had been hard-won, though, given their turbulent past. Decades earlier, with the wrongheaded desperation of people who would go to any lengths to preserve their daughter's happiness, the Lightseys had ruthlessly engineered the marriage of Philip to Pamela. And, as anyone could have predicted, the marriage hadn't lasted. But the consequences of the Lightseys' interference had. Thanks to them, Philip had never known about Jenny, until he found out by accident last summer. It was amazing, Nina thought, what people would do in order to manipulate their children's lives.

Perhaps one of the saddest victims of the debacle was Pamela herself, the mother of the bride. She had never remarried. According to Jenny, she lived a lonely life in her luxurious Fifth Avenue apartment, attending fund-raiser teas, serving on committees and collecting art. She looked fiercely proud today, though, awaiting the bride with the rest of the gathering. Her parents were not present. According to Jenny, Mr. Lightsey was in the hospital, and they'd sent a lavish tea service from Tiffany's as a wedding gift.

Nina felt a subtle change in the air, and she craned her neck around, spying Greg. Her heart kicked into overdrive, and she tried not to stare, but in his tux, he looked like a dream come true. She tried to catch his eye, but he seemed very serious and distracted. At one point, she thought he was looking at her but his gaze skimmed right past.

She suspected the cause of his seriousness was sitting across the aisle and near the back— Sophie, his ex-wife. She was coolly beautiful in a crisp linen sleeveless dress and open-toed pumps. Sophie Bellamy resembled a classical statue of a goddess, but better-dressed. Nina knew that if she was more savvy about fashion, she'd recognize the label of the couture dress. Nina had been careful not to ask Sonnet too much about Sophie. Yet now the girl noticed Nina's scrutiny. 'I knew you were curious,' she said. 'She's really smart and has this amazing job. You know how some kids pretend like their parents have these big, important jobs, like they're saving humanity? Well, Sophie really is.'

'So I heard.' Nina had expected to dislike

Sophie. To disapprove of her. After all, she'd left a husband and two hurting kids to go jetting off to Europe, hadn't she? Now Nina was forced to consider the possibility that the situation was more complicated.

Sonnet leaned over and said, 'Don't worry, people are impressed by you, too. All I've heard about since I got back is how incredible you've made the Inn at Willow Lake.'

'I don't change people's lives. Just their weekend, maybe. If anyone's impressed by me, it's because of my awesome daughter.' Nina gave her hand a squeeze. Sonnet had come back from Europe more polished and smarter than ever, yet just as wide-eyed about the world, and just as kind-hearted. Sitting with her, waiting for the wedding to begin, Nina felt a keen sense of just what she would lose when Sonnet went away for good. No one in this world held Nina in the same love and regard.

'I'm happy for you, Mom. You know that, right?' Sonnet whispered. 'I'm glad you and Greg are—'

'Greg and I are what?' Nina felt a chill of alarm. She hadn't said anything. She and Greg had barely seen each other since Sonnet had returned.

'I think he's great, Mom.'

The five-piece string ensemble ended its tender rendition of Pachelbel's Canon, leaving a pause of silence. People shifted in their seats, cleared their throats. Then the wedding march swelled in grand strains from the musicians. Heads swiveled to the aisle as the wedding party made its entrance. When Nina caught sight of Jenny on the arm of the groom's brother, Julian, she unexpectedly teared up. Jenny looked ethereal and lovely in her gown, with violet freesias in her hair, carrying a bouquet of white roses. Nina flashed on a collage of moments of their childhood together—the sleepovers, the fits of giggles, the earnest plans they'd made for their weddings. How differently things had turned out for both of them. Nina realized these were tears for the way she was feeling now, for the things she wanted to say to Greg, for all her hopes and regrets.

Olivia looked vulnerable and gorgeous at the same time. Connor made a magnificent bridegroom—towering and imposing, almost intimidating in his good looks and presence, until he smiled. Then he just glowed with goofy happiness, and it transformed him into the person Nina knew he was—a great guy who'd led a lonely life until he met Olivia. These two were so good to each other. Even a casual observer could see the caring in their eyes and hear it ringing in their voices as they spoke their vows.

Together, the two of them made love look effortless. Nina knew it hadn't been, of course—it never was—but now they shone with hope and confidence. It made her wonder what the future held for them. Yes, they adored each other now. What would it take to stay that way? What did it take for any couple to stay in love? She thought about her own parents. On the surface, it seemed that Pop was the dreamer, Ma the realist. Now she wondered if maybe Ma had dreams, too, but nobody knew what they were. Pop's big dreams and goals eclipsed them. For the first time in her life, Nina could understand why her mother was perfectly content with this, and that worried Nina. A lot.

With so many brothers and sisters, Nina had attended many weddings in her time. She tried to tally up all the occasions, but she'd lost count. The first was for her aunt Isabella. She was five years old, and a flower girl. She remembered a succession of joyful brides, weeping mothers, proud grooms, loud parties. She dearly loved weddings—the music, the ceremony, the rituals, the toasts, the emotions. Today, she felt different. For the first time ever, she didn't just want to toast the bride. She wanted to *be* the bride.

Frightened by the thought, she listened, really listened to the words and prayers of a wedding service. She was moved, yet at the same time, completely skeptical. How could two rational individuals stand there and pledge their lifelong devotion to one another? Were they crazy? Didn't they realize life was full of surprises, some of them not so welcome?

Yet today, she watched the bride and groom through new eyes. For the first time in her life, she could understand the hope and possibility that compelled two people to make those vows. For the first time, she could imagine herself saying the words, meaning them, dedicating herself to keeping a vow to love someone forever.

When the ceremony concluded, she tried again to make eye contact with Greg. He was busy with the rest of the family, being herded around by the photographer. She'd find him at the reception, then.

But the reception was a giddy whirlwind of toasting and dancing, the music so loud it was necessary to shout to be heard. Nina felt uncharacteristically subdued. No, that was putting it mildly. She was taken back to the days when she was Mrs. Romano's cheeky daughter, an outsider, a misfit who would never make it as a Bellamy.

'Hey, you,' someone said. 'Let's dance.'

'Connor! Congratulations,' she said, putting her hand in his. 'To what do I owe this honor?'

'My father stole my bride and I need consoling.' He gestured at the dance floor, where Olivia was dancing with Terry Davis. Olivia's father, Philip Bellamy, had claimed Laura Tuttle from the bakery as his partner, and the sight of them brought a smile to her lips. They were both so clearly smitten with each other. Like everyone else in town, Nina had always thought Laura would stay single her whole life. Now, at an age when some people were counting down the years to retirement, Laura was taking the ultimate leap of faith.

'Love is in the air, huh?' Connor remarked, leading her onto the floor.

'Like a virus.'

He laughed and firmed up his dance hold, making up in humor what he lacked in grace. 'Ha. You're not so tough.'

Nina scanned the room, admiring Olivia's friends with their boarding-school accents and polished social skills. She simply didn't have whatever it was these people had. It wasn't breeding but something ineffable she couldn't begin to grasp or articulate. 'I don't really fit in here,' she confessed to Connor.

He chuckled. 'I felt the same way,' he said. 'A bull in a china shop. Olivia and I come from different worlds. But that's just an excuse.'

The song ended and she wished him well, and watched him go over to reclaim his bride. Mulling over his words, she conceded he was right. She needed to get past her fears. On the one hand, she couldn't wait to talk to Greg. Yet at the same time, she felt downright afraid. She was poised on the verge of a supreme happiness, and it scared her to find herself in such a vulnerable position. The hall was crowded and maybe it wasn't the best place to tell Greg what her heart had been urging her to say to him. She tried it out in silence. I love you, Greg. I love you. I. Love. You. Iloveyou . . . Finally, finally the words made sense to her. At last she felt something she'd never understood before, and it was like freefalling out of an airplane.

*       *       *

Greg wanted to relax and enjoy the wedding. It wasn't often all the Bellamys gathered in one place, and he wished he could appreciate it more. But he was ticked-off and distracted. At the reception, he watched the dancing and toasting. He stood at the top of the stairs that led down to the dock, trying to psyche himself up to join in. Daisy sat at a table, eating a plate heaped with food and talking earnestly with her mother. At least they were talking, he thought. Then suspicion stabbed at him. Maybe now, in the wake of Daisy's big announcement, Sophie would try to convince their daughter to move overseas with her. Maybe . . . Damn, he hated this. Why wouldn't Daisy simply let him take care of her?

'Hey.' Suddenly Nina was at his side.

For a moment, he felt a spike of pure attraction. He studied her flushed face, her sparkling smile.

'Champagne?' she offered, taking two flutes from the tray of a passing waiter. The motion raised a series of memories in Greg, something he thought he'd forgotten. But standing here, taking a glass of champagne from her, he realized they were in the same place they'd been at another wedding—Greg's. It had taken place right here at Camp Kioga. He'd gotten drunk and put his fist through a wall. He could still see a slight scar where the Sheetrock had been repaired. It would never be exactly the same. An inauspicious beginning. Yet he'd been so certain it could work. So had Sophie.

This summer, Nina had turned him into a true believer all over again. He'd been inches from opening his heart to her. Then Daisy had delivered a necessary reality check. Now Nina stood there looking completely beautiful and without guile. As she had ever since he'd first met her, she represented the unattainable. The thing he couldn't have. He'd been stupid to think anything had changed.

He had intended to wait until after the wedding to confront her, but since she'd cornered him, they could have it out now. He held open the door and she stepped outside, heading down the stairs to the lakeshore. It was sunset, the lake on fire with color, mocking his mood.

Nina turned to him, her full lips moist, as though she expected him to kiss her.

'Daisy says she's moving out,' he told her bluntly. 'After the baby.'

Nina blinked, as though surprised. 'Really.'

'Yeah, just like you said. I wonder how you

knew.'

She recoiled from his anger. He had to force himself to ignore the hurt in her eyes. She said, 'I have no idea what you're talking about.'

'Right. She's going away to find her life.'

'And this is a bad thing?'

'Hell, yes, it's bad. She belongs at the inn. With me.'

'So it's all about you now.'

He glared at her. 'That's bullshit. It's about keeping my daughter safe.'

'It's about keeping her where you can control her.' A bitter laugh burst from Nina. 'You know, I had something entirely different in mind that I wanted to talk about. But you just spared me the trouble.'

'What the hell is that supposed to mean?' he demanded.

Her face looked stiff, as though she was battling to keep her emotions in check. 'Believe me, you don't want to know.'

'Just . . . keep your advice to Daisy to yourself from now on, okay?' he said. 'She's not you, Nina. She's not ready to take on the world.'

'And you think I was?'

'I think—Christ—I just wish you'd back off when it comes to my daughter.'

She narrowed her eyes at him, but he could still see the glitter of temper there. 'Did you ever think maybe *you* should back off when it came to your daughter?'

441

'Screw you, Nina.' Operating on fear, he lashed out, shocking even himself with his anger, using just a few words to trash everything they had built together throughout the summer. He watched her face turn pale, her eyes widen as anger turned to hurt. 'Look, it's not working—this, the inn—it would be better if we didn't see each other.'

She crossed her arms defensively in front of her. 'That's going to be a bit of a challenge, seeing how we work together.'

Go ahead, he told himself. Throw it all away. 'Maybe that's going to need to change.'

'You can't be serious.' Her hands dropped to her hips, drawing attention to the fact that she looked amazing tonight, dressed to the nines for the wedding. 'You *are* serious. How convenient for you, that you're able to fire someone and break up with her all in one step.'

He felt them falling apart, which was so depressing. They'd barely had a chance. Maybe it was better this way, better to cut their losses. Daisy was the issue here. He needed to keep his focus on that. At the same time, he hated what he'd just done. 'Nina,' he said.

She was halfway up the stairs. She paused, but didn't turn to look at him. Then, bracing her hand on the railing, she kept on going.

Greg eyed the smooth wall, balling his hand into a fist. At the top of the stairs, a door burst open. Sophie stepped out, barely glancing at

442

Nina. For a second, Greg found himself caught between the two of them, one his past, one his future, neither happy with him.

'It's Daisy,' Sophie said. 'We need to go to the hospital.'

## TWENTY-SEVEN

They couldn't have done a worse job planning. They should have assumed she could go into labor at any given moment. No one had allowed that the baby might make his appearance on the wedding day. Sophie had driven to the camp in her rental car—a two-door subcompact of the tiny type she'd grown accustomed to in Europe—and Greg had brought his work truck. They ended up borrowing Philip's SUV, because it was roomiest in the back. Greg helped himself to a stack of clean table linens and tea towels from the caterer's van, yelling at someone that he'd replace them. They definitely needed towels; in childbirth class they'd been advised to keep a supply in the car. In fact, the instructor had actually suggested a tarp.

Nothing went according to plan. The exodus was supposed to unfold in orderly fashion. Phone calls would be made calmly and without shouting. A prepacked suitcase would be loaded into the car. They would reach the hospital by driving at cautious speeds.

Instead, Greg roared with frustration at the lack of a cell-phone signal and sent his mother to the office to use the landline while he and Sophie helped Daisy to the car. During that process, the pains came fast and hard, and Daisy started to cry, each sob skewering Greg with panic. He started the car, but Sophie appeared at his side. 'I'll drive.'

'But—'

'Dad . . .' Daisy's voice strained toward him.

Greg swore and got out. It wasn't supposed to happen like this. But he'd signed on as her birth coach, and he couldn't do that if he was driving. He got into the backseat, realizing then why the childbirth instructor had suggested the tarp. Sorry about your upholstery, bro, he thought.

Jenny's husband, Rourke McKnight, who was chief of police, offered an escort with emergency lights, but Daisy refused. Between pains, she seemed a bit sheepish about all the attention. 'This is Olivia's day,' she said past gritted teeth. 'Let's go as quietly as possible. Just the three of us.'

Sophie pulled out of the parking lot and headed down the road, the tires spitting gravel and dust. Greg looked back just in time to see Max. He walked over to Nina. She didn't hesitate, but pulled him into a fierce hug. Then a cloud of dust obscured the small knot of family and wedding guests. Daisy half lay

444

across the seat in her now-ruined bridesmaid's dress, her hands braced against the seat. 'It'll be all right, baby,' he said to her. 'We'll be at the hospital soon.'

She went rigid with pain and fear. Her face glowed moon-white and her breath came in shallow pants. When a pain hit, he noted the time on his cell phone and guided her through the breathing they'd learned in their classes.

'It's . . . bad,' she said. 'I . . . can't . . . can't . . .' A wild fright gleamed in her eyes.

He realized the classes could only go so far to prepare them for what was to come. They hadn't addressed the bone-deep fear he saw in her, or his own supreme sense of helplessness. 'We'll be there soon,' he said inanely. 'The doc will give you something.'

'It hurts now. I can't stand it.' A note of hysteria tightened her voice.

He glanced at Sophie. She kept her eyes glued to the road and drove with grim competence, her hands clutching the steering wheel. A streak of sweat trickled down her temple, and he realized she wasn't grim at all, but terrified, every bit as scared as Daisy was.

'Daddy, help me, make it stop, make it stop.' Daisy breathed the chanted plea through her clenched teeth.

If there was a definition of hell on earth, it was this—being powerless to keep your child from hurting when she was begging you to make it stop.

'Soon, honey,' he said. 'Hang in there.'

'I can't . . . I . . . have to—'

He saw it coming a split second before she erupted. Instinctively he scrambled back, plastering himself against the door, but there was nowhere to go. She spewed up everything she'd consumed at the wedding reception. He didn't freak. He didn't gross out. He handed her a wad of tea towels he'd grabbed from the caterer and said, 'It's okay, Daze. Take it easy.'

She miserably wiped her face with one of the linen napkins. 'I was starving at the reception. I ate everything in sight.'

No kidding, thought Greg, using a towel on his trousers and shoes. He told Sophie, 'The road gets bumpy up ahead. It's another quarter mile to the paved highway.'

'Let me concentrate on driving, Greg. You look after Daisy,' she muttered. The moment her cell phone beeped, indicating it had found a signal as they approached town, she snatched it up. Without taking her eyes off the road, she put in the number of the hospital.

That was Sophie, he observed. Super-competent when it came to things like dialing a phone from touch memory. She said Daisy was all right, except that she'd thrown up, gave an estimate of their arrival time, then rang off.

'They've already heard from your Grandma Jane,' she said to Daisy. 'We'll be there soon, I promise.'

It was highly unlikely that Daisy heard this,

446

since she was in the grip of another pain.

'Breathe, honey,' he coached her, exactly the way they'd learned in the class, but the one thing he couldn't do was take her pain away. She clutched Greg's hand and squeezed, and it was as though she was squeezing his heart. He ached for his little girl, so frightened and in such agony. He knew then that he would not let her leave, despite what she'd said earlier. He wanted—needed—to keep her safe with him.

Sophie brought the car to a stop under the covered walkway at the hospital entrance. Greg jumped out and ran around to help Daisy. Between contractions, she wore a benumbed look of confusion. The doors *whooshed* open, yet there didn't seem to be anyone around. Sophie rolled down the window. 'Why don't you wait here, and I'll go get someone with a gurney or wheelchair?'

Daisy moaned a little. Greg wasn't waiting another second. 'Just park the goddamned car, Sophie,' he barked, and swept Daisy up as though she was five years old again, carrying her through the door.

*     *     *

Someone—an orderly or nurse—showed Greg where to clean up and don a set of scrubs. He changed in a hurry, stuffing his wedding clothes in a bin marked Biohazard. They were,

447

he rationalized. He should have known better than to wear that tux. It was freaking bad luck, that was for sure. Good riddance.

With his feet covered by disposable booties, he skidded along a marked hallway, making his way to labor and delivery. The efficient staff had already helped Daisy change into a hospital gown, and someone assured him the doctor and anaesthesiologist were on the way. Daisy looked small and weak, imprisoned by the barred bed and all the monitoring equipment. She still had wilted flowers in her hair from the wedding, which now seemed as though it had taken place a hundred years ago. Greg wedged himself between a monitor on a cart and the head of the bed. He touched her shoulder. 'How you doing, Daze?'

Before long, the doctor arrived. It wasn't Daisy's regular doctor but the woman on night duty, yet she seemed calm and efficient as she examined the chart and checked a computer screen. 'You the father?' she asked Greg.

'Yeah,' he said, 'I mean, no, I'm—uh—Daisy's father. The patient's father.'

'He's my dad,' Daisy said, 'and birth coach.'

All the same, Greg stepped outside while the doctor did an assessment. While he was waiting, Sophie arrived, now also clad in scrubs, her face porcelain pale in contrast to the greenish fabric.

'So far so good, I think,' he told her.

'When can we go in?' she asked.

448

'It won't be long.'

She nodded, studied the gleaming tiled floor. Watching her, he felt a gentle nudge of regret. 'Pretty amazing driving, Soph,' he told her. 'I didn't get a chance to tell you that. And you even knew the way.'

'I memorized the route.'

Of course she had.

He cleared his throat. 'And, uh, about what I said before . . . I didn't mean to yell at you about parking the car.'

She nodded again, which didn't exactly signify forgiveness or understanding. It probably signified, 'But you still yelled at me.'

'All things considered,' he said with forced heartiness, 'we make a pretty good team.'

She stared at him. 'No,' she said. 'We don't. But we're both on Daisy's side, and I assume that's what she needs from us.'

The door opened, and they went inside. The doctor gave them a rundown. Things were progressing. The baby was in position, his vital signs normal, and Daisy would be getting an epidural. 'Could be a long night,' the doctor said.

Greg positioned himself on one side of the bed, Sophie on the other. They regarded each other across their laboring daughter, bound for the time being by wordless solidarity.

The minutes dragged into hours. Greg offered ice chips and cool cloths. Personnel came in and out, checking on Daisy. An

449

epidural was administered. Sophie stepped out occasionally to phone Max, reassuring him that everything was fine. Daisy slept a little, cried a little, and spent most of her time staring straight ahead at a photograph of Ayers Rock, which hung incongruously on the wall opposite the bed. At some point in the middle of the night, the doctor declared that it was time to push. The bed was repositioned, the lower half rolled away, handles and foot rests raised.

Daisy nodded. She grabbed Greg's hand, and at last, he saw, the fear and the pain were gone. She wore an expression of steely determination, and for a moment she looked so much like Sophie that he thought he was seeing things.

'Let's go, Daddy-O,' she said.

'You got it, Daisy-O,' he replied.

She pushed like a champ, coordinating her efforts with the contractions, just like they'd been taught. Greg's world shrank to the expression on his daughter's face—red and scrunched, teeth gritted, tears squeezing from her eyes, sweat soaking her hair. It broke his heart to watch her, but he didn't waver; he murmured encouragement. He heard the doctor narrating the progress, and finally, when it seemed Daisy was about to give out from exertion, a collective gasp went up. 'And here he is,' the doctor announced. There was a gurgling suction sound, followed by a thin, vibrato cry. 'He looks gorgeous.'

Sophie began to sob, a sound so alien to Greg that at first he didn't know what it was. Then he saw her pull the mask from her face so she could bend and kiss Daisy's forehead.

A blood-streaked bundle lay atop Daisy. For the shadow of a second, stark terror shone in her eyes. Then her arms went around the little bundle in a powerful embrace. 'Hello, baby,' she whispered. 'Hello, my precious little baby.'

Greg's knees felt weak. He felt weak all over as he stared in wonder. Someone put an instrument in his hands.

'You want to do the honor?'

He looked down at his trembling hand. Oh, yeah. Oh, shit, he had to cut the cord. He gritted his teeth, forced his hand to stop shaking and stepped forward. Someone held the tied-off cord between two gloved hands. Steady as a rock, he severed it with a decisive clip.

\*     \*     \*

Among her friends and family, Daisy temporarily achieved the status of minor celebrity. By the next evening, nearly everyone they knew had stopped by with flowers or a gift, leaving good wishes. At the hospital's birthing center, patients weren't treated as though they were sick. Visitors were allowed to come and go at will, instructed to scrub with

451

disinfectant and take their cue from the new mother.

Greg and Sophie took turns sitting with their daughter. Emile Charles Bellamy was declared perfect and healthy, and was allowed to room in with his mother. He'd been examined, inoculated, bathed and swaddled and now he slept in a clear Lucite bassinet on a rolling cart, his tiny head covered by a pale blue cap. A fine fringe of reddish peach-fuzz hair peeked out from beneath the cap. The sight of it came as something of a shock to everyone who saw the baby. It was the first concrete evidence of something the Bellamys hadn't really thought much about—somewhere, the baby had a father. With red hair.

Sophie went back to her hotel to shower and change, and Max arrived with Greg's parents. All three of them stood by the bassinet, staring as though frozen in an enchantment. Finally Greg's mother, Jane, looked up, beaming and crying at the same time. 'He's just glorious.'

Max concurred. 'Pretty cute,' he said.

Daisy grinned. 'You think?'

'Totally. When's he going to wake up?'

'I think he's supposed to sleep for a while. We had a long night.'

To Greg it felt surreal, standing there and watching his kids converse—rather than bicker—like adults. His heart felt enormous, as though it had grown too big for his chest.

He was wrung out; he could barely even look at his parents. If he did, he was worried he might break down like everyone else around here.

'Do me a favor,' Daisy said to Max. 'Tell Olivia I'm sorry I disrupted her wedding.'

'Are you kidding? She's totally happy for you. Said she can't wait to come and see you. She and Connor want to stop in and see the baby before they take off for St. Croix.'

'Oh, I hope they do.'

'So can we wake him up?' Max asked.

'Don't you dare,' Daisy said. 'But . . . hand him to me, will you? I just feel like holding him.'

Max reached into the bassinet, then stepped back. 'I don't really know how to pick him up.'

Greg patted him on the shoulder. 'Same way you do everything for a baby. Really, really gently.' He bent down and curled his hands under the soft bundle. Warmth seeped into his bones as he passed the baby to Max. 'Easy now,' he said. 'You'll be amazed at how light he feels.'

'Nine pounds isn't so light,' Greg's mother said. 'Dear, we're very happy for you, aren't we, Charles.'

'Proudest great-grandparents in the world,' Greg's father agreed.

Max held the baby awkwardly, and shuffled over to the bed as though carrying a stick of dynamite. 'Here you go,' he said to Daisy.

453

'Here we go,' she said, settling the blanket into the crook of her arm. The baby stirred, stretching his head back and emitting a puppylike sound, but he didn't wake up. His tiny red fists clutched the edge of the blanket. Daisy gazed down at him, smiling. One minute, she looked as vulnerable as the baby, and the next, as fierce and protective as a mother bear.

Her grandparents kissed her and the baby, and took Max to the cafeteria to get something to eat. Greg lingered, stealing glances at the baby. With each passing minute, he felt something growing in his heart—a peculiar kind of joy, the kind that lifted him up off the floor, made everything suddenly seem effortless. Daisy seemed to be feeling it, too. She held the swaddled bundle, gazing down with an expression on her face that reminded Greg of every Christmas morning they'd ever shared, all rolled into one.

Then she lifted her eyes, and the smile disappeared as she looked at something over his shoulder. He turned to see a stranger in the doorway.

'Logan,' Daisy said.

Greg stiffened. So this was Logan O'Donnell. Al O'Donnell's boy. He had the look of his father—broad and handsome, blue-eyed, with a shock of flame-colored hair. A sharp sense of protectiveness seized Greg.

'Logan, this is my dad,' Daisy said.

'Mr. Bellamy.' Logan held out his hand.

Greg hesitated. He felt a sharp spike of aversion. Then he remembered himself, eighteen years ago, a sudden father greeting Sophie's parents for the first time. He took the proffered hand. 'Logan.'

'Sir, I didn't come to cause trouble,' Logan said. 'I need to see Daisy and . . . the baby.'

'It's okay, Dad,' Daisy said. 'I called him.'

With leaden reluctance, he left them alone. As he turned to shut the door, he saw Logan approach the bed as though approaching a wild animal, slowly, his gaze never wavering. Daisy angled the baby toward him and said something, and he took a step closer, his face lit with reverence.

As Greg quietly closed the door, the joy he felt over the baby—his *grandson*—darkened as he felt Daisy being torn from him. She'd called Logan O'Donnell. She was already making her own decisions, her own connections, without consulting him. On the one hand, Greg understood that this was healthy, a necessary step away from him, from home. She needed to take control, make decisions on her own.

Just like Nina had told him. Oh, man. *Nina.* He was in agony as he paced the hospital corridor. He lost track of time, and was in thought when Logan came out of Daisy's room. He looked chastened, his eyes damp. 'I want you to know, Daisy and I are going to figure out a way to make this work,' he said. 'I know you want what's best for her. It's what I

455

want, too.'

Greg rubbed his jaw. He hadn't shaved in a hundred years. 'You're saying the right things, Logan. I hope that means you'll do the right thing.'

'I will,' the boy said. He glanced down at a handwritten list on a scrap of paper. 'She wants a pizza.'

Greg nodded. 'It's a start.'

As soon as Logan left, Greg went back in to see Daisy. Her eyes were damp, too, but she looked calm. 'I'm fine, Dad,' she said. 'It's going to be all right.'

'I hope so, Daze. Just, please. Don't rush into anything.'

'I won't. Logan and I haven't decided anything yet. We need to do a lot more talking.' She hugged the sleeping baby closer. 'At first, I thought I never wanted to see him again. I didn't want him to have anything to do with Charlie.'

'Charlie?'

'Logan says people might mispronounce Emile.'

'You think?'

Her eyes misty, she leaned back against the pillows. 'Anyway, Dad, you mean the world to me. I can't imagine what my life would have been like without you, and so I started thinking, what about Emile? What if he needs Logan the way I've always needed you?'

Greg had to clear his throat. He prayed his

voice wouldn't break. 'You know I'll always be there for you, no matter what.'

'I do, Dad. And . . . you can go, you know,' Daisy said to Greg.

'I know.' He stayed where he was.

'We're going to be okay, this little guy and me.'

'I know that, too. I thought I'd wait until your mother gets back.'

'You don't have to.' She toyed with a corner of the baby's blanket. 'I was so glad you were both with me last night,' she said.

'We'll always be with you.'

'I thought, I don't know, just for a minute I thought the baby and I would bring the two of you together, heal something.'

'We aren't together,' he told her. 'But something was healed.'

She smiled. 'That's good. And seriously, I want you to know, that even after everything that happened yesterday, I meant what I said to you and Mom before the wedding.'

'Daze, we don't need to talk about that, not now.'

'Maybe not, but I don't want you to forget or pretend it's news to you that I want to be on my own.' He started to say something, but she stopped him with a look. 'I know you. That's what you do, you act like you never heard this before. I want to make sure this doesn't get put on the back burner. It's my life. I do love you, Daddy, and there are some things that are just so much easier when I'm with you. But that's not living my life. That's being your daughter. There's a difference. I need to be my own person—for myself, and now for Emile.'

'I'm not opposed to that,' he said.

'Yes, you are. And you need to get used to it. And another thing. Don't be all pissed at Nina for giving me advice.' She smiled with a peculiar female wisdom. 'I know all about Nina.'

'No idea what you're talking about,' he stated, although his stomach was churning. How the hell did she do it? He had a glass head.

'We both know. Listen, when you went out with other women, I couldn't quite figure out why it was hard for me to like them. I thought it was probably because deep down, I only wanted you to be with Mom. Or by yourself. And now there's Nina.'

Nina, he thought. The hell with Nina. The hell with anyone who would tell Daisy to go off on her own. He should not even be thinking of Nina at a time like this, but for some reason, she stayed on his mind. She'd looked so happy and breathless at the wedding, moments before he ripped into her. She'd been dewy-eyed, wearing an expression he'd seen on her face only rarely, like when they'd been making love. Why couldn't she be that woman? His lover, his confidante. Not someone who would encourage his daughter to leave home.

But then . . . Greg pictured her smile. The way she got so excited about things. Her open manner with everyone she met. Her quick temper, quicker laughter and her swift, honest passion for the things she did . . . for him.

'I'm happy for you, Dad.' Daisy's face glowed as though she was in possession of some kind of mystical feminine wisdom. 'Really. I think you and Nina are great together. I can tell you're crazy about each other, and I just feel like this is different, you know. I love seeing you with her. She brings you alive, Dad, really.'

Oh. Well, shit.

'What's that look, Dad?'

'I, um, I kind of broke up with her at the wedding reception.'

'Tell me you didn't. Tell me you did not do this incredibly stupid thing.'

'I did this incredibly stupid thing.'

'Then go undo it, Dad. Hurry.'

### TWENTY-EIGHT

Late at night, Nina stood on the dock of the Inn at Willow Lake, maybe for the last time. She was bidding farewell to a long-held dream, but more than that, to something infinitely richer and deeper. To the love she'd found with Greg. She suspected his 'you're fired' was

459

blurted out in haste. But Nina didn't actually need to hear the words. She knew she had made the decision in her heart before she consciously thought it—*I can't stay here.*

It was hard on every single level to say goodbye. But the Inn at Willow Lake was just a place, she reminded herself. A place she'd dreamed about, a place she'd lived and worked at for a while. Now it was time to move on, taking her dreams with her. She hoped she would always remember the sound of the loons on the lake, the glassy path of the full moon on the water, the stirring of the breeze through the maples and the gentle ripples across the surface.

It was a beautiful summer night, the kind of night that closed around you and made you feel safe, but she didn't feel that now. She walked out to the very end of the dock, her heart full of nostalgia. It was as though her tethers had been cut. She was flying free, aimlessly, with no thought as to where she would land. Maybe that was a good thing, but it didn't feel so good. She felt overwhelmed and . . . damaged somehow, as if a part of her had been ripped away, not by the thought of leaving this place, but by the thought of leaving Greg Bellamy.

How crazy was that, to fall in love with him? She'd spent the whole summer talking herself out of it, and in the end, her heart had pulled her in over her head anyway. Love. It was something she thought she knew. She loved her family, her friends. She loved her daughter with a depth and commitment that had no end. But this was something wholly different, heady and consuming, yet . . . fragile. Uncertain. Why had she let herself believe loving Greg could be enough to hold them together?

She wasn't sure how long she'd been standing there when she heard someone behind her. One of the guests? No, it was—

'Nina.' Greg walked toward her. She recognized his voice and his easy, loose-limbed gait. The moonlight outlined his form in precise detail. The silvery glow cast everything in shades of gray, as though they were images from an old movie.

She felt her heart speed up. Just the sight of him, even now, made her happy. Yet at the same time, she was on the verge of tears. Stop it, she told herself. Not now. She cleared her throat and asked him, 'How's Daisy?'

'She's great. The baby's great, too.' He seemed to have come fresh from the shower, she noticed, in a Hawaiian shirt and shorts, his hair damp and fragrant. 'She named him Emile. It's French.'

'I know.'

'Don't ask me why she picked it. His middle name's Charles, after my dad.'

'That's good.' She silently begged him to stop telling her about his life; she had to learn not to care about these things. 'And how are

461

you?'

'Relieved. Happy. Completely freaked. I have a grandson, for chrissakes.'

'Congratulations, Greg. It's going to be wonderful for all of you. I just know it.'

A long, tense silence stretched out between them, and suddenly she was yearning for the inane chitchat. She tried not to think about the fact that she knew so much about this man, and she'd given him so much of herself. She had opened the door to her heart and let him in where she'd never let anyone else, ever. She didn't want to regret that. She hoped she never would.

'Nina—'

'Greg—'

They both spoke at once. All right, she told herself. Deep breath. Get it over with, like ripping a Band-Aid off a wound. 'I've been trying to think about where I'm going next.'

'Don't go anywhere. I didn't mean what I said. I was a complete ass. I'm sorry.'

*I'm sorry.* Such sweet, simple words. They came from the heart and she believed him completely. But she also believed that whatever they had together was tenuous. When it came to intimacy, her track record was almost nonexistent, and she had to believe there was a reason for that. 'I'm not mad, Greg, but I do have to go. We don't need to talk about it. It's just something that needs to happen.' She refused to say I told you so, but

462

hadn't she? Hadn't she said that if they got involved and it didn't go well, their troubles would interfere with their work at the inn?

'You're not leaving,' he said.

'I am. Let's not argue about it.'

'Okay, we won't argue. There's something I want to be sure you understand, though. The things I said at the wedding reception . . . I spoke out of panic and fear and anger that didn't have anything to do with you.'

'I realize that. The things you said were still pretty cruel.'

'I'm sorry,' he said again. 'I was freaking out and pissed and none of it was about you.'

God forbid that she should mistake her own importance to him. 'Greg, what is it you're trying to say?'

'You can't leave. You love this place. You belong here.'

She felt hollowed out by hurt. She wanted to hear that she belonged with *him*. She wanted to feel that, to know it beyond a doubt. 'That doesn't matter,' she said.

'Hell, yes, it matters. If it doesn't matter, then I don't know what does.'

A terrible silence, weighted by doubts, stretched out between them. She could hear the water lapping at the pilings of the dock, the soughing of the wind through the trees. Then he made a tortured, wordless sound and pulled her into his arms. She resisted, but then something made her melt and she lifted her

463

face to his. Make me believe, she thought.

He kissed her then, and it was a kiss of possession and searing honesty that left her breathless and stunned. It made her remember the ways he'd touched her, the times they'd laughed together and the times they'd lain quiet, listening to the night. When he came up for air, he said, 'That's pretty much what I've been trying to say, only I'm not so good with words.'

For a fleeting moment, a heartbeat of hope, she soared. Then she remembered all the roadblocks in their way. 'It's not about words,' she managed to say in a broken whisper, trying to pull away from him. 'It's about the fact that we're in such different places in our lives.'

'Damn, Nina, you've spent the whole summer dwelling on all the reasons we can't be together. All the reasons things won't work out for us. And while you were doing that, everything was working out. Except for yesterday. I said I was sorry but you've got no reason to believe that. Stay, Nina. Just . . . stay, and I'll make you believe. I swear I will.'

She looked up at him, and wondered how he'd guessed at her thoughts. *Make me believe.* Slowly but undeniably, the hollowed-out place inside her began to fill. This was his great strength, the thing she could never resist. He had an uncanny ability to jump back into love and commitment even after a failed marriage and painful divorce. He wasn't afraid of relationships, not the way Nina was. She needed his courage when it came to matters of the heart. She needed *him*. The summer had been amazing, she conceded, and full of surprises. This was nothing new to Nina. Things never seemed to turn out the way she expected. This appeared to be the way life had always revealed itself to her.

She looked at him and thought, they turned out *better*. She'd wanted the inn; instead she found herself with a partner. She'd wanted her independence, and she'd fallen head-over-heels for Greg *and* his kids. Throughout the autumn and winter, Nina and Greg had grown closer with each passing day. She wasn't afraid of this relationship anymore, and she no longer worried about the complications in his life.

She took a deep breath and said, 'I've lived in the same town my whole life. I was thinking, tonight, that maybe I need to live a different life, do something else.'

'You've done plenty, Nina. But I can think of something you haven't done.'

'Yeah? What's that?'

'You've never been in love. Remember? You told me that, a long time ago.'

'It's not true anymore.' She blurted it out, just like that. The words were out there, not the way she'd planned to tell him, but she couldn't snatch them back. Nor did she want to. Starting over didn't mean she would struggle as she had before. This new beginning was a joyful one.

He didn't even look surprised. 'It's about time you said something. I've been waiting.'

'You knew?'

At that, he laughed. *Laughed.* 'You're not exactly a poker face.'

'Then why didn't you say anything?'

'I won't lie to you. I was married for a long time.' He grinned. 'We can't all be virgins, you know.'

'Very funny.'

'Nina. I said I was married for a long time. And clearly, it ended badly. For a while, I lost any faith I might have had in my ability to trust anybody. Including myself. Including my own feelings.'

'Which are?' She knew asking the question was a risk, but she had to find out what he was thinking.

'What I'm saying is, you can't go through something like that and not learn anything. I know what love is. And what it isn't.' He held her close, tenderly now, and leaned down to whisper in her ear. 'I know I'm just completely in love with you. I plan on staying that way for good, so get used to it.'

She didn't realize she'd been holding her breath until she let it out on a long wave of relief. It was enough, she realized. It was everything.

## EPILOGUE

Nina heard the thud of a trunk lid slamming shut. She saw Greg's shoulders stiffen, as though he was bracing himself for a blow. They were in the foyer of his house, bracing themselves to say goodbye to Daisy.

Outside, the exhaust from Daisy's idling car plumed into the overcast sky of the wintry afternoon. Early twilight was coming on, and a cold quiet settled over the landscape. Greg had spent half the day checking and re-checking the car to make sure it was winterized, the tires checked, the windows scraped, everything in working order, as though his daughter was about to make a cross-country trek rather than a drive to the other side of the river, to a small house of her own on the road to New Paltz.

It wasn't the distance, though. Nina understood that. It was the fact that Daisy was leaving Greg's house, a transition far more wrenching and complicated than a mere change of venue. She'd lived at home for five months after the baby was born, but now she was eager to move on to her new life. She had spent the past hour loading the last of her things. The baby, thickly bundled into his carseat, was already sound asleep. In a few minutes, they would soon be on their way.

Nina studied Greg's face, noting the tension

in his jaw, and wished there was something she could say to ease his mind. They had known for a long time that Daisy was leaving. Now that the actual day had arrived, his apprehension was palpable.

Her heart squeezed in sympathy for him. Loving someone meant more than hearts and flowers. Sometimes it meant hurting when he hurt. There had been a time when she'd been afraid of this, afraid of the complications in his life. She wasn't afraid now. She zipped up her parka and went to the door with him.

'It's going to be okay,' she said. 'You know that, don't you?'

He pulled her in close, kissed her temple. 'Yeah. I do.'

'She's got everything she needs from you,' Nina told him, thinking of Sonnet, so far away at college. Nina had given herself the same advice, every time her stomach clenched with worry and her heart ached with missing her daughter.

He took her hand, and they stepped out into the cold afternoon to tell Daisy goodbye. Nina bent down and gently touched the sleeping bundle in the backseat. Emile—whom everyone called Charlie, thank God—was the center of Daisy's world, and Nina knew he always would be.

Greg gave his daughter a long hug, cupping his hand around the back of her head, the way he'd probably done when Daisy was a little

468

girl. 'Be careful on the road,' he said.

'Always,' she promised. 'Tell Max to call when he gets home from school. See you around, Daddy-O.'

'Count on it.'

And just like that, she was gone, tires crunching along the driveway. Nina and Greg watched until the car rounded the bend to the main road, leaving a vacuum of silence behind. There were no guests at the inn today; the season was at its lowest ebb, and the parking lot was empty. A few lights glowed in the boathouse above the dock, reminding her that she'd planned to spend the afternoon working at the computer.

She shivered and glanced up to find Greg watching her, a peculiar expression on his face. 'You all right?' she asked him.

'I'm okay.'

'Are you sure?'

He nodded, turning to her and resting his hands on her shoulders. 'I'm so damn glad you're here, Nina.'

She smiled, tilting her head to the side, trying to figure out what was going on with him.

'Nina,' he said, 'the first time I saw you, you were just a kid, hanging around Camp Kioga. But even back then, I knew that somehow you were going to be special to me. And you were. You are. Every day I wake up more in love with you than I was the day before, and that's not going to end for me, ever.'

She forgot to breathe. She knew where this was going, and she couldn't even move. She hoped her mouth wasn't hanging open in amazement. She hoped her expression was as bright with love as his.

He was endearingly anxious as he went down on one knee, his hand reaching into a pocket and bringing out a ring. His hand trembled, and he gave an unsteady laugh. 'Sorry, I'm nervous. I've been carrying this around for days, trying to figure out the best time to ask you.'

'Now would be good,' she whispered, her breath freezing in the winter air. 'Ask me now. *Please.*'

He pressed his lips to the back of her hand, then looked steadily up at her. 'I've never done this before, and I don't plan on doing it again. You're my one shot. Nina Romano, will you marry me?'

She'd imagined this moment so many times since last summer. She'd dreamed about it, wished for it. She knew she'd be consumed by emotion when she heard the actual words, but she hadn't realized she would be too happy to speak. So she nodded her head, and then the tears came, the tears she'd sworn she wouldn't shed, and finally, she managed to answer. 'Yes, I'll marry you. I love you, Greg. I always will.'

Without taking his eyes off her, he rose to his feet and slipped the ring on her finger.

It was a simple solitaire, the gold quickly warming to her flesh.

'It's a perfect fit,' Greg said. He kissed her gently, and she could feel his lips curving into a smile. He lifted his mouth from hers and said, 'Whew. That went well.'

She put her arms around his waist and laughed with joy. 'I'd say so.' Then she stepped back and studied their joined hands, her finger now encircled with his ring, a glittering promise of their future. She wasn't cold at all now, wrapped in happiness as she pictured them together in the boxy, old-fashioned house at the Inn at Willow Lake.

'Let's go inside,' Greg said, taking her hand and leading her up the path. 'I've got big plans for us.'

# Chivers Large Print Direct

If you have enjoyed this Large Print book and would like to build up your own collection of Large Print books and have them delivered direct to your door, please contact **Chivers Large Print Direct**.

**Chivers Large Print Direct** offers you a full service:

☆ **Created to support your local library**

☆ **Delivery direct to your door**

☆ **Easy-to-read type and attractively bound**

☆ **The very best authors**

☆ **Special low prices**

For further details either call Customer Services on 01225 443400 or write to us at

**Chivers Large Print Direct**
**FREEPOST (BA 1686/1)**
**Bath**
**BA1 3QZ**